Far ~~Out~~ Autumn

Brent Bowman-Art

Terry Eisele-Story

www.terryeisele.com

Cover art by Brent Bowman.
https://sites.google.com/site/thebrentbowmanproject/

Cover design by John Novak.
www.novakarts.com/

T.E.

-Far Tune is dedicated to all the Fartuns, Libans, Hodans, Aminas, and Ibrahims--Somalis everywhere who have survived what most people cannot imagine and who continue to strive for better.

B.B.

-I want to dedicate this book to my amazing sons, Nayson and Nevan. Thanks for all of the love and support.

Prologue

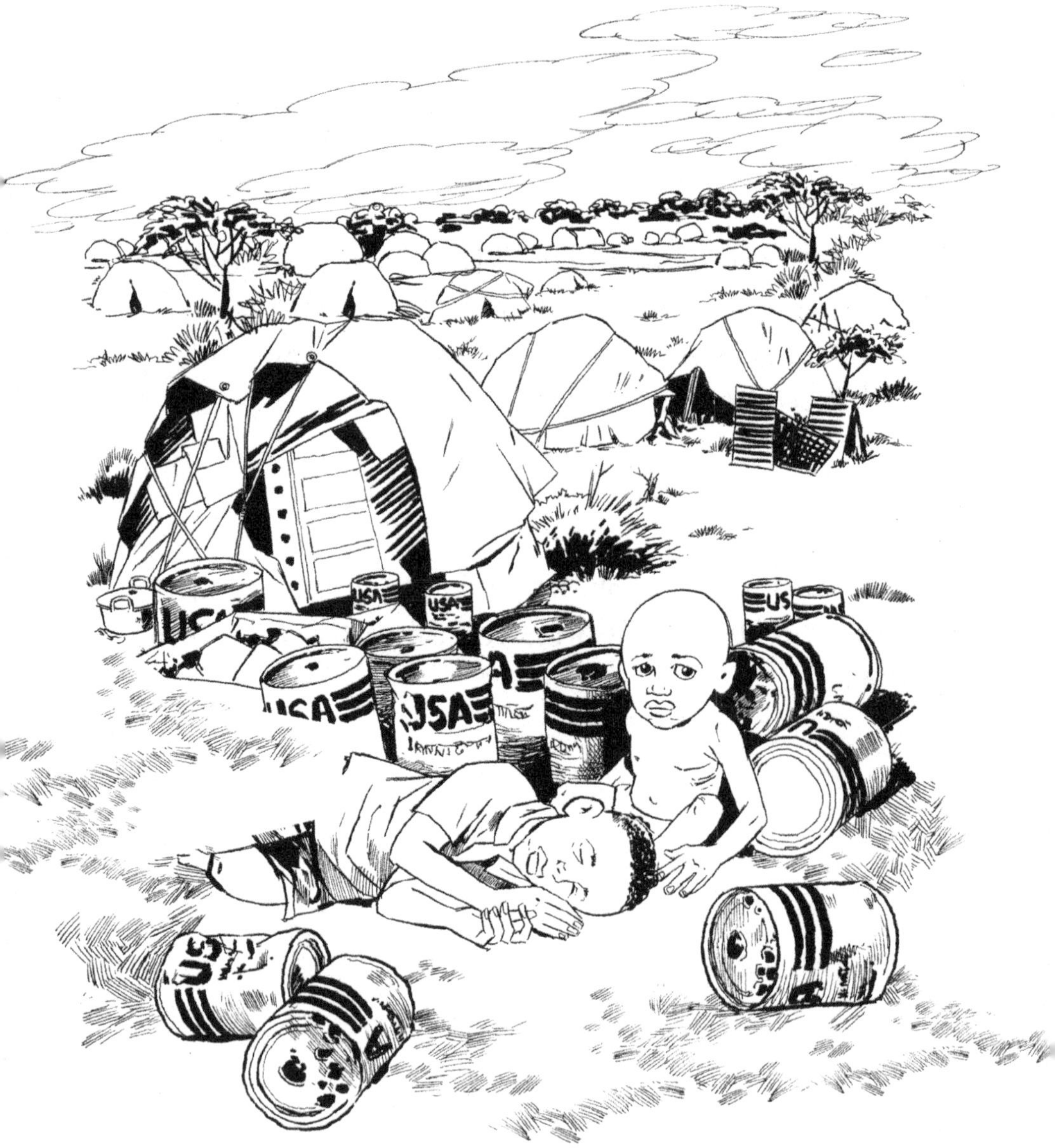
USA
USA
USA
USA

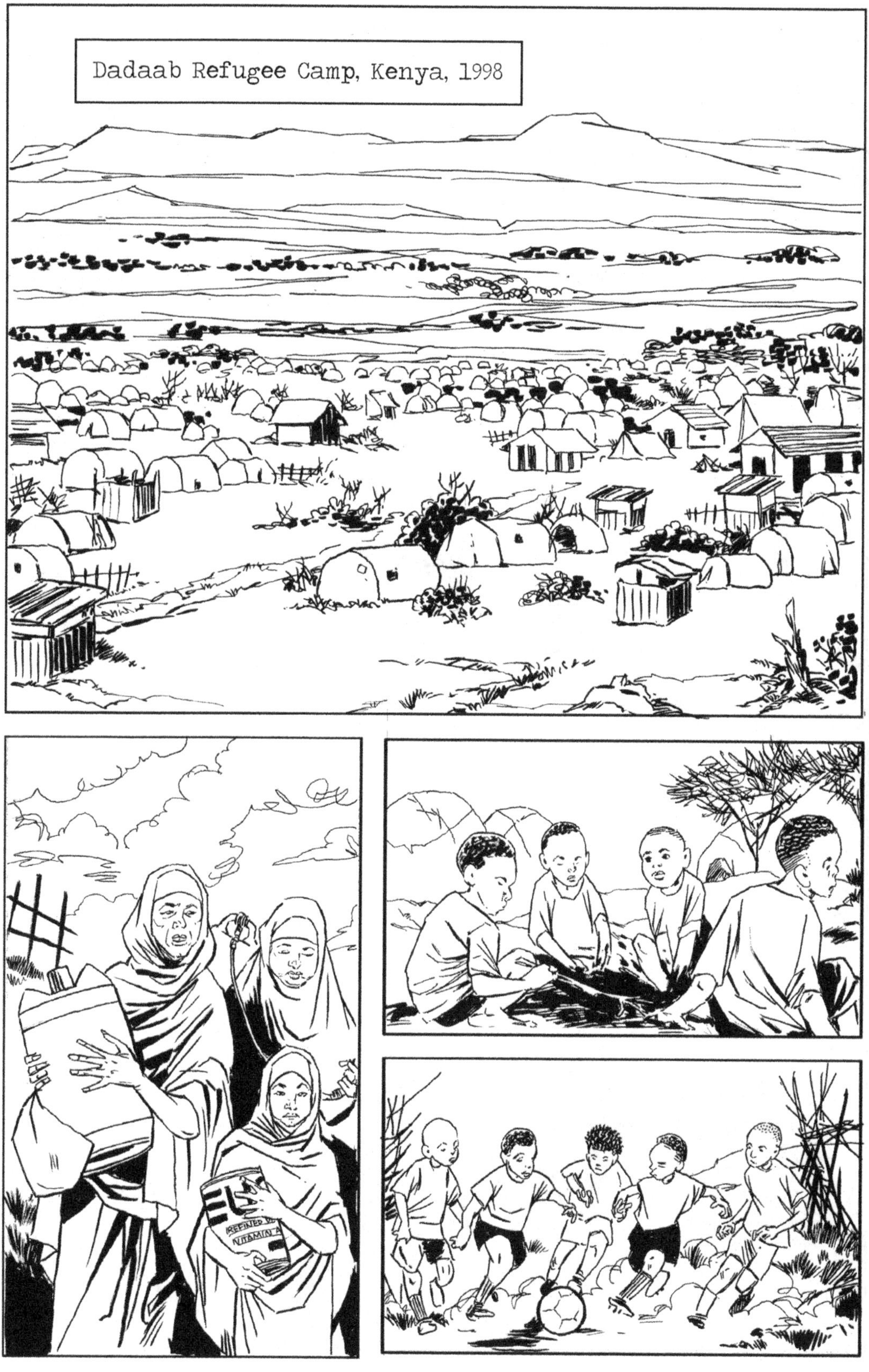
Dadaab Refugee Camp, Kenya, 1998

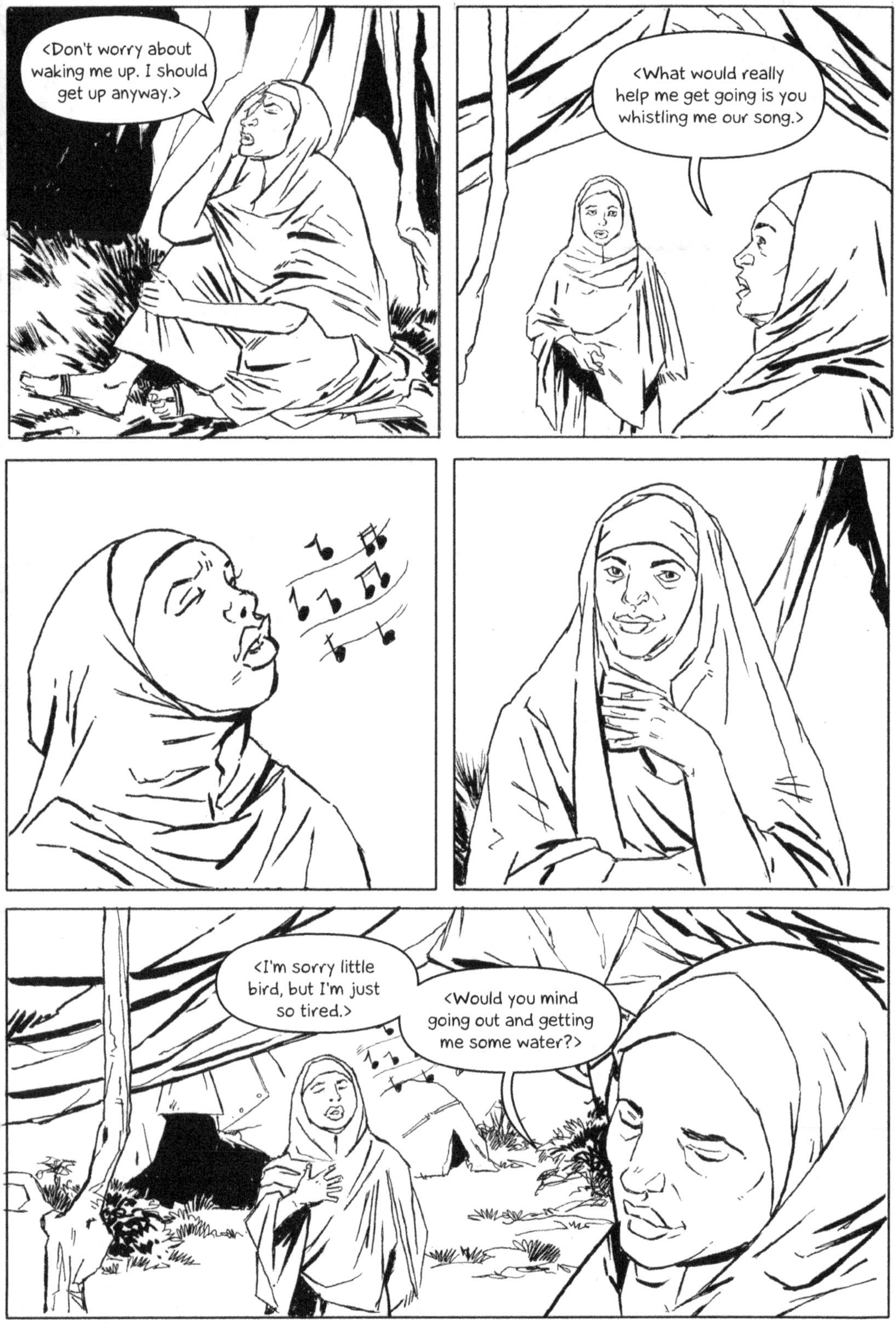
<Don't worry about waking me up. I should get up anyway.>
<What would really help me get going is you whistling me our song.>
<I'm sorry little bird, but I'm just so tired.>
<Would you mind going out and getting me some water?>

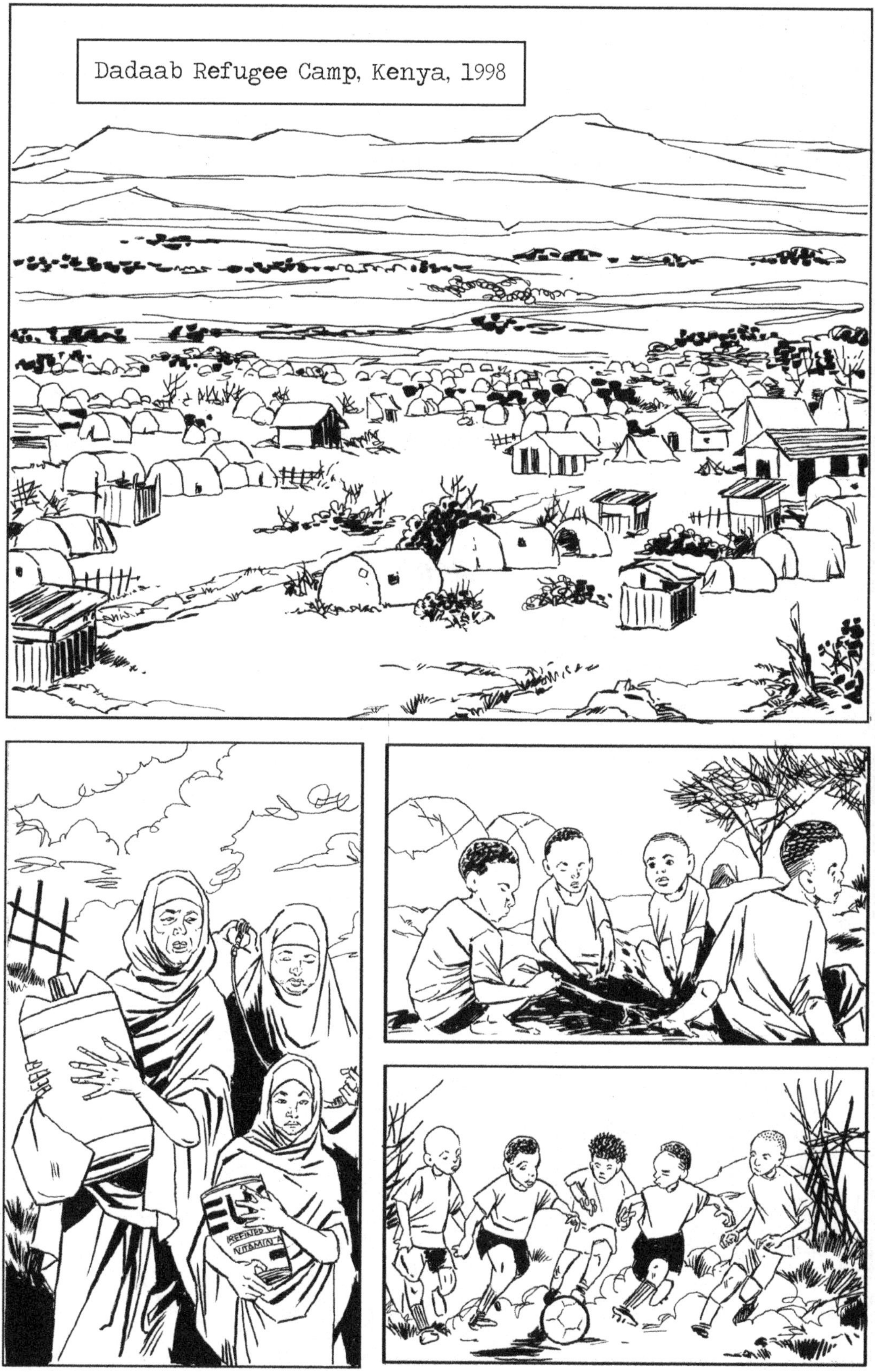
Dadaab Refugee Camp, Kenya, 1998

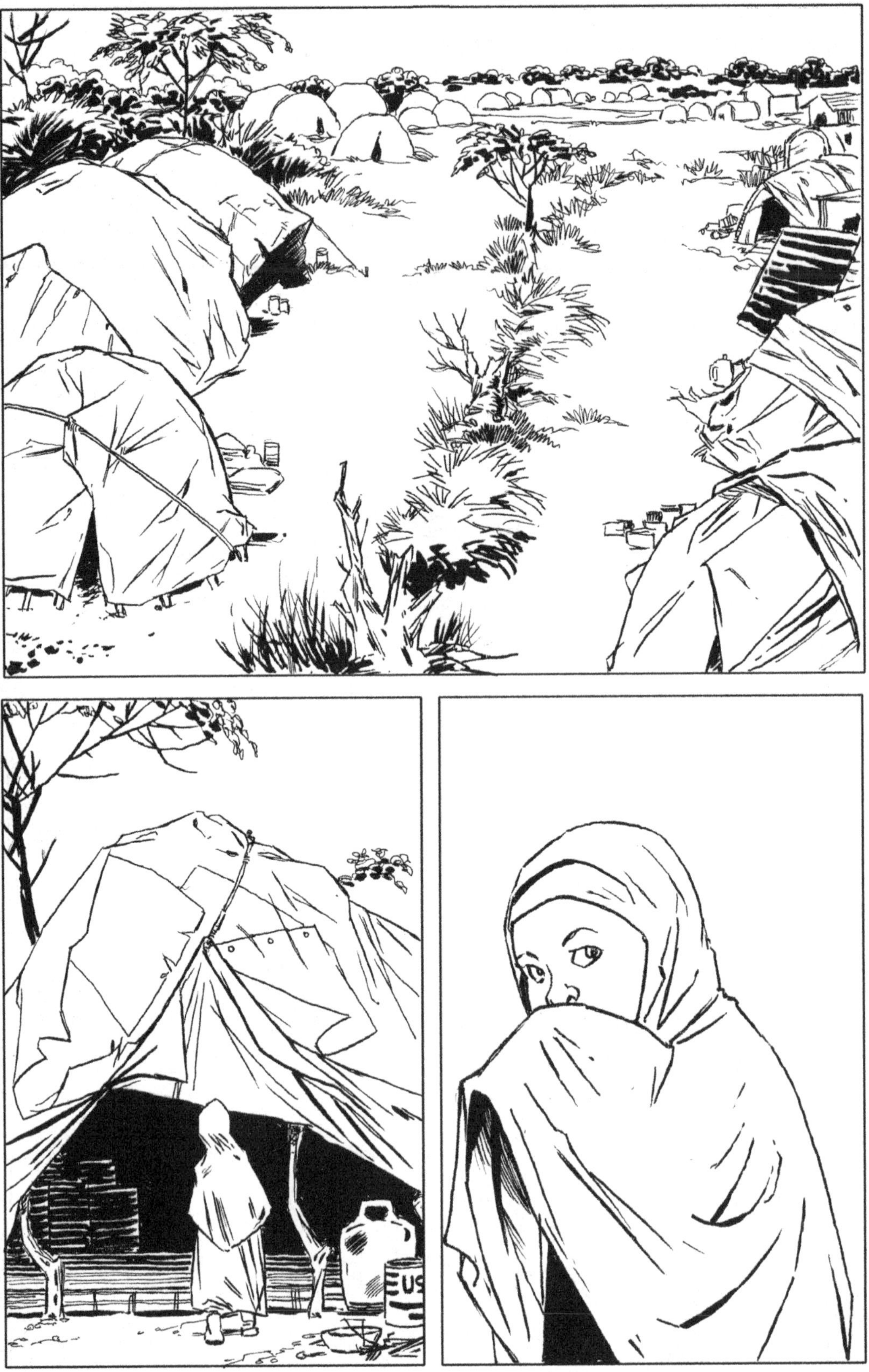
US

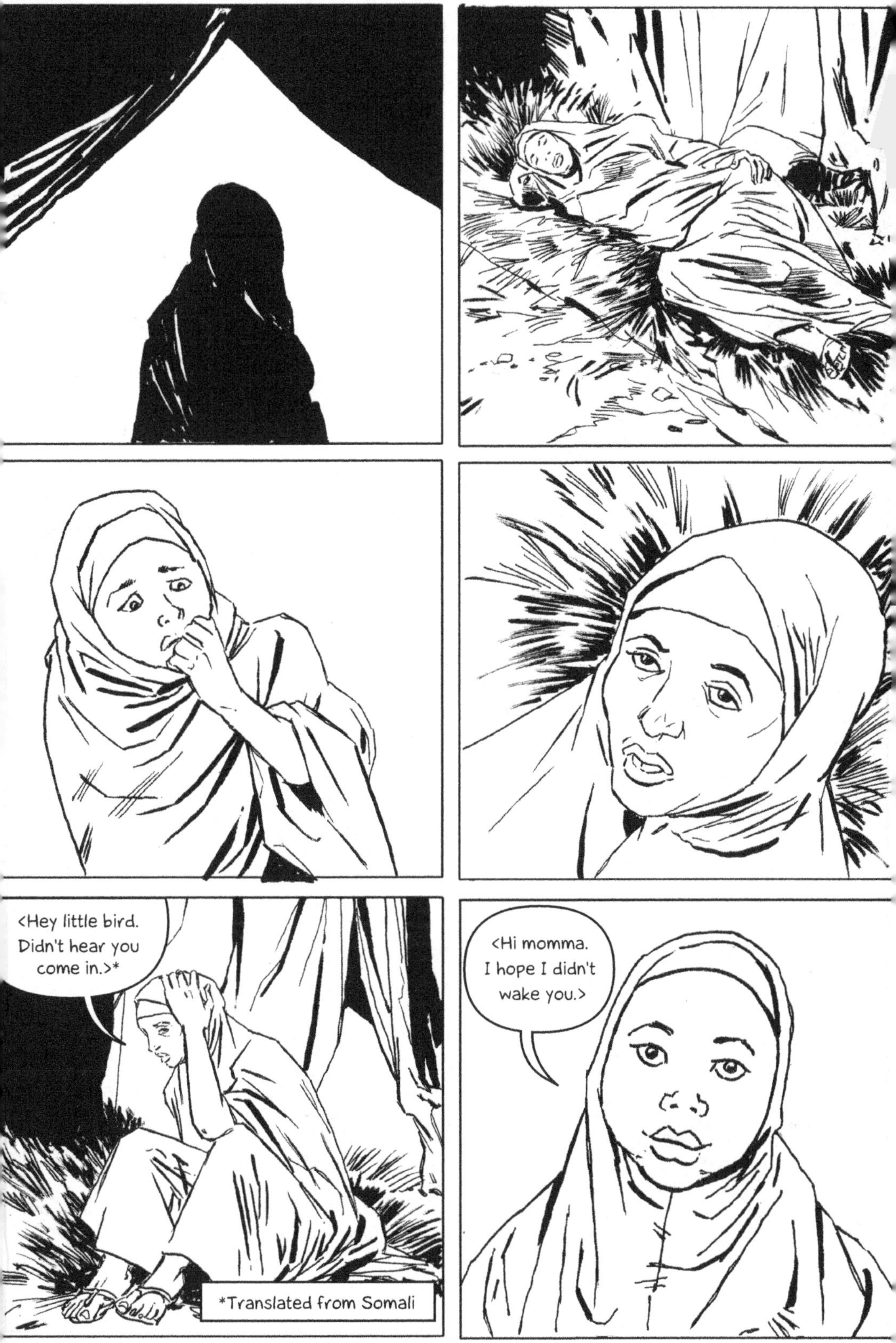
<Hey little bird. Didn't hear you come in.>*
*Translated from Somali
<Hi momma. I hope I didn't wake you.>

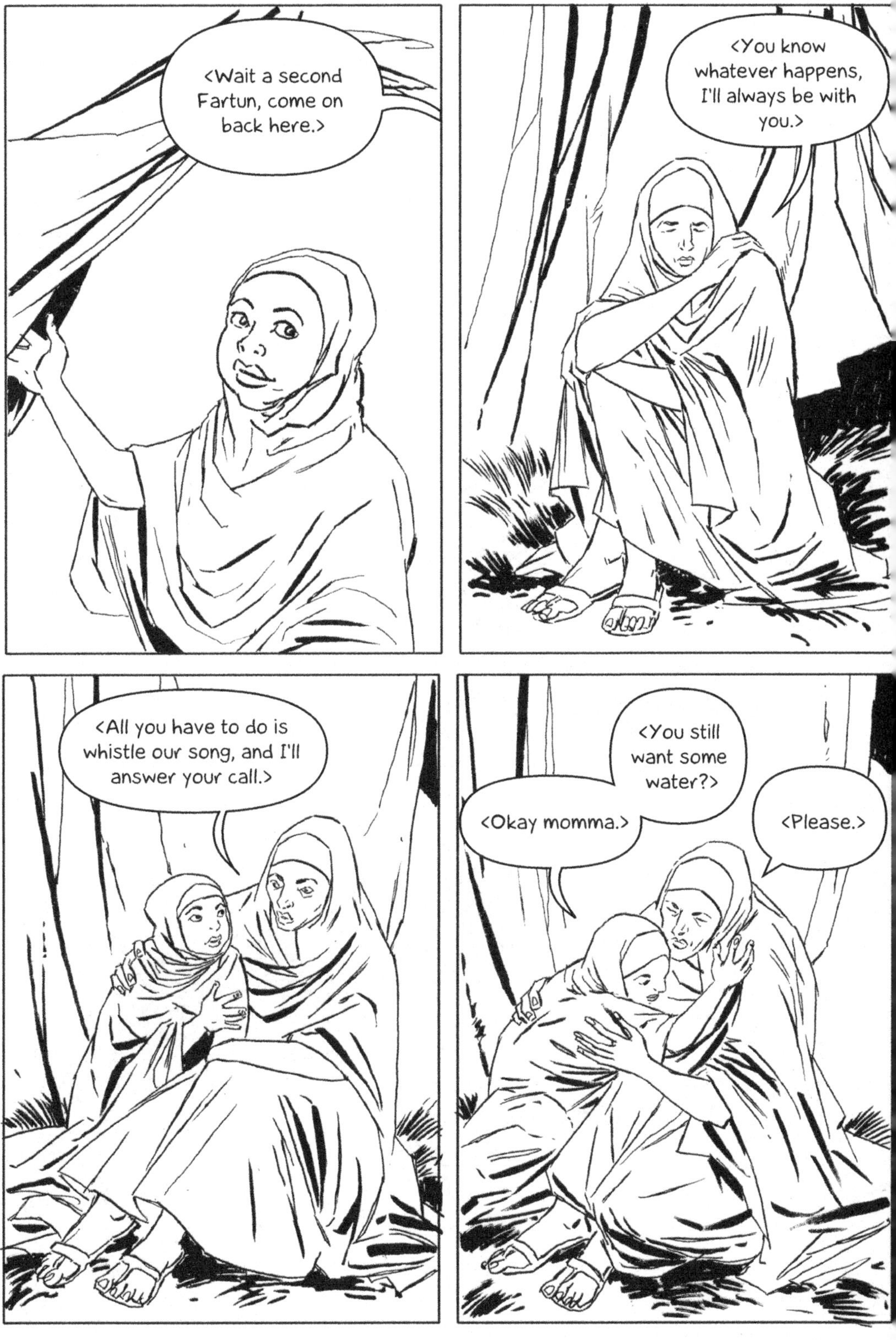
<Wait a second Fartun, come on back here.>
<You know whatever happens, I'll always be with you.>
<All you have to do is whistle our song, and I'll answer your call.>
<Okay momma.>
<You still want some water?>
<Please.>

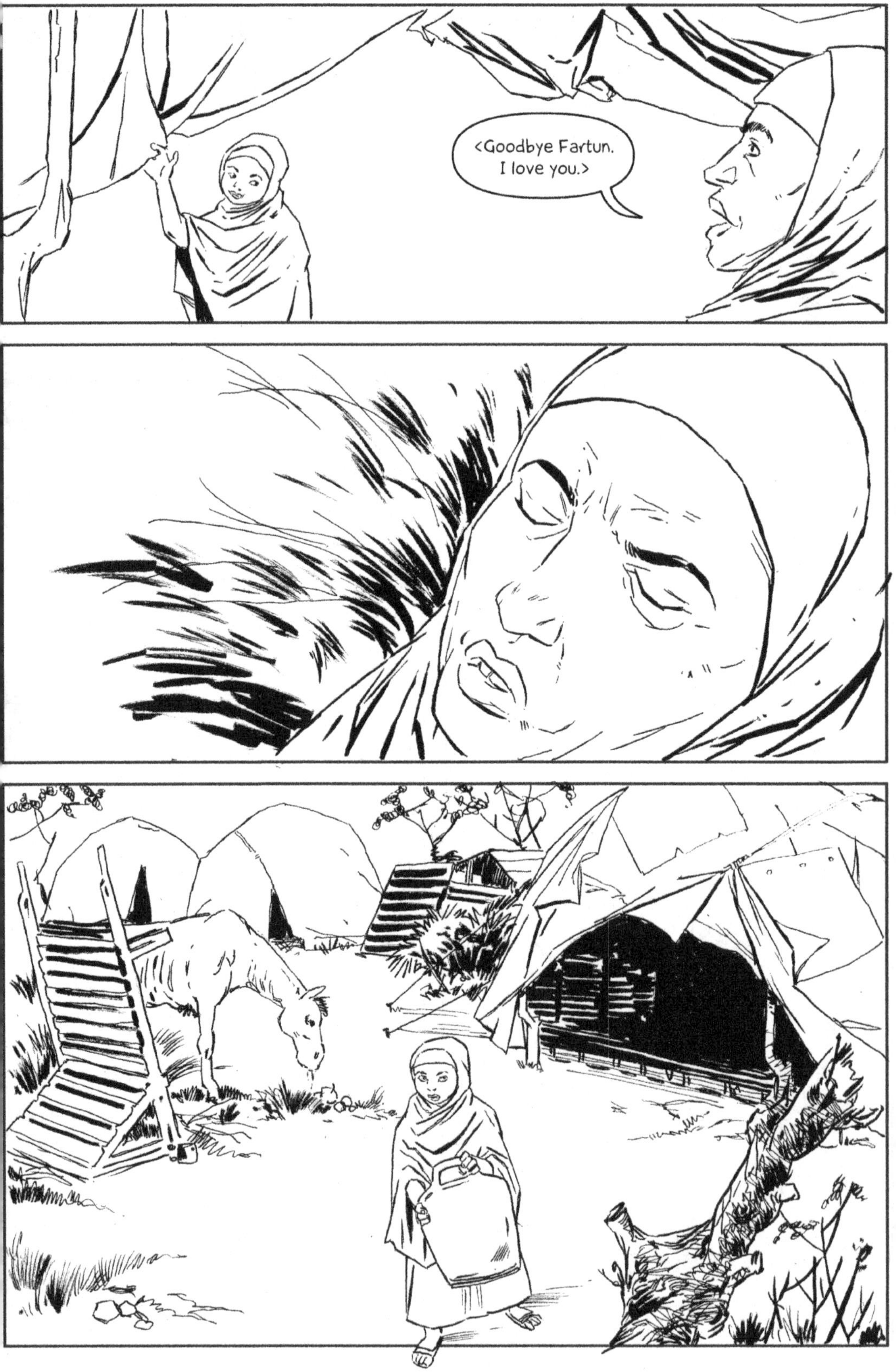
<Goodbye Fartun.
I love you.>

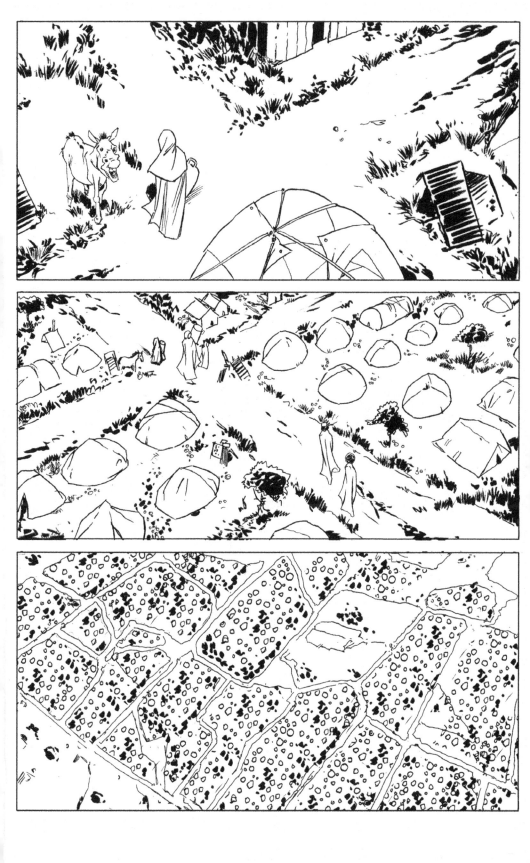

Part One

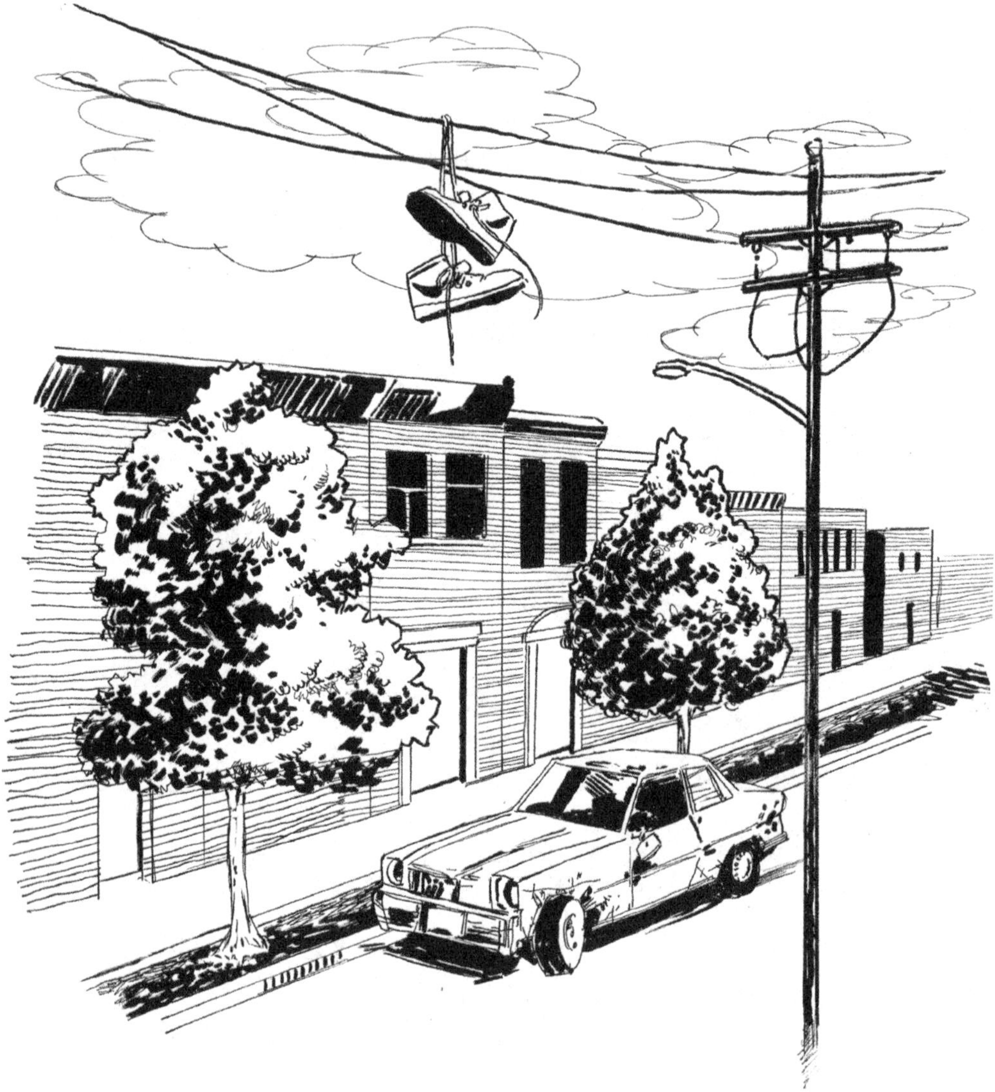

Autumn

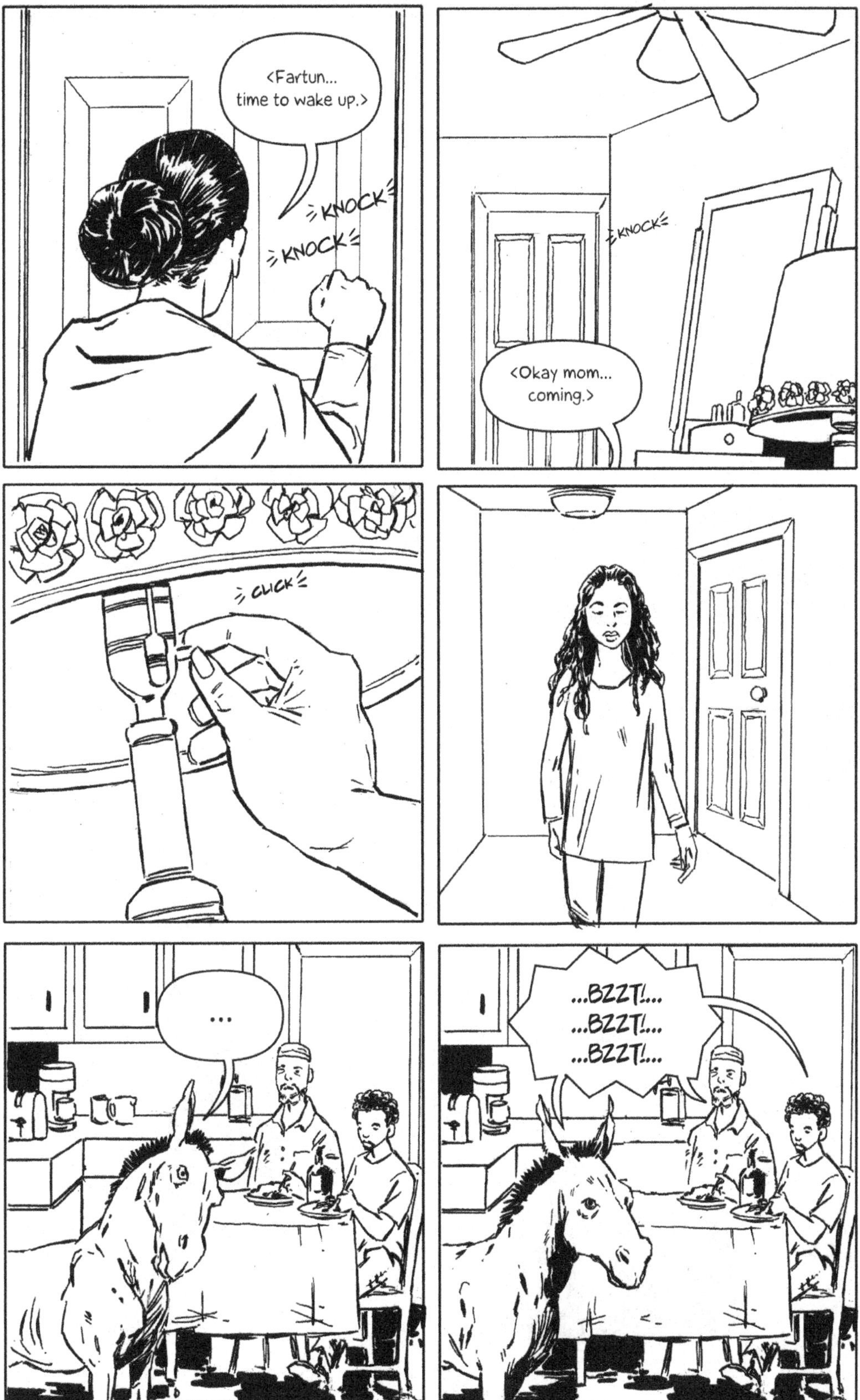
<Fartun...
time to wake up.>
KNOCK
KNOCK
KNOCK
<Okay mom...
coming.>
CLICK
...
...BZZT!...
...BZZT!...
...BZZT!...

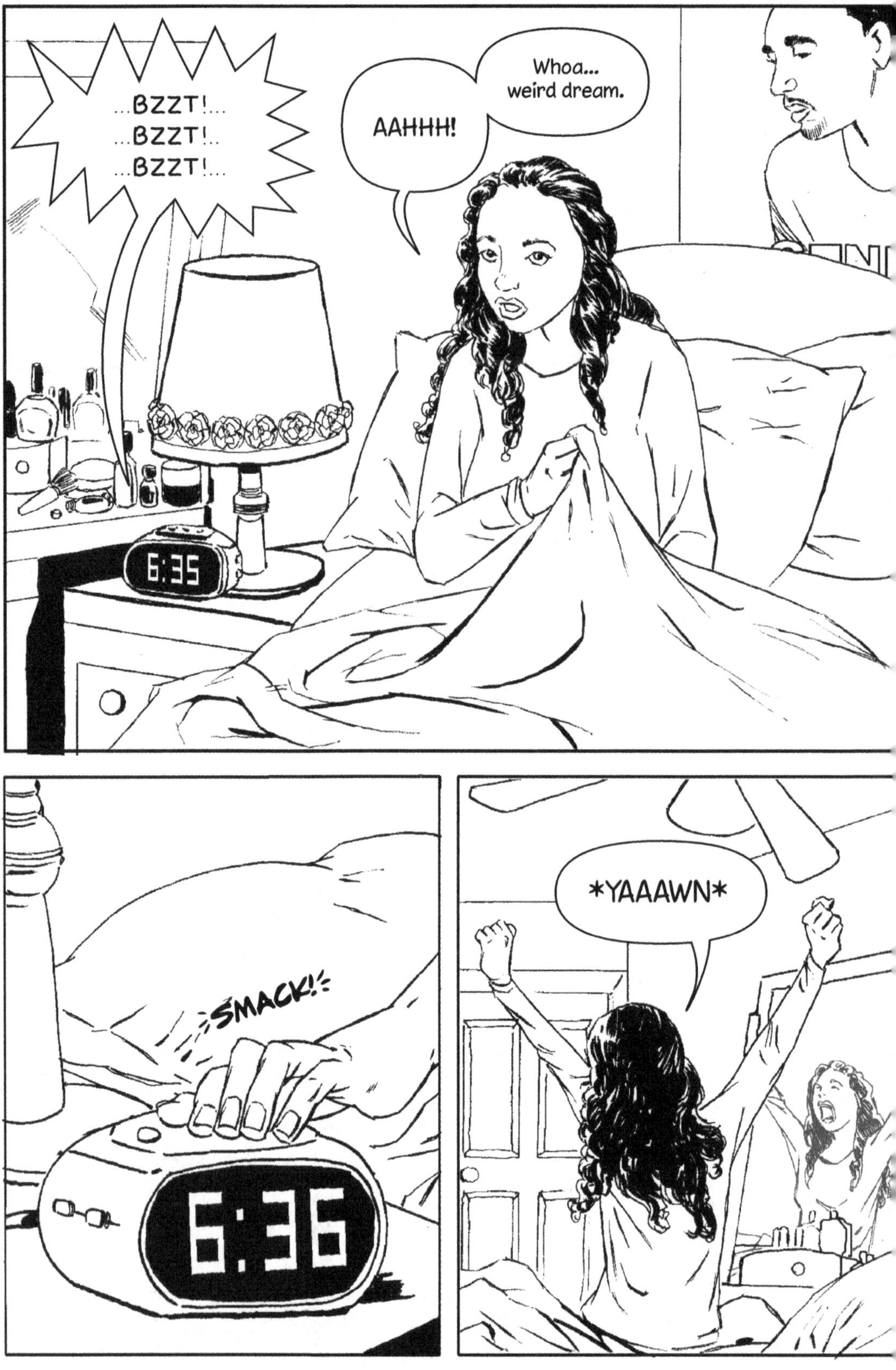
...BZZT!...
...BZZT!...
...BZZT!...
6:35
AAHHH!
Whoa...
weird dream.
SMACK!
6:36
YAAAWN

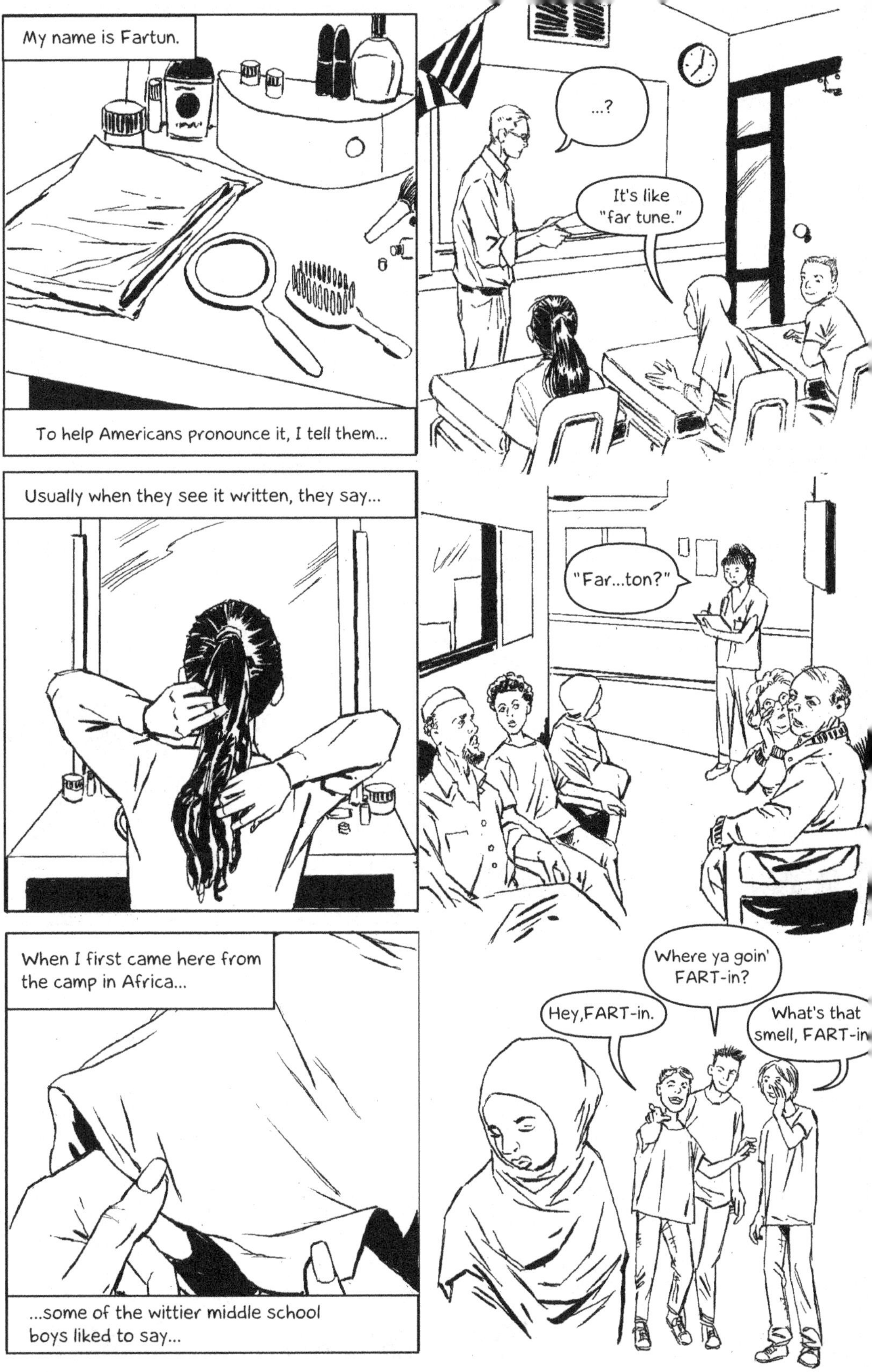
My name is Fartun.
To help Americans pronounce it, I tell them...
...?
It's like "far tune."
Usually when they see it written, they say...
"Far...ton?"
When I first came here from the camp in Africa...
...some of the wittier middle school boys liked to say...
Hey,FART-in.
Where ya goin' FART-in?
What's that smell, FART-in

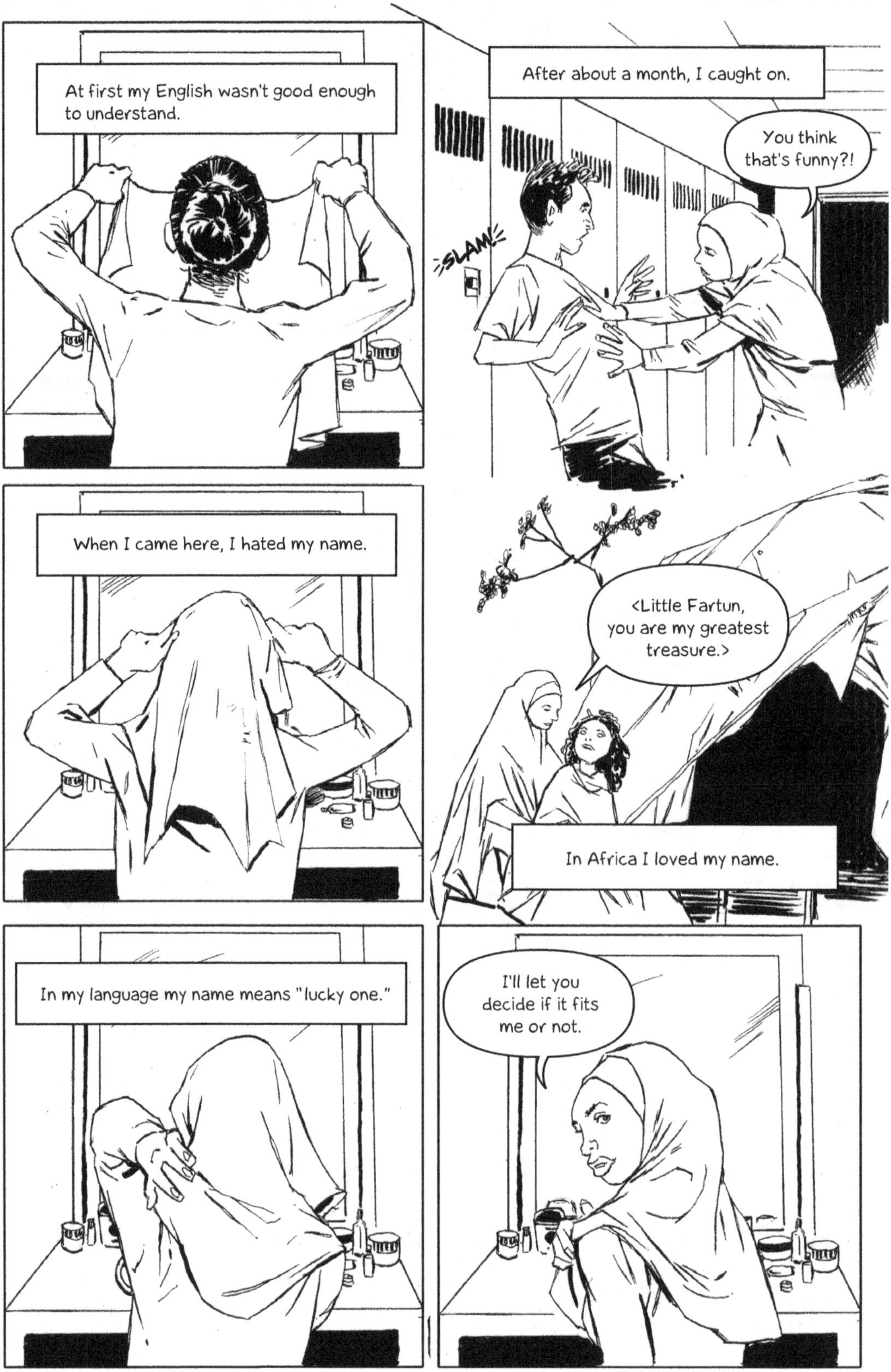
At first my English wasn't good enough to understand.
After about a month, I caught on.
SLAM!
You think that's funny?!
When I came here, I hated my name.
<Little Fartun, you are my greatest treasure.>
In Africa I loved my name.
In my language my name means "lucky one."
I'll let you decide if it fits me or not.

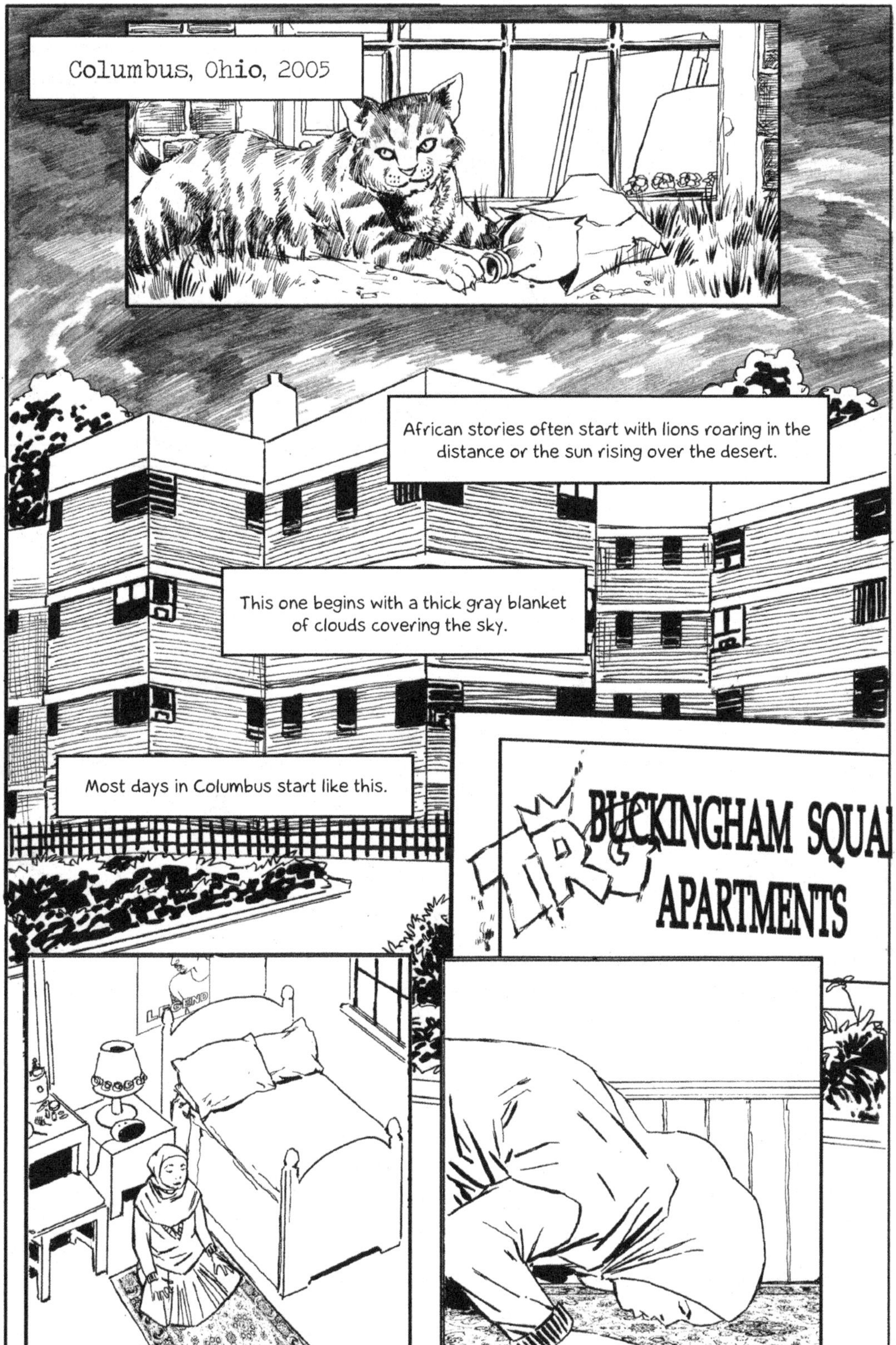
Columbus, Ohio, 2005
African stories often start with lions roaring in the distance or the sun rising over the desert.
This one begins with a thick gray blanket of clouds covering the sky.
Most days in Columbus start like this.
BUCKINGHAM SQUA
APARTMENTS
LEGEND

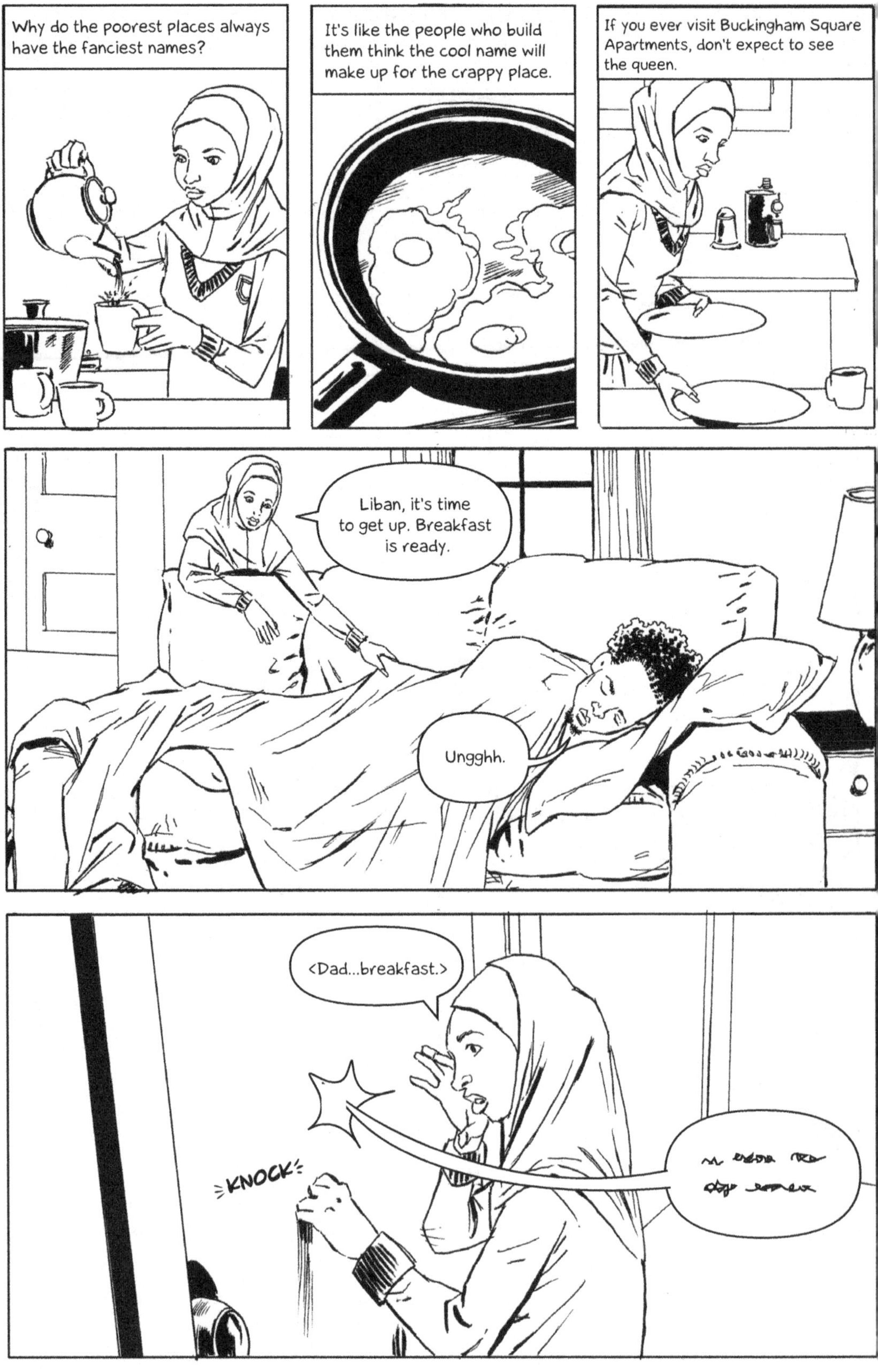
Why do the poorest places always have the fanciest names?
It's like the people who build them think the cool name will make up for the crappy place.
If you ever visit Buckingham Square Apartments, don't expect to see the queen.
Liban, it's time to get up. Breakfast is ready.
Ungghh.
<Dad...breakfast.>
KNOCK

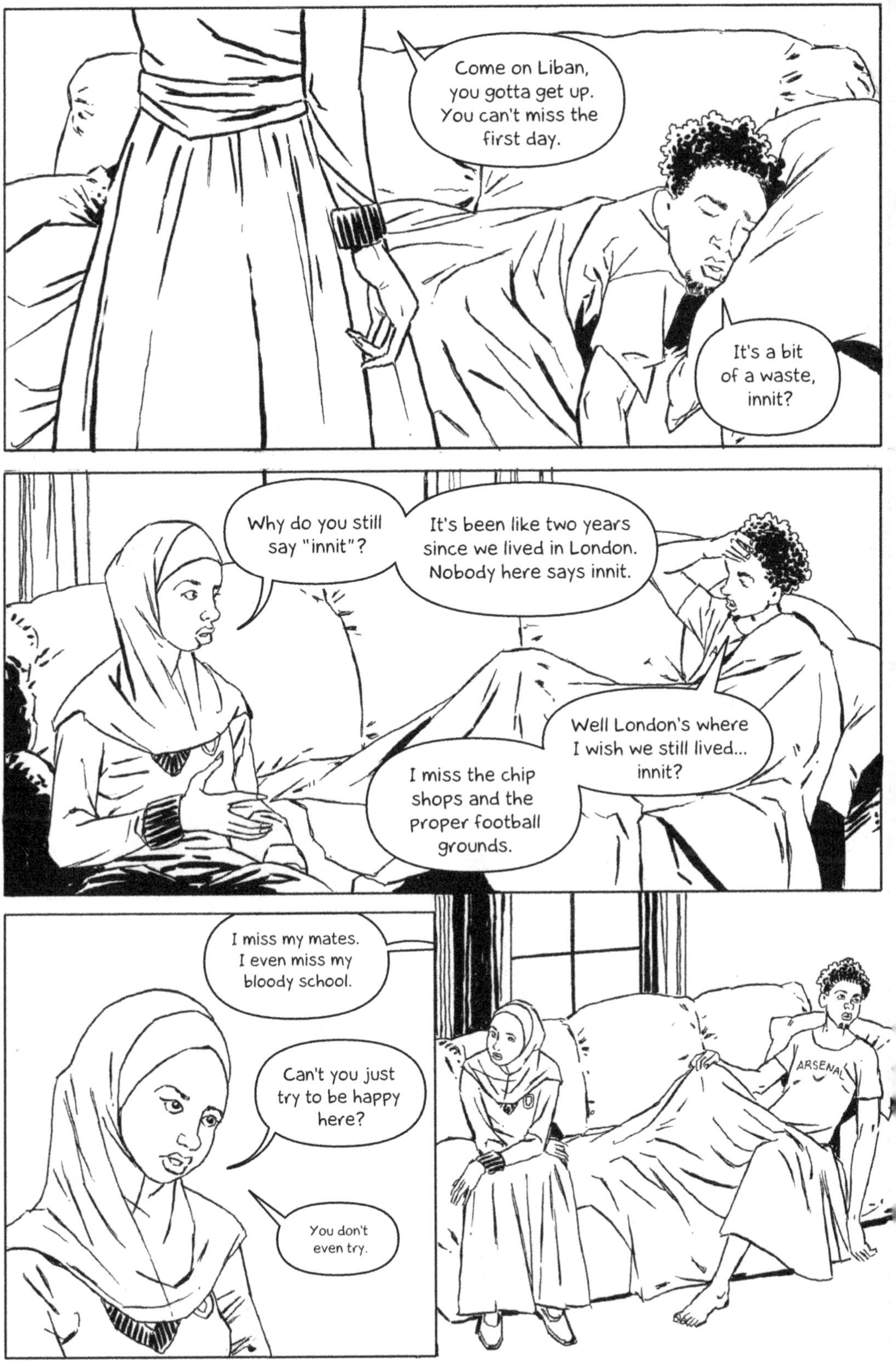
Come on Liban, you gotta get up. You can't miss the first day.
It's a bit of a waste, innit?
Why do you still say "innit"?
It's been like two years since we lived in London. Nobody here says innit.
Well London's where I wish we still lived... innit?
I miss the chip shops and the proper football grounds.
I miss my mates. I even miss my bloody school.
Can't you just try to be happy here?
You don't even try.
ARSENAL

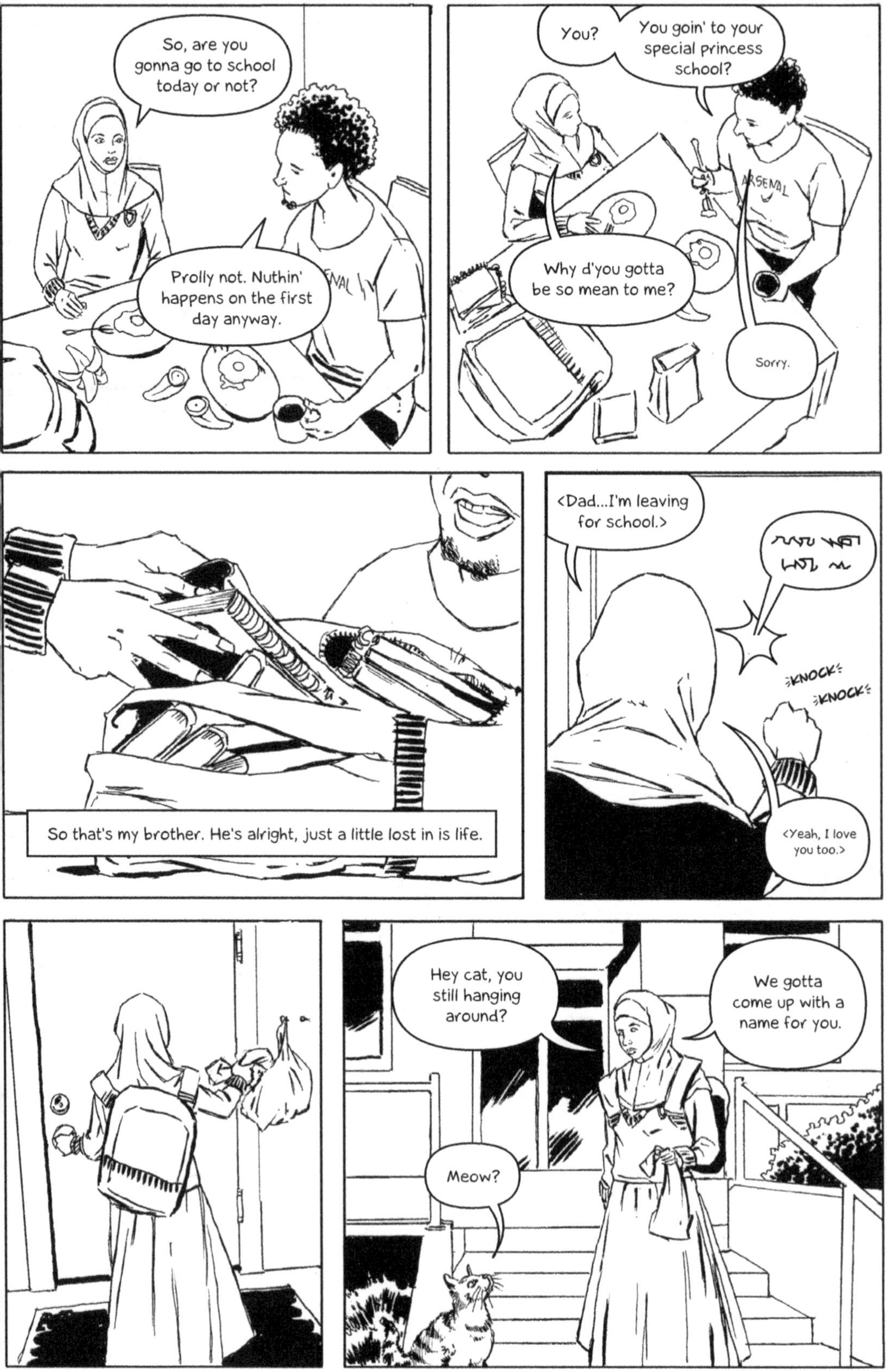
So, are you gonna go to school today or not?
Prolly not. Nuthin' happens on the first day anyway.
You?
You goin' to your special princess school?
Why d'you gotta be so mean to me?
Sorry.
So that's my brother. He's alright, just a little lost in is life.
<Dad...I'm leaving for school.>
KNOCK
KNOCK
<Yeah, I love you too.>
Hey cat, you still hanging around?
We gotta come up with a name for you.
Meow?

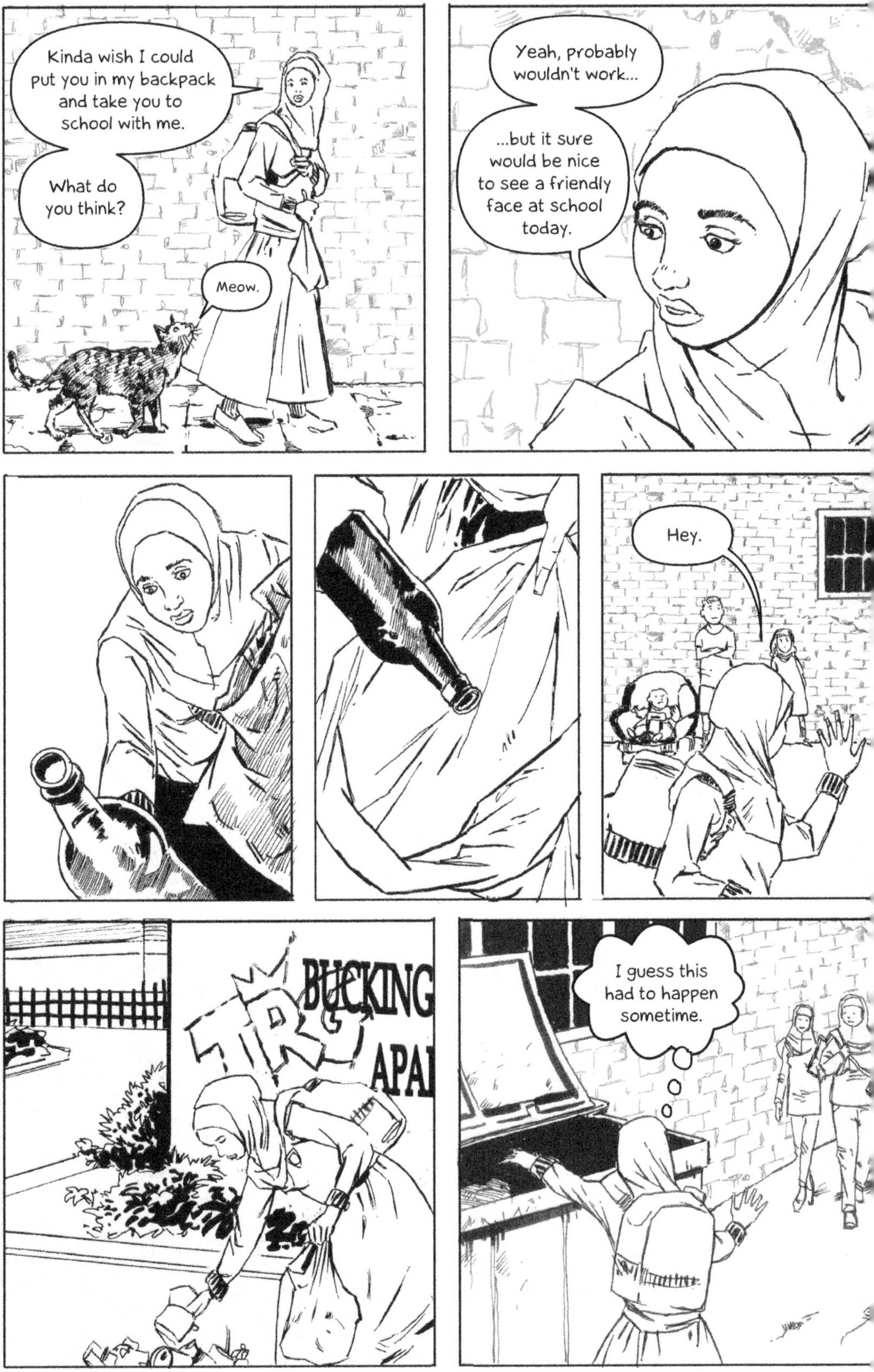
Kinda wish I could put you in my backpack and take you to school with me.
What do you think?
Meow.
Yeah, probably wouldn't work...
...but it sure would be nice to see a friendly face at school today.
Hey.
I guess this had to happen sometime.

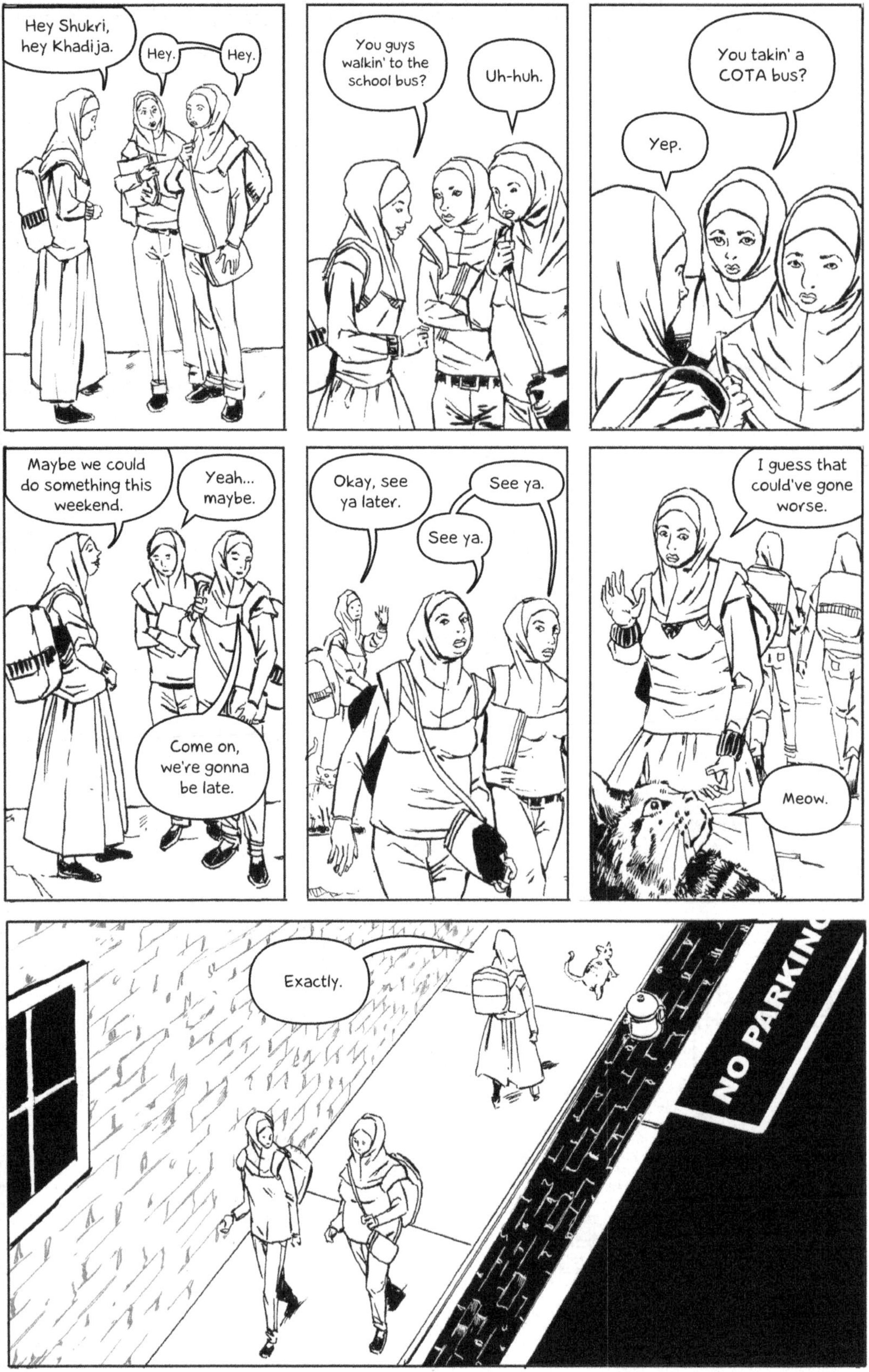
Hey Shukri, hey Khadija.
Hey.
Hey.
You guys walkin' to the school bus?
Uh-huh.
You takin' a COTA bus?
Yep.
Maybe we could do something this weekend.
Yeah... maybe.
Come on, we're gonna be late.
Okay, see ya later.
See ya.
See ya.
I guess that could've gone worse.
Meow.
Exactly.
NO PARKING

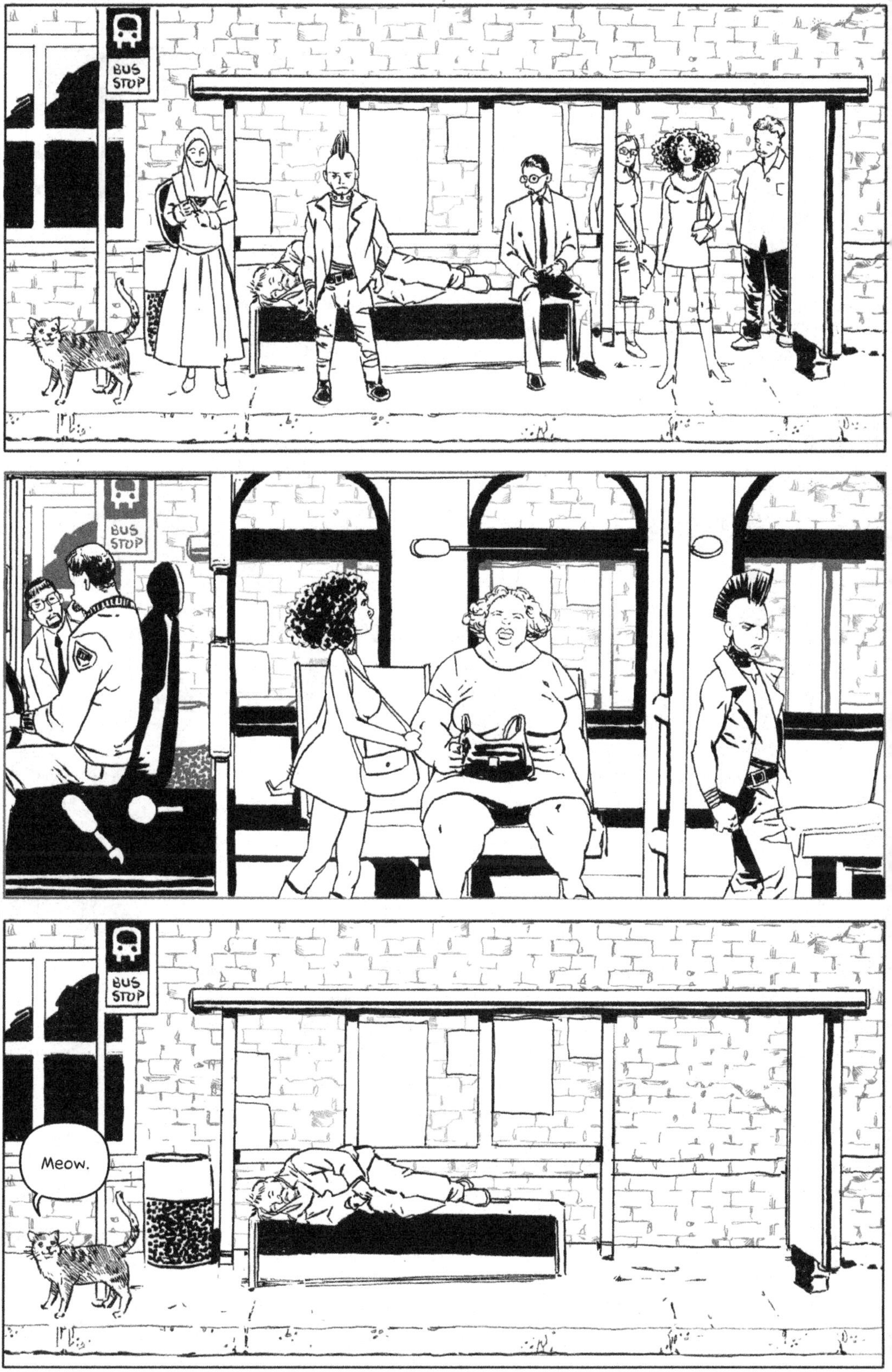
BUS STOP
BUS STOP
BUS STOP
Meow.

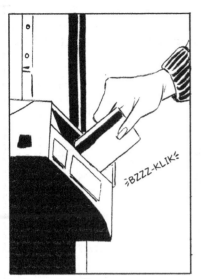

=BZZZ-KLIK=

Moment of truth #1...

...can I find an open seat that's not next to a weirdo.

Yes, two open ones!

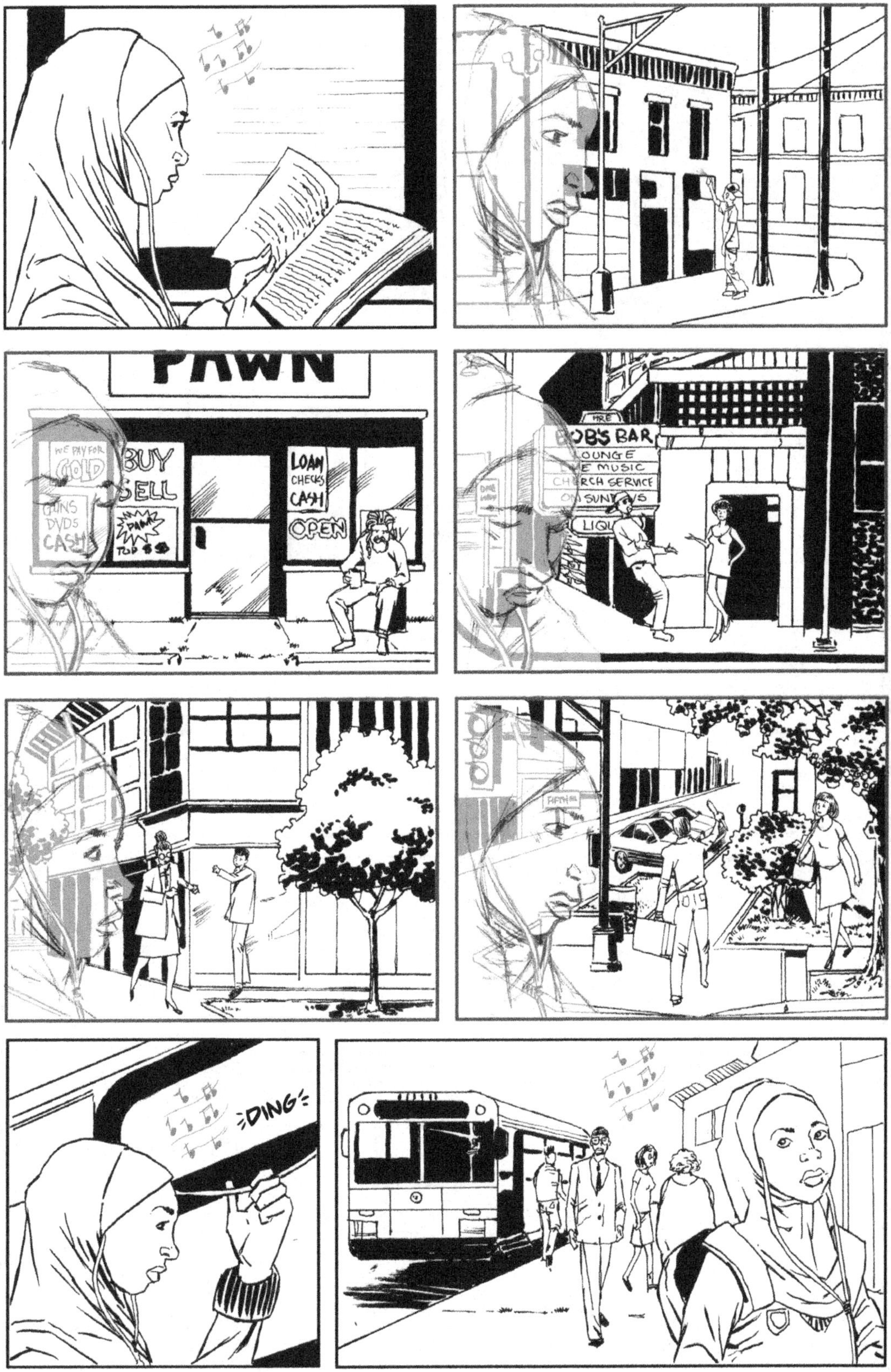
PAWN
WE PAY FOR GOLD
GUNS DVDS CASH
BUY
SELL
LOAN CHECKS CASH
OPEN
BOB'S BAR
LOUNGE
CHURCH SERVICE
DING

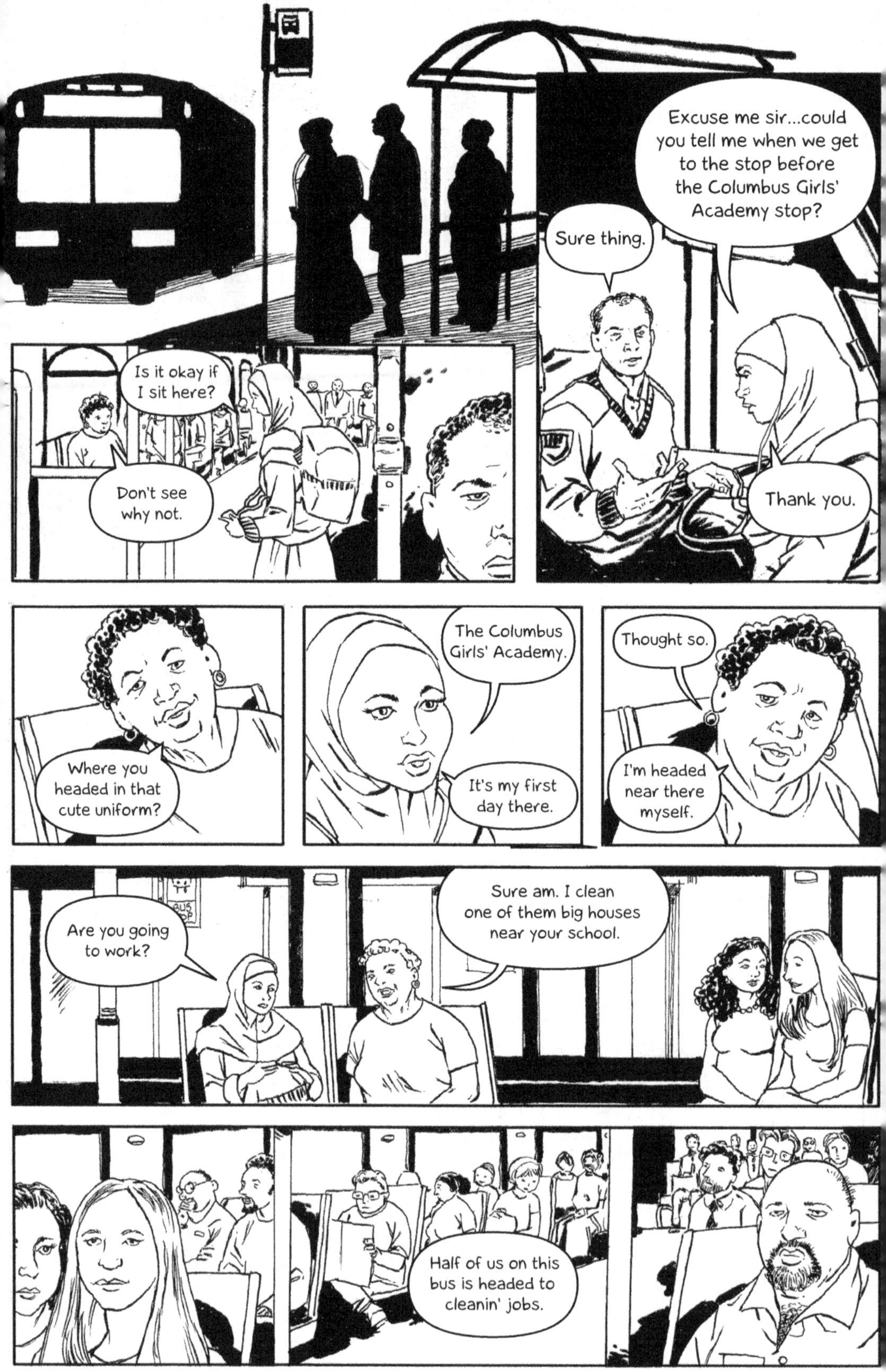
Excuse me sir...could you tell me when we get to the stop before the Columbus Girls' Academy stop?
Sure thing.
Is it okay if I sit here?
Don't see why not.
Thank you.
Where you headed in that cute uniform?
The Columbus Girls' Academy.
It's my first day there.
Thought so.
I'm headed near there myself.
Are you going to work?
Sure am. I clean one of them big houses near your school.
Half of us on this bus is headed to cleanin' jobs.

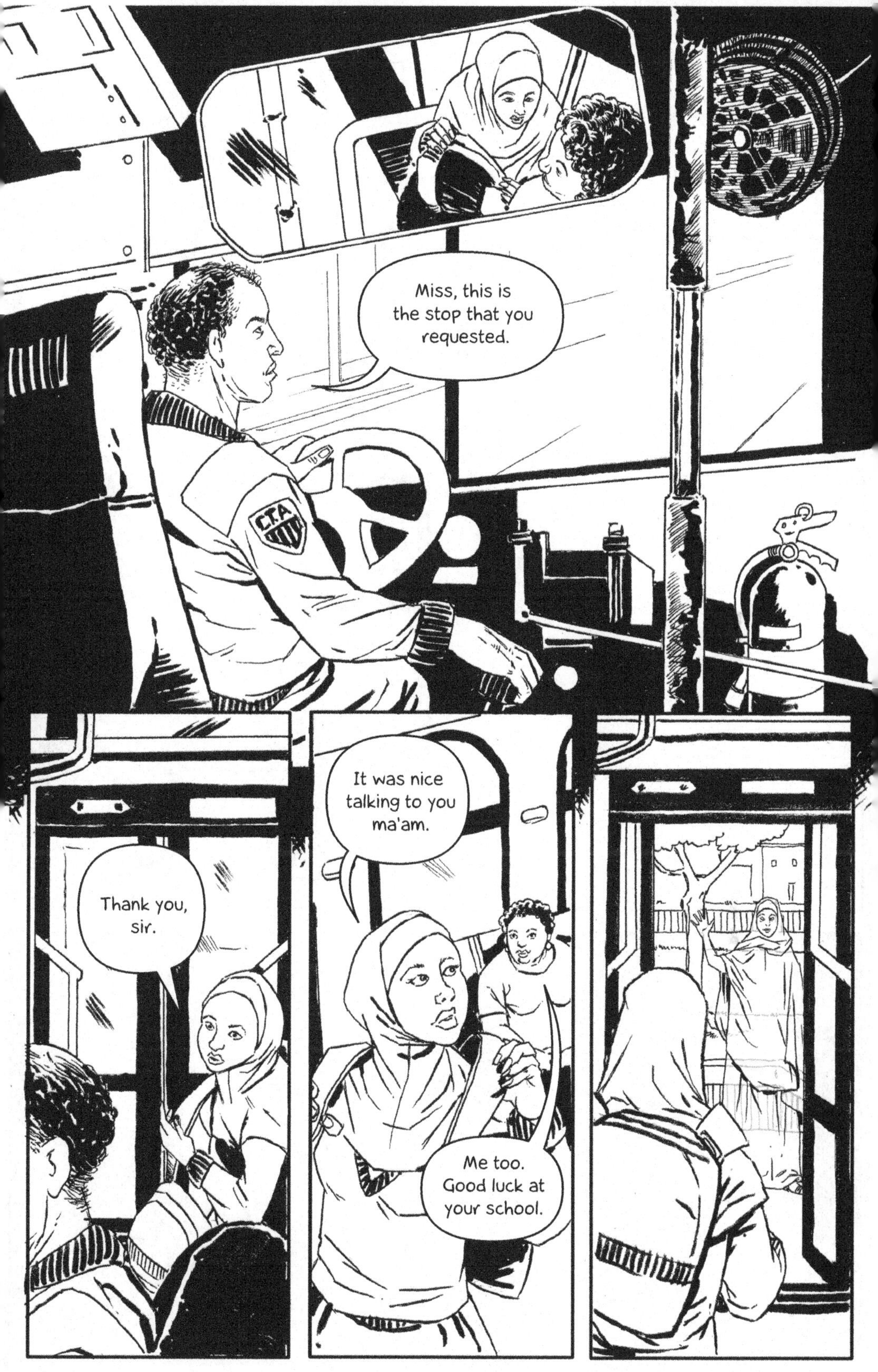
Miss, this is the stop that you requested.
Thank you, sir.
It was nice talking to you ma'am.
Me too. Good luck at your school.

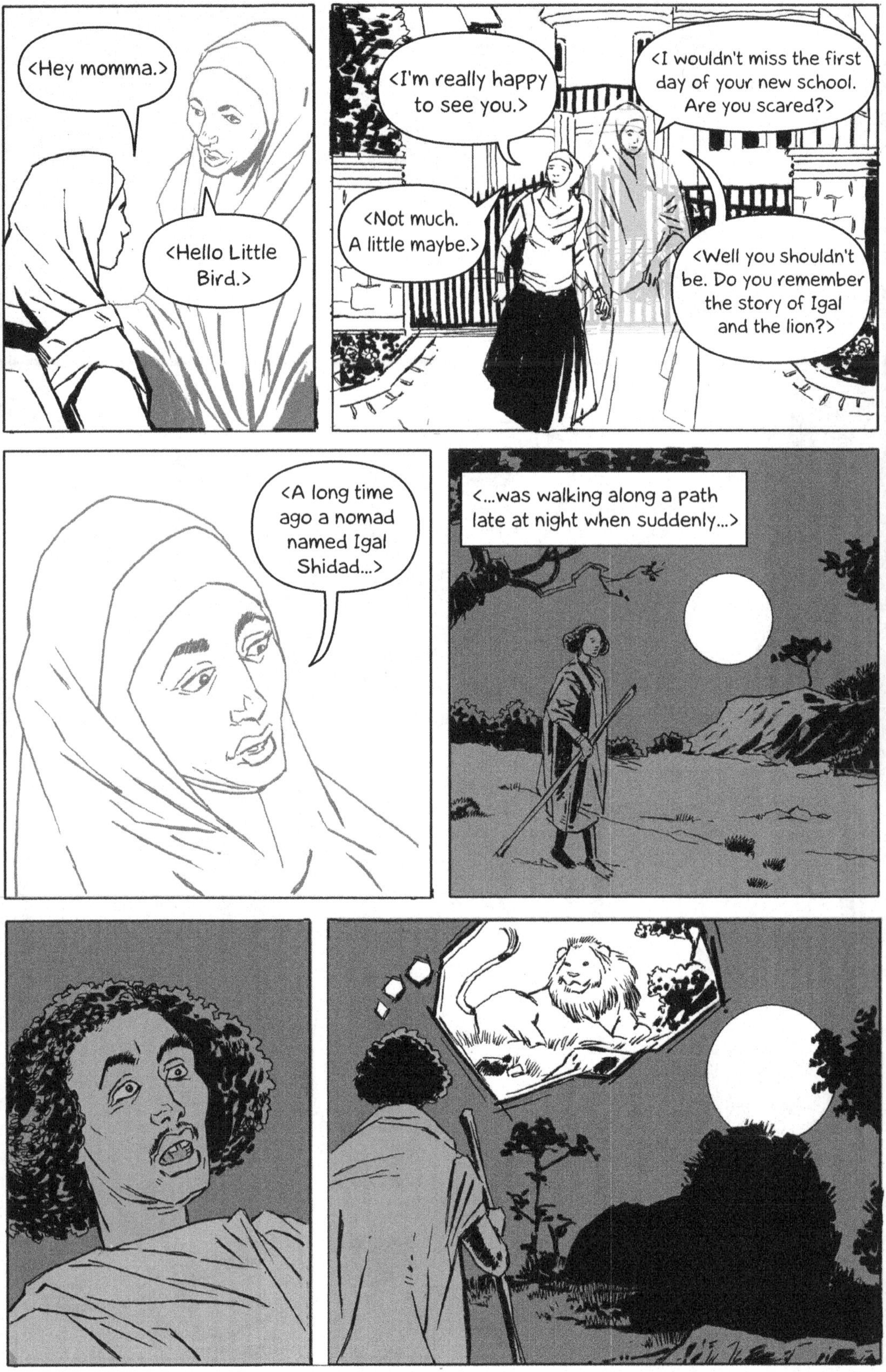
<Hey momma.>
<Hello Little Bird.>
<I'm really happy to see you.>
<I wouldn't miss the first day of your new school. Are you scared?>
<Not much. A little maybe.>
<Well you shouldn't be. Do you remember the story of Igal and the lion?>
<A long time ago a nomad named Igal Shidad...>
<...was walking along a path late at night when suddenly...>

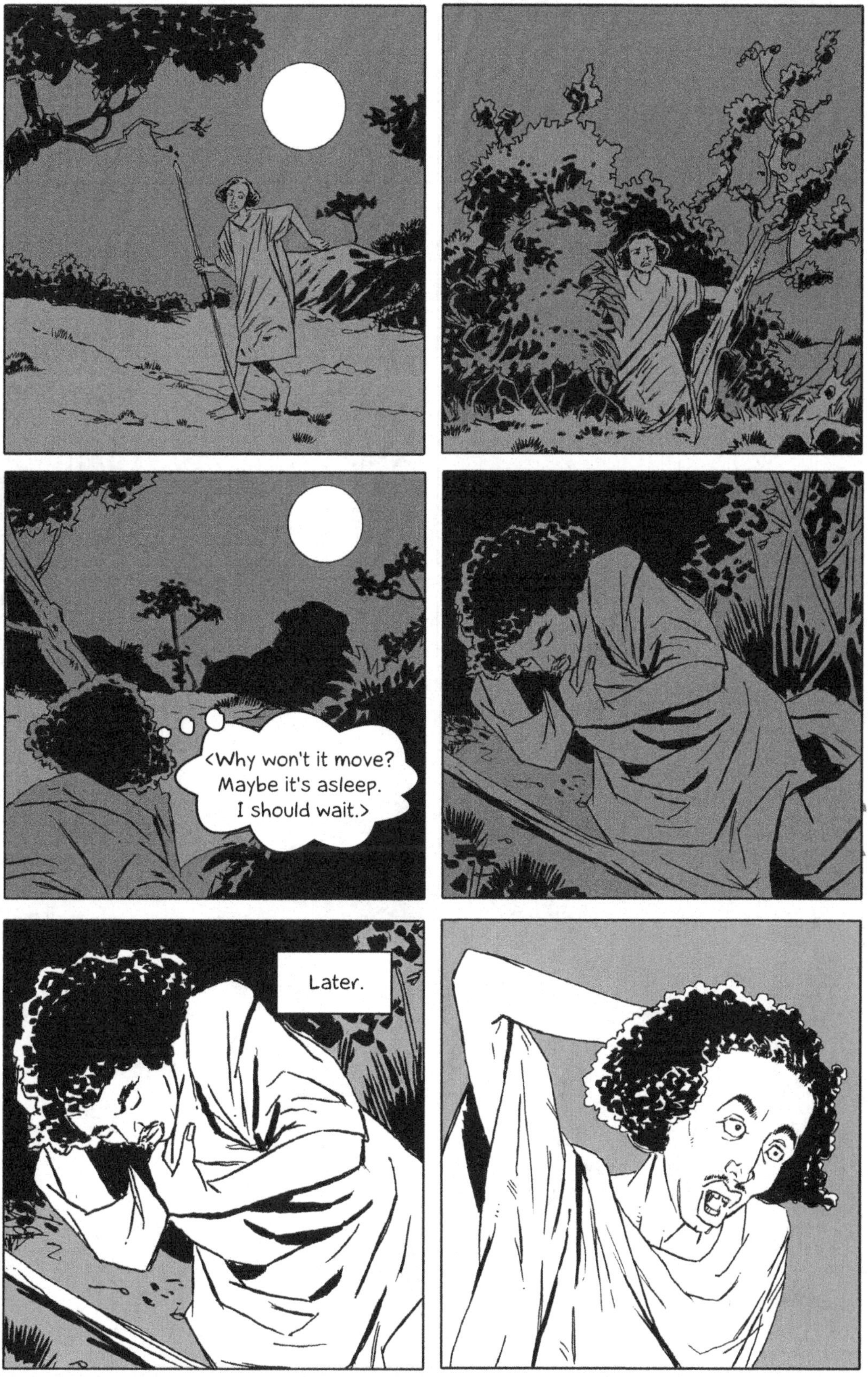

<Why won't it move?
Maybe it's asleep.
I should wait.>
Later.

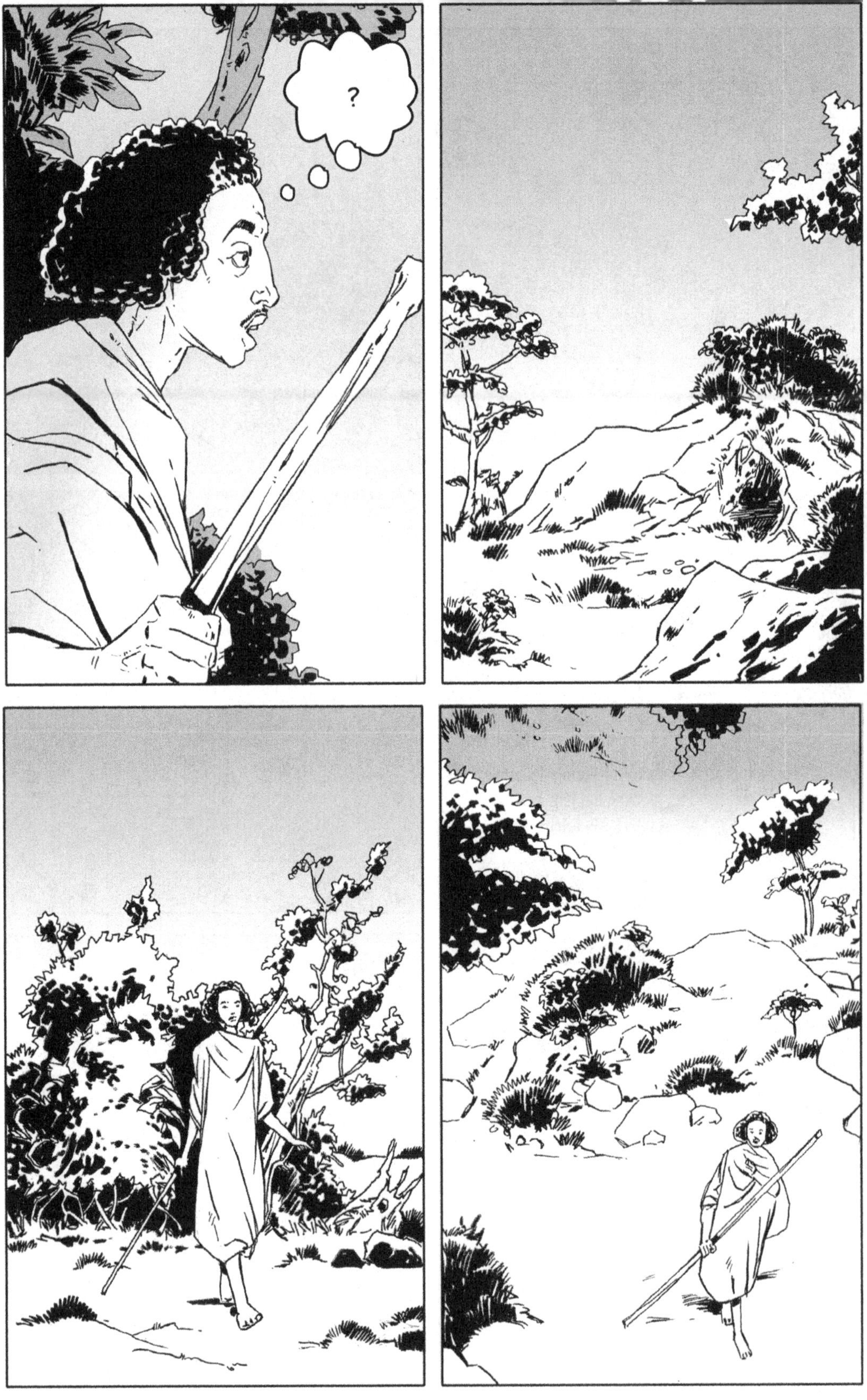
?

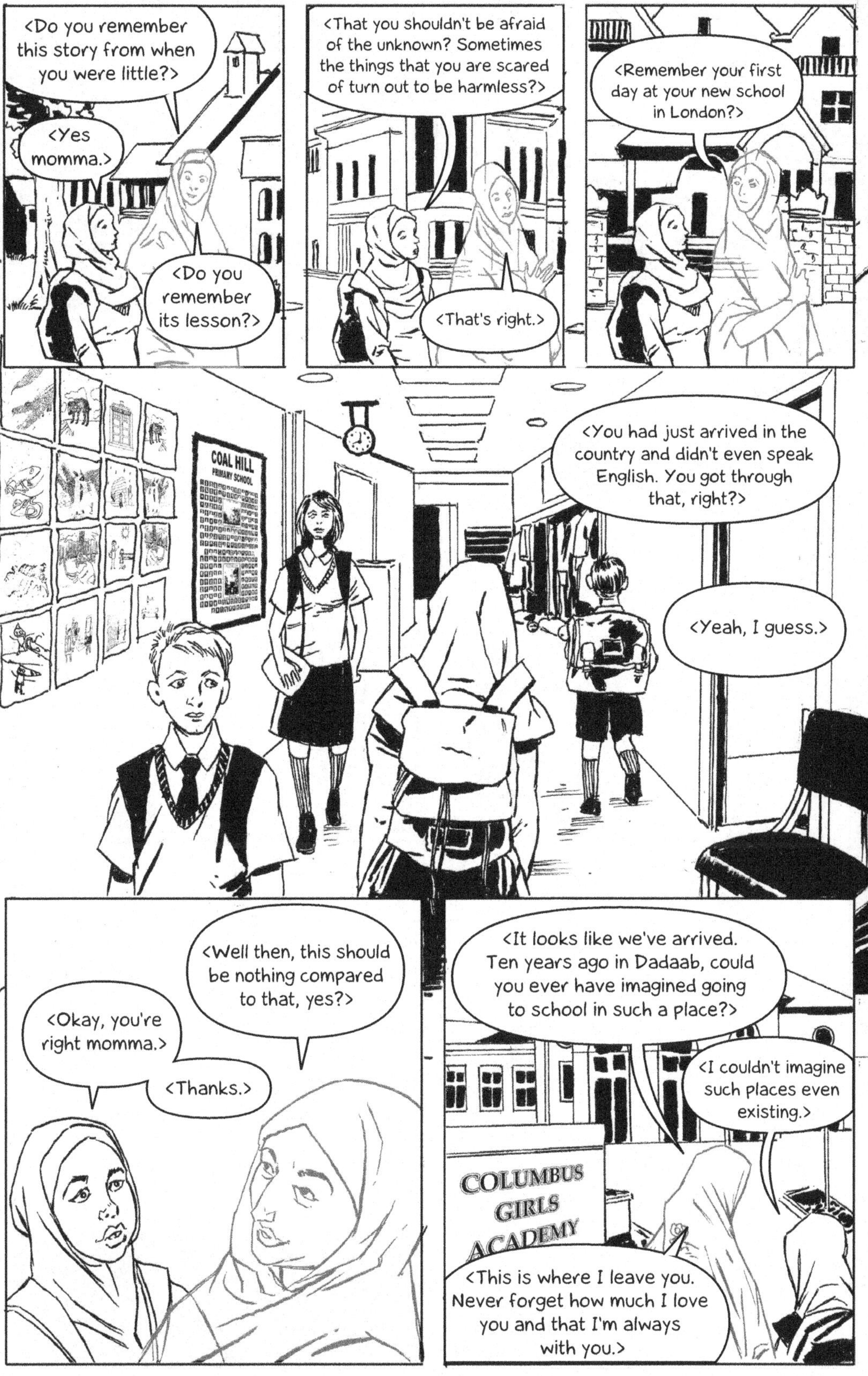
<Do you remember this story from when you were little?>
<Yes momma.>
<Do you remember its lesson?>
<That you shouldn't be afraid of the unknown? Sometimes the things that you are scared of turn out to be harmless?>
<That's right.>
<Remember your first day at your new school in London?>
COAL HILL
PRIMARY SCHOOL
<You had just arrived in the country and didn't even speak English. You got through that, right?>
<Yeah, I guess.>
<Well then, this should be nothing compared to that, yes?>
<Okay, you're right momma.>
<Thanks.>
<It looks like we've arrived. Ten years ago in Dadaab, could you ever have imagined going to school in such a place?>
<I couldn't imagine such places even existing.>
COLUMBUS
GIRLS
ACADEMY
<This is where I leave you. Never forget how much I love you and that I'm always with you.>

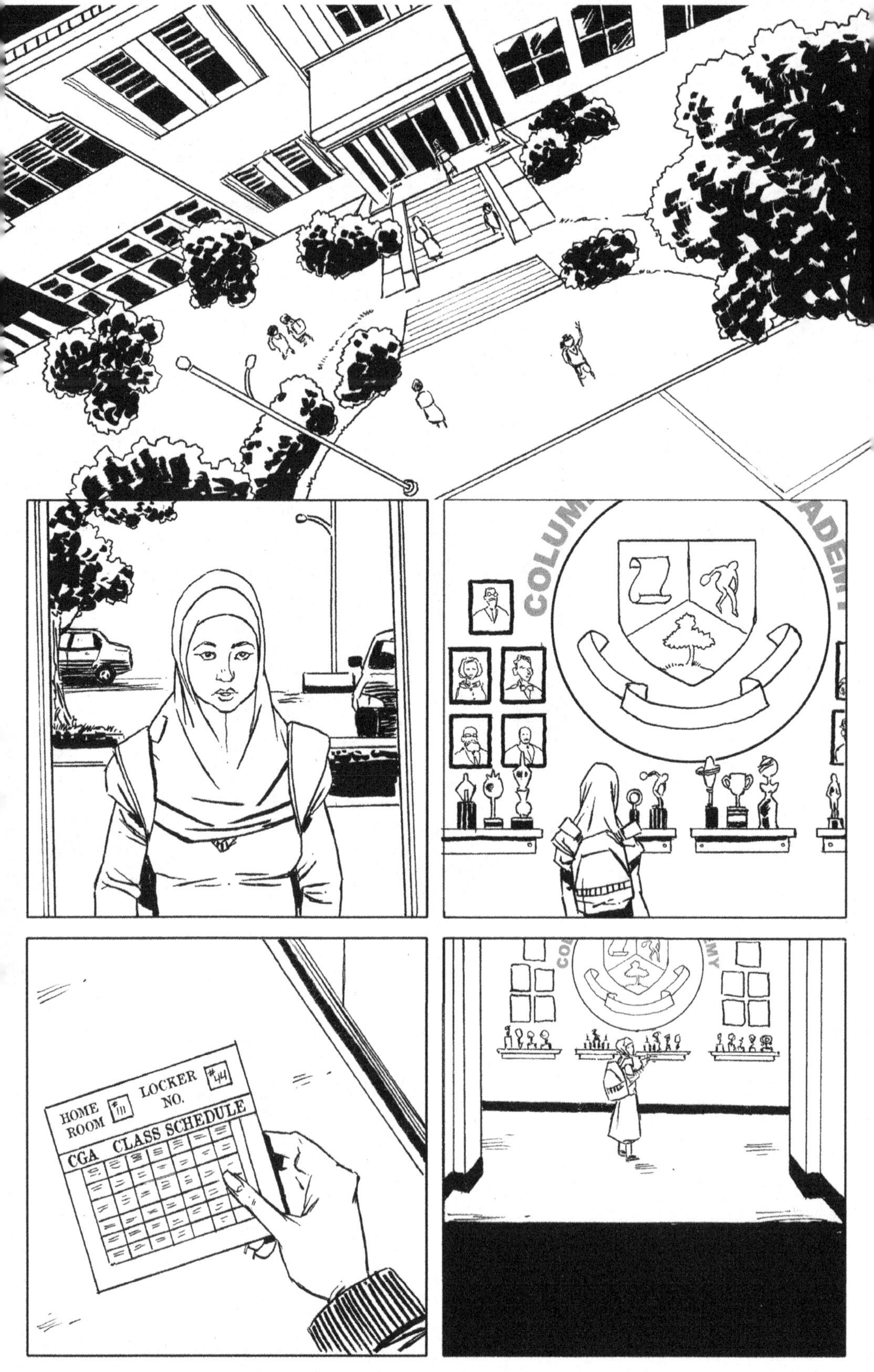
COLUM
ADEMY
HOME ROOM #111
LOCKER NO. #44
CGA CLASS SCHEDULE

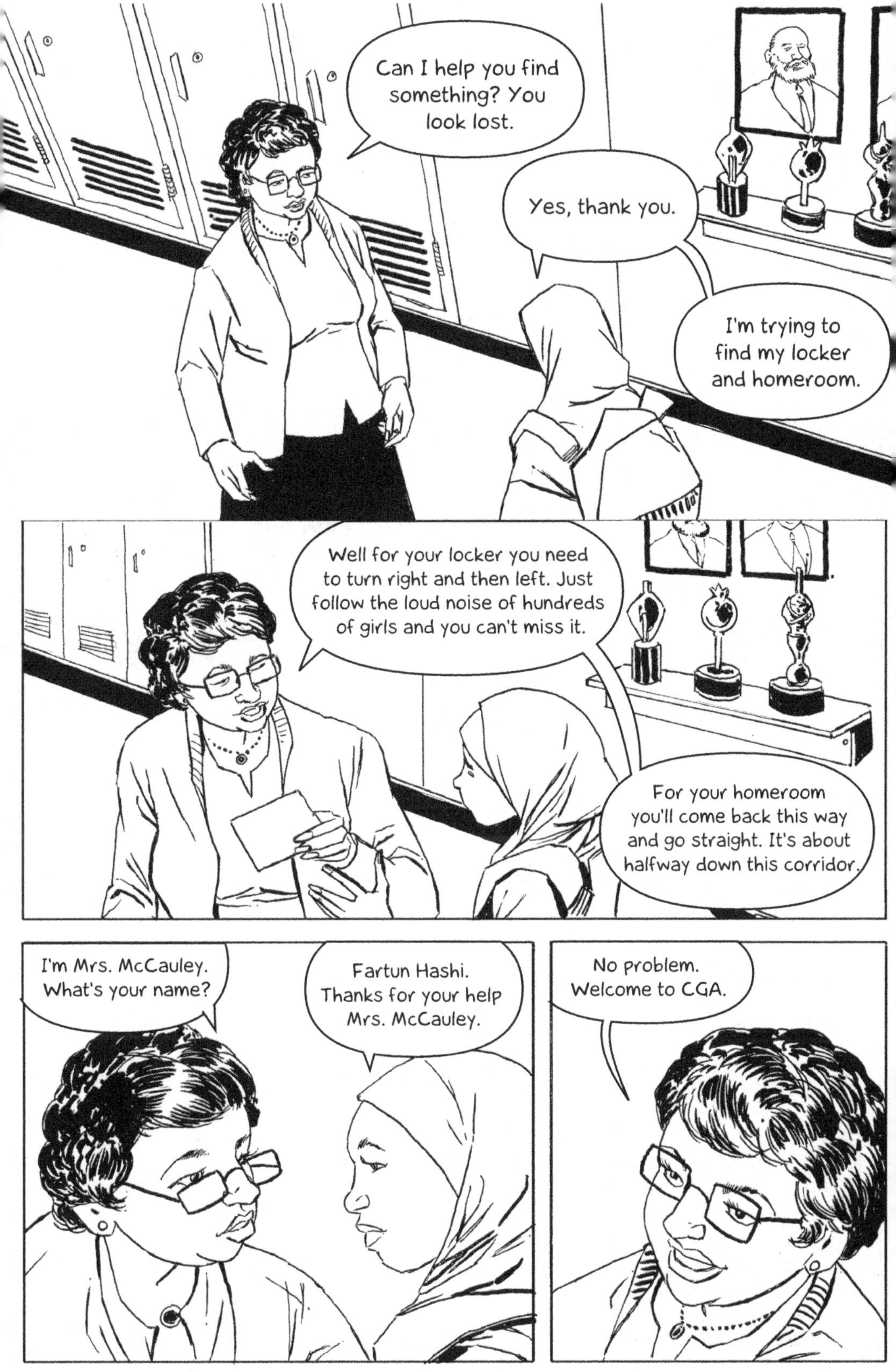
Can I help you find something? You look lost.
Yes, thank you.
I'm trying to find my locker and homeroom.
Well for your locker you need to turn right and then left. Just follow the loud noise of hundreds of girls and you can't miss it.
For your homeroom you'll come back this way and go straight. It's about halfway down this corridor.
I'm Mrs. McCauley. What's your name?
Fartun Hashi. Thanks for your help Mrs. McCauley.
No problem. Welcome to CGA.

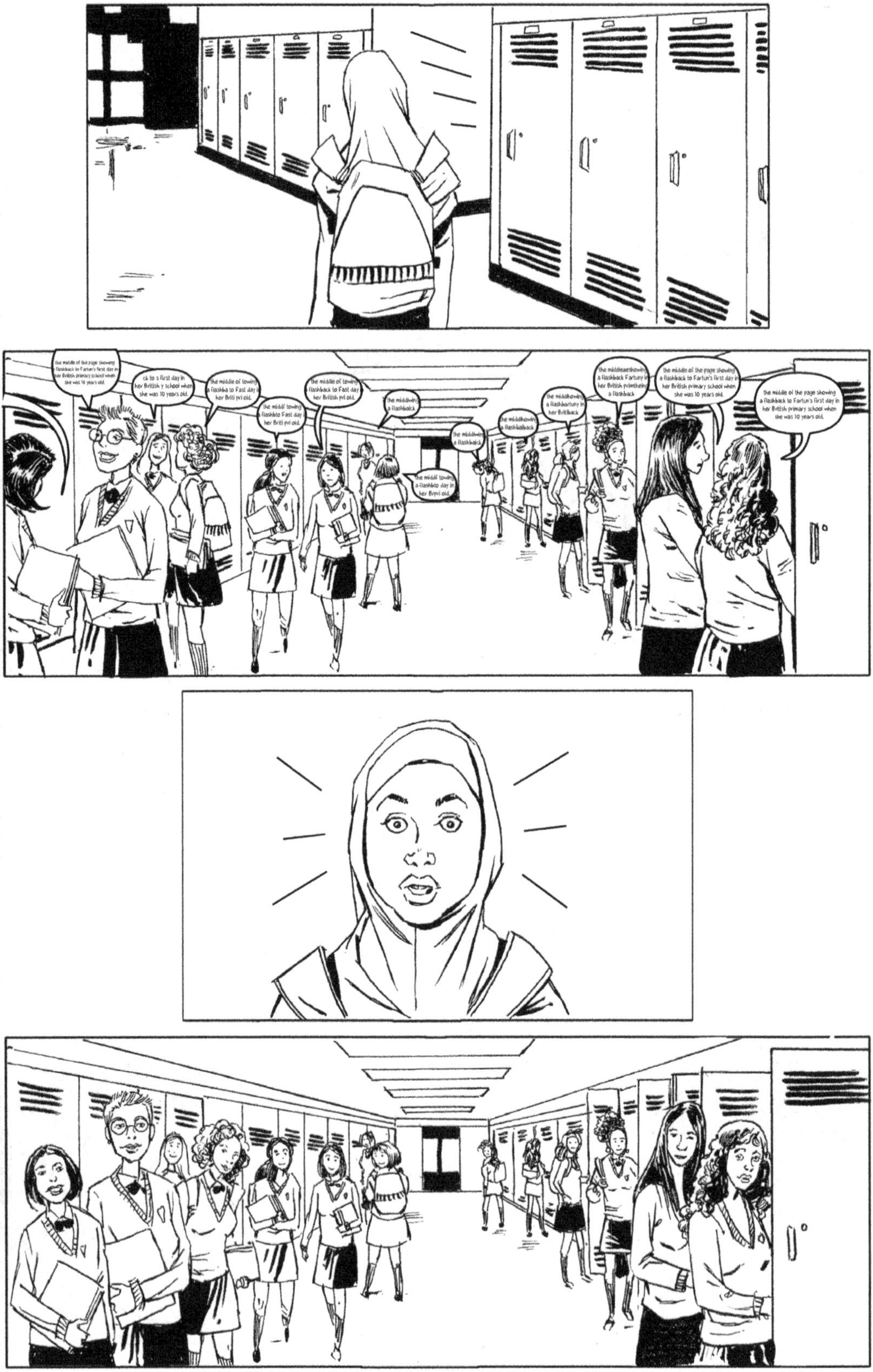
the middle of the page showing flashback to Fartun's first day in her British primary school when she was 10 years old.
ck to s first day in her British y school when she was 10 years old.
the middle of towing a flashba to Fast day in her Briti pri old.
the middl towing a flashbto Fast day her Briti pri old.
the middle of towing flashback to Fast day her British pri old.
the middiwing a flashbaick
the middl towing a flashbto day in her Brpri old.
the middiwing a flashbaick
the middhowing a flashbalback
the middhowing a flashbartuny in her Britback
the middieaeshowing a flashback Fartuny in her British primtheing a flashback
the middle of the page showing a flashback to Fartun's first day in her British primary school when she was 10 years old.
the middle of the page showing a flashback to Fartun's first day in her British primary school when she was 10 years old.

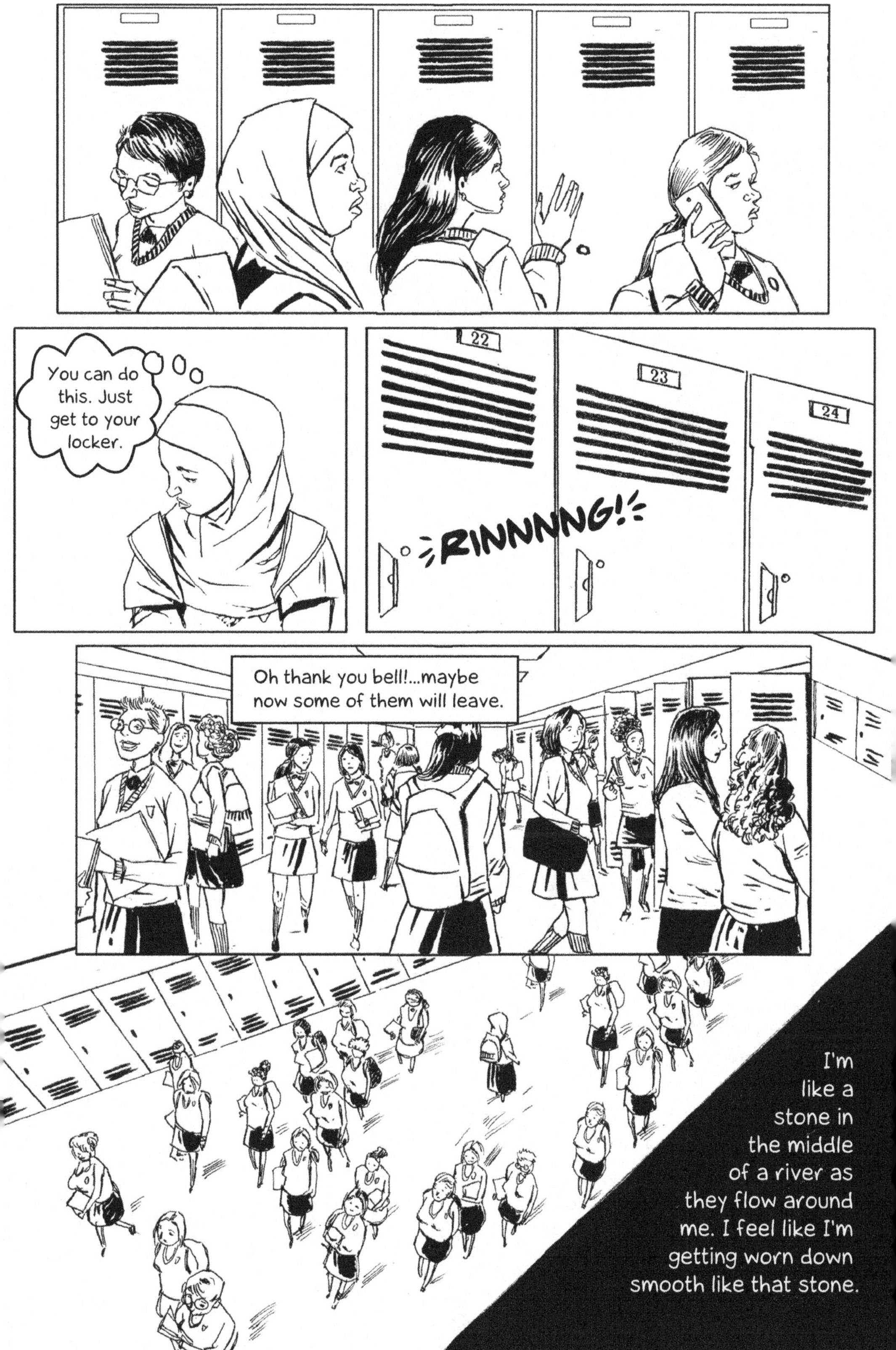
You can do this. Just get to your locker.
22
23
24
RINNNNG!
Oh thank you bell!...maybe now some of them will leave.
I'm like a stone in the middle of a river as they flow around me. I feel like I'm getting worn down smooth like that stone.

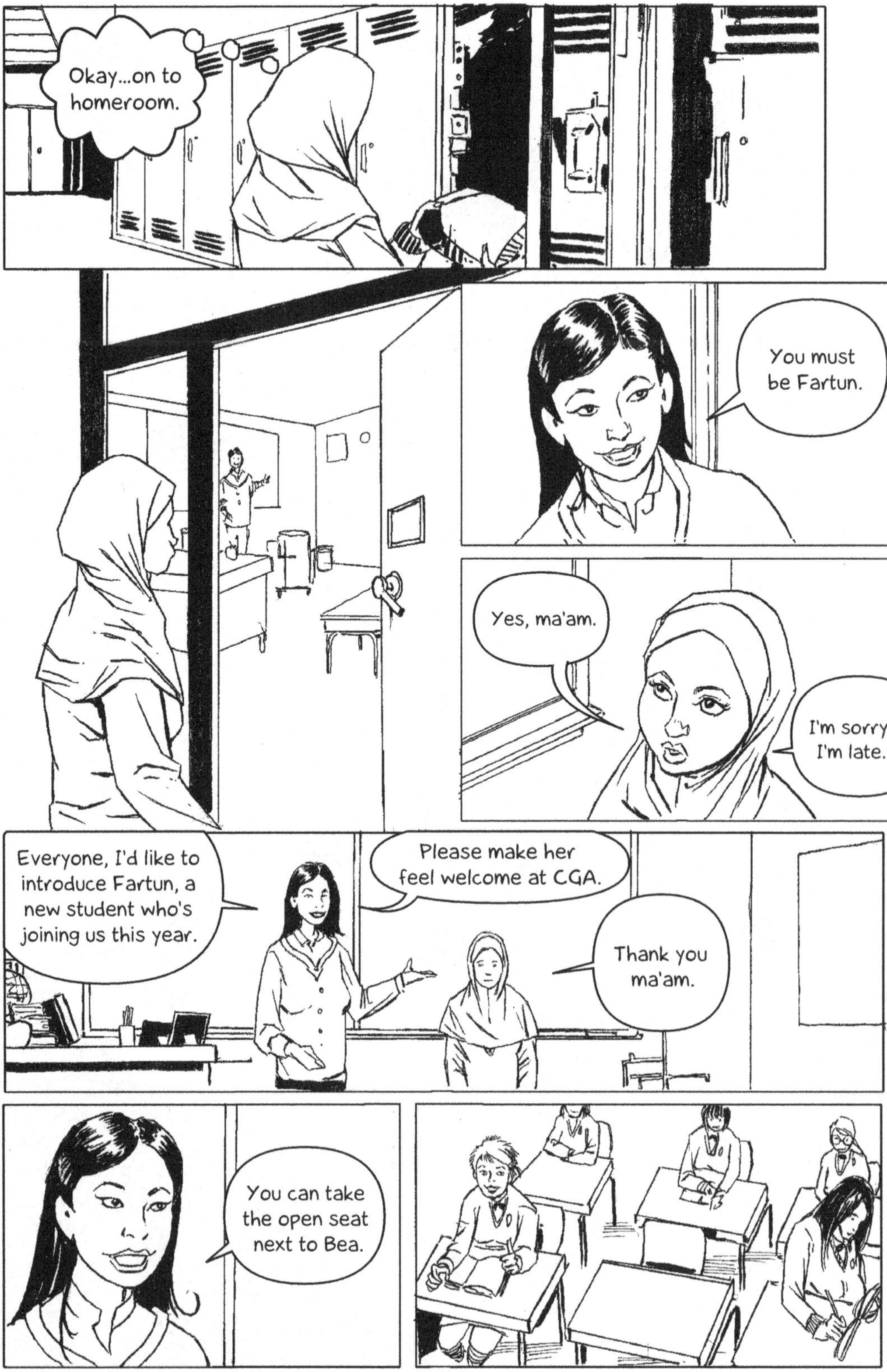
Okay...on to homeroom.
You must be Fartun.
Yes, ma'am.
I'm sorry I'm late.
Everyone, I'd like to introduce Fartun, a new student who's joining us this year.
Please make her feel welcome at CGA.
Thank you ma'am.
You can take the open seat next to Bea.

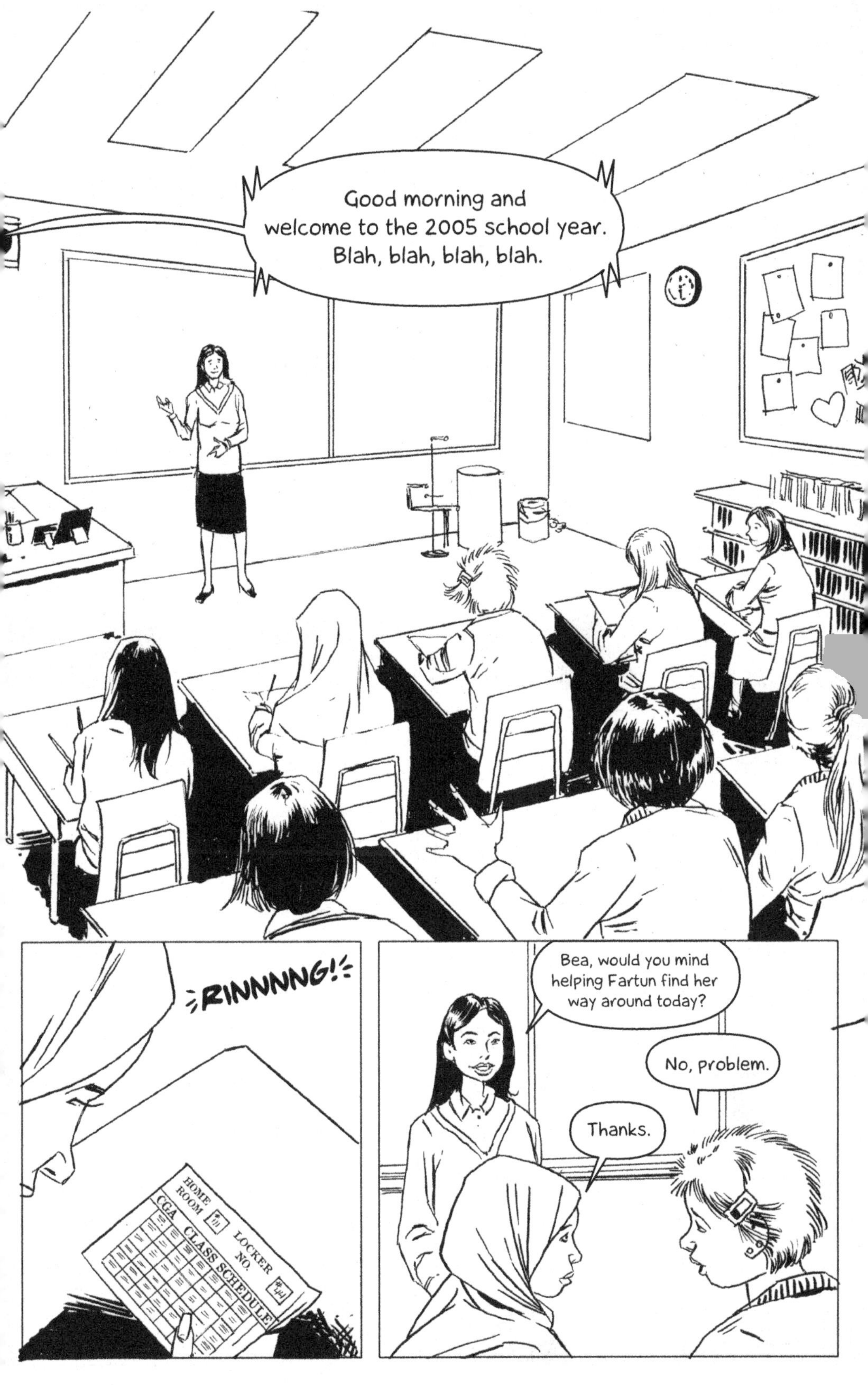
Good morning and welcome to the 2005 school year. Blah, blah, blah, blah.
RINNNNG!
HOME ROOM
LOCKER NO.
CGA CLASS SCHEDULE
Bea, would you mind helping Fartun find her way around today?
No, problem.
Thanks.

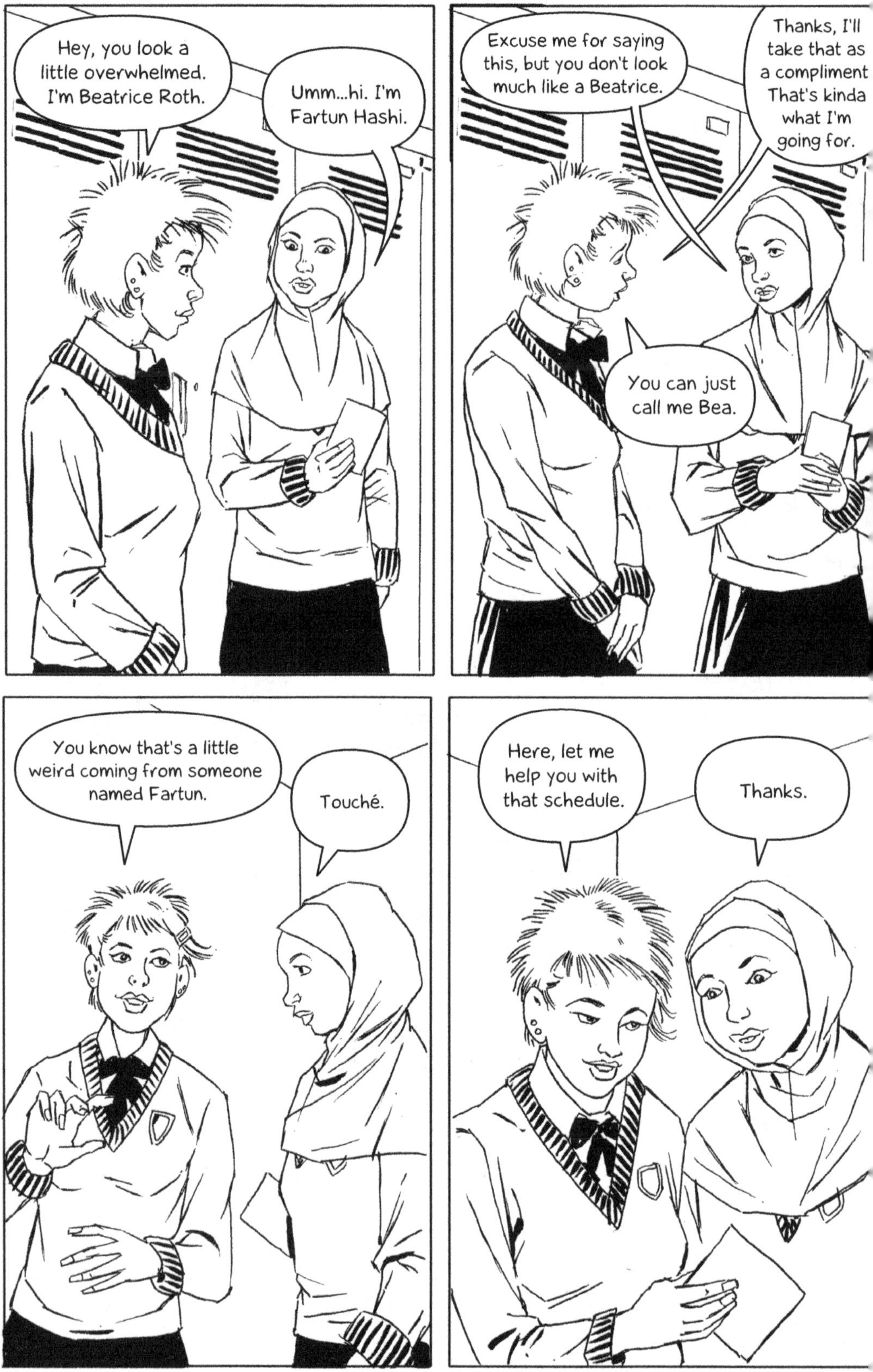
Hey, you look a little overwhelmed. I'm Beatrice Roth.
Umm...hi. I'm Fartun Hashi.
Excuse me for saying this, but you don't look much like a Beatrice.
Thanks, I'll take that as a compliment That's kinda what I'm going for.
You can just call me Bea.
You know that's a little weird coming from someone named Fartun.
Touché.
Here, let me help you with that schedule.
Thanks.

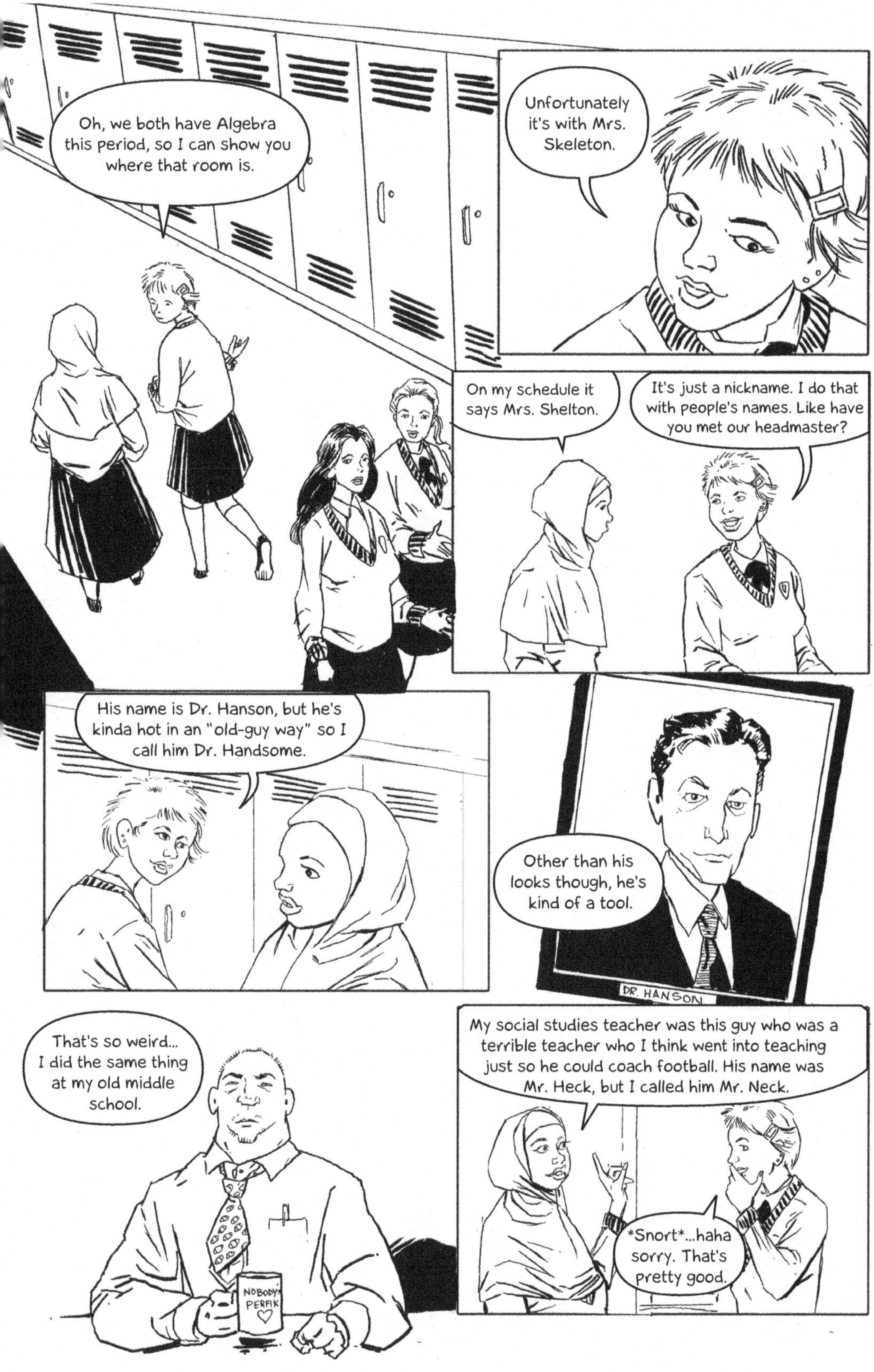
Oh, we both have Algebra this period, so I can show you where that room is.
Unfortunately it's with Mrs. Skeleton.
On my schedule it says Mrs. Shelton.
It's just a nickname. I do that with people's names. Like have you met our headmaster?
His name is Dr. Hanson, but he's kinda hot in an "old-guy way" so I call him Dr. Handsome.
Other than his looks though, he's kind of a tool.
DR. HANSON
That's so weird... I did the same thing at my old middle school.
NOBODY'S PERFIK
My social studies teacher was this guy who was a terrible teacher who I think went into teaching just so he could coach football. His name was Mr. Heck, but I called him Mr. Neck.
Snort...haha sorry. That's pretty good.

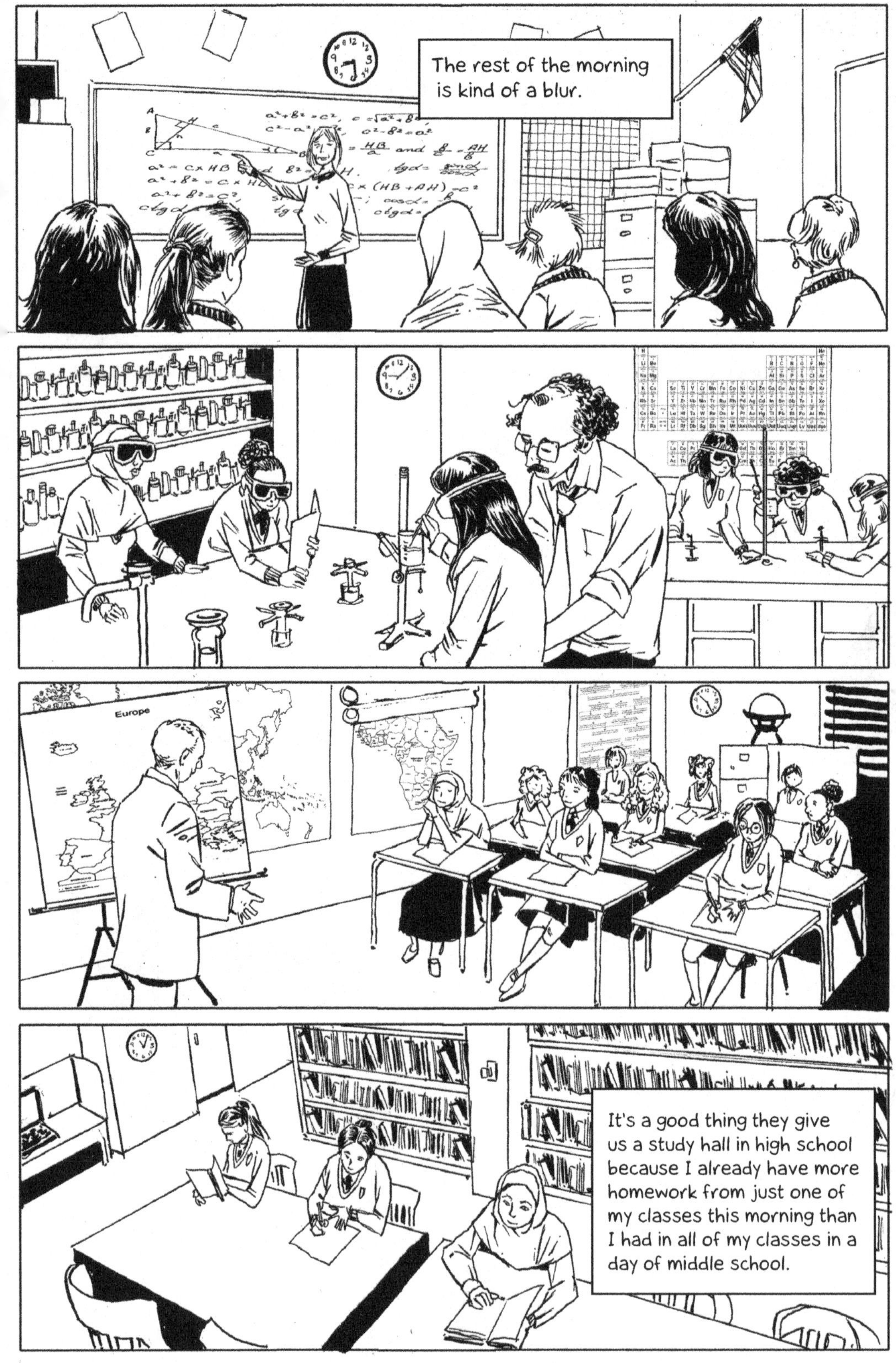
The rest of the morning is kind of a blur.
Europe
It's a good thing they give us a study hall in high school because I already have more homework from just one of my classes this morning than I had in all of my classes in a day of middle school.

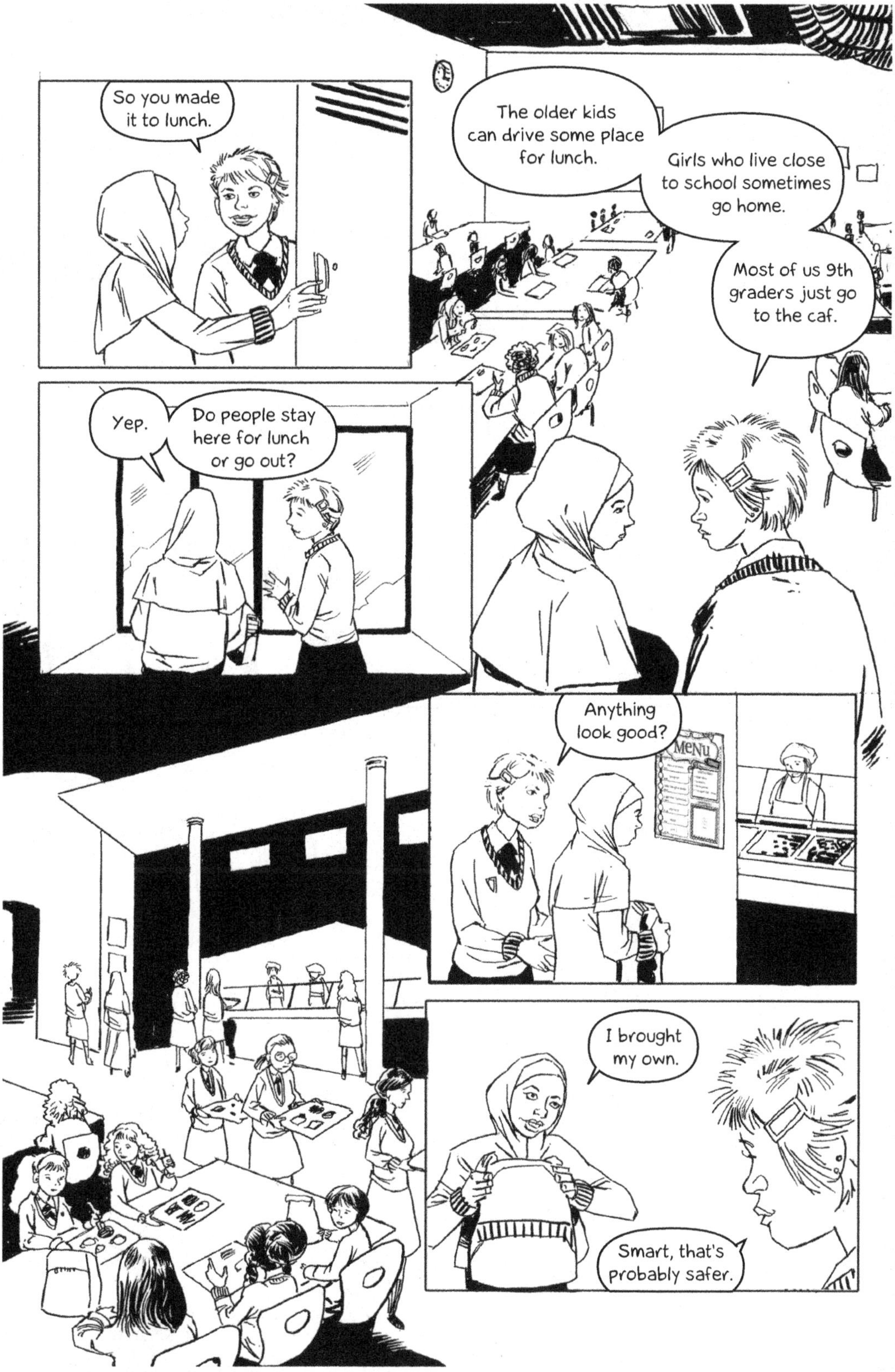
So you made it to lunch.
Yep.
Do people stay here for lunch or go out?
The older kids can drive some place for lunch.
Girls who live close to school sometimes go home.
Most of us 9th graders just go to the caf.
Anything look good?
MENU
I brought my own.
Smart, that's probably safer.

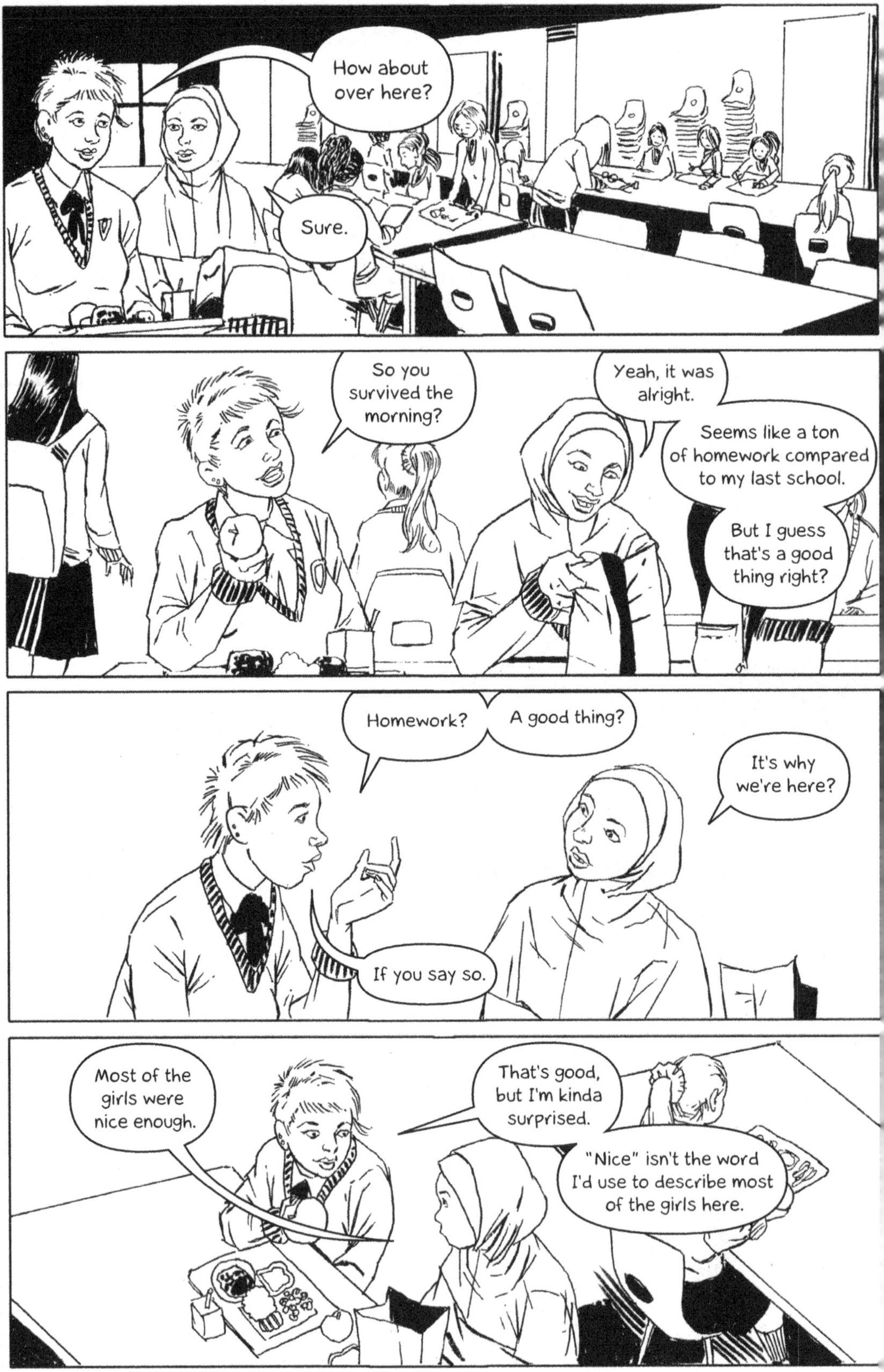
How about over here?
Sure.
So you survived the morning?
Yeah, it was alright.
Seems like a ton of homework compared to my last school.
But I guess that's a good thing right?
Homework?
A good thing?
It's why we're here?
If you say so.
Most of the girls were nice enough.
That's good, but I'm kinda surprised.
"Nice" isn't the word I'd use to describe most of the girls here.

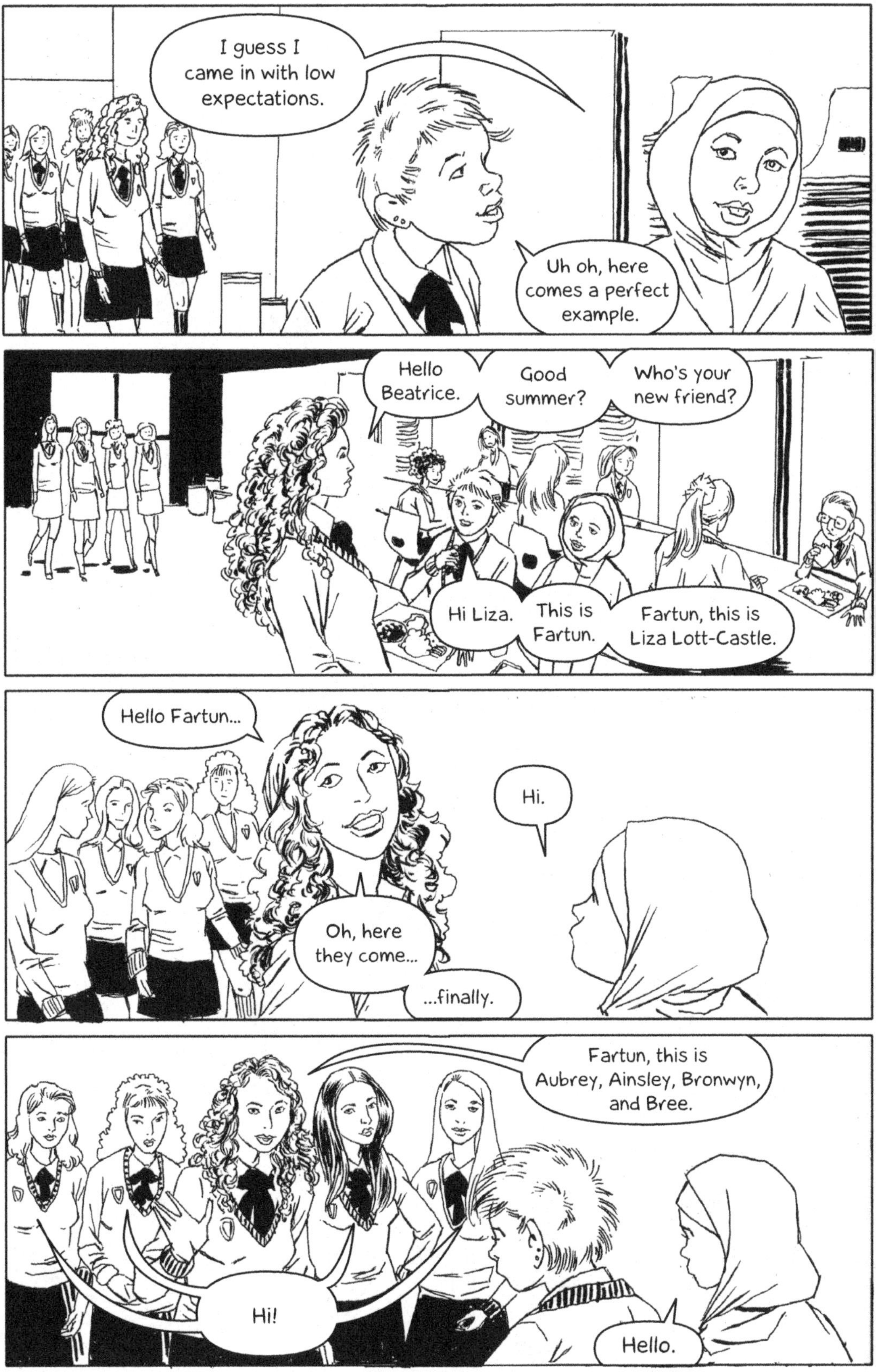
I guess I came in with low expectations.
Uh oh, here comes a perfect example.
Hello Beatrice.
Good summer?
Who's your new friend?
Hi Liza.
This is Fartun.
Fartun, this is Liza Lott-Castle.
Hello Fartun...
Hi.
Oh, here they come...
...finally.
Fartun, this is Aubrey, Ainsley, Bronwyn, and Bree.
Hi!
Hello.

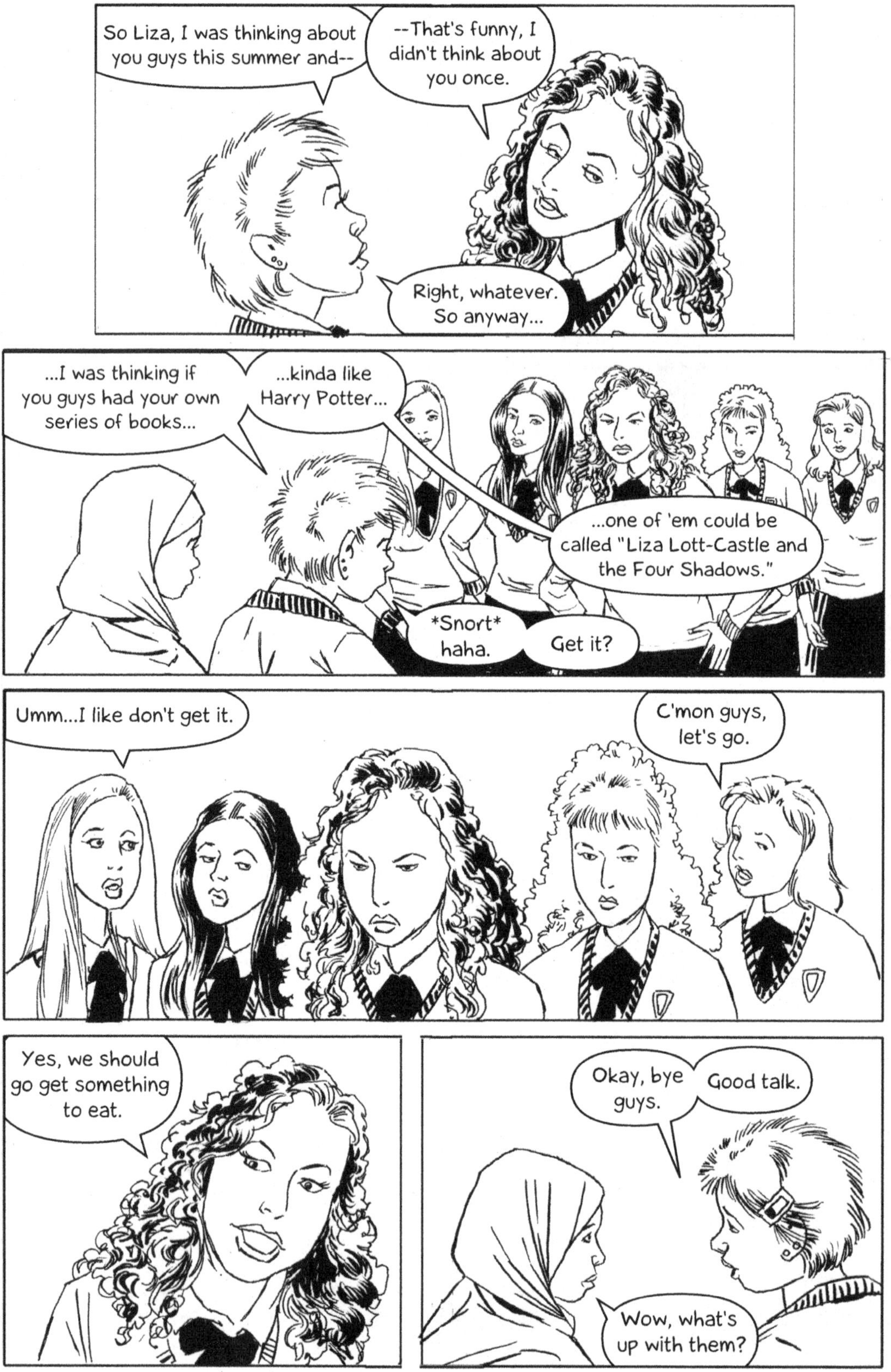
So Liza, I was thinking about you guys this summer and--
--That's funny, I didn't think about you once.
Right, whatever. So anyway...
...I was thinking if you guys had your own series of books...
...kinda like Harry Potter...
...one of 'em could be called "Liza Lott-Castle and the Four Shadows."
Snort haha.
Get it?
Umm...I like don't get it.
C'mon guys, let's go.
Yes, we should go get something to eat.
Okay, bye guys.
Good talk.
Wow, what's up with them?

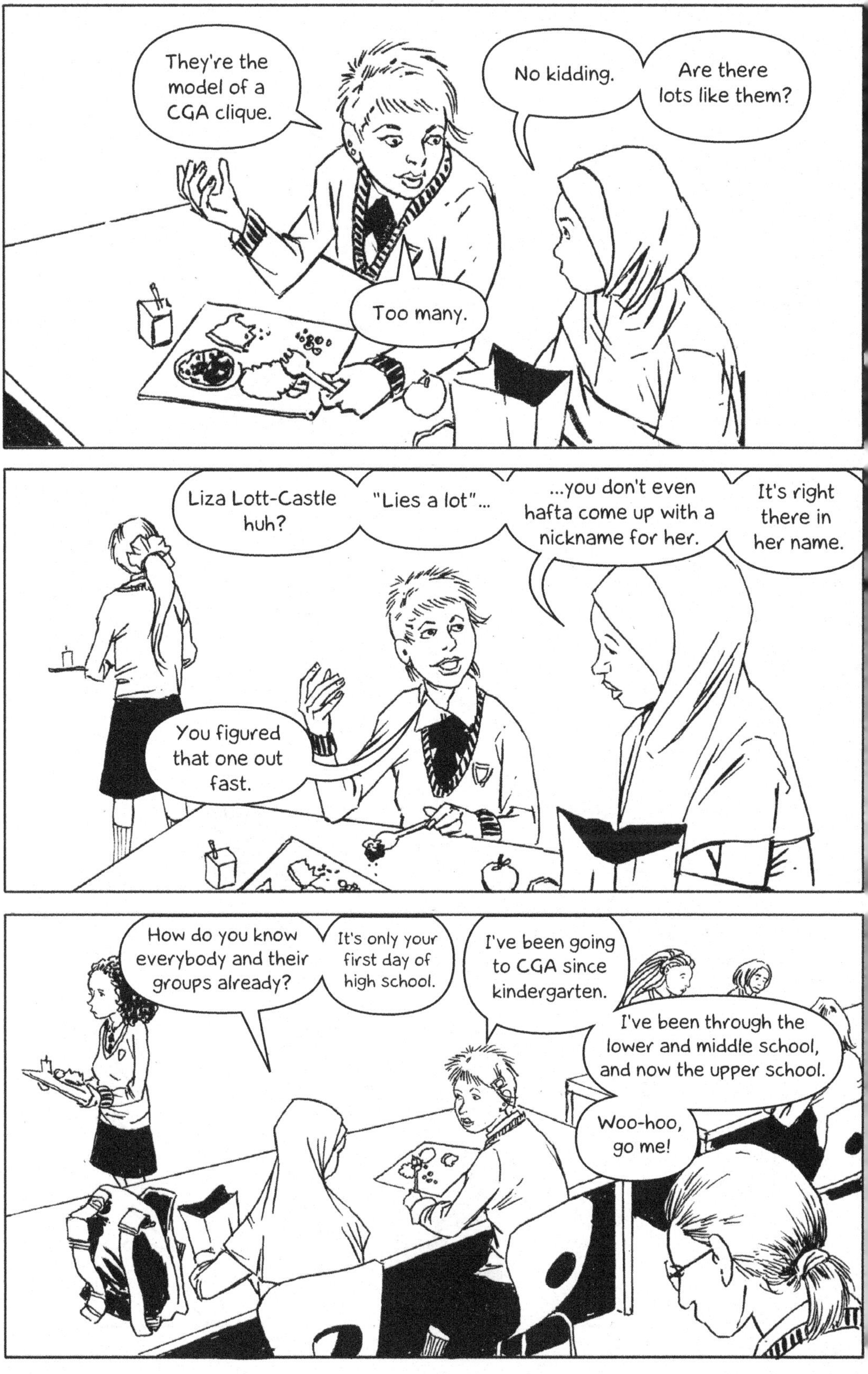
They're the model of a CGA clique.
No kidding.
Are there lots like them?
Too many.
Liza Lott-Castle huh?
"Lies a lot"...
...you don't even hafta come up with a nickname for her.
It's right there in her name.
You figured that one out fast.
How do you know everybody and their groups already?
It's only your first day of high school.
I've been going to CGA since kindergarten.
I've been through the lower and middle school, and now the upper school.
Woo-hoo, go me!

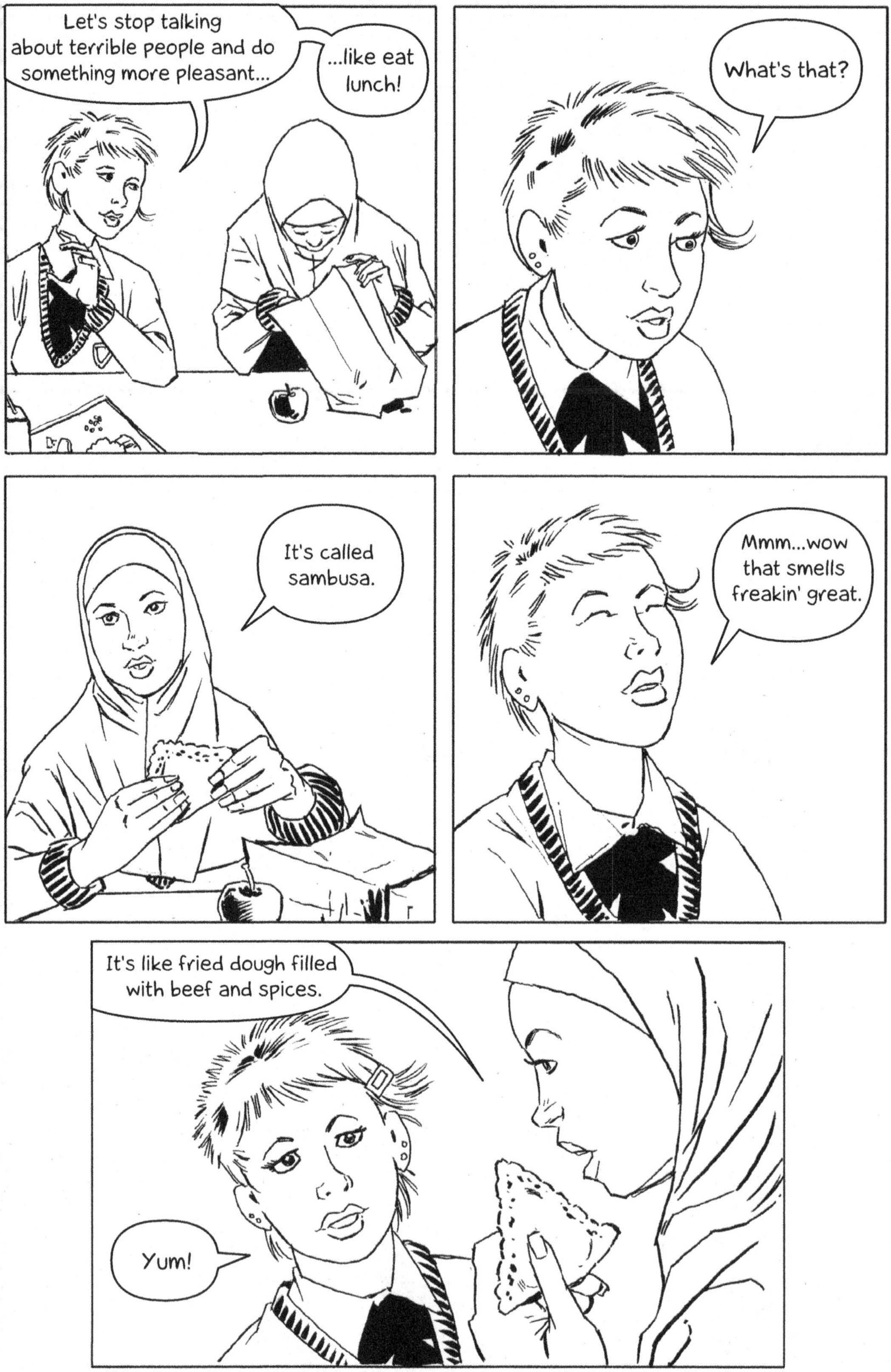
Let's stop talking about terrible people and do something more pleasant...
...like eat lunch!
What's that?
It's called sambusa.
Mmm...wow that smells freakin' great.
It's like fried dough filled with beef and spices.
Yum!

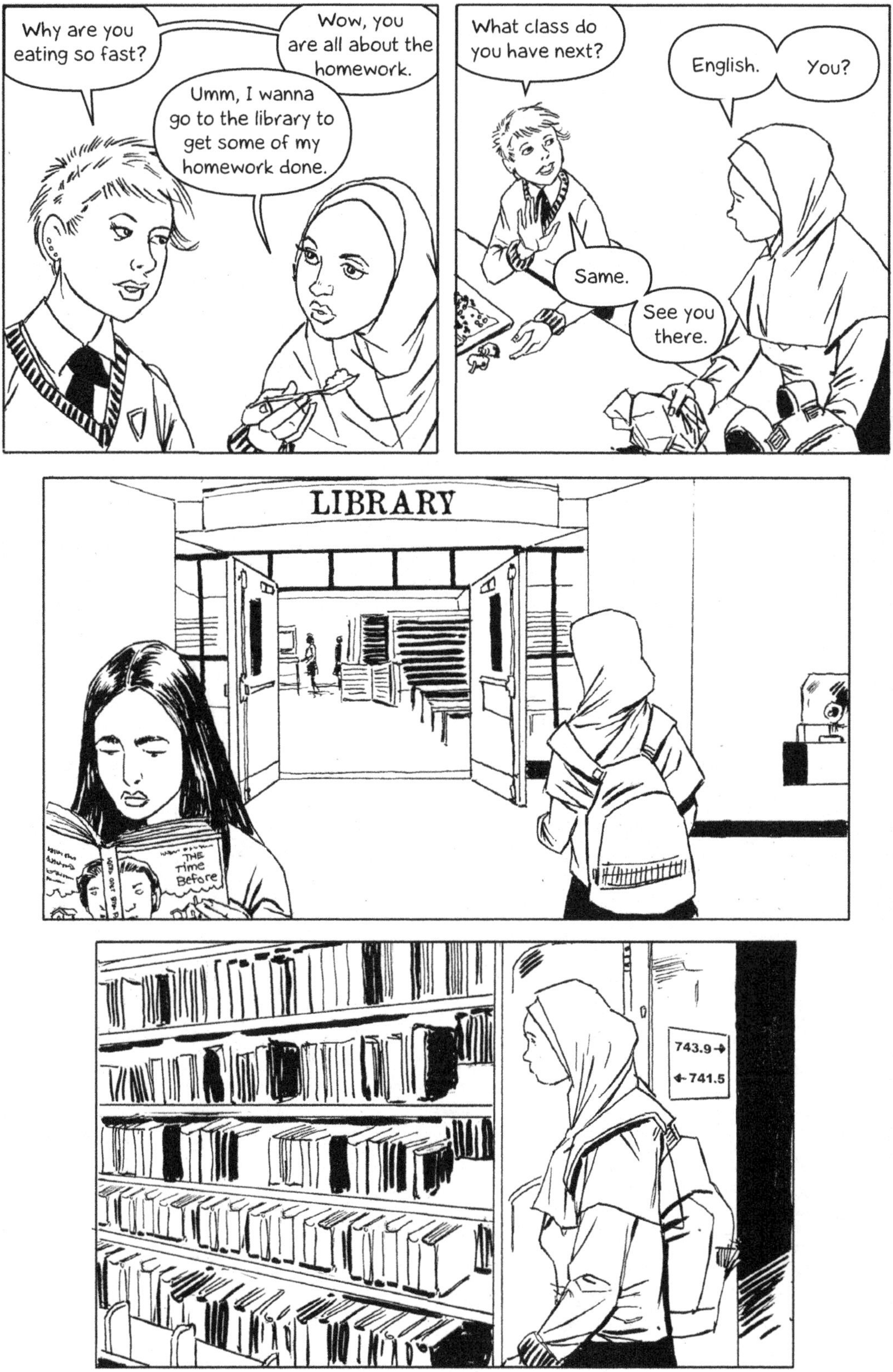
Why are you eating so fast?
Umm, I wanna go to the library to get some of my homework done.
Wow, you are all about the homework.
What class do you have next?
English.
You?
Same.
See you there.
LIBRARY
THE Time Before
743.9 →
← 741.5

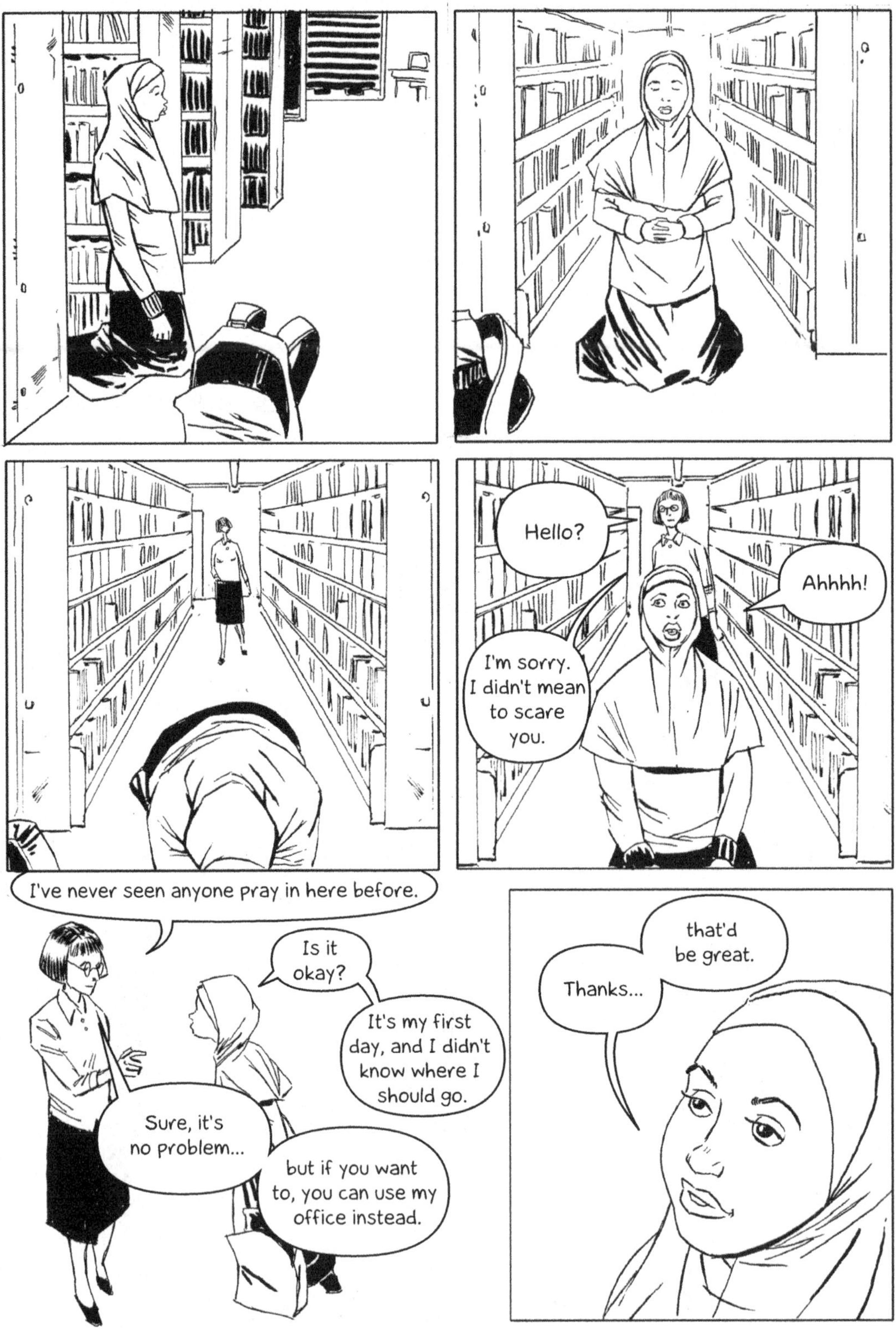
Hello?
Ahhhh!
I'm sorry. I didn't mean to scare you.
I've never seen anyone pray in here before.
Is it okay?
It's my first day, and I didn't know where I should go.
Sure, it's no problem...
but if you want to, you can use my office instead.
Thanks...
that'd be great.

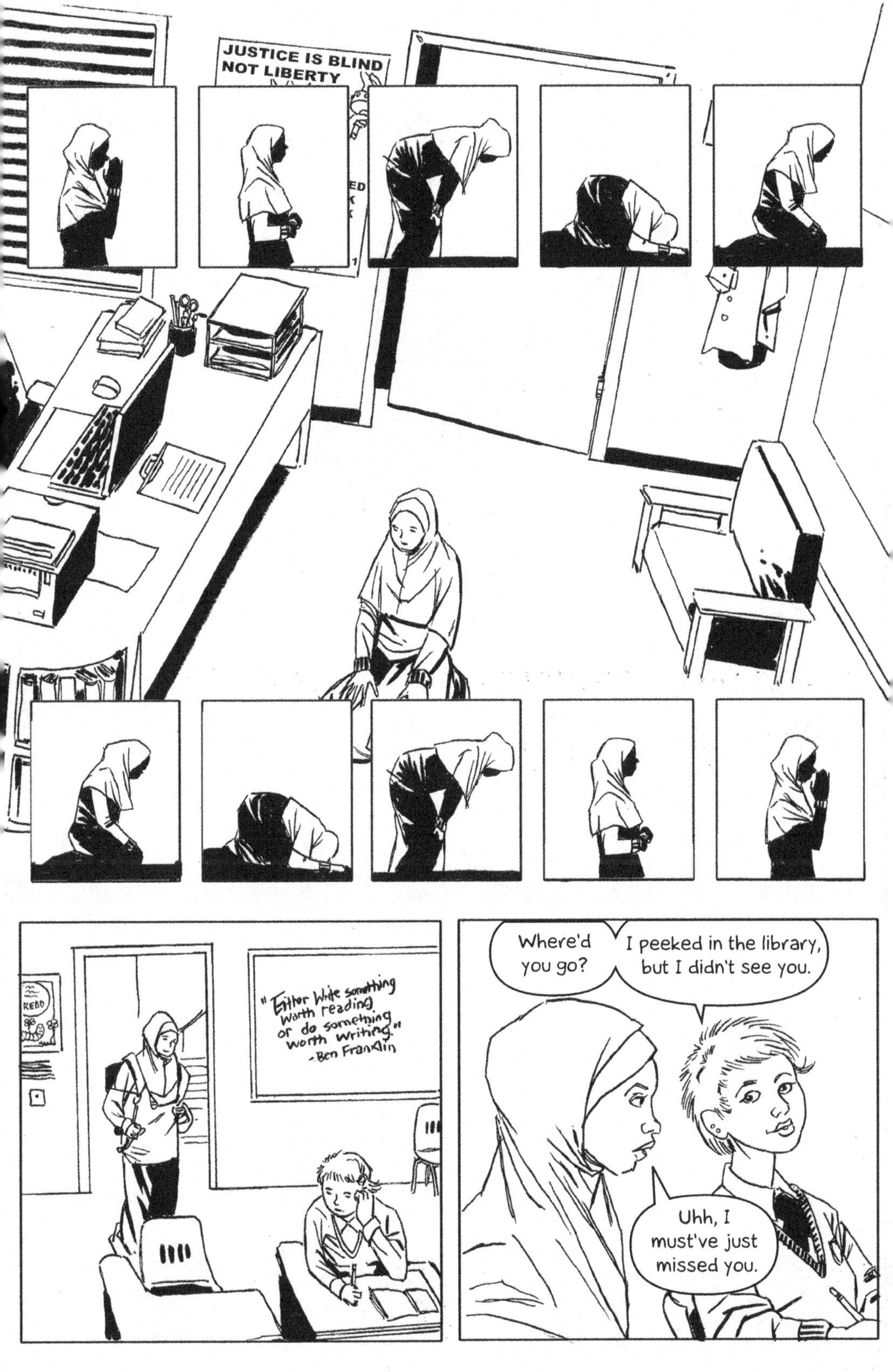
JUSTICE IS BLIND
NOT LIBERTY
READ
"Either Write something worth reading or do something worth writing."
-Ben Franklin
Where'd you go?
I peeked in the library, but I didn't see you.
Uhh, I must've just missed you.

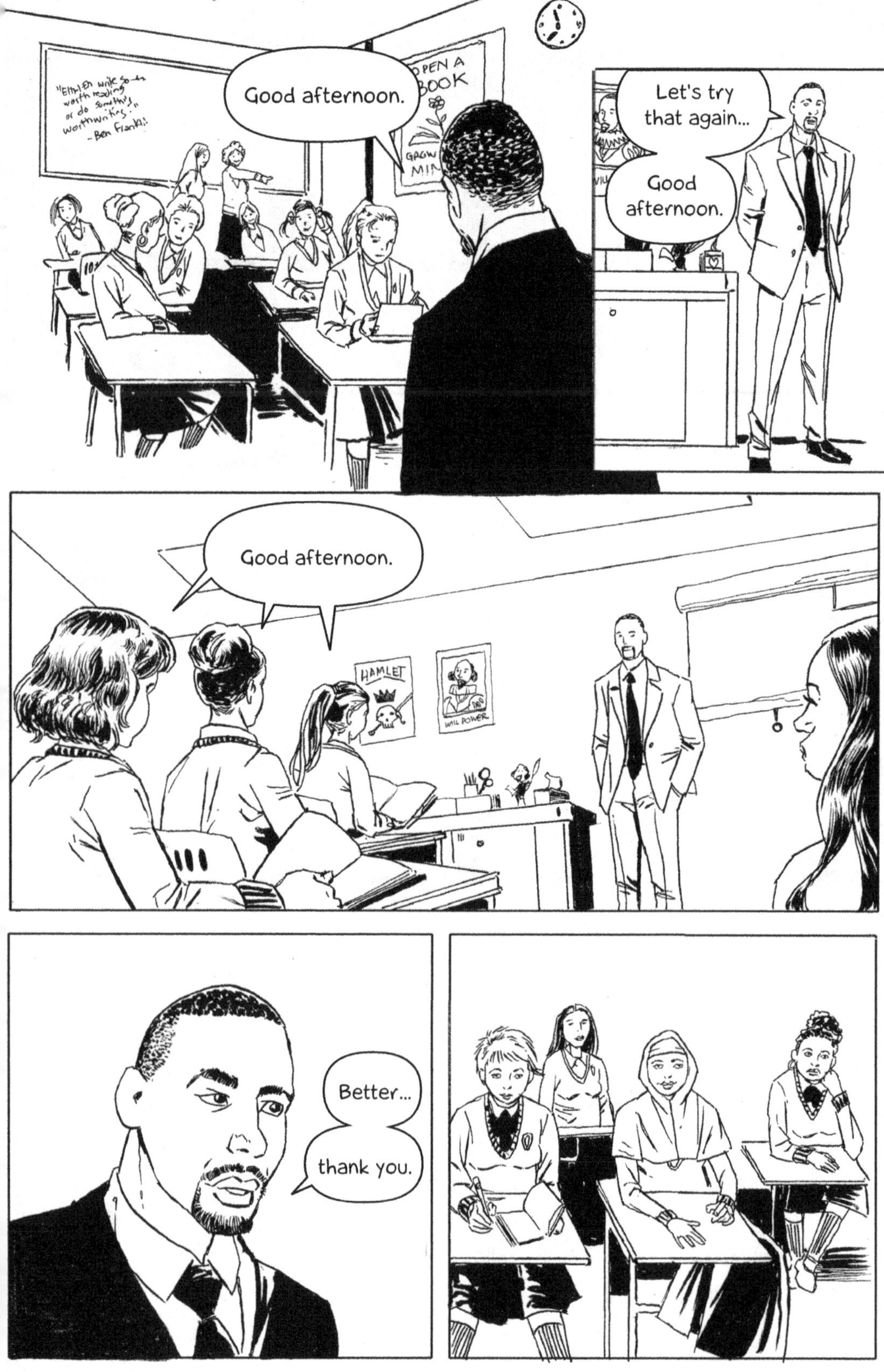

OPEN A BOOK
Good afternoon.
Let's try that again...
Good afternoon.
Good afternoon.
HAMLET
WILL POWER
Better...
thank you.

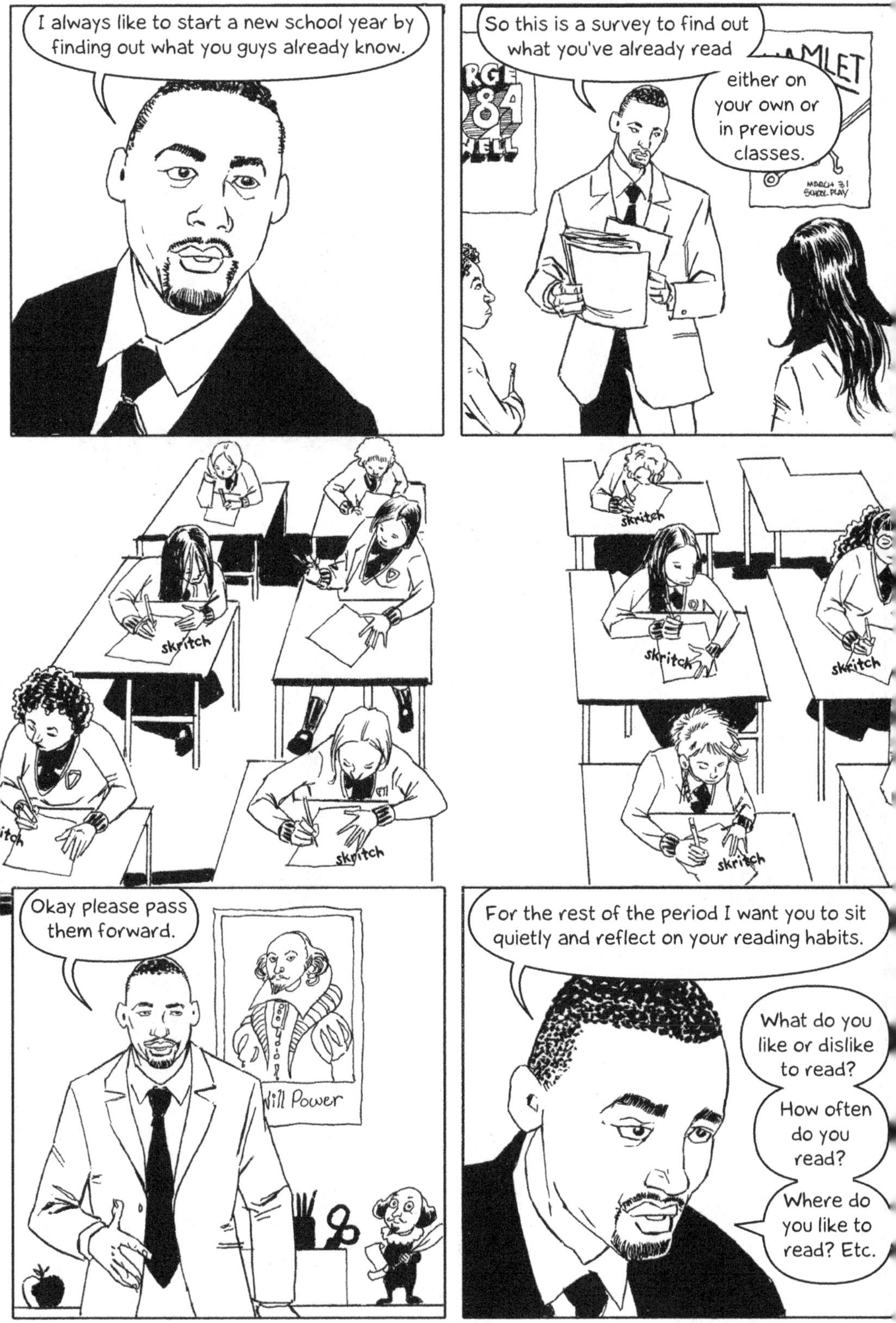
I always like to start a new school year by finding out what you guys already know.
So this is a survey to find out what you've already read
either on your own or in previous classes.
HAMLET
MARCH 31 SCHOOL PLAY
skritch
skritch
skritch
skritch
skritch
skritch
Okay please pass them forward.
Will Power
For the rest of the period I want you to sit quietly and reflect on your reading habits.
What do you like or dislike to read?
How often do you read?
Where do you like to read? Etc.

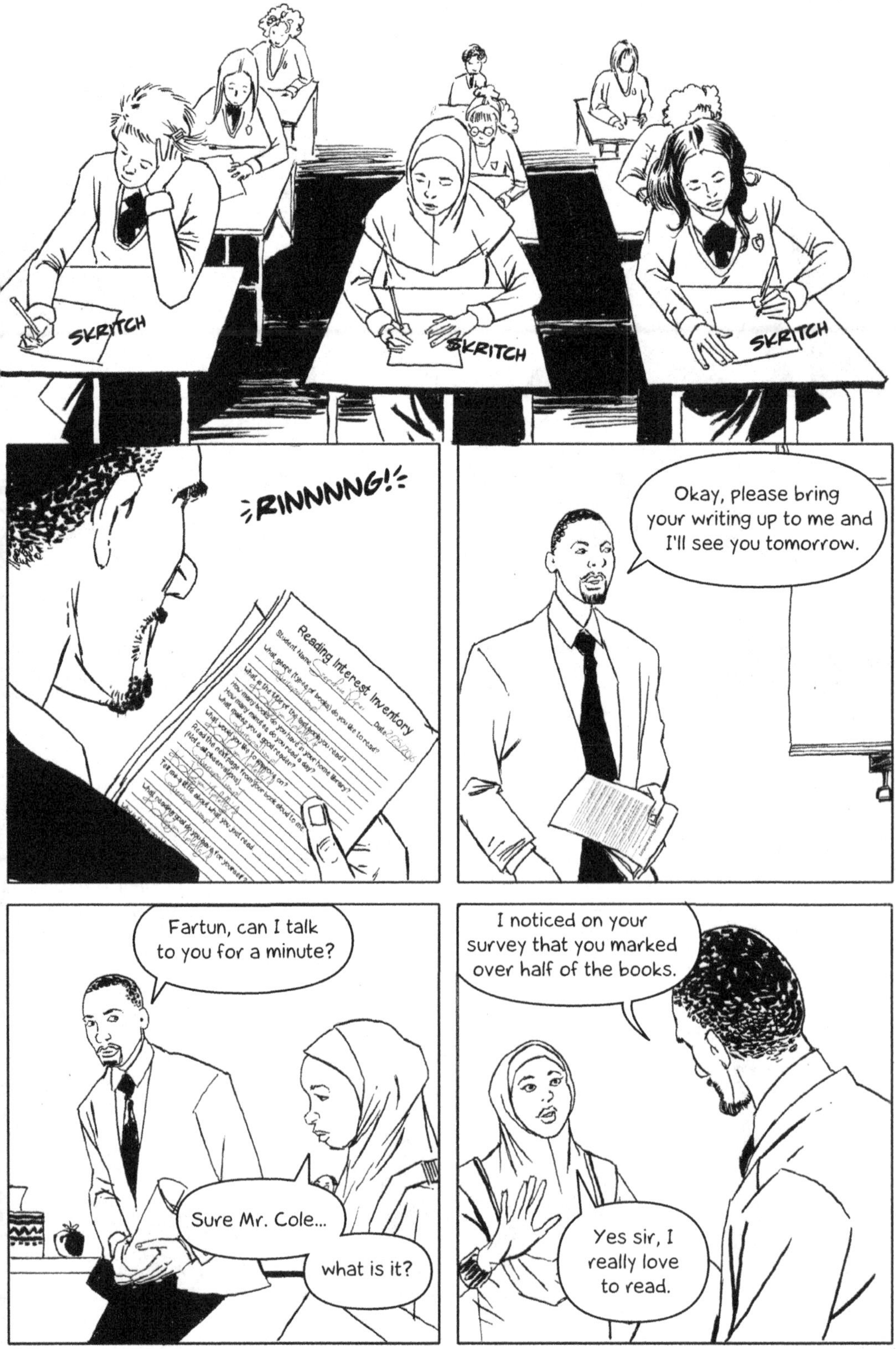
SKRITCH
SKRITCH
SKRITCH
RINNNNG!
Reading Interest Inventory
Okay, please bring your writing up to me and I'll see you tomorrow.
Fartun, can I talk to you for a minute?
Sure Mr. Cole...
what is it?
I noticed on your survey that you marked over half of the books.
Yes sir, I really love to read.

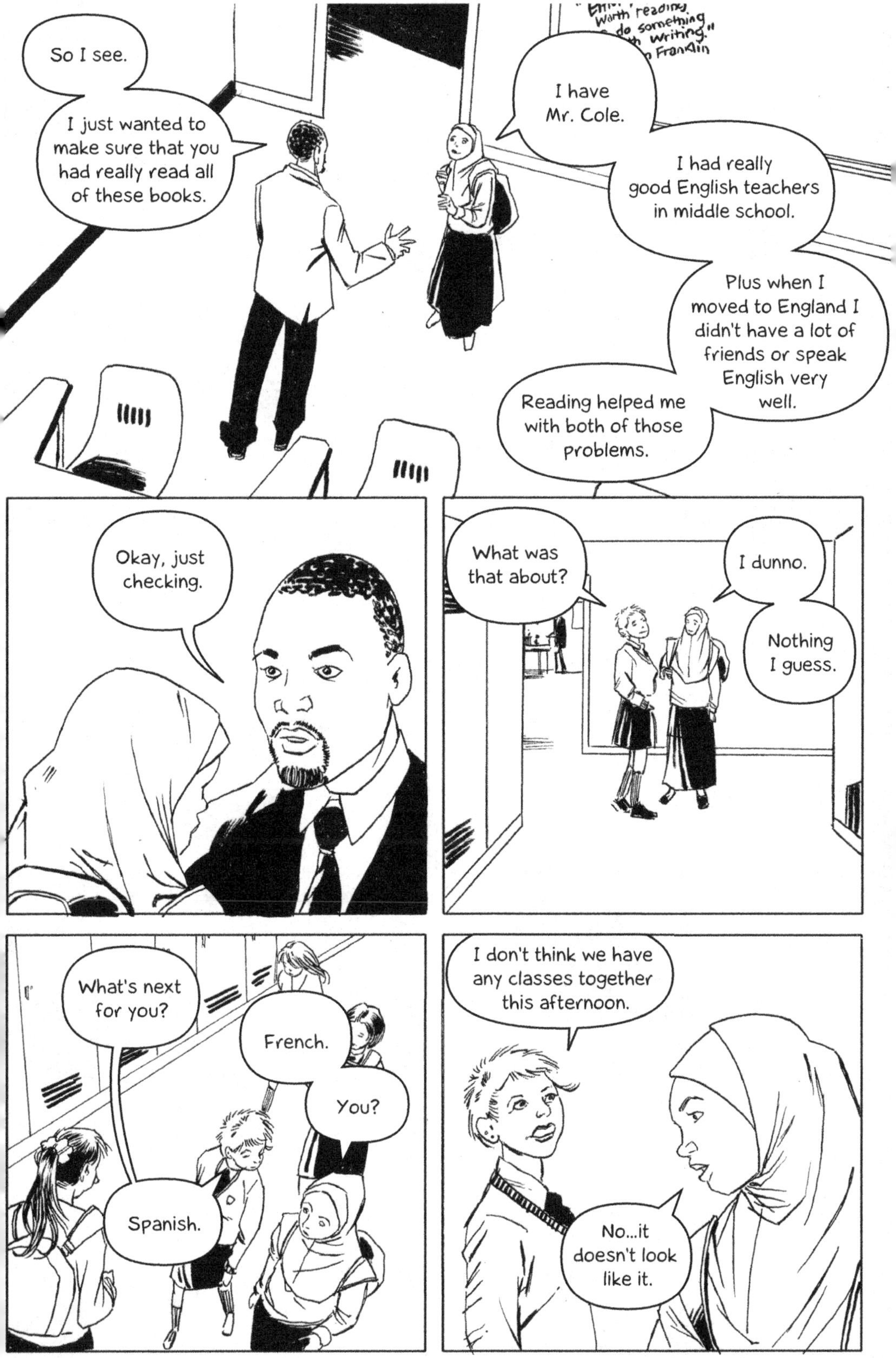
So I see.
I just wanted to make sure that you had really read all of these books.
I have Mr. Cole.
I had really good English teachers in middle school.
Plus when I moved to England I didn't have a lot of friends or speak English very well.
Reading helped me with both of those problems.
Okay, just checking.
What was that about?
I dunno.
Nothing I guess.
What's next for you?
French.
You?
Spanish.
I don't think we have any classes together this afternoon.
No...it doesn't look like it.

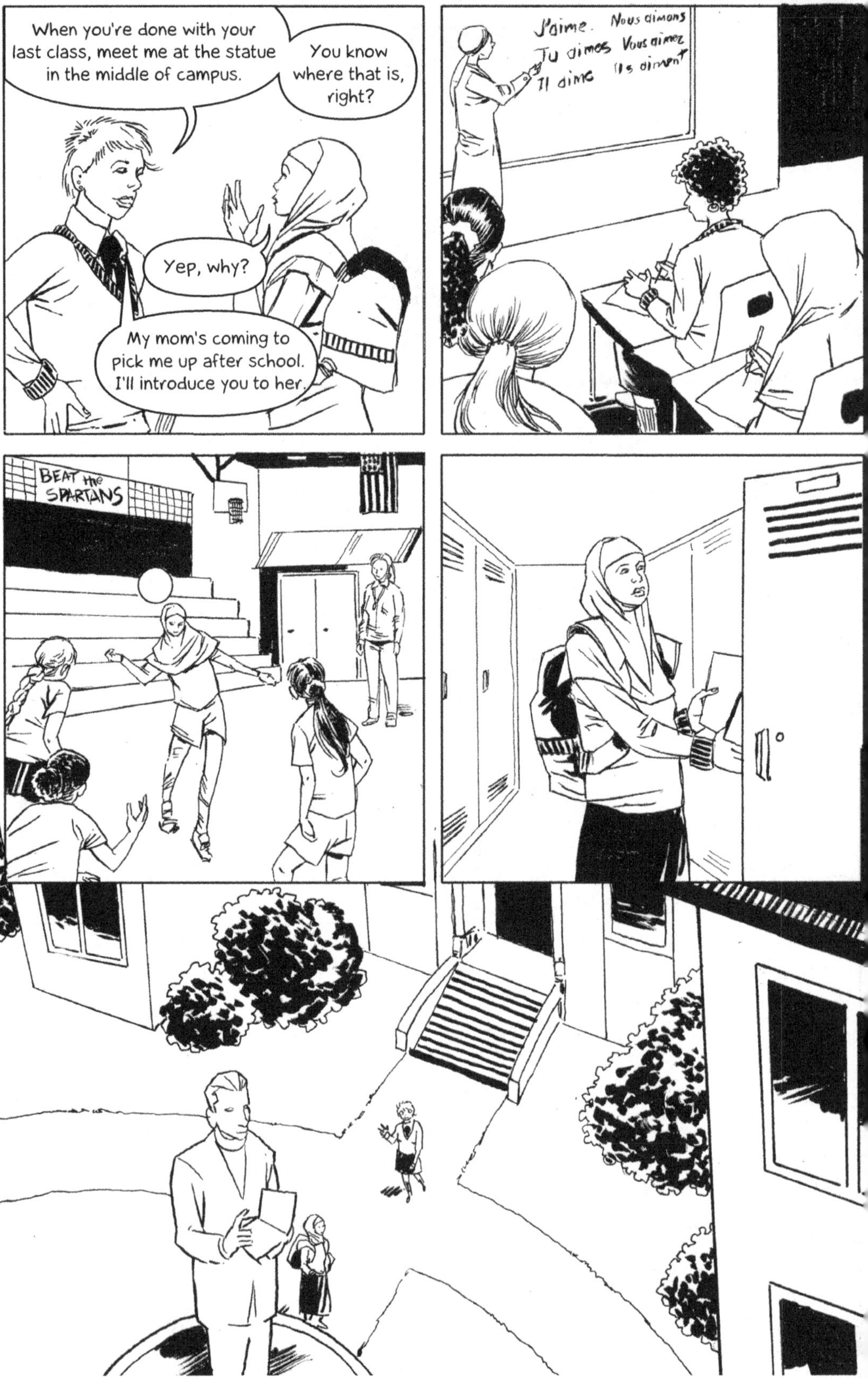
When you're done with your last class, meet me at the statue in the middle of campus.
You know where that is, right?
Yep, why?
My mom's coming to pick me up after school. I'll introduce you to her.
J'aime. Nous aimons
Tu aimes Vous aimez
Il aime Ils aiment
BEAT the SPARTANS

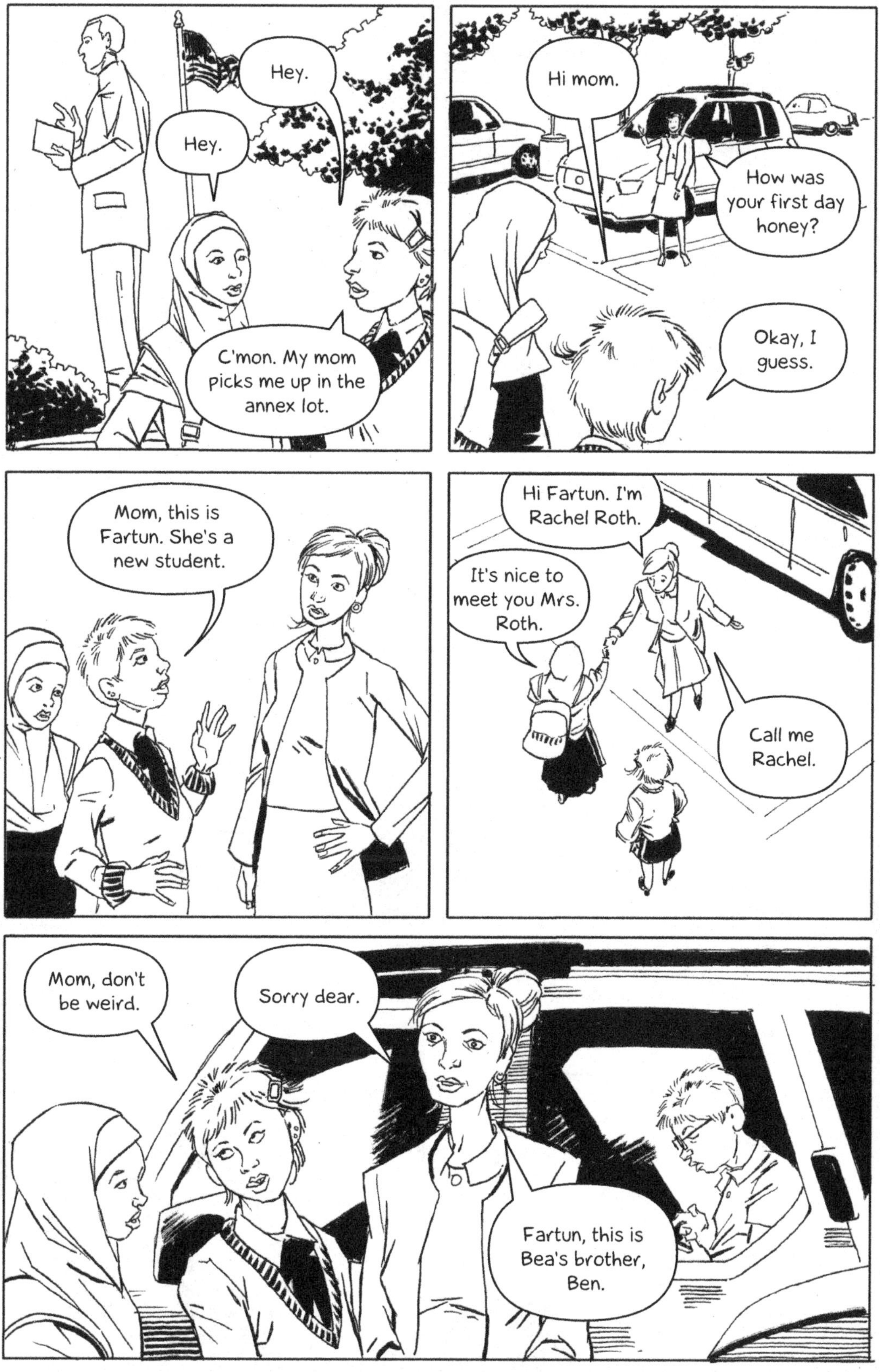
Hey.
Hey.
C'mon. My mom picks me up in the annex lot.
Hi mom.
How was your first day honey?
Okay, I guess.
Mom, this is Fartun. She's a new student.
Hi Fartun. I'm Rachel Roth.
It's nice to meet you Mrs. Roth.
Call me Rachel.
Mom, don't be weird.
Sorry dear.
Fartun, this is Bea's brother, Ben.

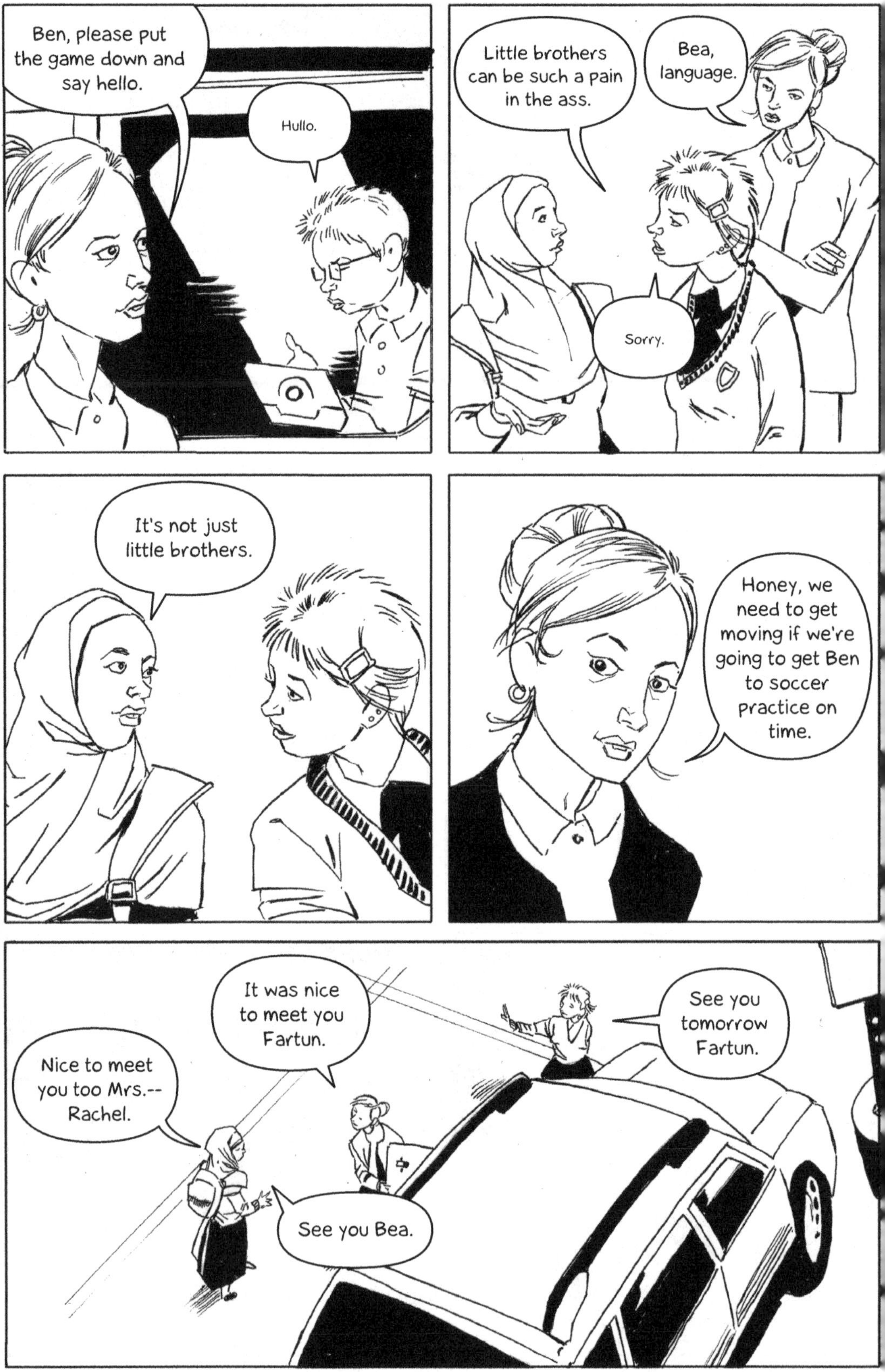
Ben, please put the game down and say hello.
Hullo.
Little brothers can be such a pain in the ass.
Bea, language.
Sorry.
It's not just little brothers.
Honey, we need to get moving if we're going to get Ben to soccer practice on time.
It was nice to meet you Fartun.
See you tomorrow Fartun.
Nice to meet you too Mrs.-- Rachel.
See you Bea.

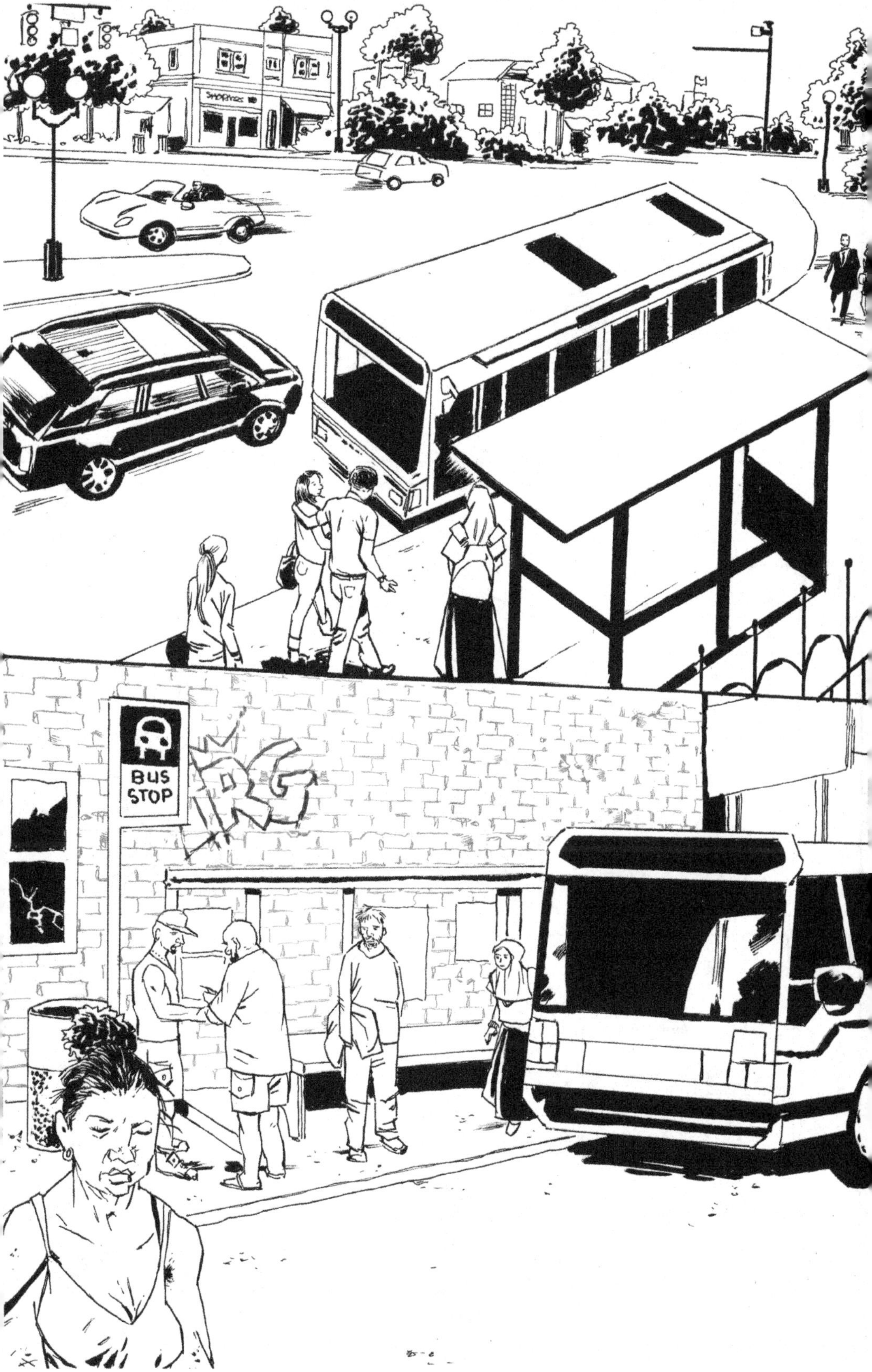
BUS
STOP

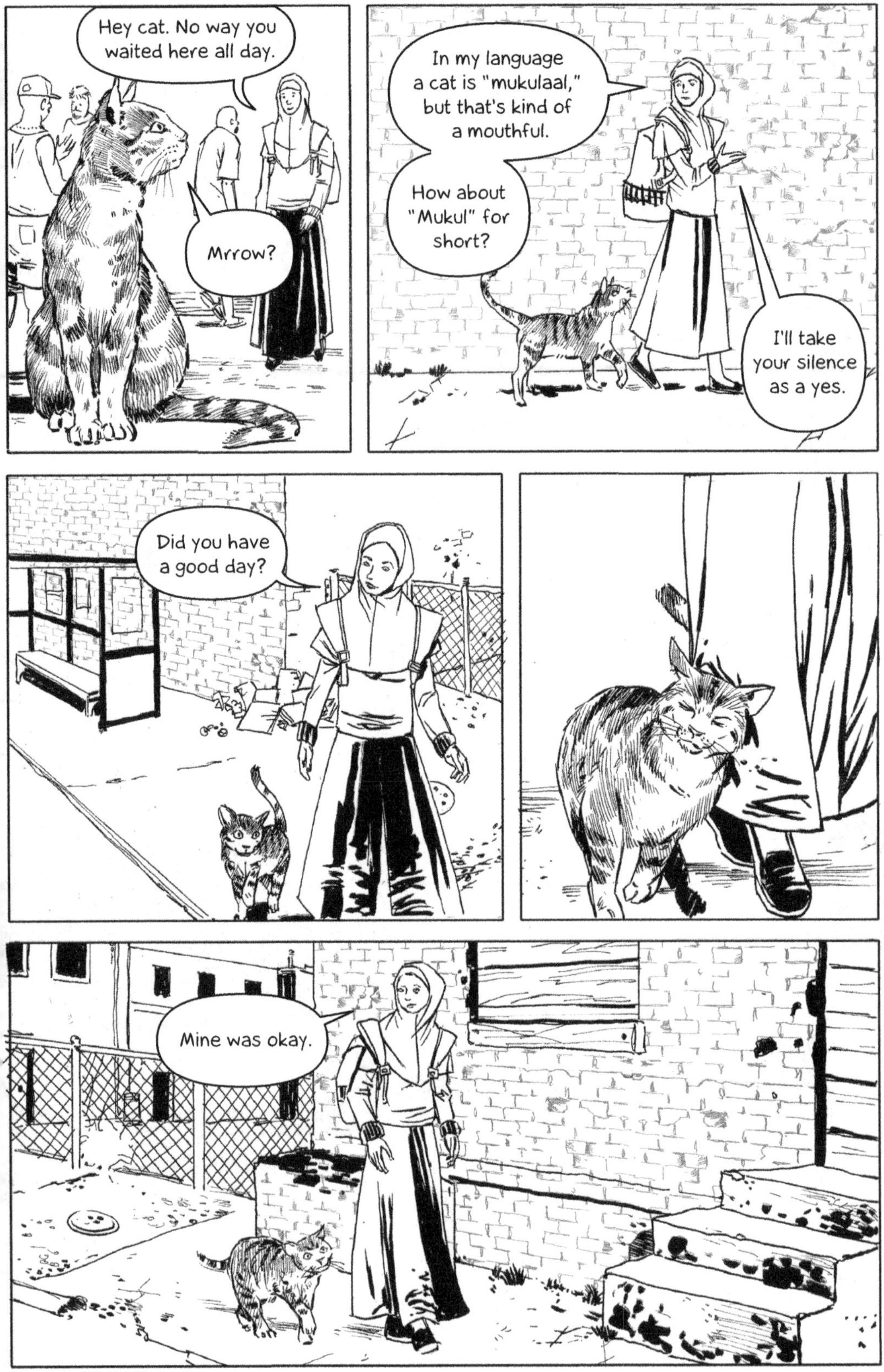
Hey cat. No way you waited here all day.
Mrrow?
In my language a cat is "mukulaal," but that's kind of a mouthful.
How about "Mukul" for short?
I'll take your silence as a yes.
Did you have a good day?
Mine was okay.

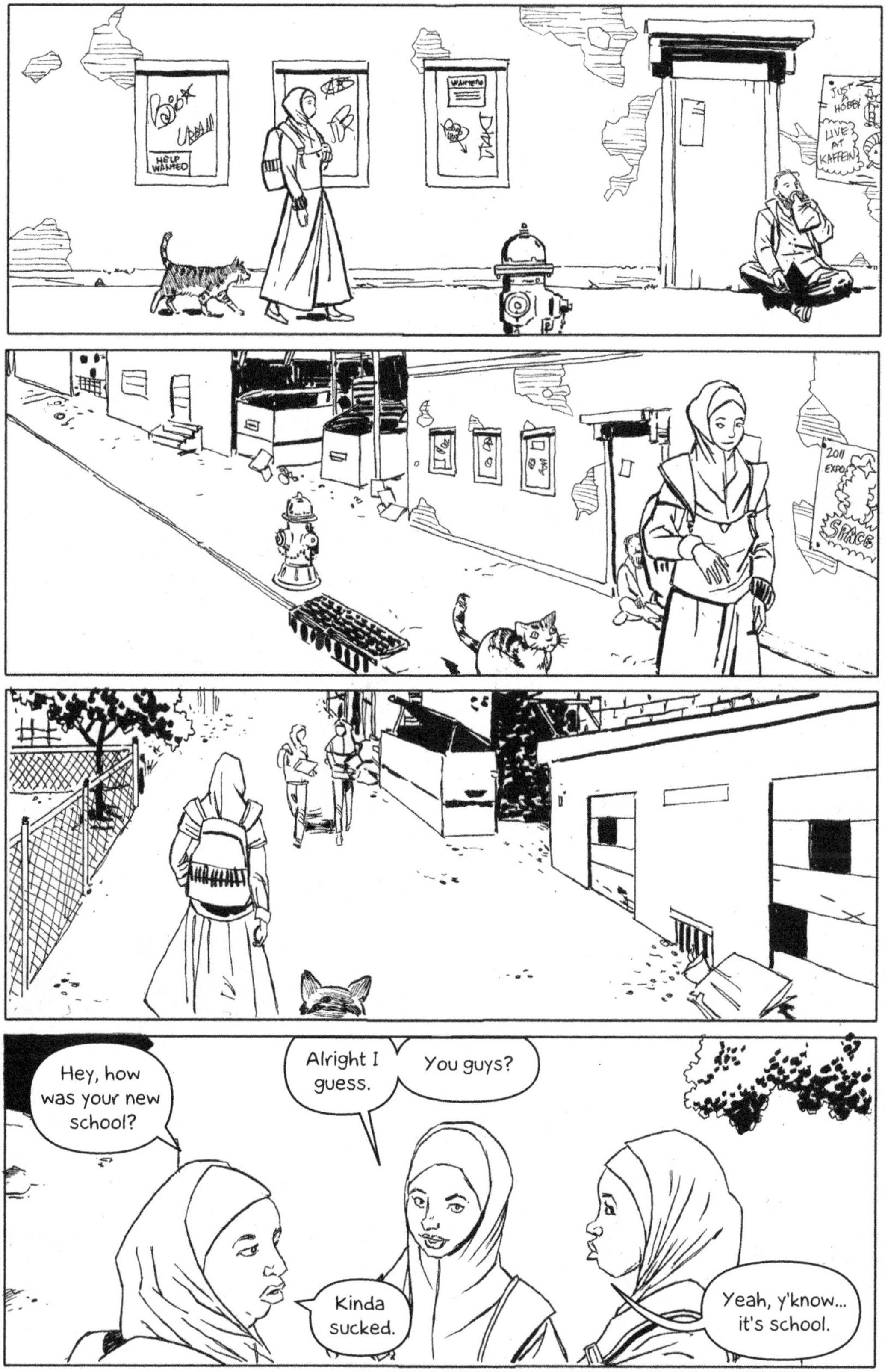
HELP WANTED
WANTED
JUST A HOBBY
LIVE AT KAFFEIN
2011 EXPO
SPACE
Hey, how was your new school?
Alright I guess.
You guys?
Kinda sucked.
Yeah, y'know... it's school.

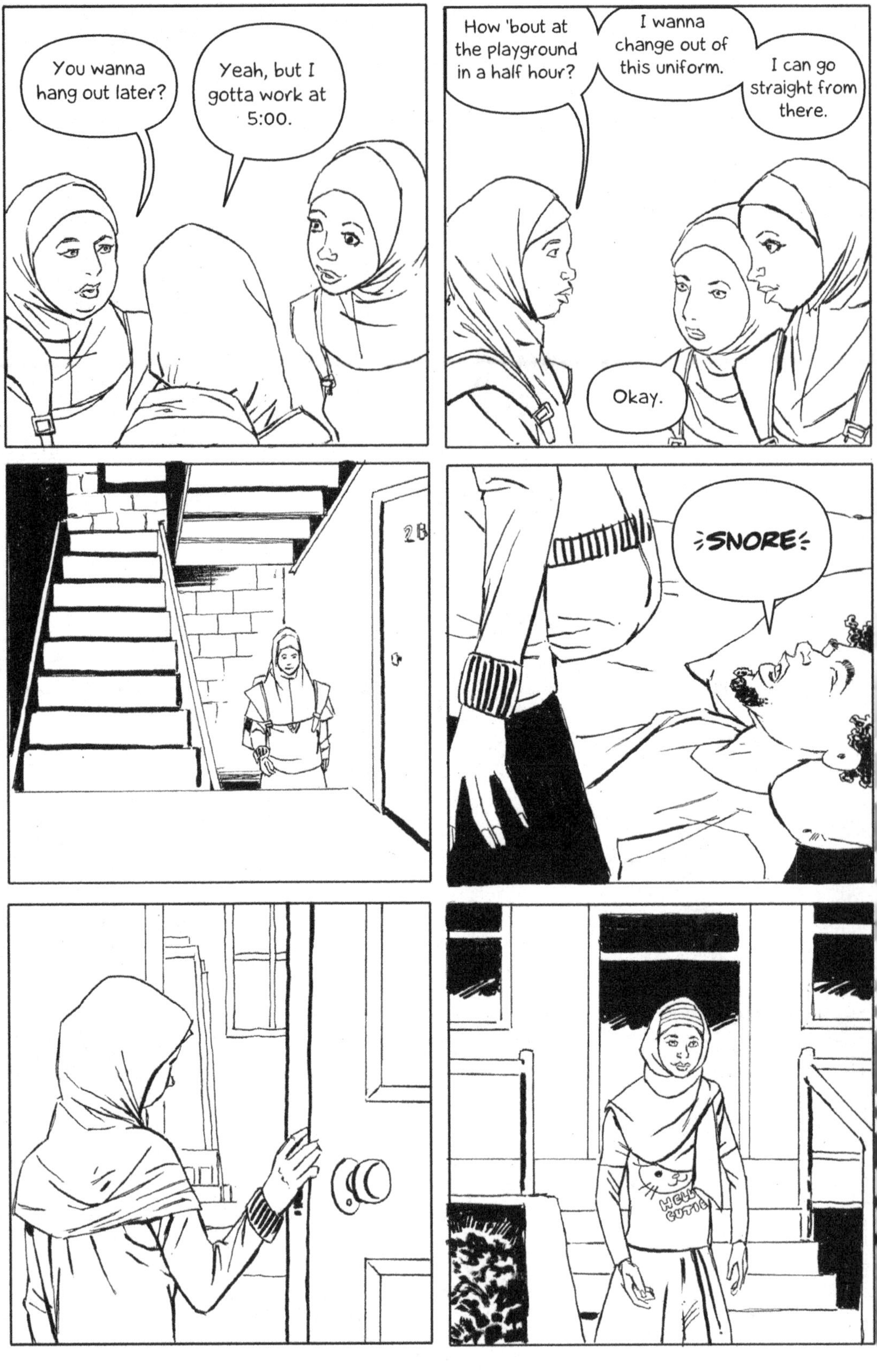
You wanna hang out later?
Yeah, but I gotta work at 5:00.
How 'bout at the playground in a half hour?
I wanna change out of this uniform.
I can go straight from there.
Okay.
2B
SNORE
HELLO CUTIE

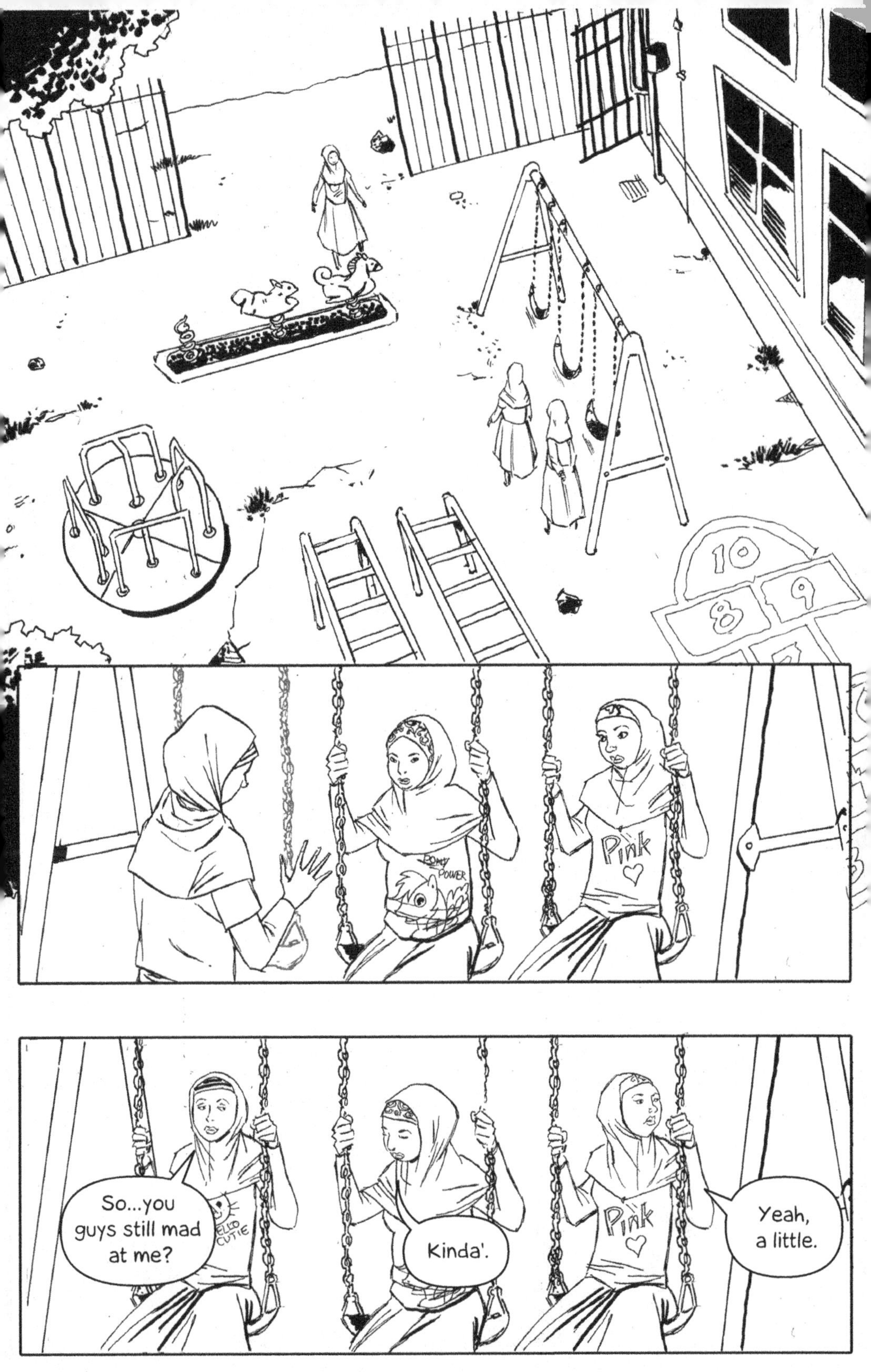

Pink
So...you guys still mad at me?
Kinda'.
Yeah, a little.

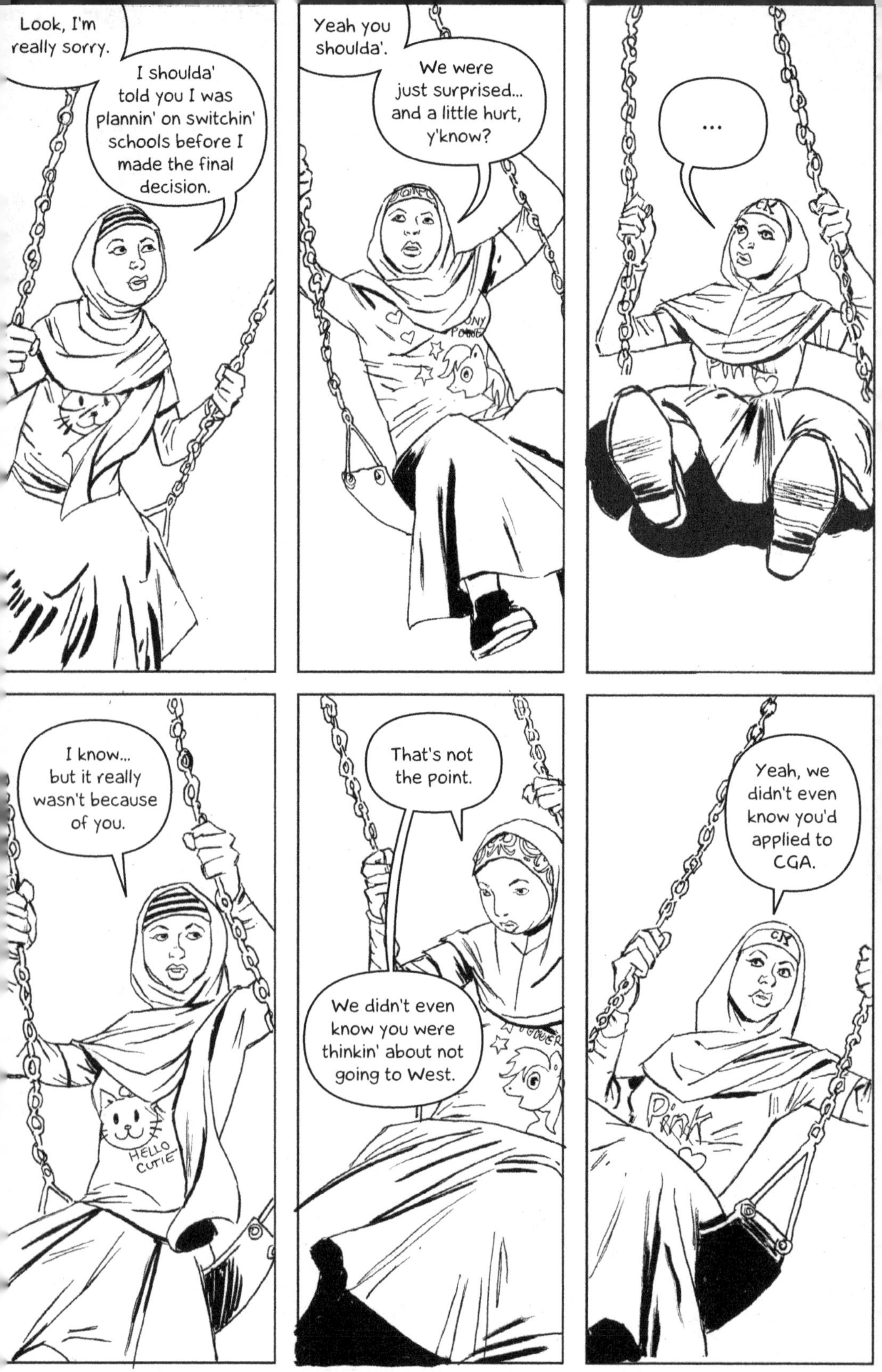
Look, I'm really sorry.
I shoulda' told you I was plannin' on switchin' schools before I made the final decision.
Yeah you shoulda'.
We were just surprised... and a little hurt, y'know?
...
I know... but it really wasn't because of you.
That's not the point.
We didn't even know you were thinkin' about not going to West.
Yeah, we didn't even know you'd applied to CGA.

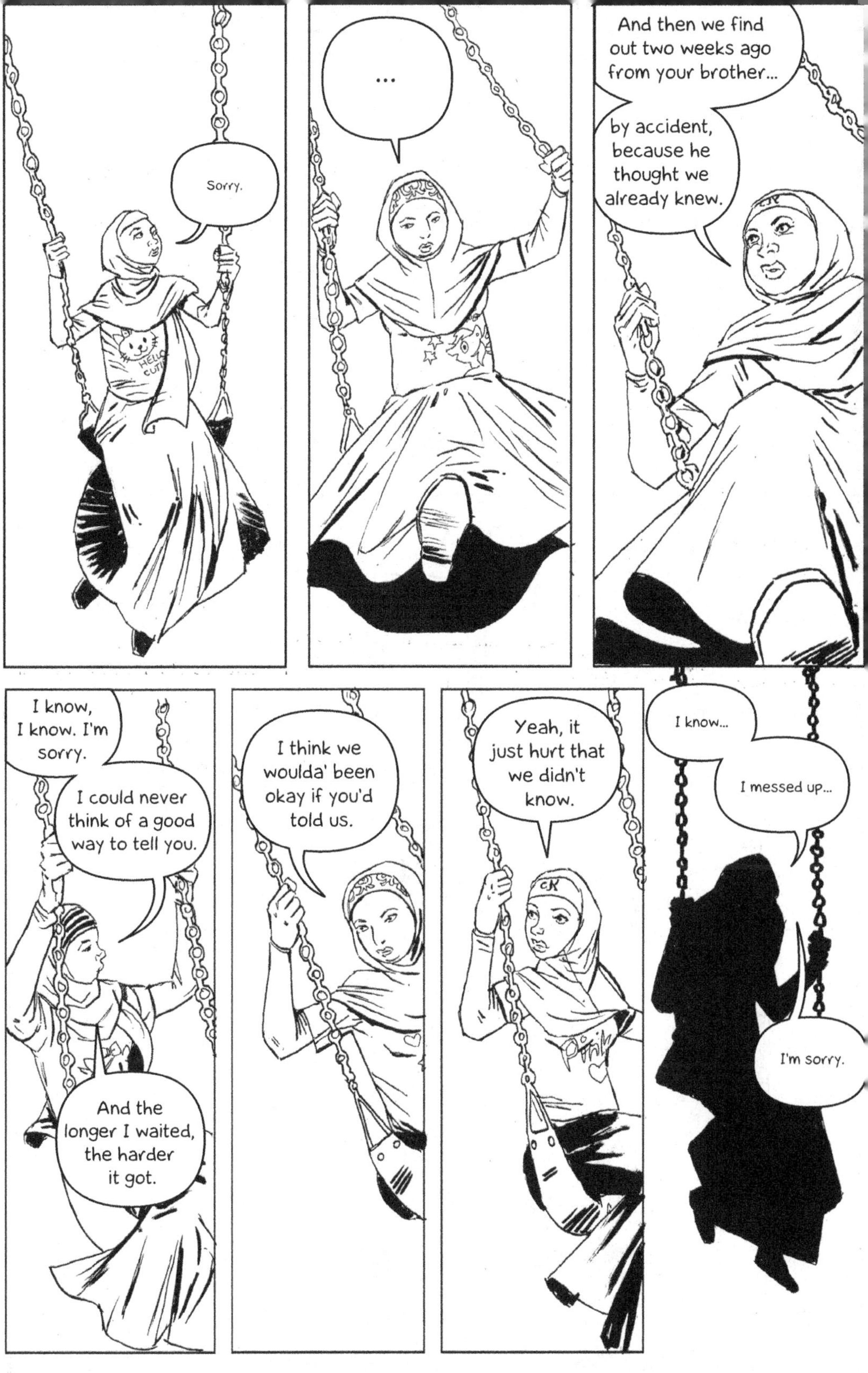
Sorry.
...
And then we find out two weeks ago from your brother...
by accident, because he thought we already knew.
I know, I know. I'm sorry.
I could never think of a good way to tell you.
And the longer I waited, the harder it got.
I think we woulda' been okay if you'd told us.
Yeah, it just hurt that we didn't know.
I know...
I messed up...
I'm sorry.

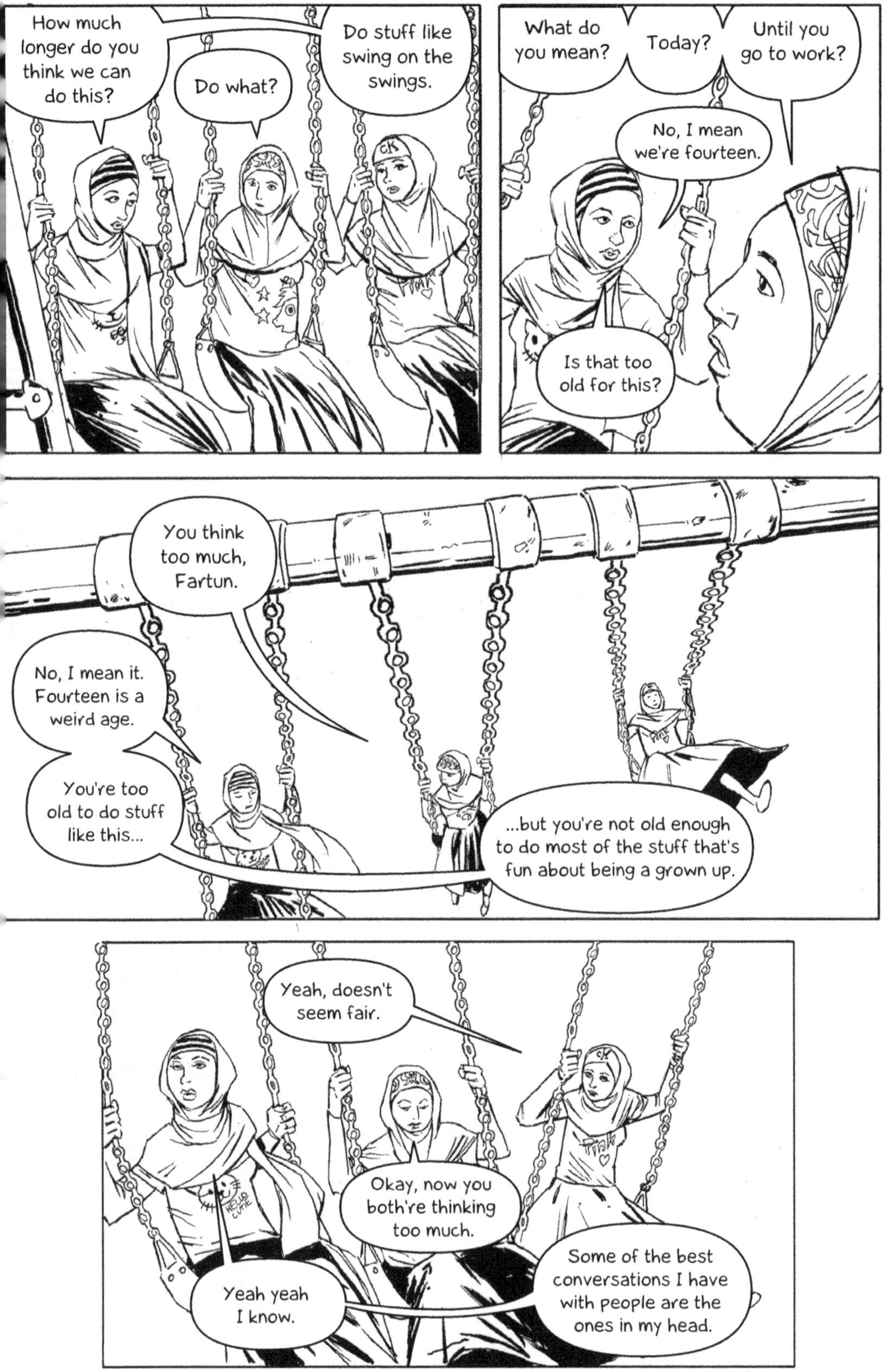
How much longer do you think we can do this?
Do what?
Do stuff like swing on the swings.
What do you mean?
Today?
Until you go to work?
No, I mean we're fourteen.
Is that too old for this?
You think too much, Fartun.
No, I mean it. Fourteen is a weird age.
You're too old to do stuff like this...
...but you're not old enough to do most of the stuff that's fun about being a grown up.
Yeah, doesn't seem fair.
Okay, now you both're thinking too much.
Yeah yeah I know.
Some of the best conversations I have with people are the ones in my head.

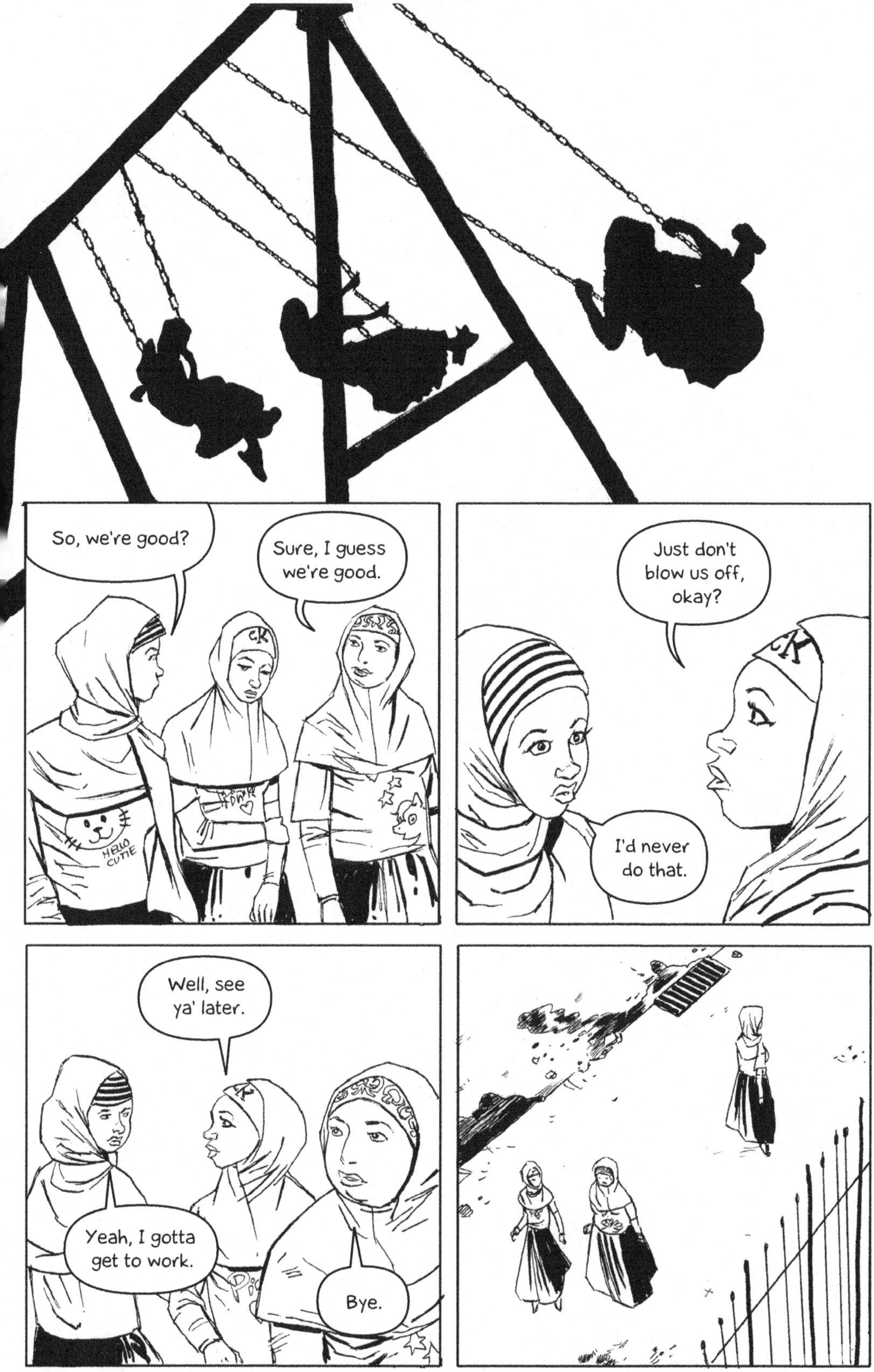
So, we're good?
Sure, I guess we're good.
HELLO CUTIE
Just don't blow us off, okay?
I'd never do that.
Well, see ya' later.
Yeah, I gotta get to work.
Bye.

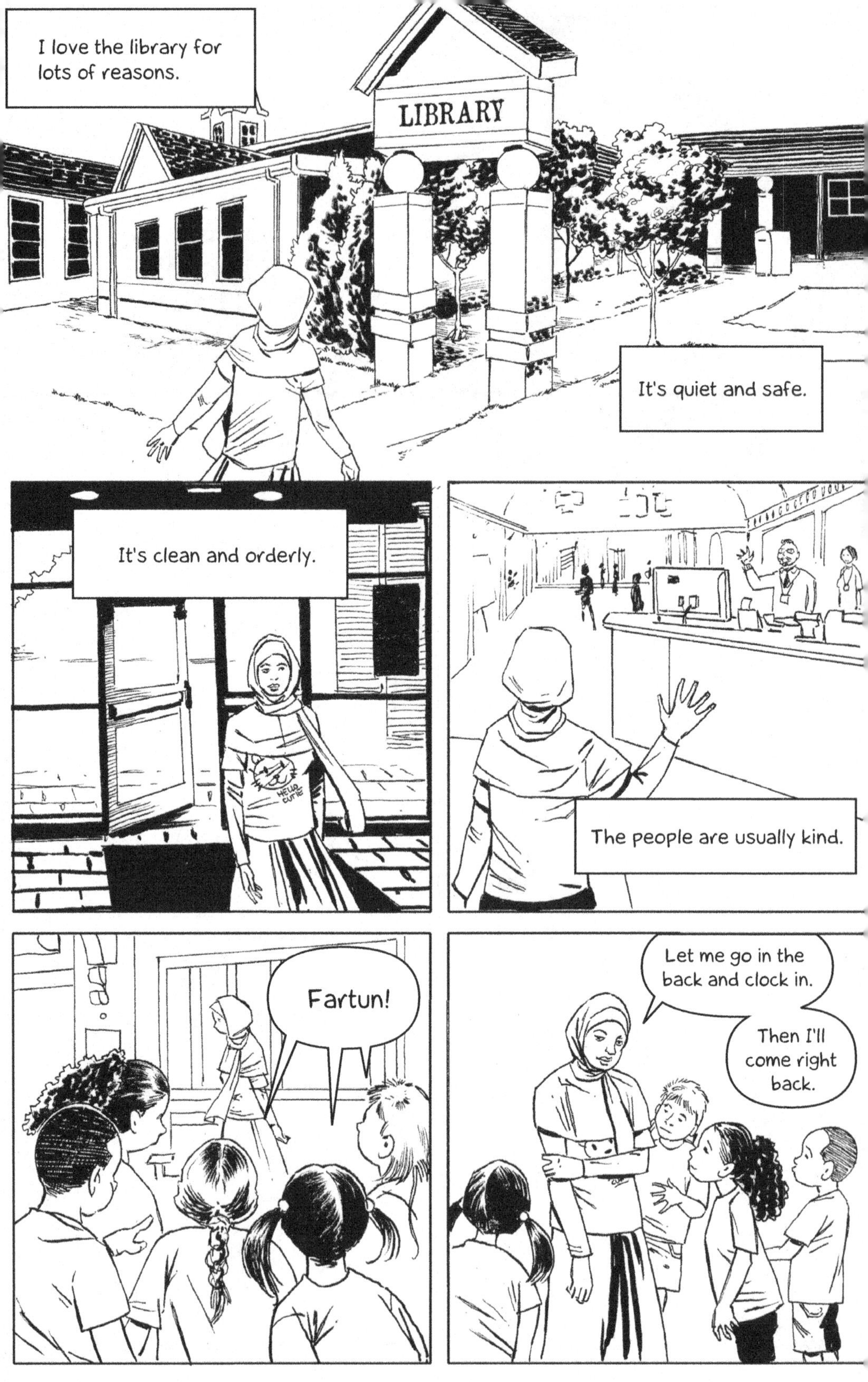

I love the library for lots of reasons.
LIBRARY
It's quiet and safe.
It's clean and orderly.
HELLO CUTIE
The people are usually kind.
Fartun!
Let me go in the back and clock in.
Then I'll come right back.

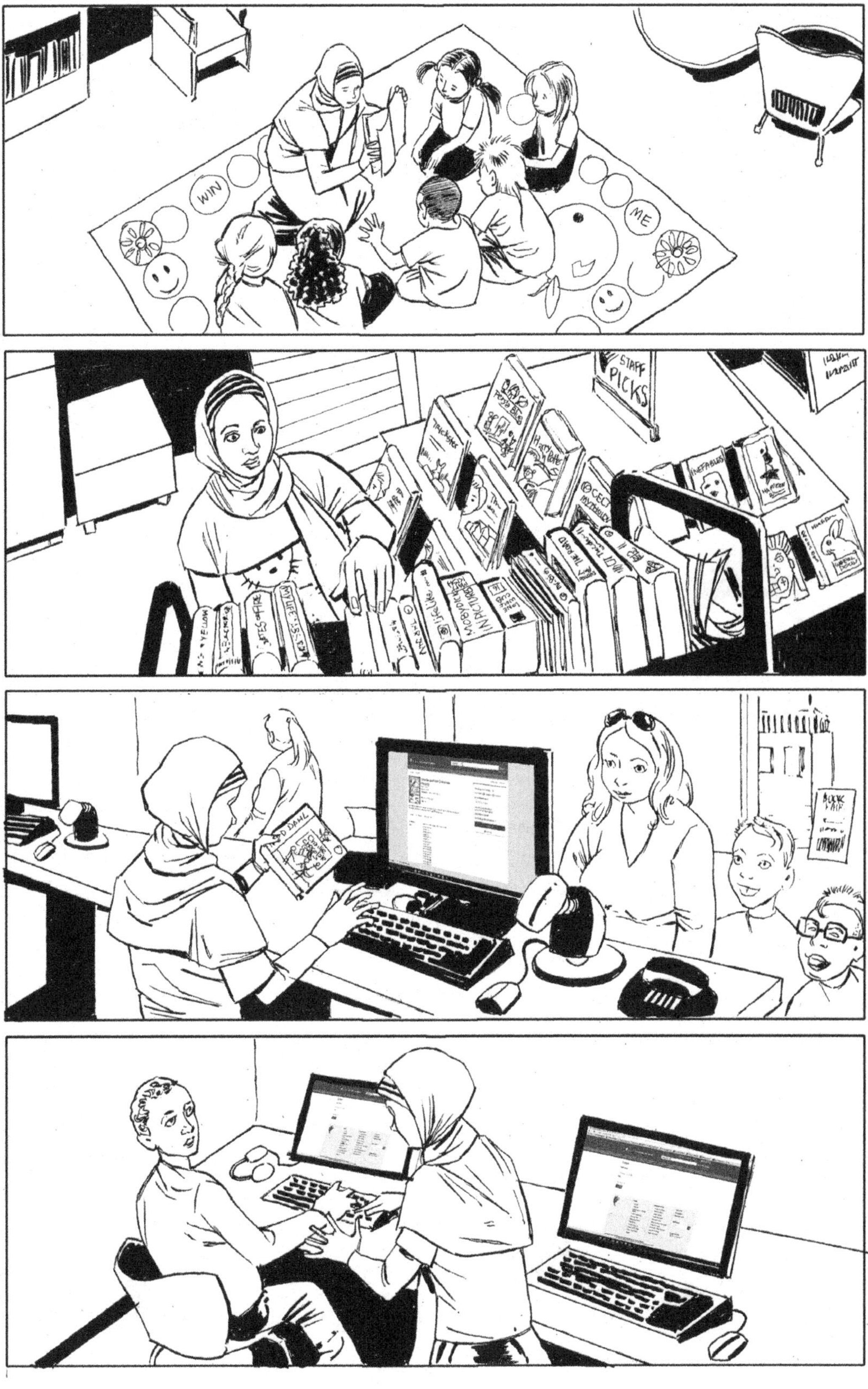

WIN
ME
STAFF PICKS
Harry Potter
THE ROAD

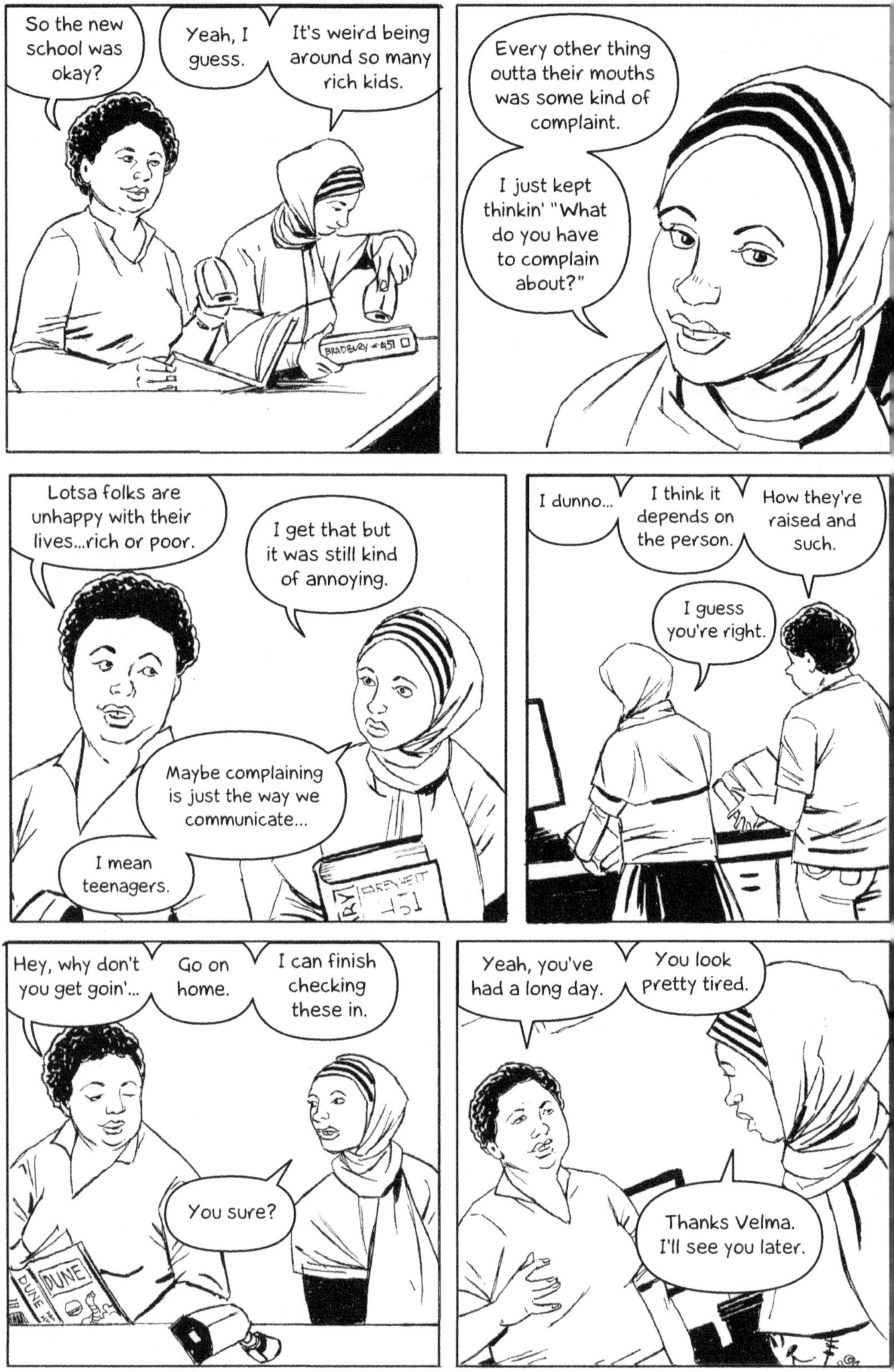
So the new school was okay?
Yeah, I guess.
It's weird being around so many rich kids.
BRADBURY 451
Every other thing outta their mouths was some kind of complaint.
I just kept thinkin' "What do you have to complain about?"
Lotsa folks are unhappy with their lives...rich or poor.
I get that but it was still kind of annoying.
Maybe complaining is just the way we communicate...
I mean teenagers.
I dunno...
I think it depends on the person.
How they're raised and such.
I guess you're right.
Hey, why don't you get goin'...
Go on home.
I can finish checking these in.
You sure?
DUNE
Yeah, you've had a long day.
You look pretty tired.
Thanks Velma. I'll see you later.

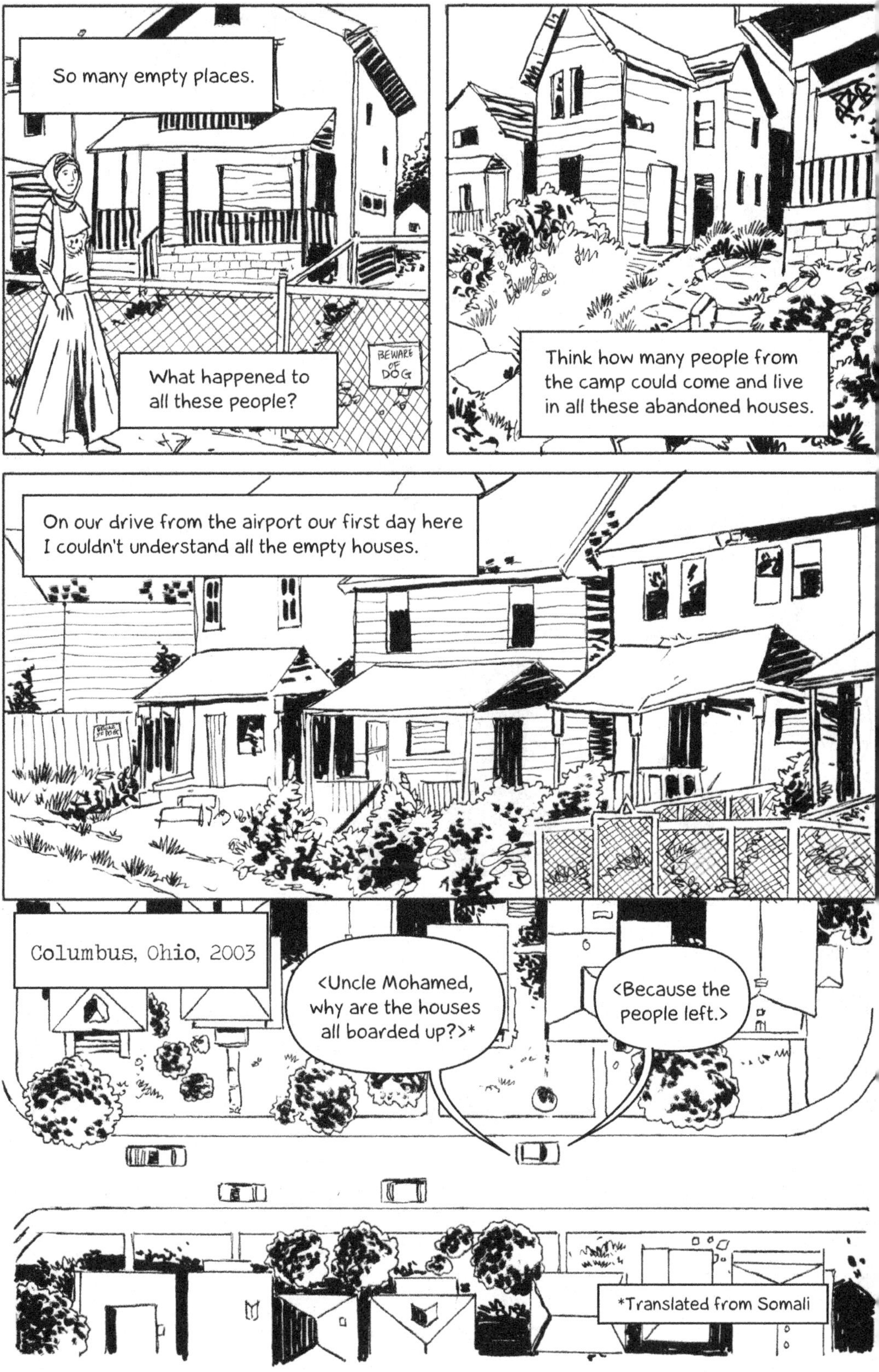
So many empty places.
What happened to all these people?
BEWARE OF DOG
Think how many people from the camp could come and live in all these abandoned houses.
On our drive from the airport our first day here I couldn't understand all the empty houses.
Columbus, Ohio, 2003
<Uncle Mohamed, why are the houses all boarded up?>*
<Because the people left.>
*Translated from Somali

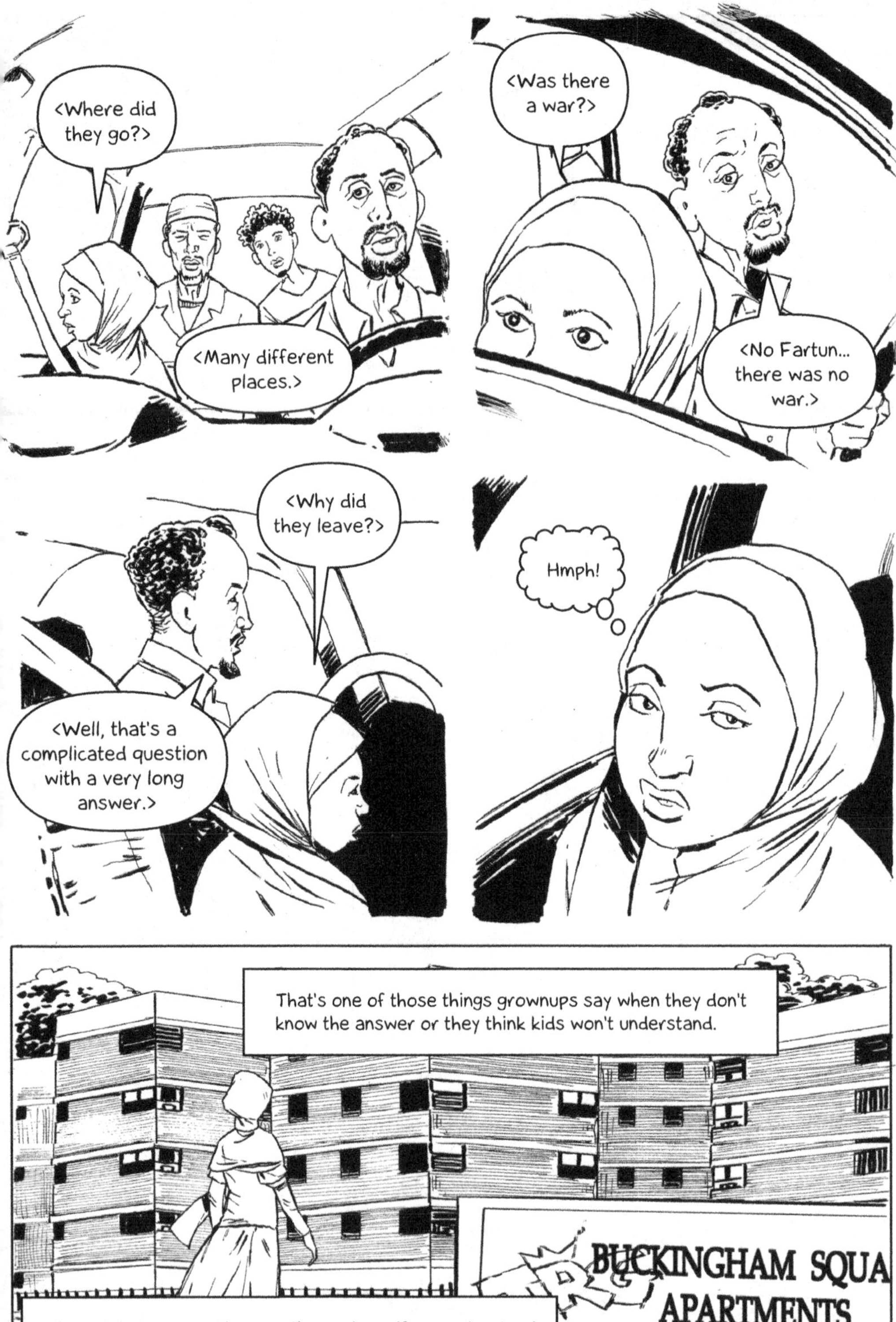
<Where did they go?>
<Many different places.>
<Was there a war?>
<No Fartun... there was no war.>
<Why did they leave?>
<Well, that's a complicated question with a very long answer.>
Hmph!
That's one of those things grownups say when they don't know the answer or they think kids won't understand.
BUCKINGHAM SQUA
APARTMENTS
Why not just answer the question and see if we understand. Or just say that you don't know the answer.

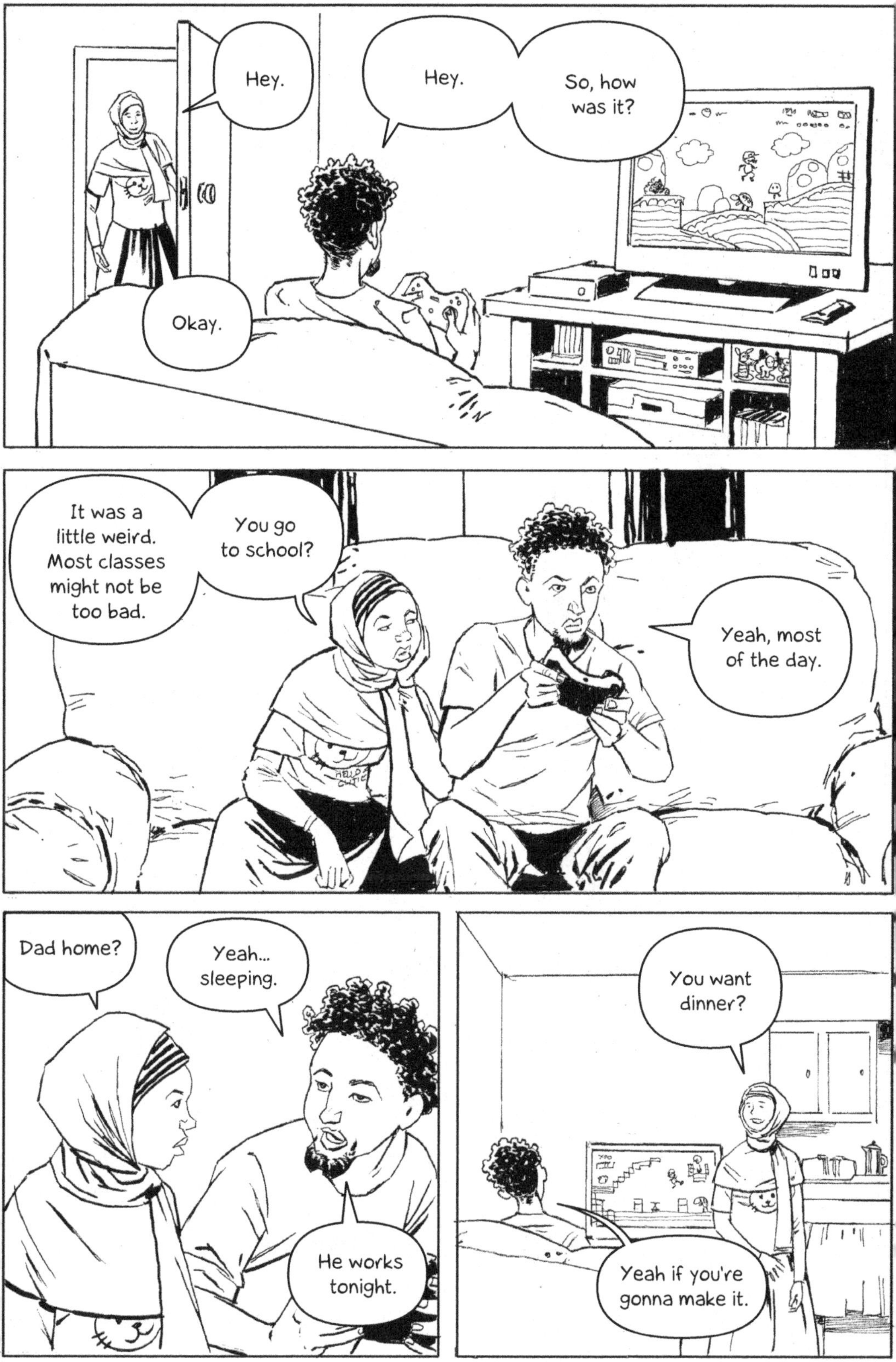
Hey.
Hey.
So, how was it?
Okay.
It was a little weird. Most classes might not be too bad.
You go to school?
Yeah, most of the day.
Dad home?
Yeah... sleeping.
He works tonight.
You want dinner?
Yeah if you're gonna make it.

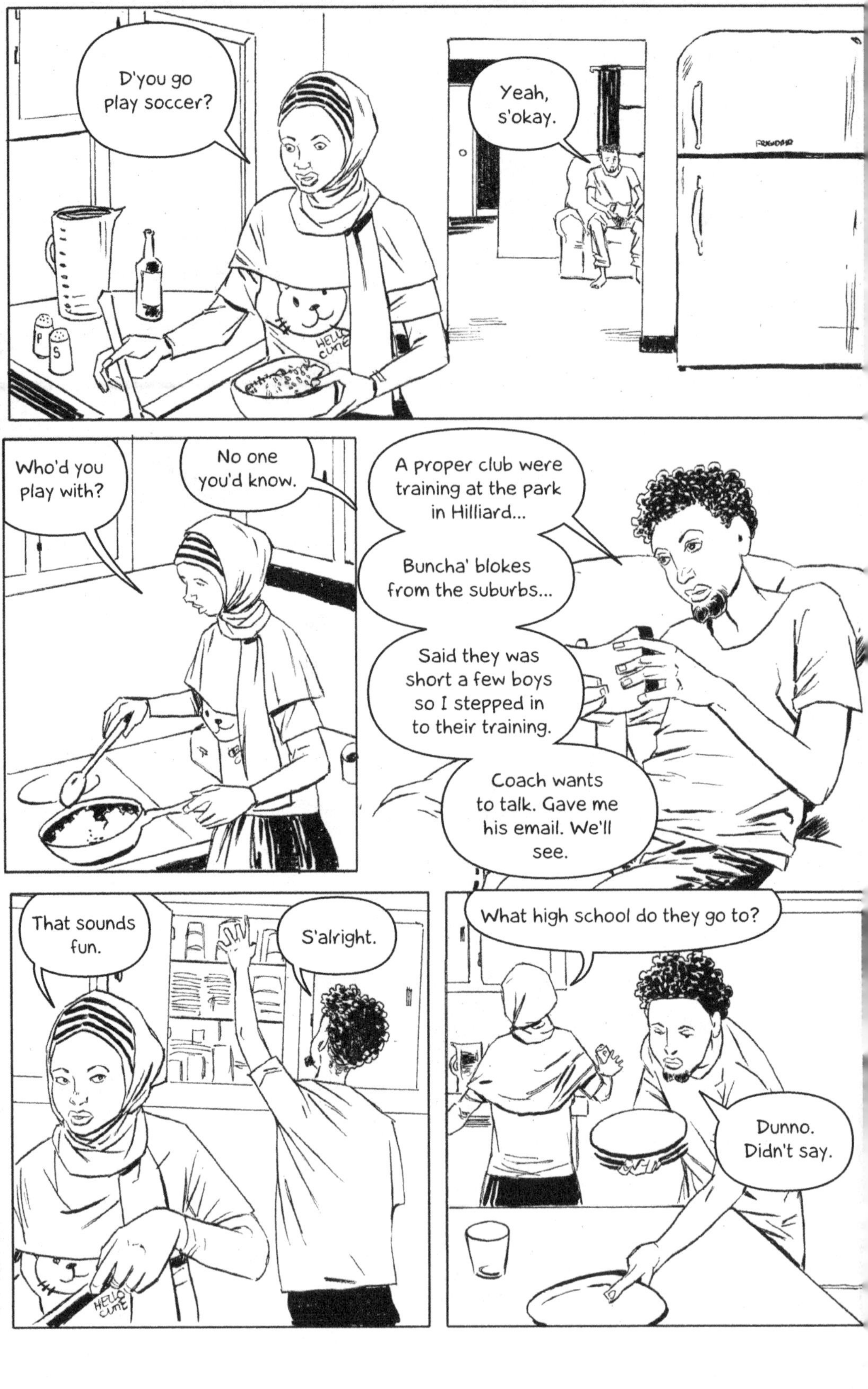
D'you go play soccer?
Yeah, s'okay.
FRIGIDAIR
Who'd you play with?
No one you'd know.
A proper club were training at the park in Hilliard...
Buncha' blokes from the suburbs...
Said they was short a few boys so I stepped in to their training.
Coach wants to talk. Gave me his email. We'll see.
That sounds fun.
S'alright.
HELLO CUTIE
What high school do they go to?
Dunno. Didn't say.

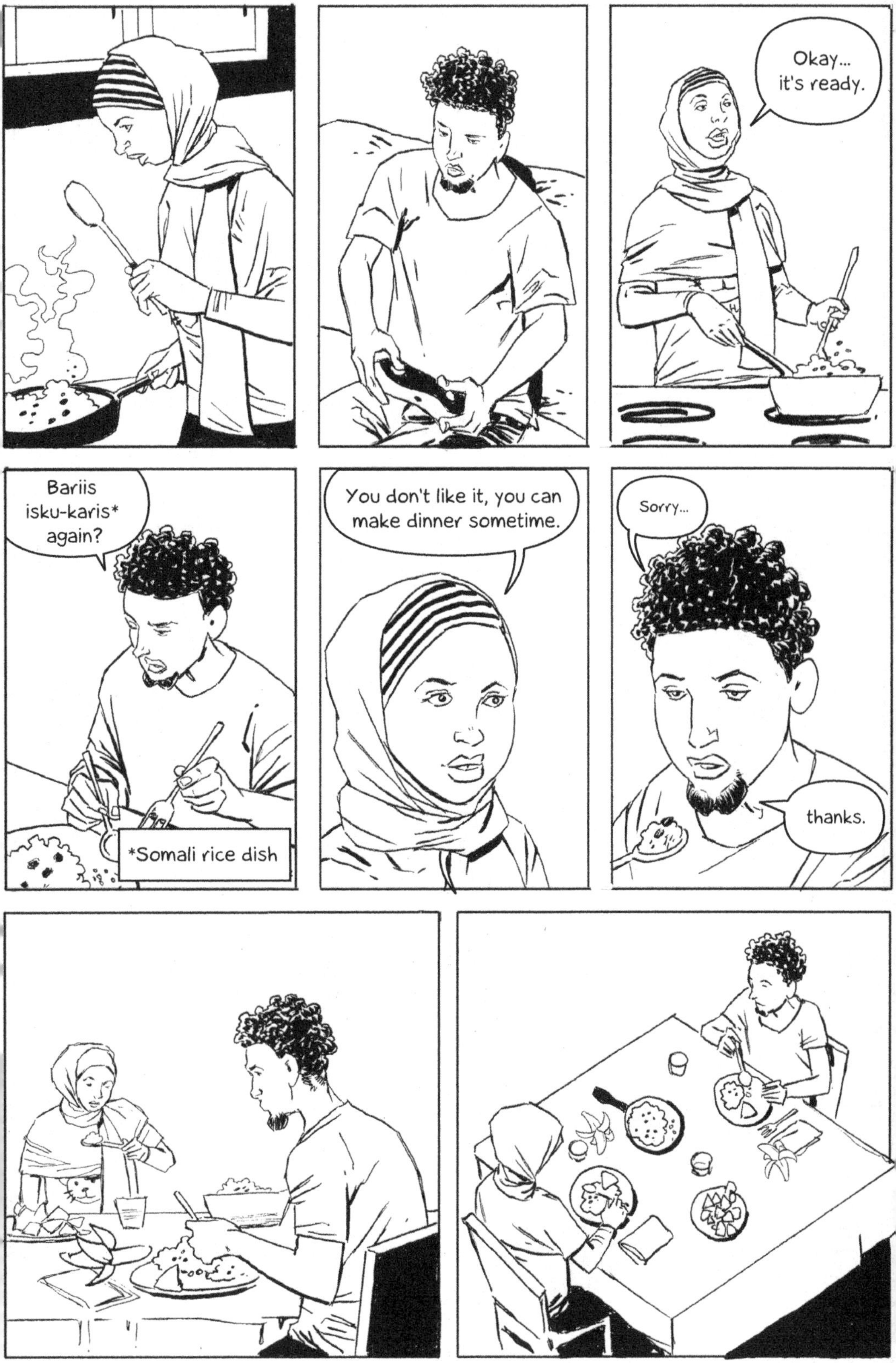
Okay... it's ready.
Bariis isku-karis* again?
*Somali rice dish
You don't like it, you can make dinner sometime.
Sorry...
thanks.

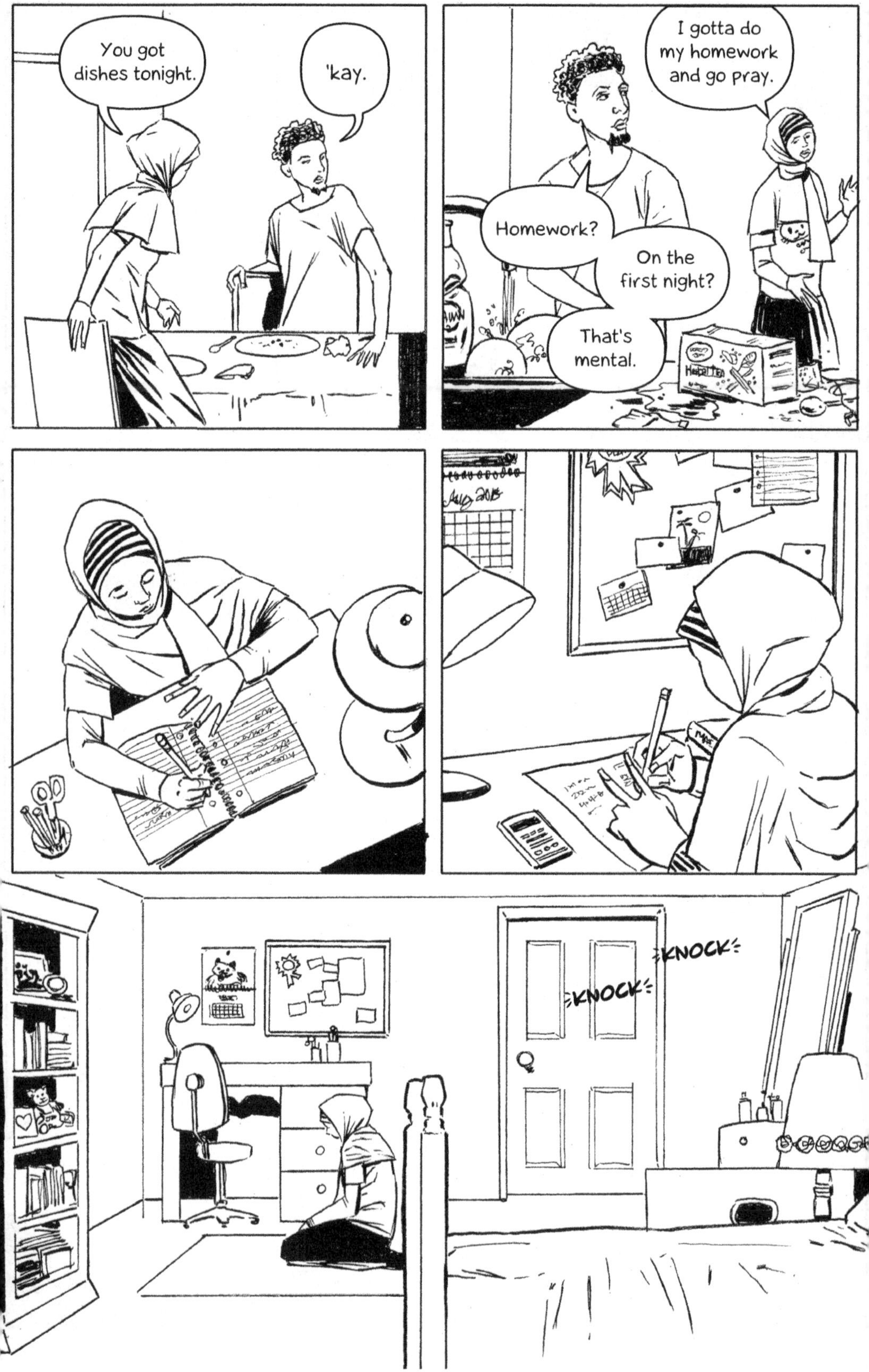
You got dishes tonight.
'kay.
I gotta do my homework and go pray.
Homework?
On the first night?
That's mental.
KNOCK
KNOCK

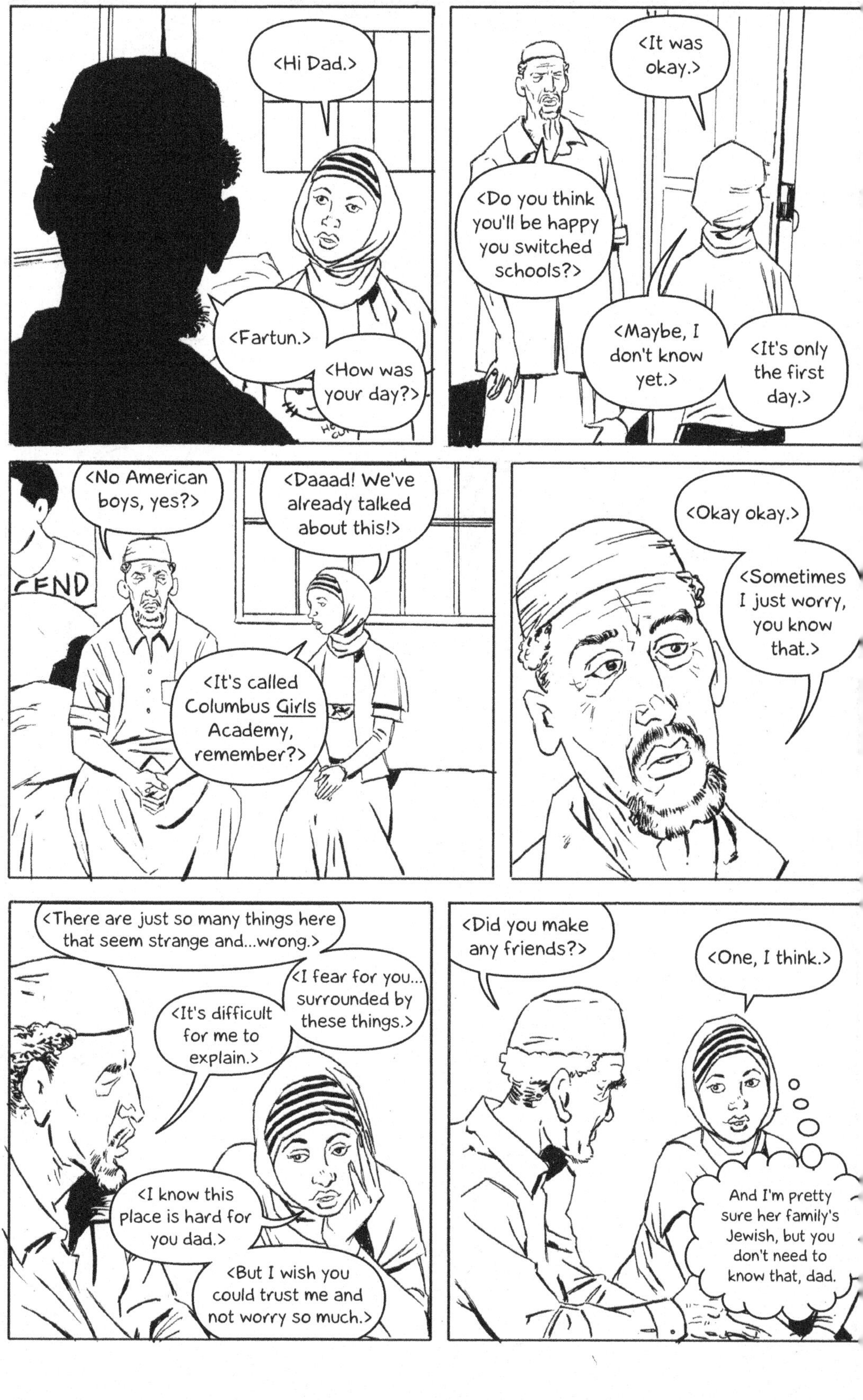

<Hi Dad.>
<Fartun.>
<How was your day?>
<It was okay.>
<Do you think you'll be happy you switched schools?>
<Maybe, I don't know yet.>
<It's only the first day.>
<No American boys, yes?>
<Daaad! We've already talked about this!>
<It's called Columbus Girls Academy, remember?>
<Okay okay.>
<Sometimes I just worry, you know that.>
<There are just so many things here that seem strange and...wrong.>
<I fear for you... surrounded by these things.>
<It's difficult for me to explain.>
<I know this place is hard for you dad.>
<But I wish you could trust me and not worry so much.>
<Did you make any friends?>
<One, I think.>
And I'm pretty sure her family's Jewish, but you don't need to know that, dad.

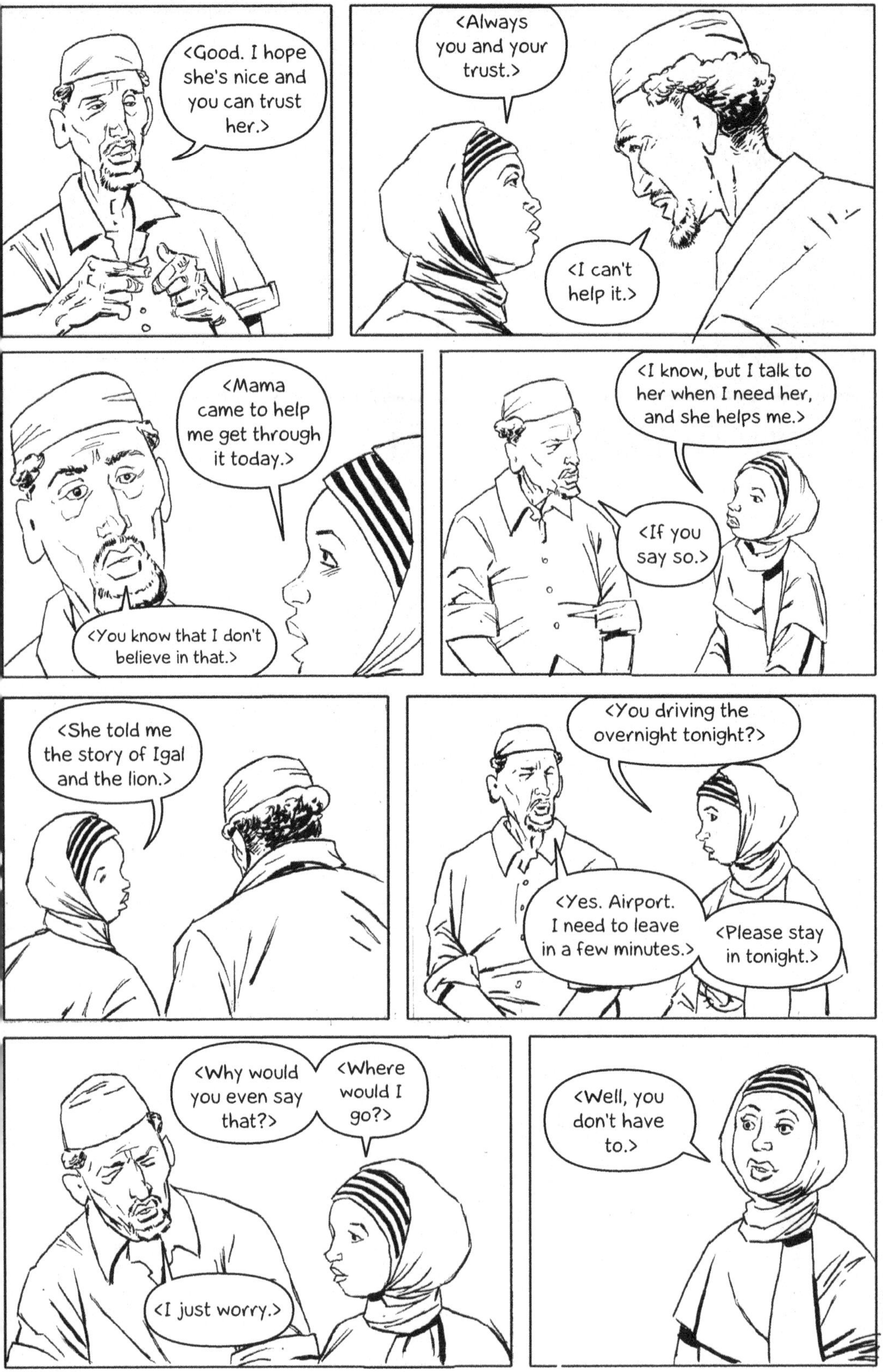
<Good. I hope she's nice and you can trust her.>
<Always you and your trust.>
<I can't help it.>
<Mama came to help me get through it today.>
<You know that I don't believe in that.>
<I know, but I talk to her when I need her, and she helps me.>
<If you say so.>
<She told me the story of Igal and the lion.>
<You driving the overnight tonight?>
<Yes. Airport. I need to leave in a few minutes.>
<Please stay in tonight.>
<Why would you even say that?>
<Where would I go?>
<I just worry.>
<Well, you don't have to.>

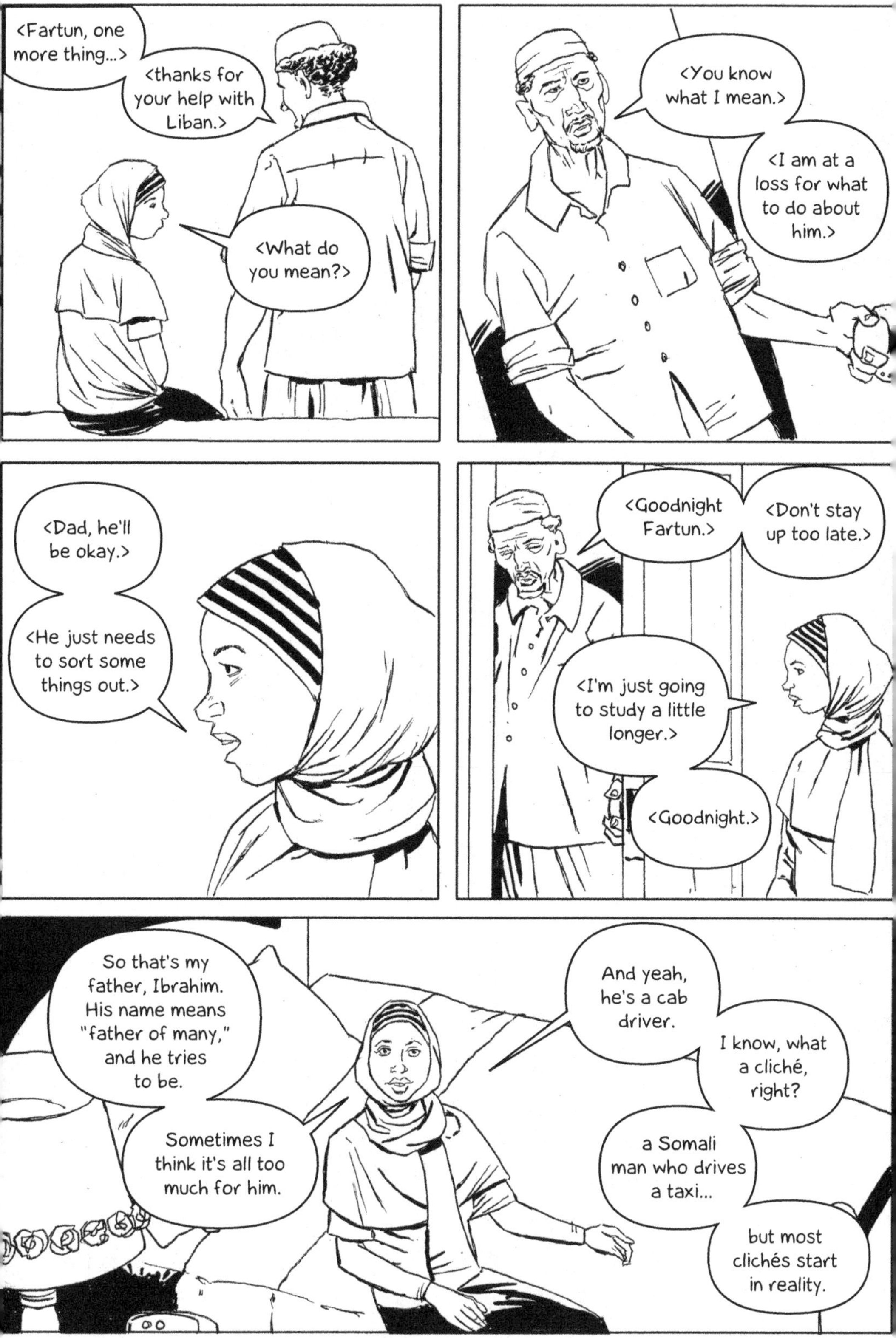
<Fartun, one more thing...>
<thanks for your help with Liban.>
<What do you mean?>
<You know what I mean.>
<I am at a loss for what to do about him.>
<Dad, he'll be okay.>
<He just needs to sort some things out.>
<Goodnight Fartun.>
<Don't stay up too late.>
<I'm just going to study a little longer.>
<Goodnight.>
So that's my father, Ibrahim. His name means "father of many," and he tries to be.
Sometimes I think it's all too much for him.
And yeah, he's a cab driver.
I know, what a cliché, right?
a Somali man who drives a taxi...
but most clichés start in reality.

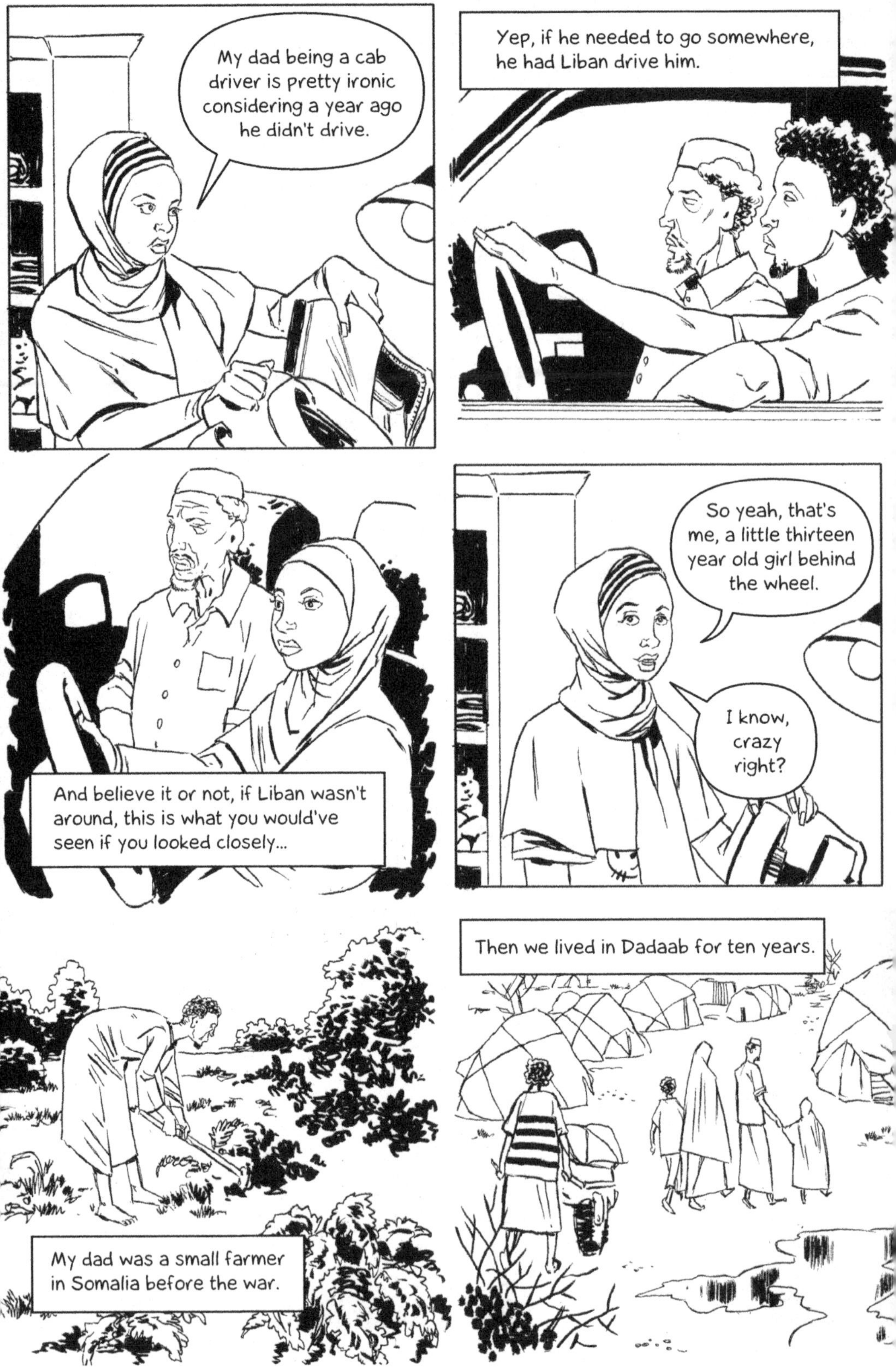
My dad being a cab driver is pretty ironic considering a year ago he didn't drive.
Yep, if he needed to go somewhere, he had Liban drive him.
And believe it or not, if Liban wasn't around, this is what you would've seen if you looked closely...
So yeah, that's me, a little thirteen year old girl behind the wheel.
I know, crazy right?
My dad was a small farmer in Somalia before the war.
Then we lived in Dadaab for ten years.

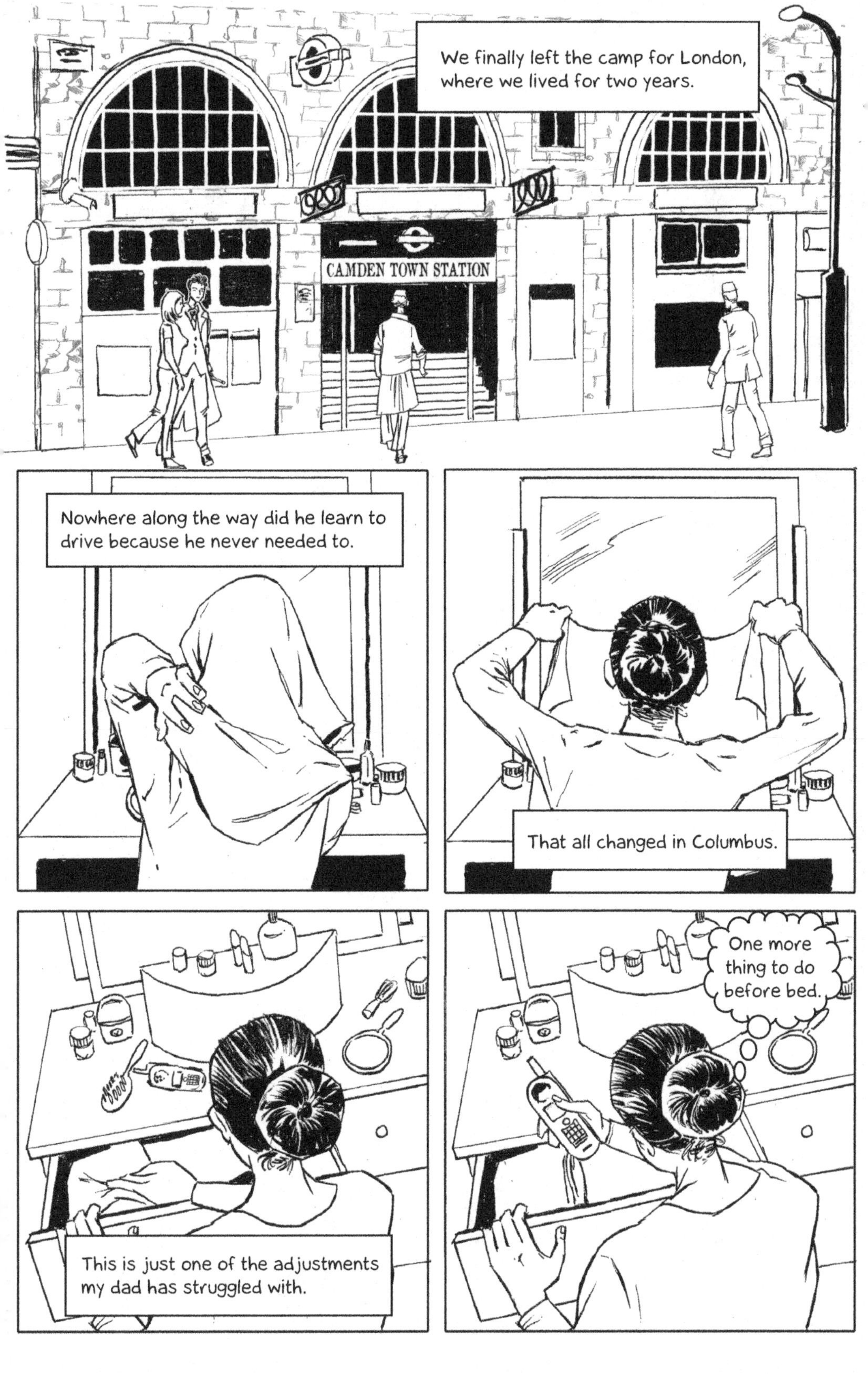
We finally left the camp for London, where we lived for two years.
CAMDEN TOWN STATION
Nowhere along the way did he learn to drive because he never needed to.
That all changed in Columbus.
This is just one of the adjustments my dad has struggled with.
One more thing to do before bed.

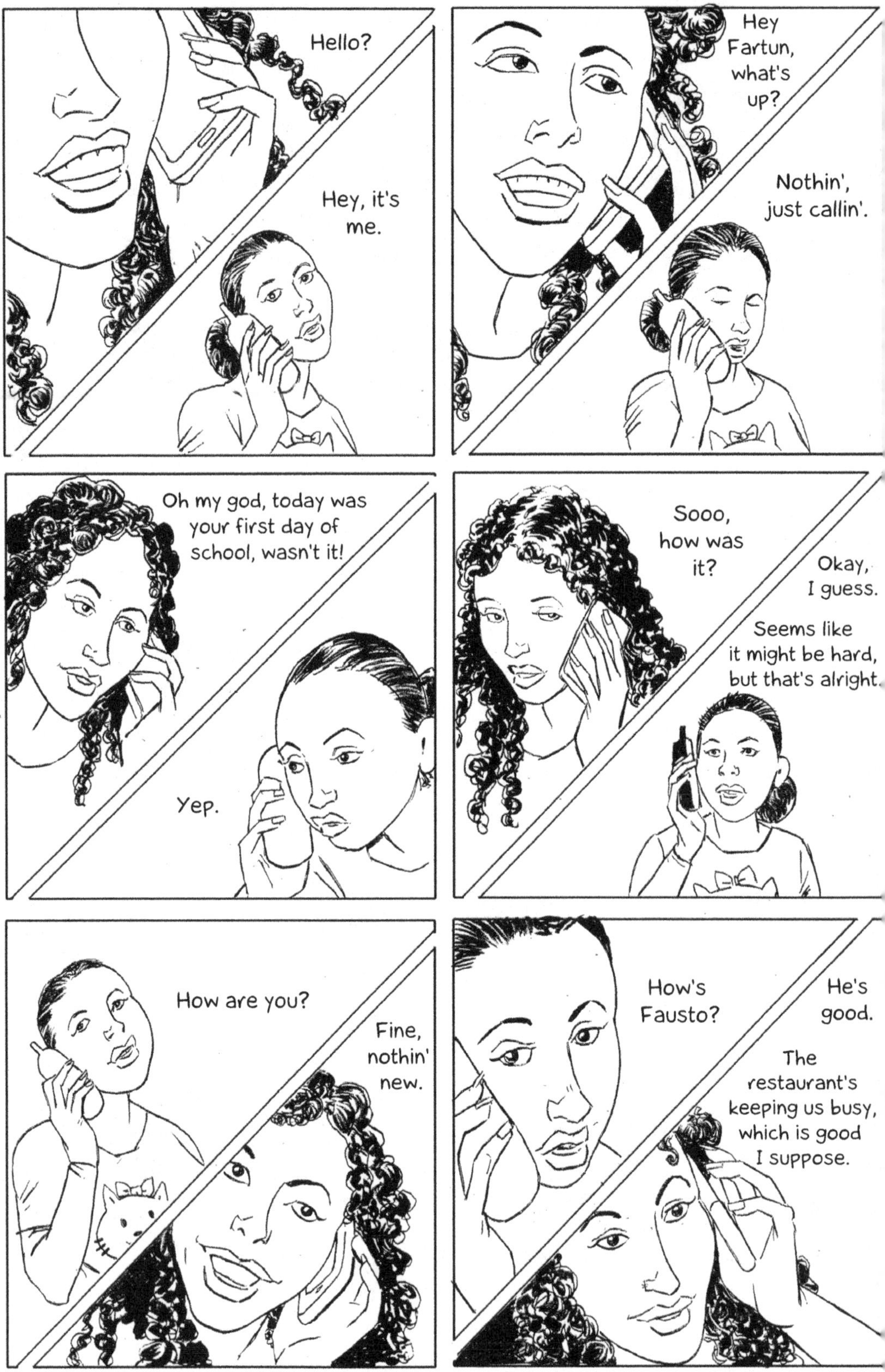
Hello?
Hey, it's me.
Hey Fartun, what's up?
Nothin', just callin'.
Oh my god, today was your first day of school, wasn't it!
Yep.
Sooo, how was it?
Okay, I guess.
Seems like it might be hard, but that's alright.
How are you?
Fine, nothin' new.
How's Fausto?
He's good.
The restaurant's keeping us busy, which is good I suppose.

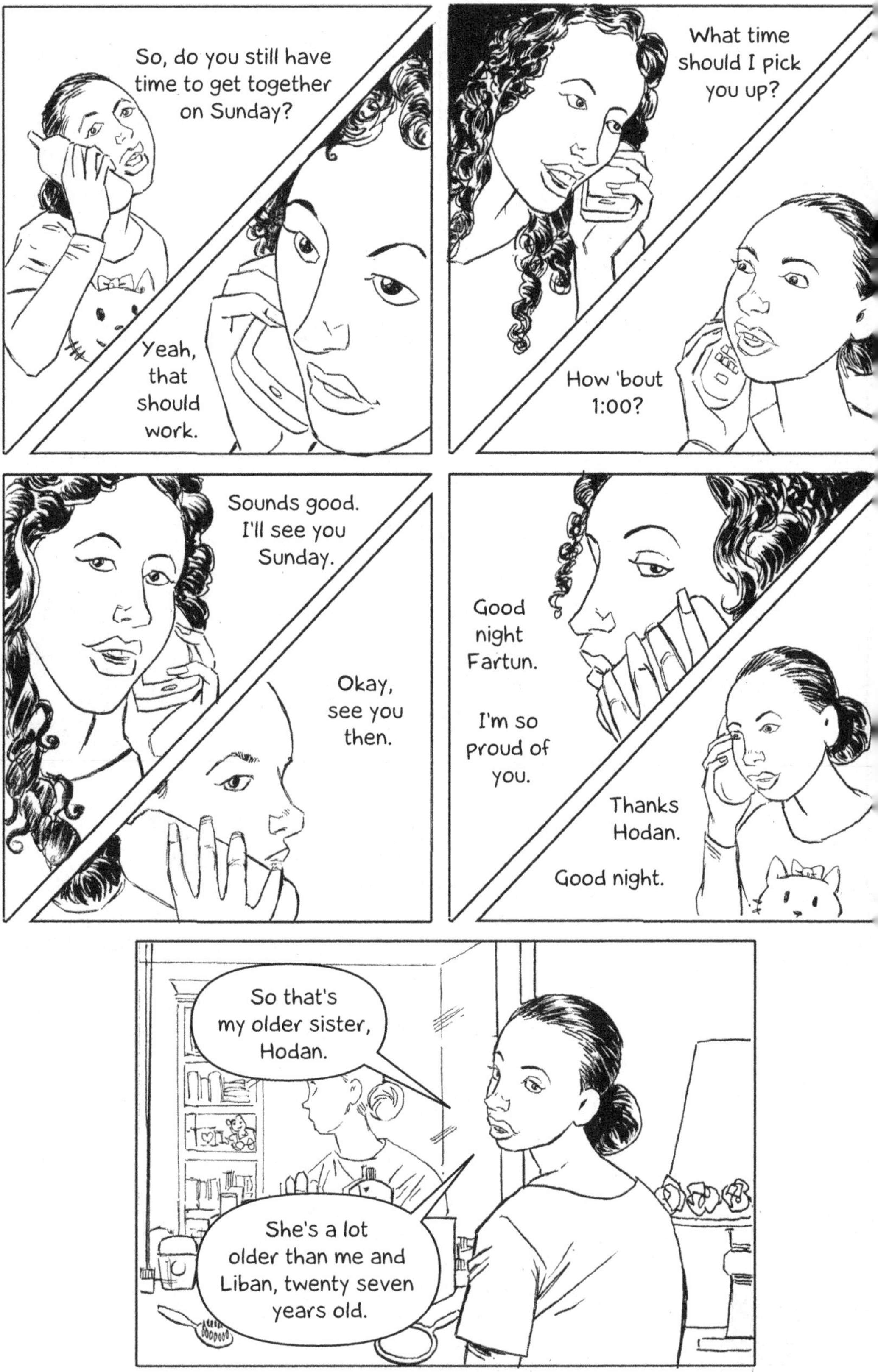

So, do you still have time to get together on Sunday?
Yeah, that should work.
What time should I pick you up?
How 'bout 1:00?
Sounds good. I'll see you Sunday.
Okay, see you then.
Good night Fartun.
I'm so proud of you.
Thanks Hodan.
Good night.
So that's my older sister, Hodan.
She's a lot older than me and Liban, twenty seven years old.

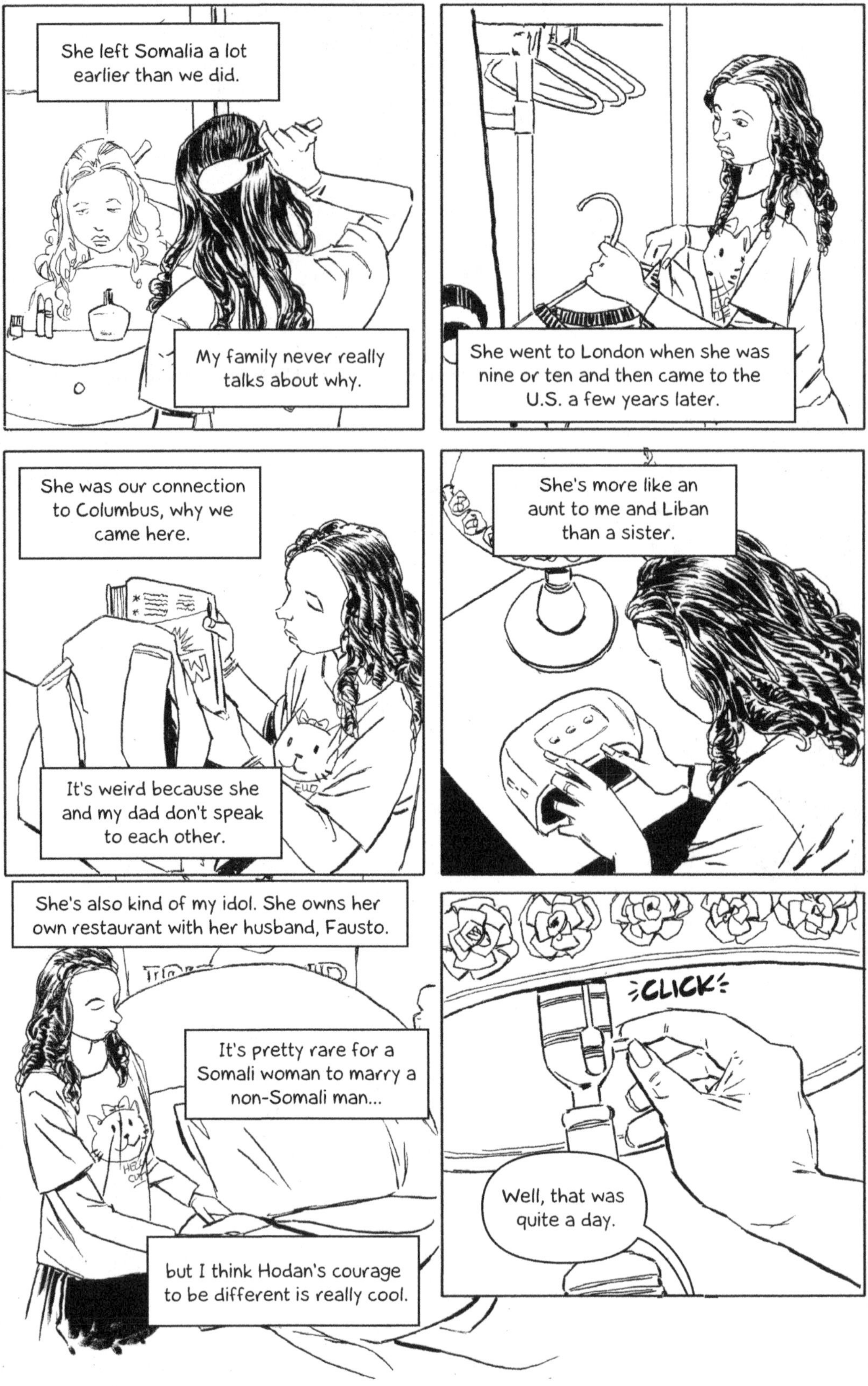
She left Somalia a lot earlier than we did.
My family never really talks about why.
She went to London when she was nine or ten and then came to the U.S. a few years later.
She was our connection to Columbus, why we came here.
It's weird because she and my dad don't speak to each other.
She's more like an aunt to me and Liban than a sister.
She's also kind of my idol. She owns her own restaurant with her husband, Fausto.
It's pretty rare for a Somali woman to marry a non-Somali man...
but I think Hodan's courage to be different is really cool.
CLICK
Well, that was quite a day.

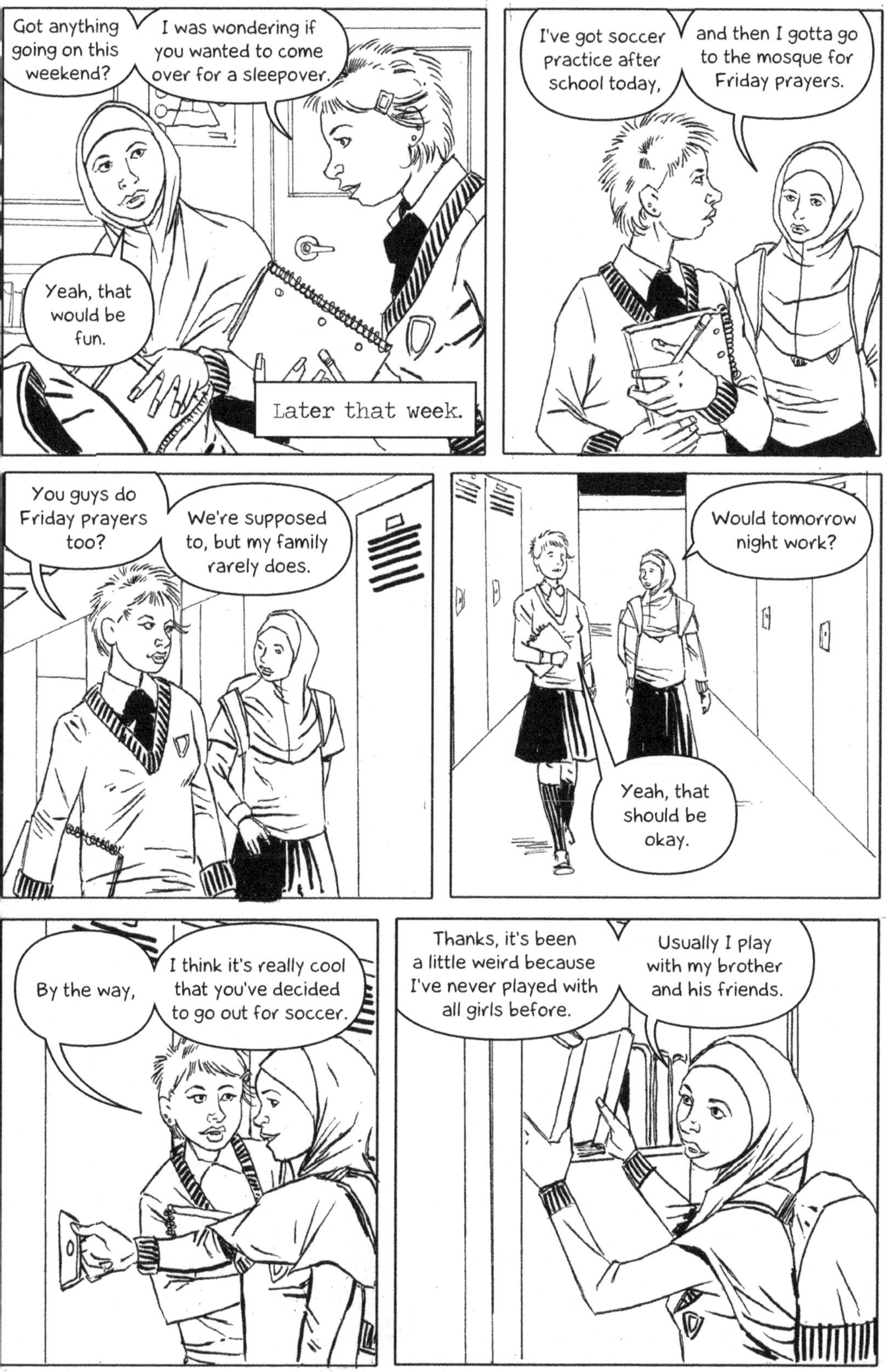
Got anything going on this weekend?
I was wondering if you wanted to come over for a sleepover.
Yeah, that would be fun.
Later that week.
I've got soccer practice after school today,
and then I gotta go to the mosque for Friday prayers.
You guys do Friday prayers too?
We're supposed to, but my family rarely does.
Would tomorrow night work?
Yeah, that should be okay.
By the way,
I think it's really cool that you've decided to go out for soccer.
Thanks, it's been a little weird because I've never played with all girls before.
Usually I play with my brother and his friends.

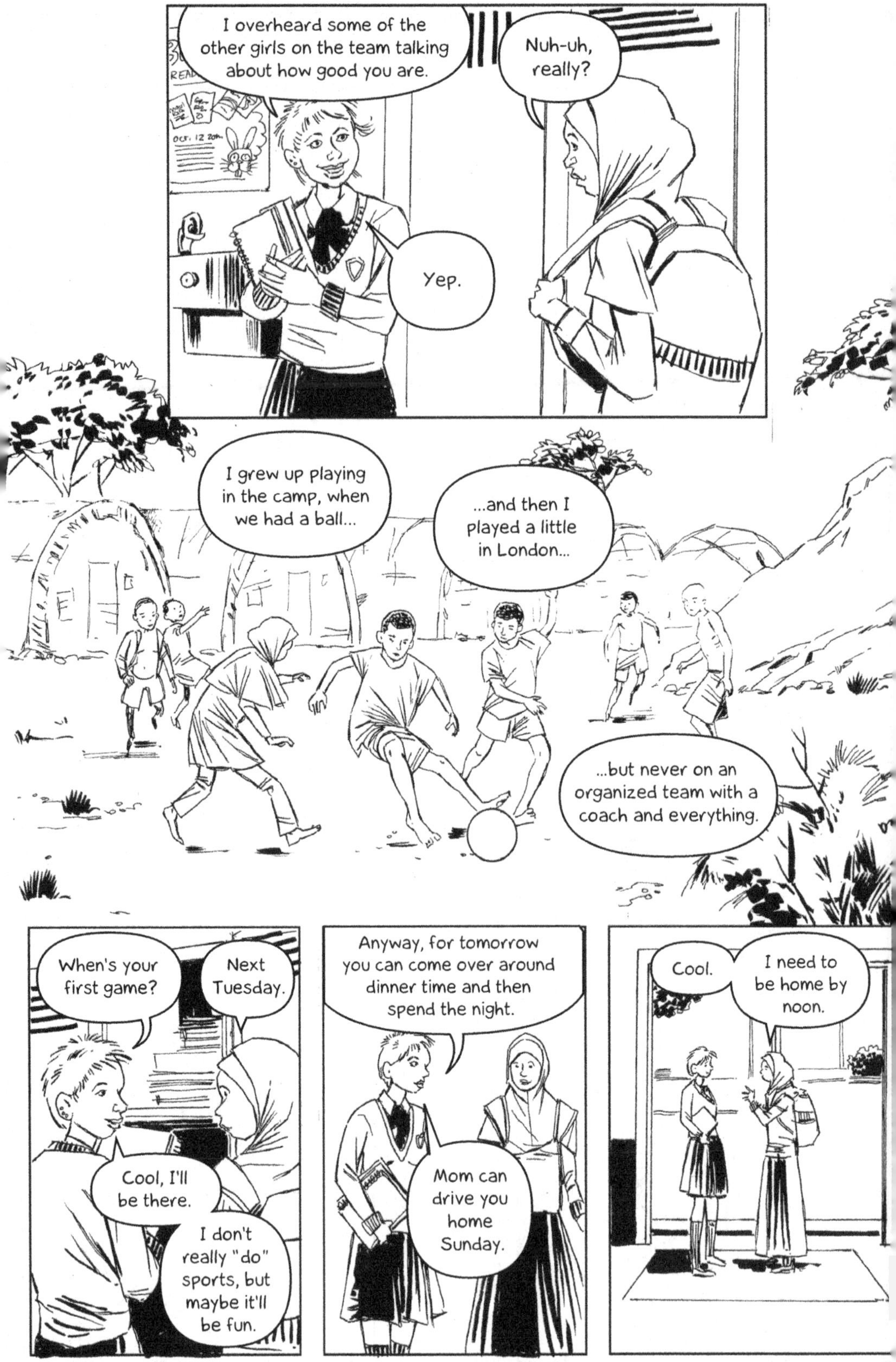
I overheard some of the other girls on the team talking about how good you are.
Nuh-uh, really?
Yep.
I grew up playing in the camp, when we had a ball...
...and then I played a little in London...
...but never on an organized team with a coach and everything.
When's your first game?
Next Tuesday.
Cool, I'll be there.
I don't really "do" sports, but maybe it'll be fun.
Anyway, for tomorrow you can come over around dinner time and then spend the night.
Mom can drive you home Sunday.
Cool.
I need to be home by noon.

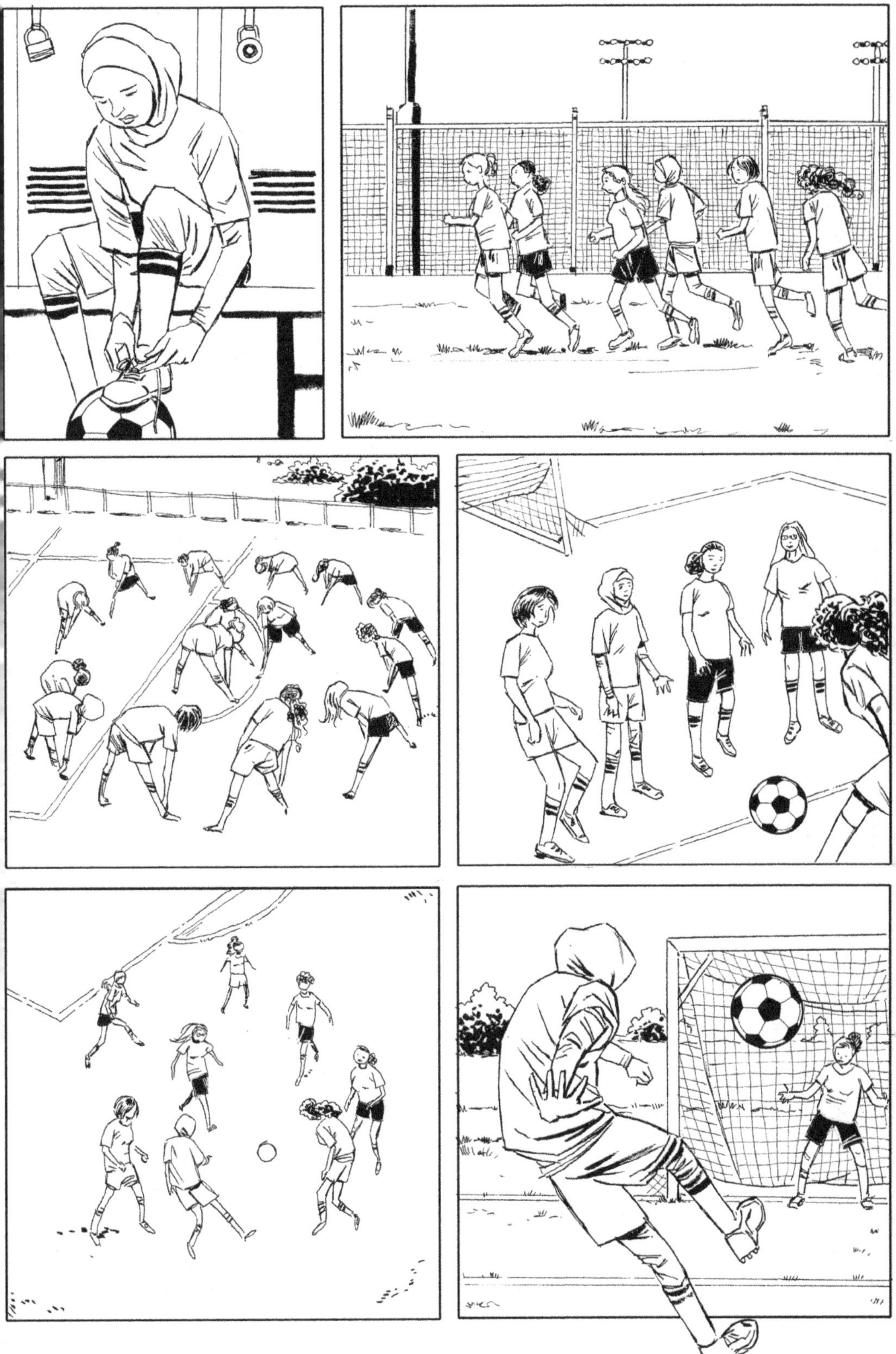

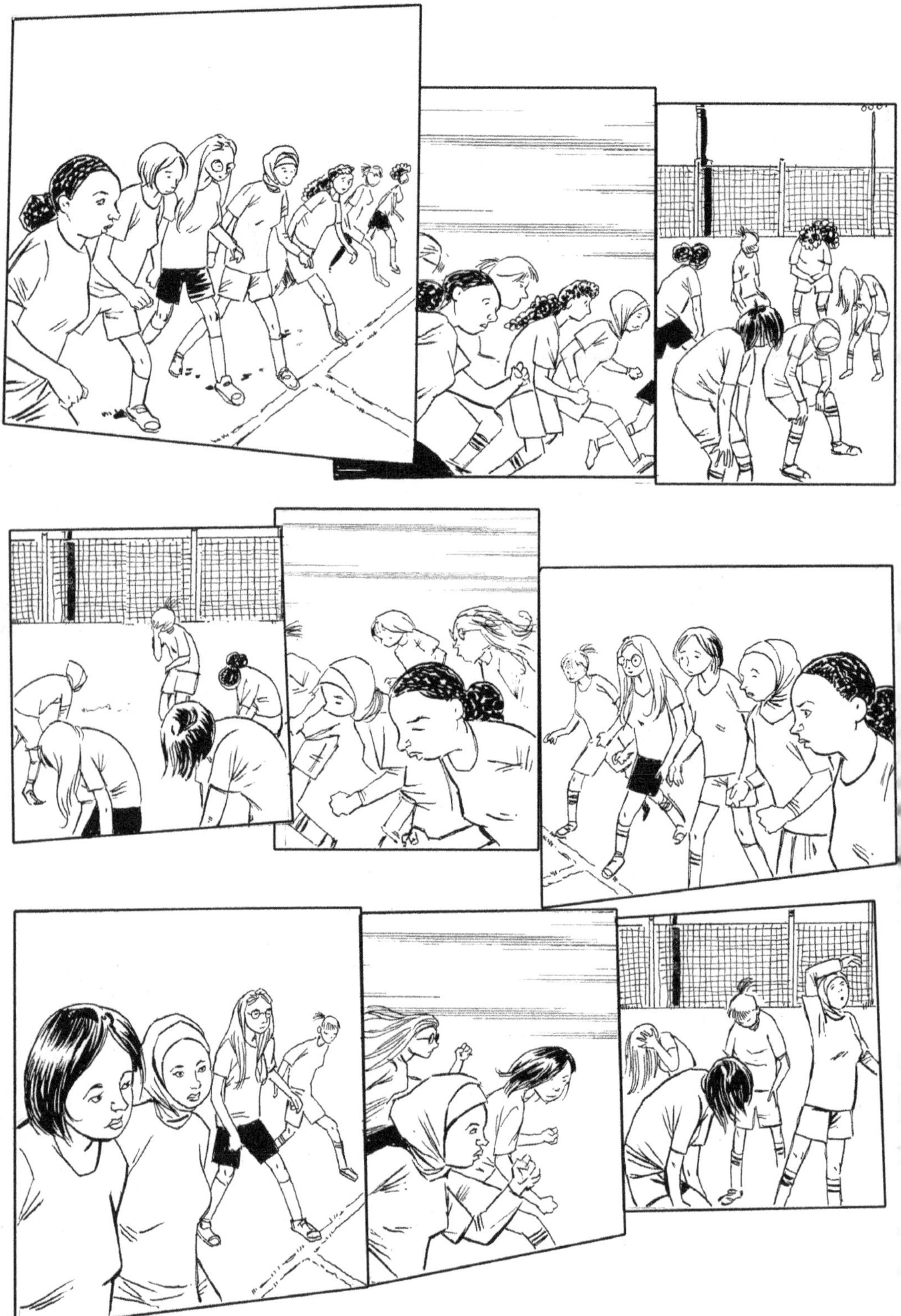

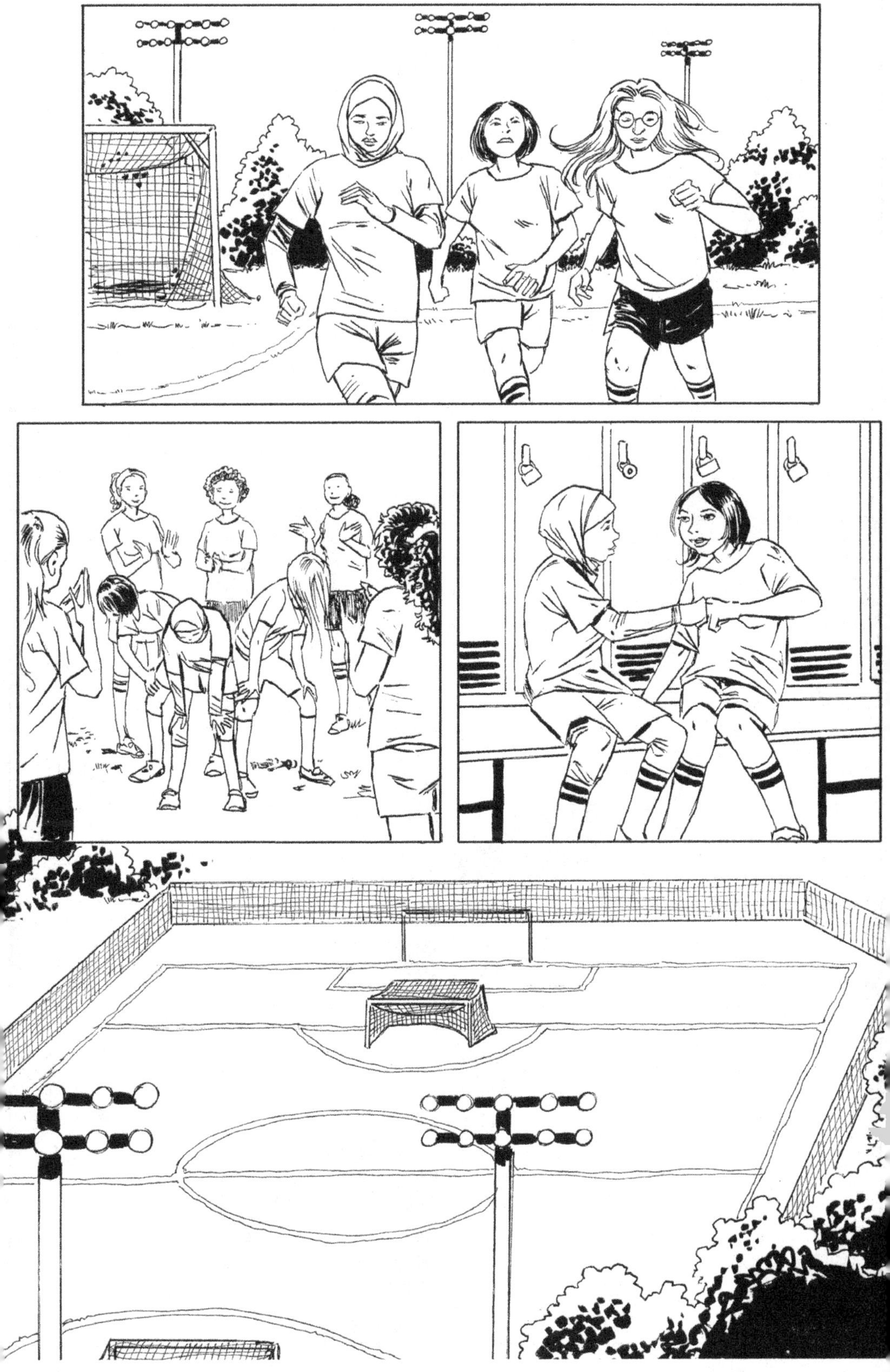

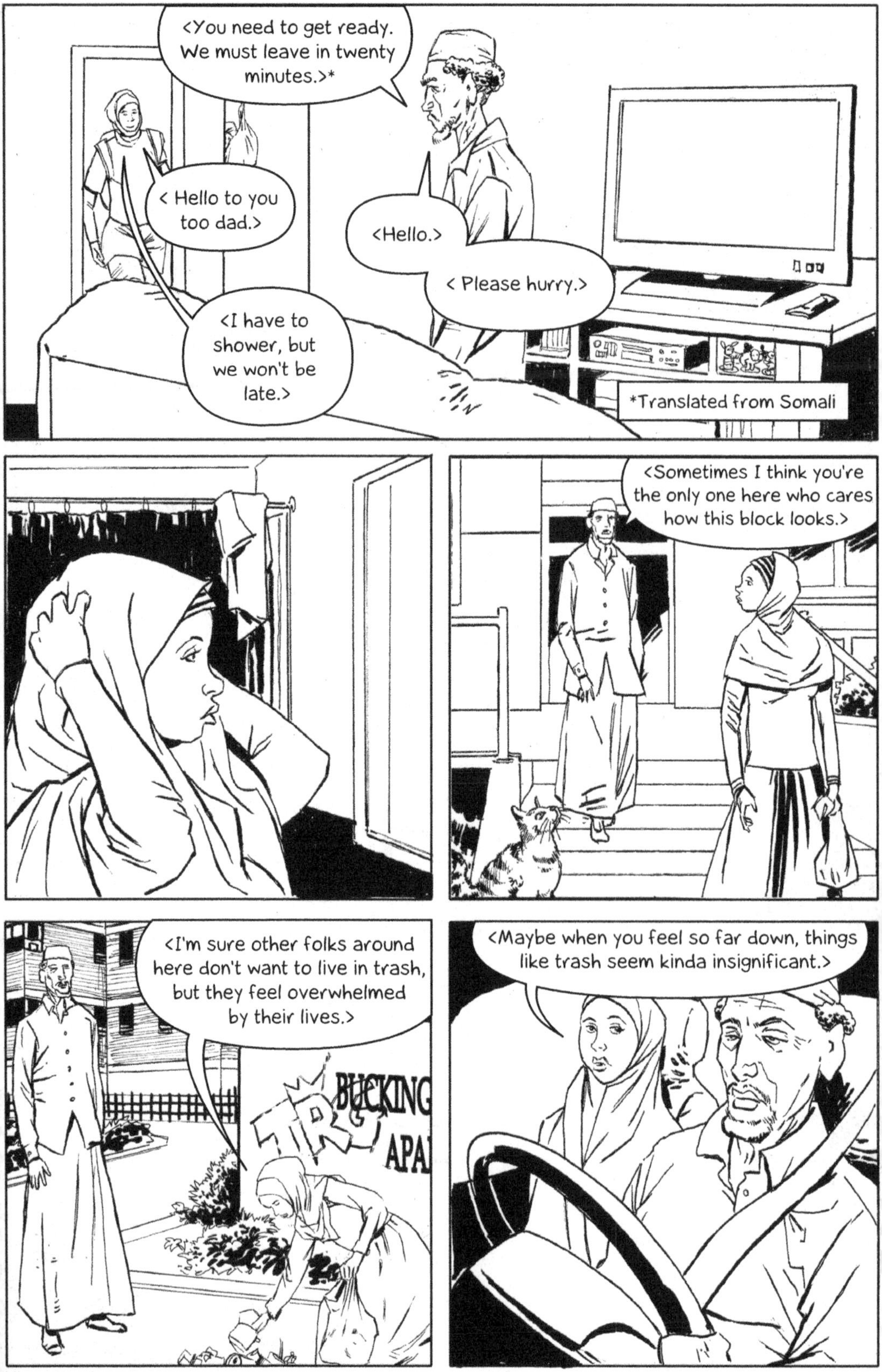
<You need to get ready. We must leave in twenty minutes.>*
< Hello to you too dad.>
<Hello.>
< Please hurry.>
<I have to shower, but we won't be late.>
*Translated from Somali
<Sometimes I think you're the only one here who cares how this block looks.>
<I'm sure other folks around here don't want to live in trash, but they feel overwhelmed by their lives.>
BUCKING
<Maybe when you feel so far down, things like trash seem kinda insignificant.>

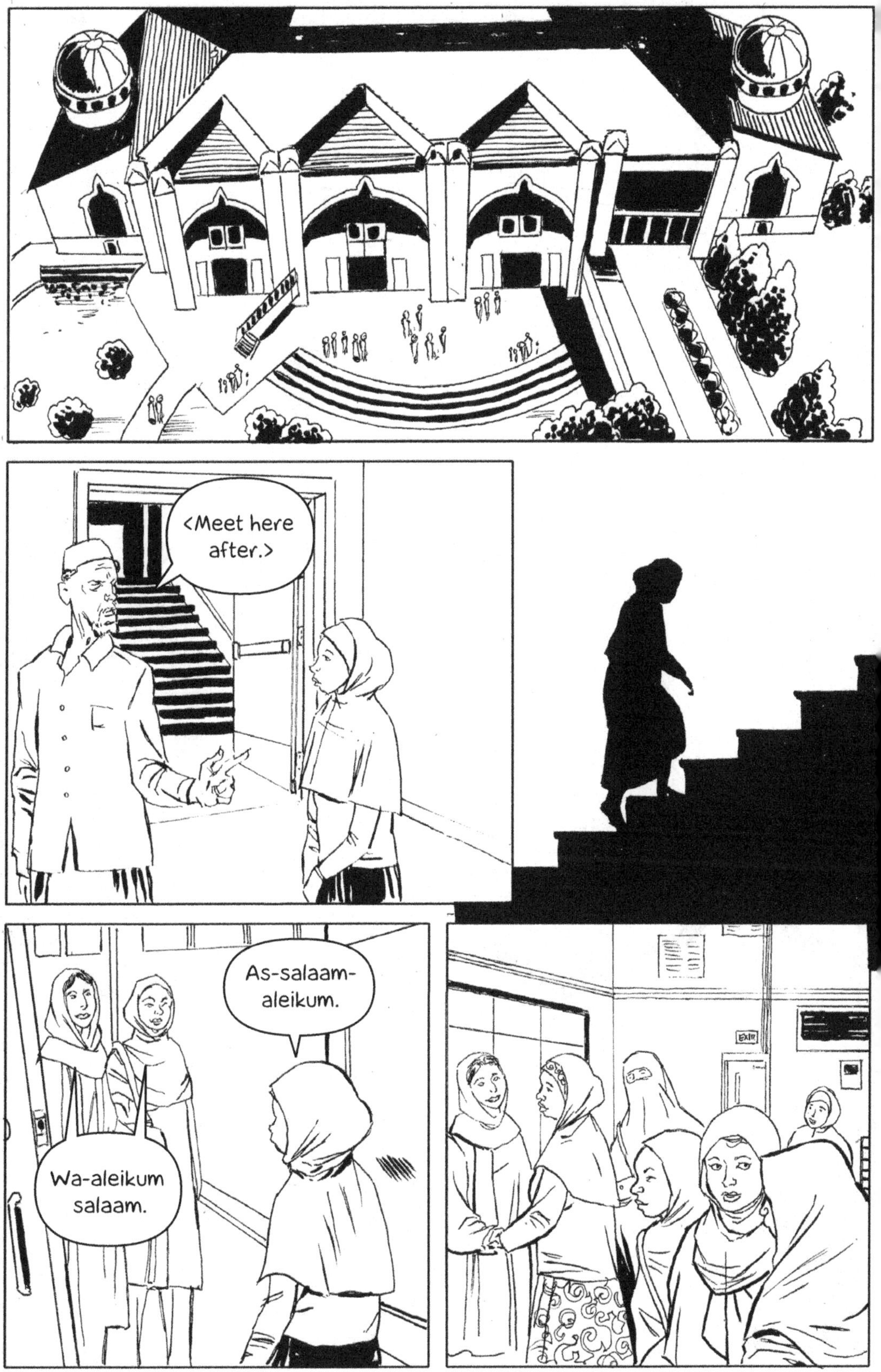
<Meet here after.>
As-salaam-aleikum.
Wa-aleikum salaam.

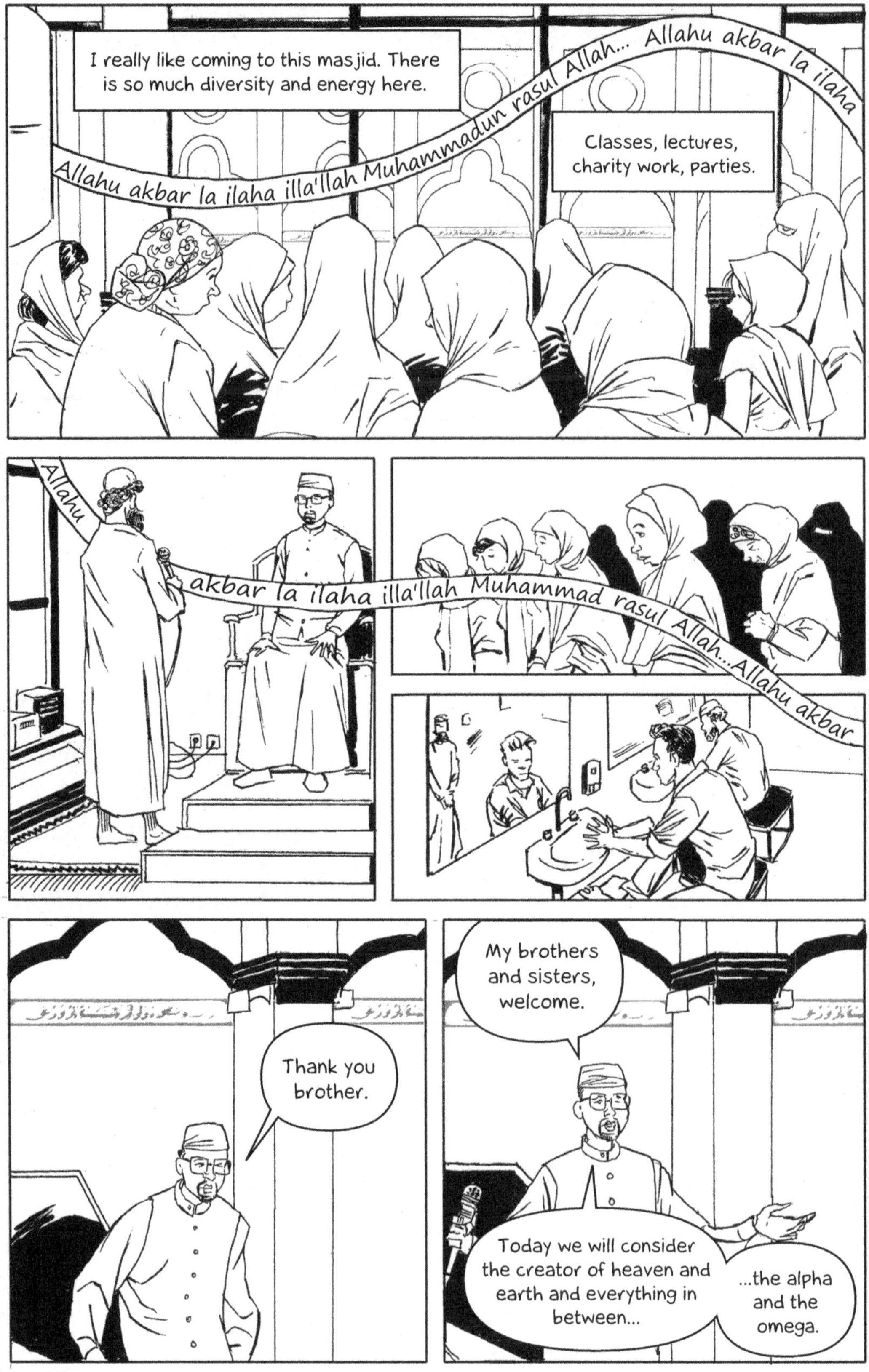
I really like coming to this masjid. There is so much diversity and energy here.
Allahu akbar la ilaha illa'llah Muhammadun rasul Allah... Allahu akbar la ilaha
Classes, lectures, charity work, parties.
Allahu akbar la ilaha illa'llah Muhammad rasul Allah...Allahu akbar
Thank you brother.
My brothers and sisters, welcome.
Today we will consider the creator of heaven and earth and everything in between...
...the alpha and the omega.

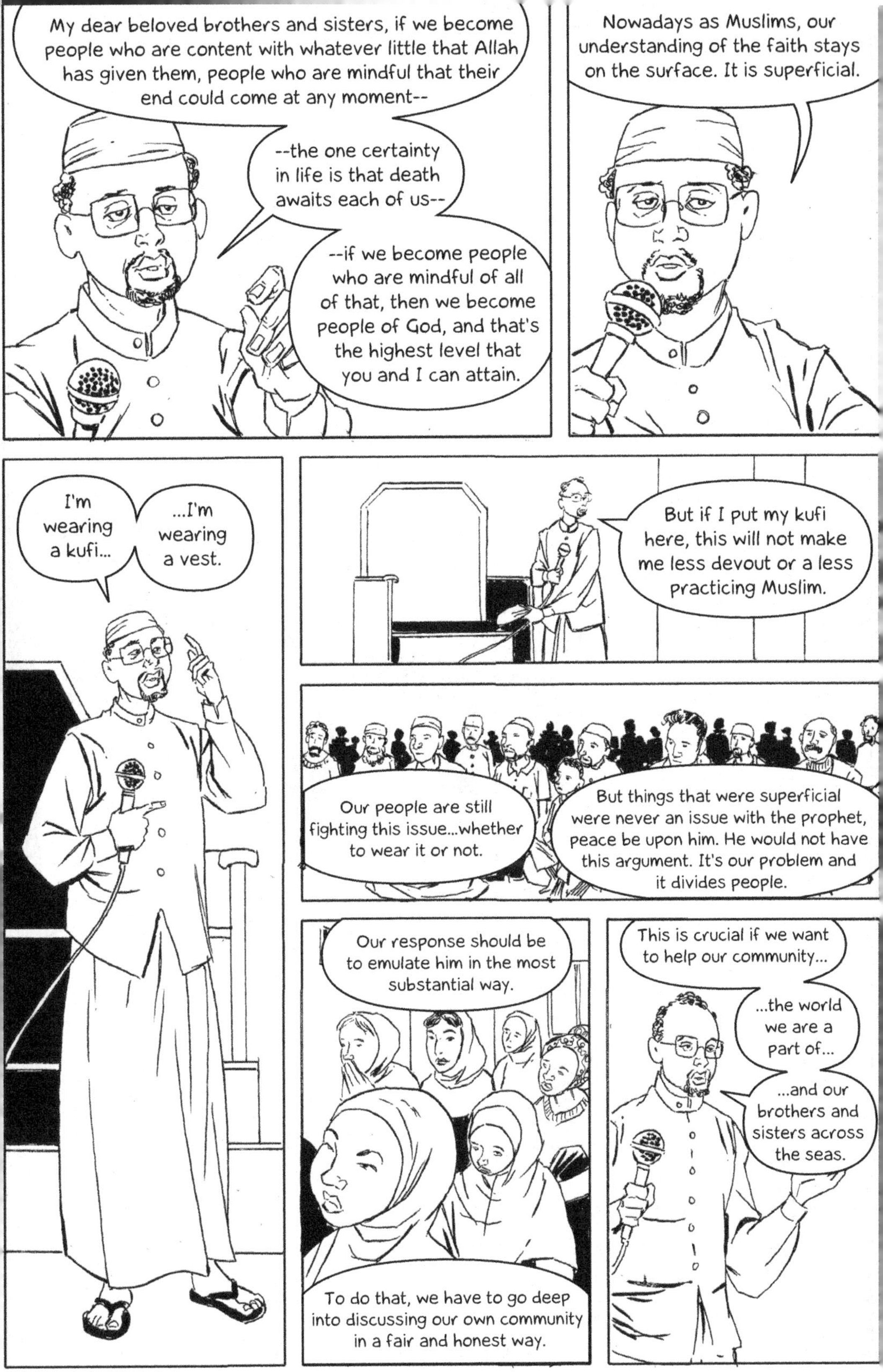
My dear beloved brothers and sisters, if we become people who are content with whatever little that Allah has given them, people who are mindful that their end could come at any moment--
--the one certainty in life is that death awaits each of us--
--if we become people who are mindful of all of that, then we become people of God, and that's the highest level that you and I can attain.
Nowadays as Muslims, our understanding of the faith stays on the surface. It is superficial.
I'm wearing a kufi...
...I'm wearing a vest.
But if I put my kufi here, this will not make me less devout or a less practicing Muslim.
Our people are still fighting this issue...whether to wear it or not.
But things that were superficial were never an issue with the prophet, peace be upon him. He would not have this argument. It's our problem and it divides people.
Our response should be to emulate him in the most substantial way.
To do that, we have to go deep into discussing our own community in a fair and honest way.
This is crucial if we want to help our community...
...the world we are a part of...
...and our brothers and sisters across the seas.

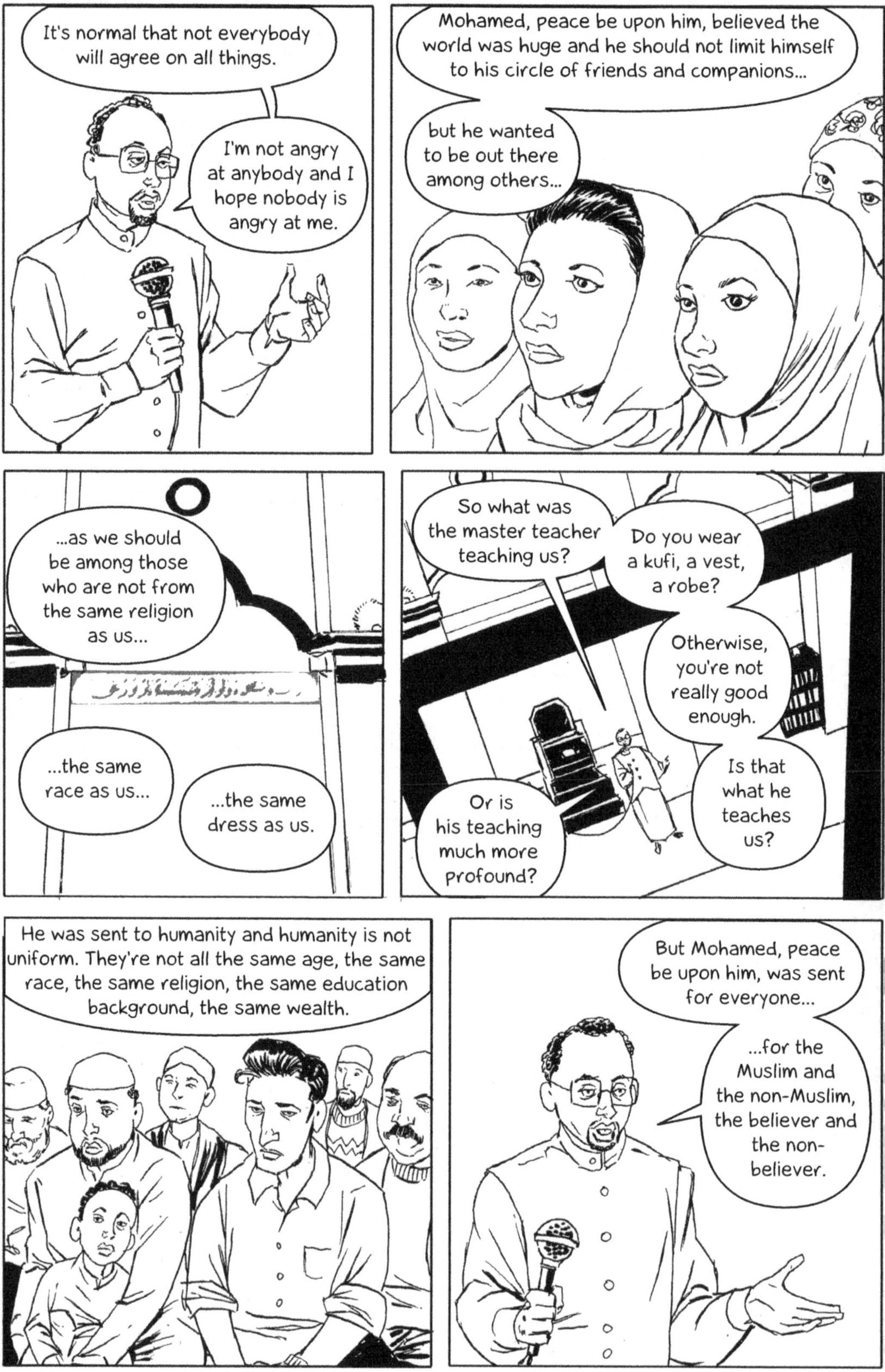
It's normal that not everybody will agree on all things.
I'm not angry at anybody and I hope nobody is angry at me.
Mohamed, peace be upon him, believed the world was huge and he should not limit himself to his circle of friends and companions...
but he wanted to be out there among others...
...as we should be among those who are not from the same religion as us...
...the same race as us...
...the same dress as us.
So what was the master teacher teaching us?
Do you wear a kufi, a vest, a robe?
Otherwise, you're not really good enough.
Is that what he teaches us?
Or is his teaching much more profound?
He was sent to humanity and humanity is not uniform. They're not all the same age, the same race, the same religion, the same education background, the same wealth.
But Mohamed, peace be upon him, was sent for everyone...
...for the Muslim and the non-Muslim, the believer and the non-believer.

Some wanted him to curse those who were different...

...but he wouldn't because he knew he wasn't sent to curse anybody.

He was sent as a mercy to all living beings...

...to all creation, not just mankind.

Therefore, we need to stop focusing on the insignificant, the superficial. We need to figure out how to be good human beings who can share life and space with other people.

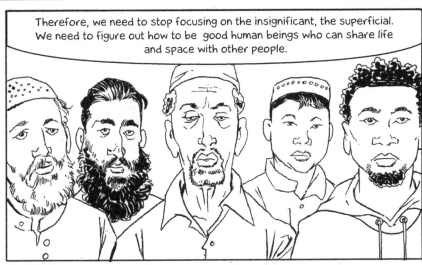

This begins with your own house and family and moves out from there, simple as that. That's what his message was.

So changing the course of history depends on you and me, insha'Allah...

...not the people who say curse this group or curse that group.

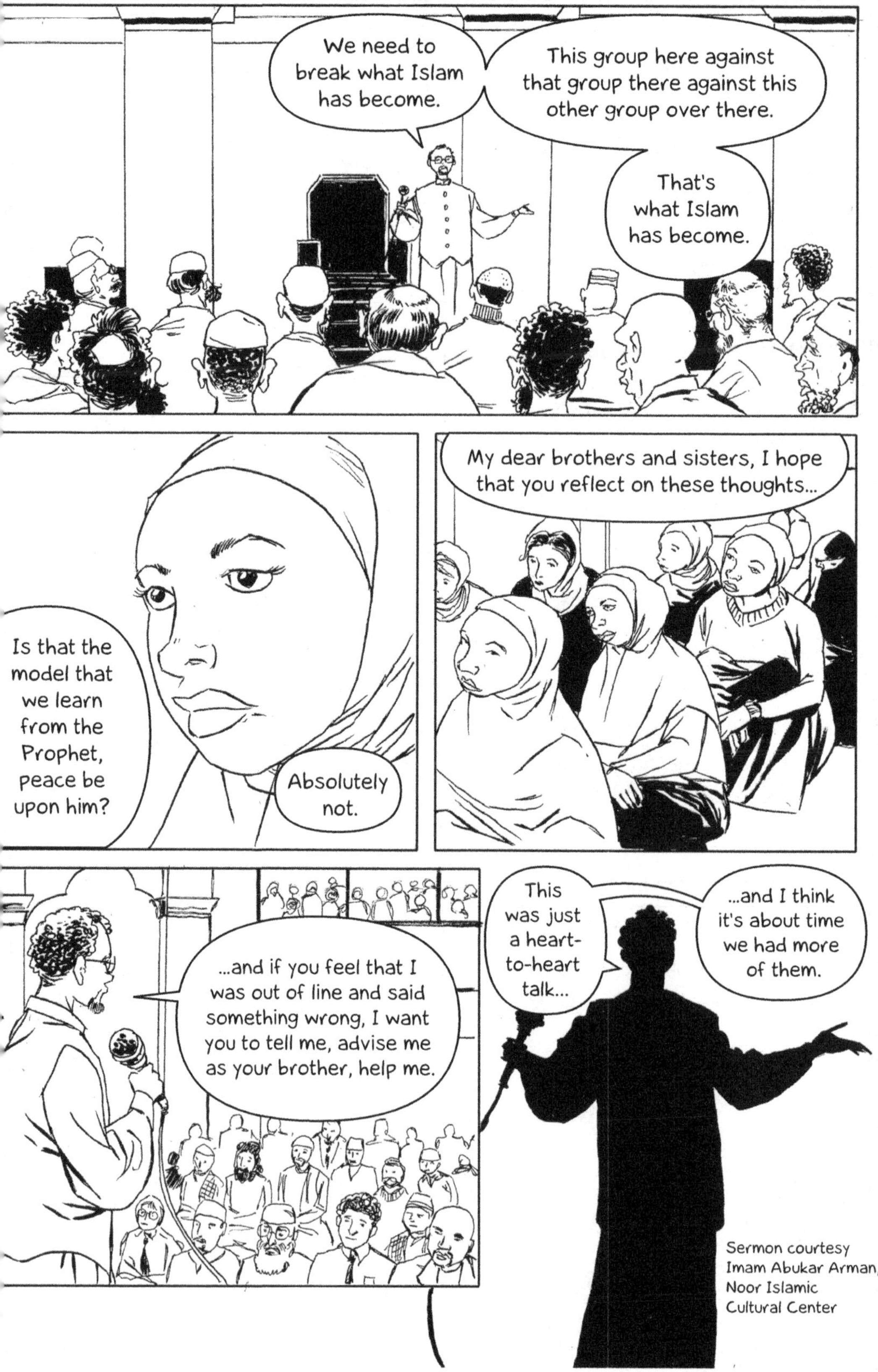
We need to break what Islam has become.
This group here against that group there against this other group over there.
That's what Islam has become.
Is that the model that we learn from the Prophet, peace be upon him?
Absolutely not.
My dear brothers and sisters, I hope that you reflect on these thoughts...
...and if you feel that I was out of line and said something wrong, I want you to tell me, advise me as your brother, help me.
This was just a heart-to-heart talk...
...and I think it's about time we had more of them.

Sermon courtesy Imam Abukar Arman, Noor Islamic Cultural Center

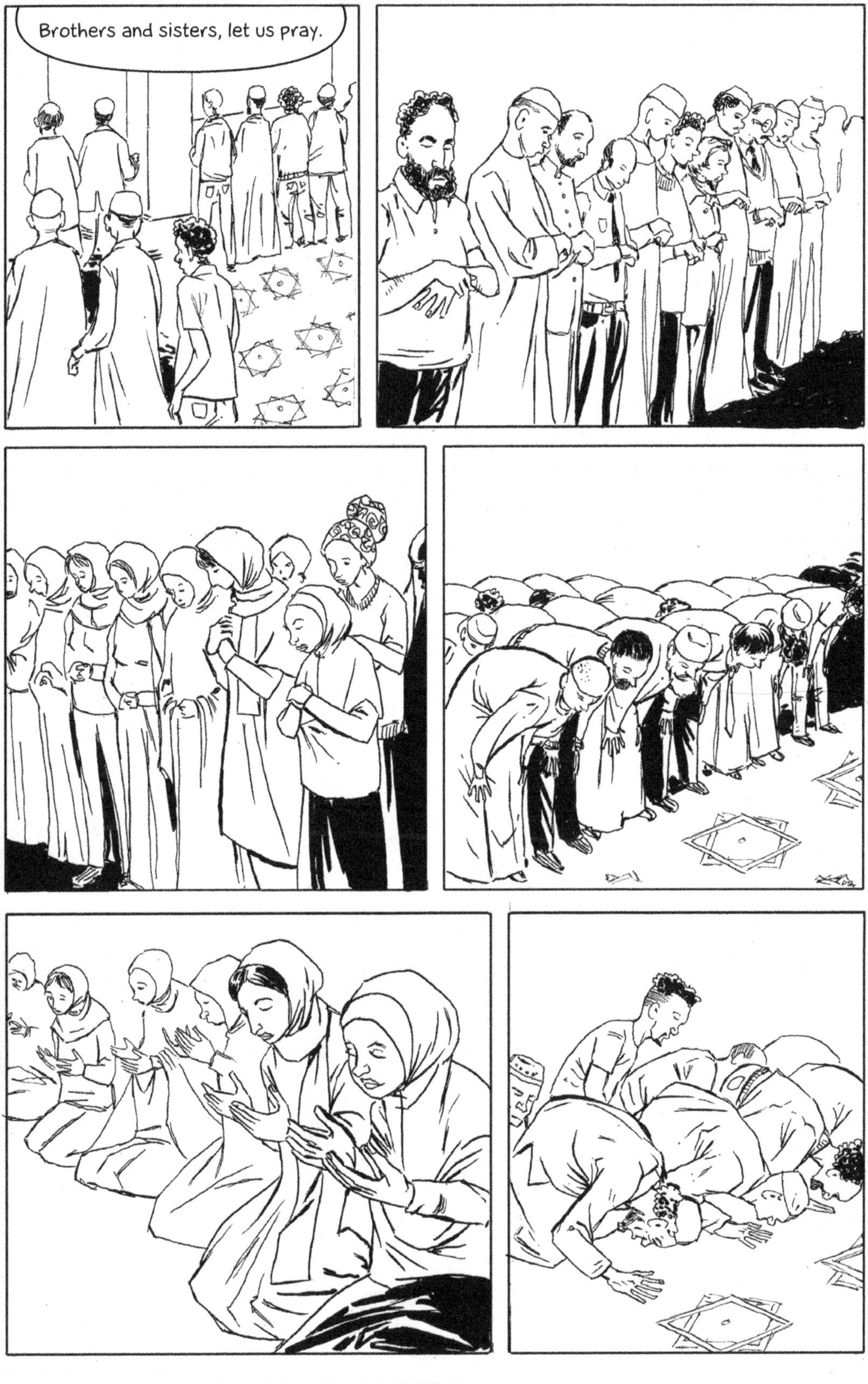
Brothers and sisters, let us pray.

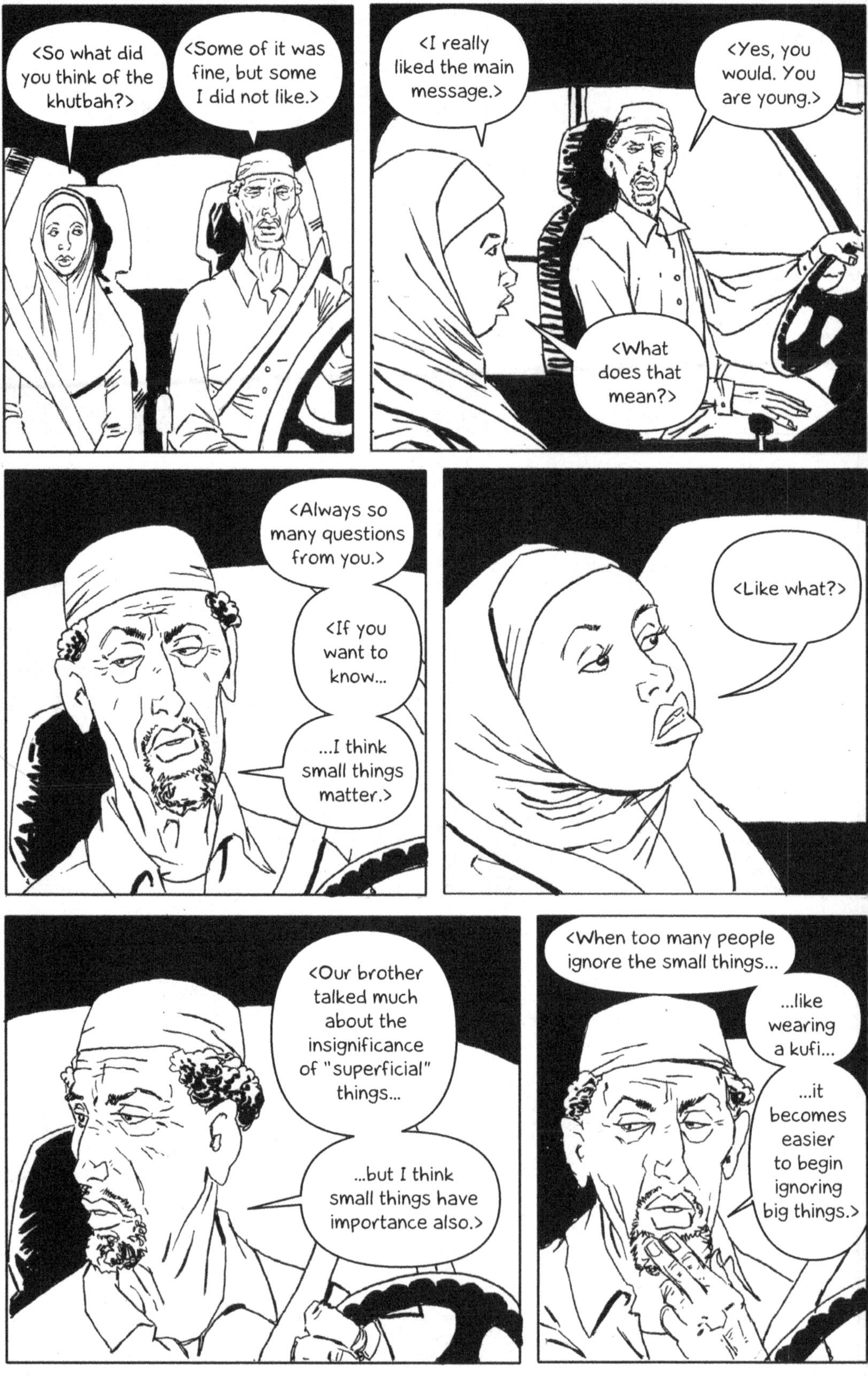
<So what did you think of the khutbah?>
<Some of it was fine, but some I did not like.>
<I really liked the main message.>
<Yes, you would. You are young.>
<What does that mean?>
<Always so many questions from you.>
<If you want to know...
...I think small things matter.>
<Like what?>
<Our brother talked much about the insignificance of "superficial" things...
...but I think small things have importance also.>
<When too many people ignore the small things...
...like wearing a kufi...
...it becomes easier to begin ignoring big things.>

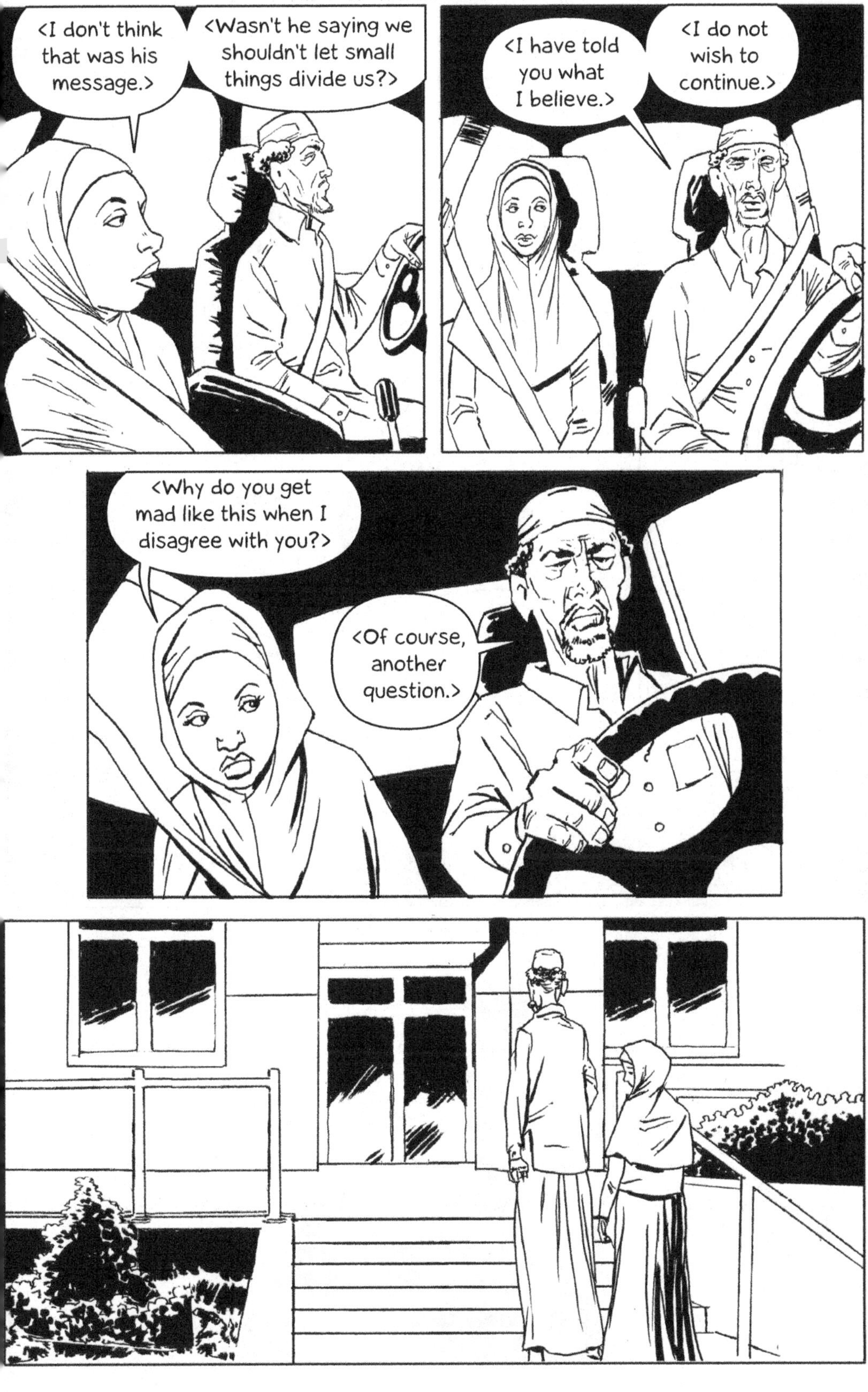

<I don't think that was his message.>
<Wasn't he saying we shouldn't let small things divide us?>
<I have told you what I believe.>
<I do not wish to continue.>
<Why do you get mad like this when I disagree with you?>
<Of course, another question.>

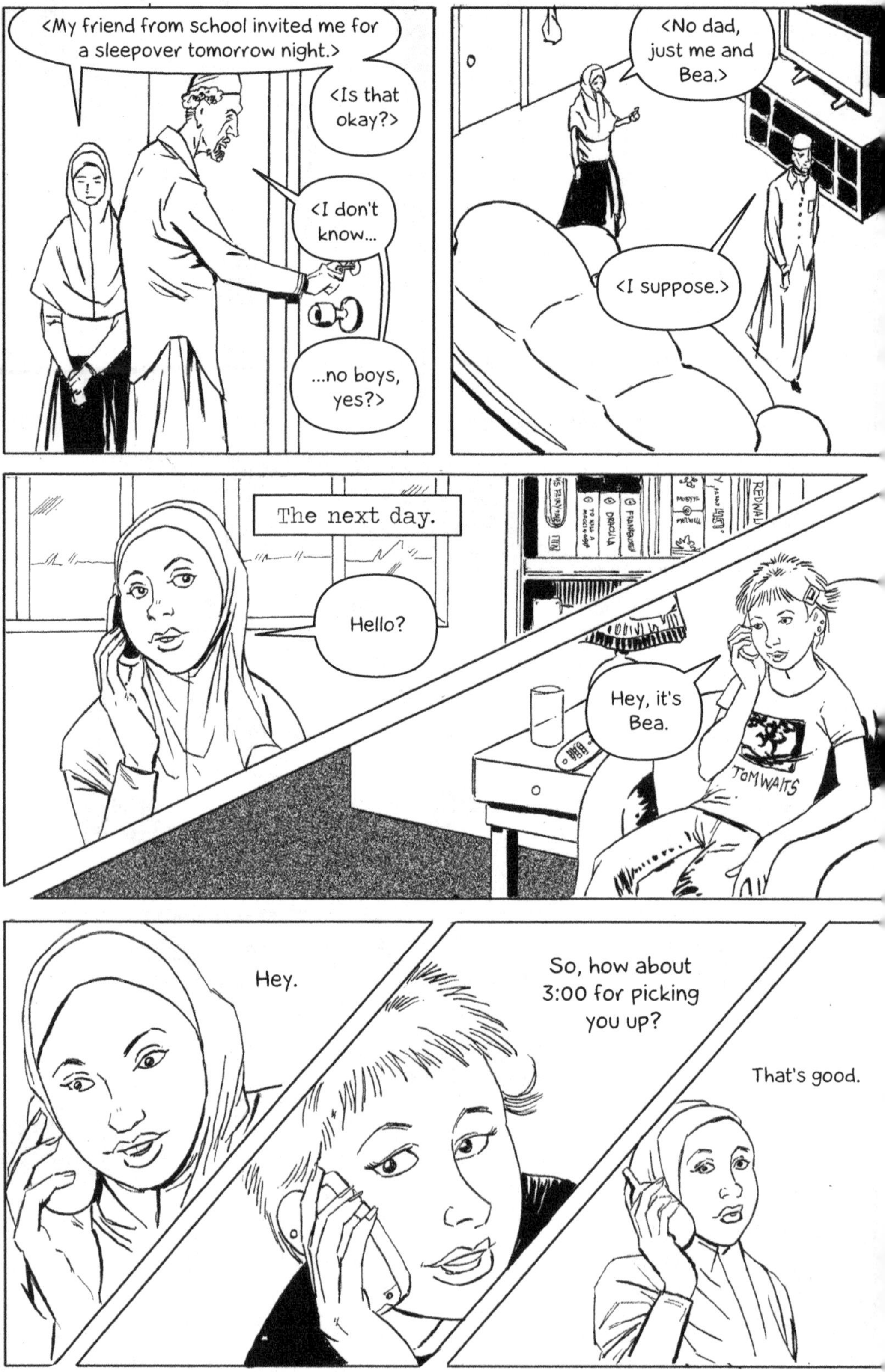
<My friend from school invited me for a sleepover tomorrow night.>
<Is that okay?>
<I don't know...
...no boys, yes?>
<No dad, just me and Bea.>
<I suppose.>
The next day.
Hello?
Hey, it's Bea.
TOMWAITS
Hey.
So, how about 3:00 for picking you up?
That's good.

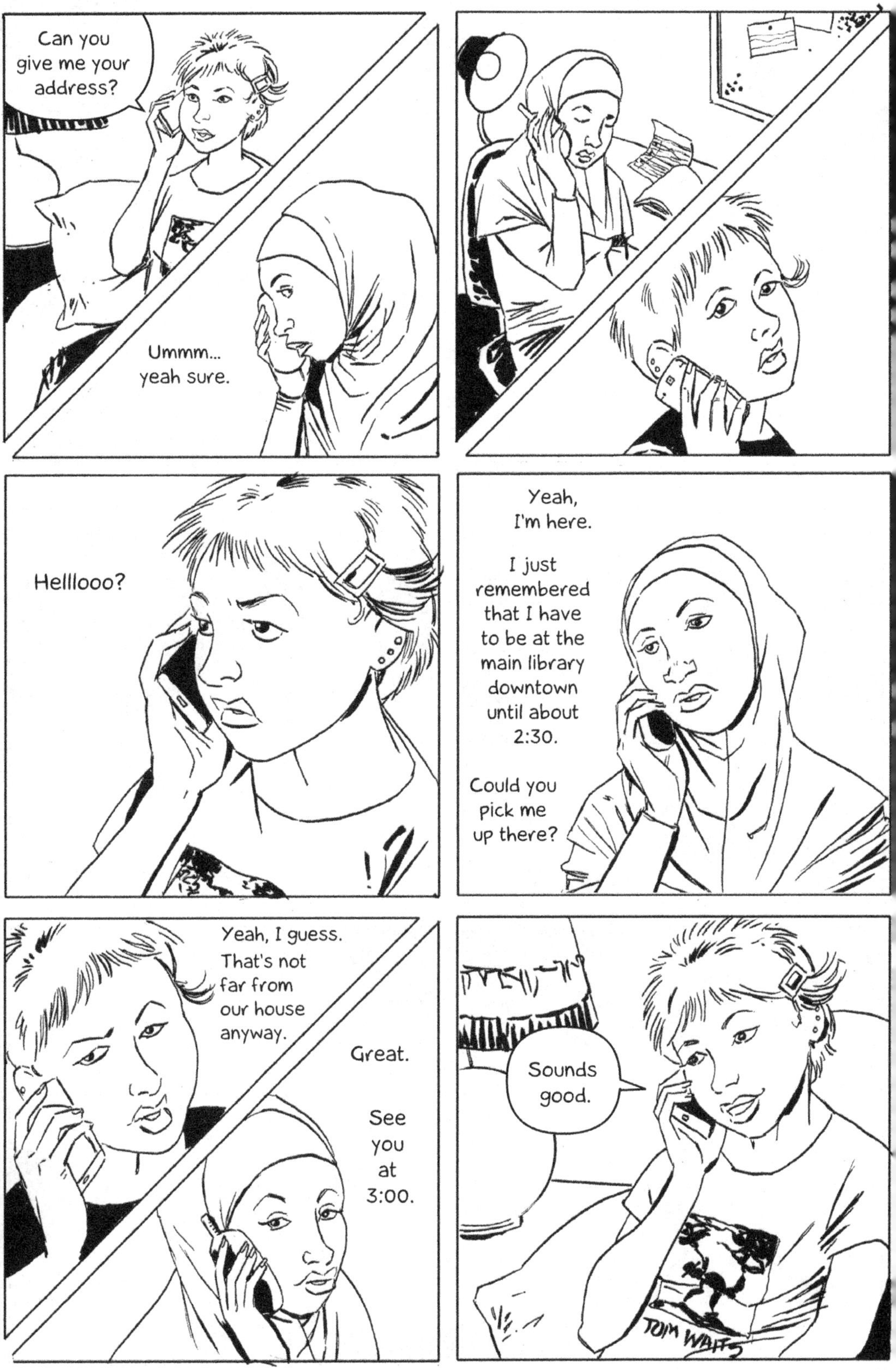
Can you give me your address?
Ummm... yeah sure.
Helllooo?
Yeah, I'm here.
I just remembered that I have to be at the main library downtown until about 2:30.
Could you pick me up there?
Yeah, I guess. That's not far from our house anyway.
Great.
See you at 3:00.
Sounds good.
TOM WAITS

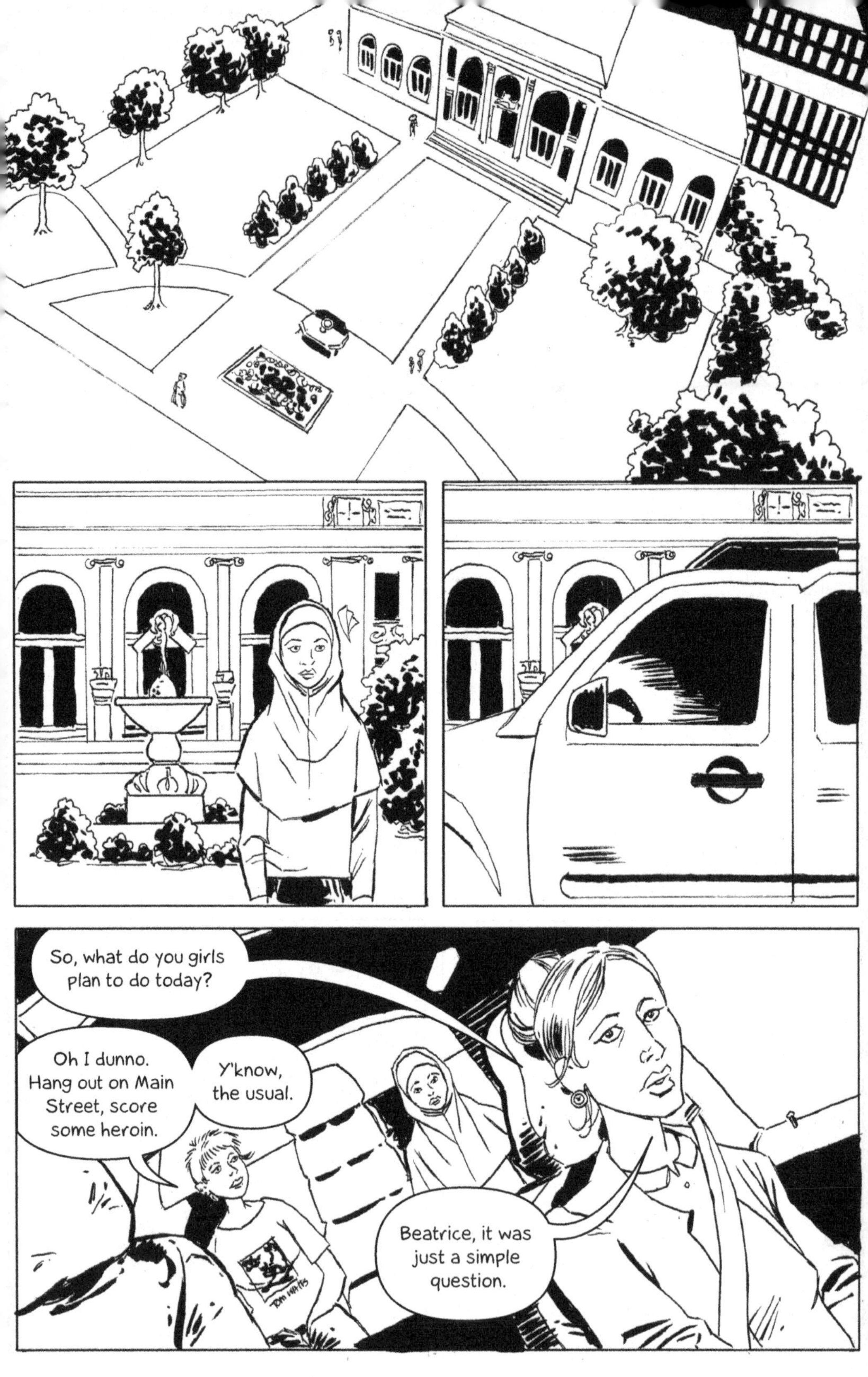
So, what do you girls plan to do today?
Oh I dunno. Hang out on Main Street, score some heroin.
Y'know, the usual.
Beatrice, it was just a simple question.

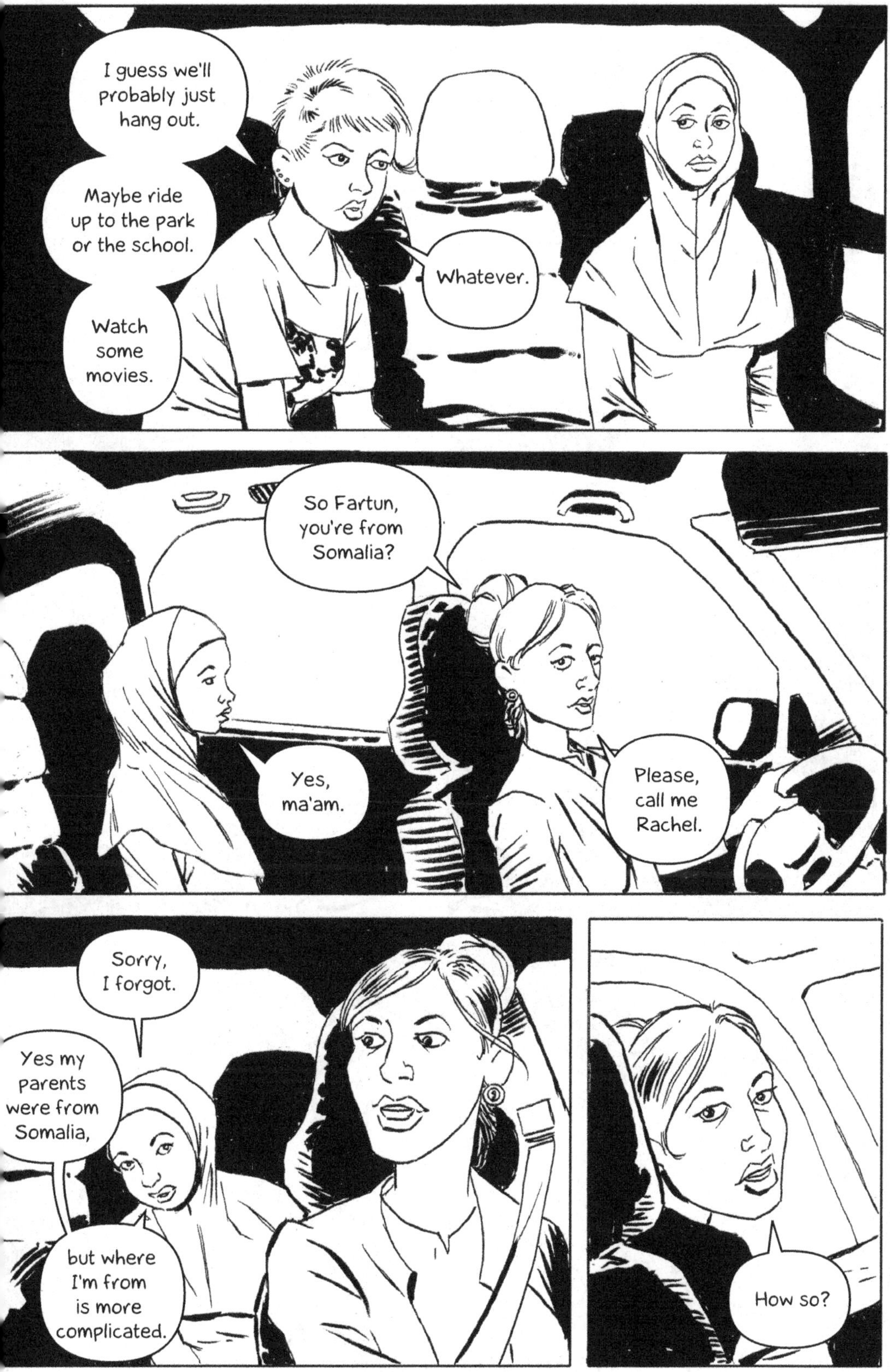
I guess we'll probably just hang out.
Maybe ride up to the park or the school.
Watch some movies.
Whatever.
So Fartun, you're from Somalia?
Yes, ma'am.
Please, call me Rachel.
Sorry, I forgot.
Yes my parents were from Somalia,
but where I'm from is more complicated.
How so?

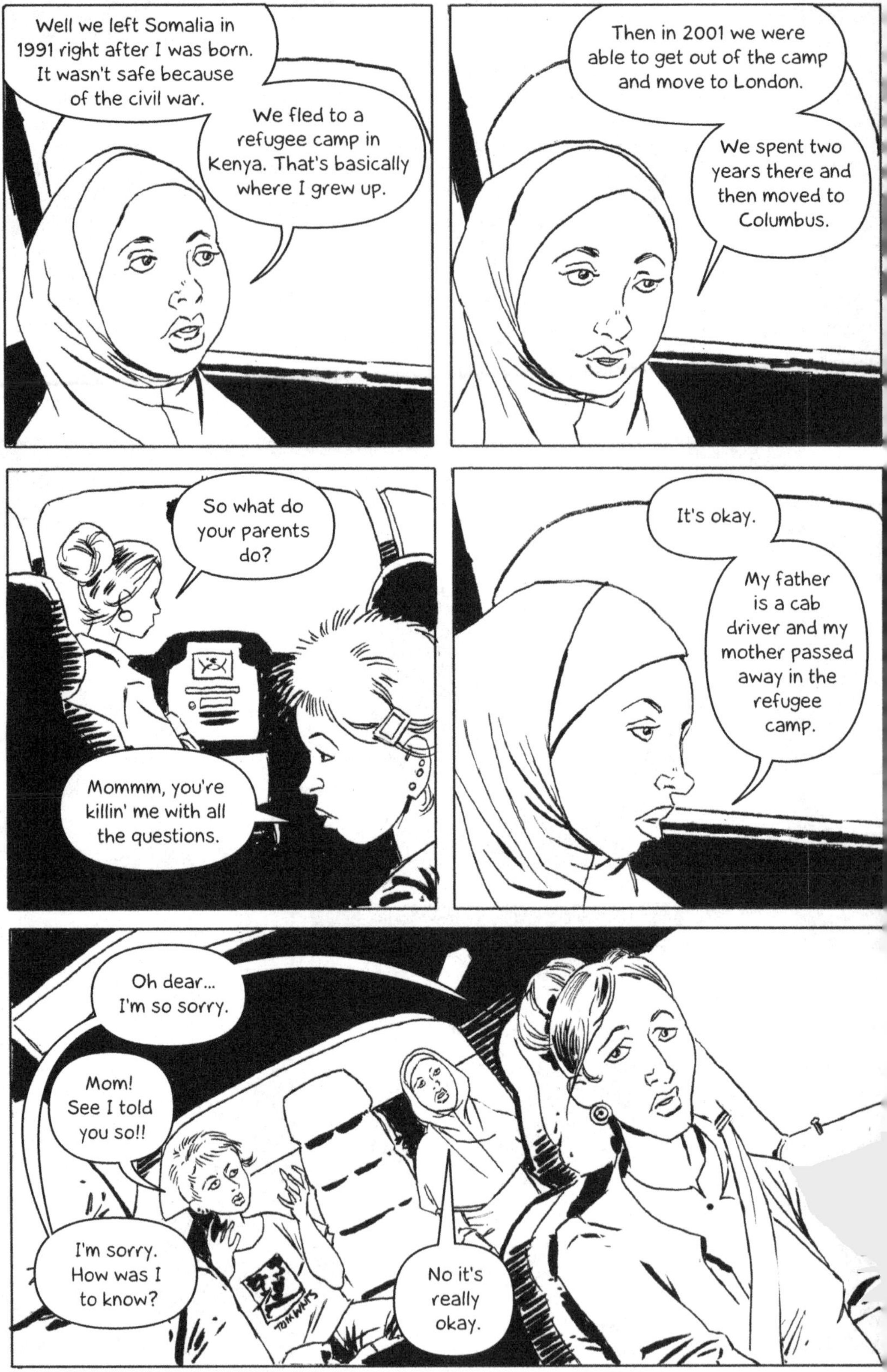
Well we left Somalia in 1991 right after I was born. It wasn't safe because of the civil war.
We fled to a refugee camp in Kenya. That's basically where I grew up.
Then in 2001 we were able to get out of the camp and move to London.
We spent two years there and then moved to Columbus.
So what do your parents do?
Mommm, you're killin' me with all the questions.
It's okay.
My father is a cab driver and my mother passed away in the refugee camp.
Oh dear... I'm so sorry.
Mom! See I told you so!!
I'm sorry. How was I to know?
No it's really okay.

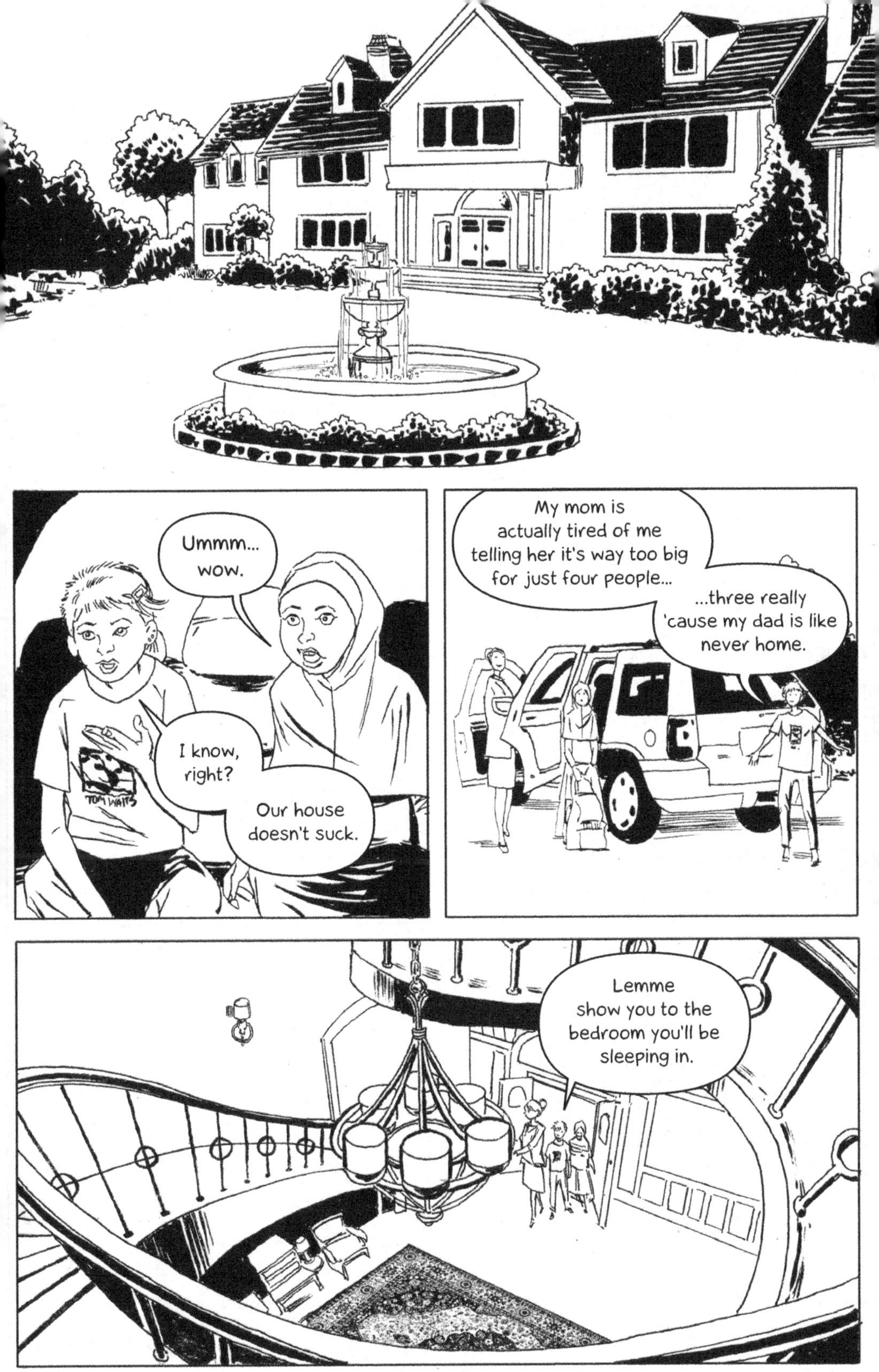
Ummm... wow.
I know, right?
Our house doesn't suck.
TOM WAITS
My mom is actually tired of me telling her it's way too big for just four people...
...three really 'cause my dad is like never home.
Lemme show you to the bedroom you'll be sleeping in.

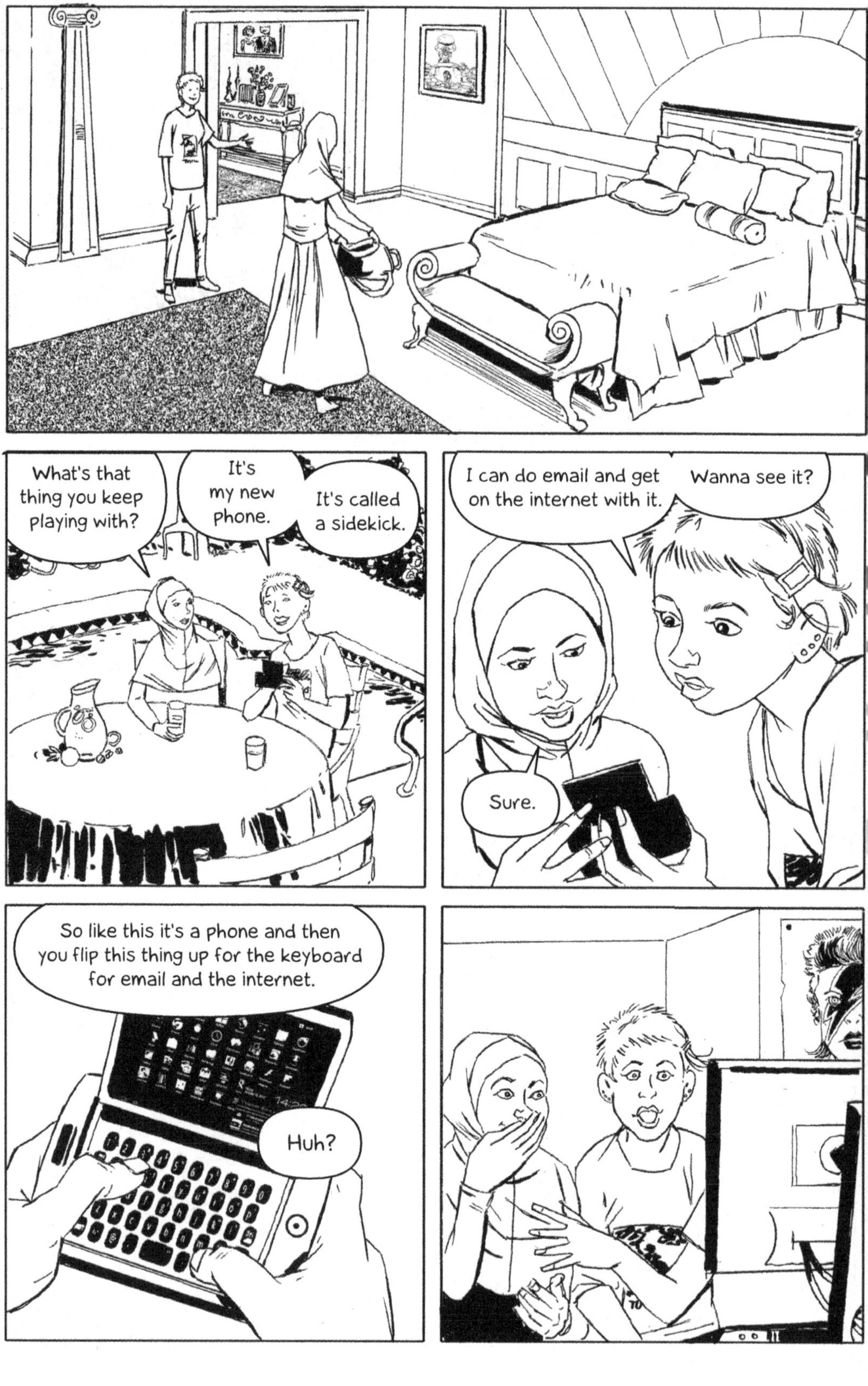
What's that thing you keep playing with?
It's my new phone.
It's called a sidekick.
I can do email and get on the internet with it.
Wanna see it?
Sure.
So like this it's a phone and then you flip this thing up for the keyboard for email and the internet.
Huh?

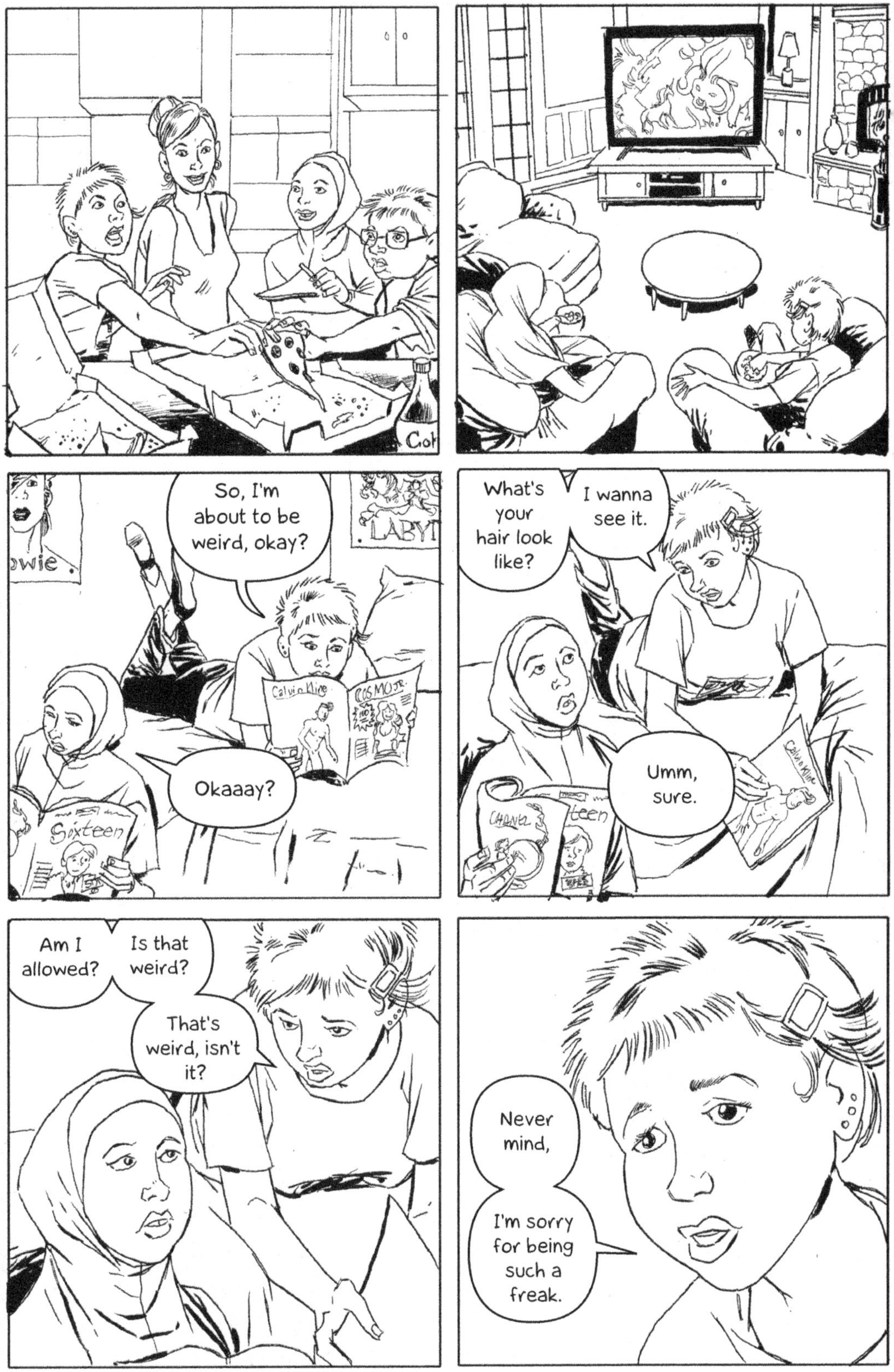
So, I'm about to be weird, okay?
Calvin Kline
COSMO JR.
Sixteen
Okaaay?
What's your hair look like?
I wanna see it.
Umm, sure.
Calvin Kline
Am I allowed?
Is that weird?
That's weird, isn't it?
Never mind,
I'm sorry for being such a freak.

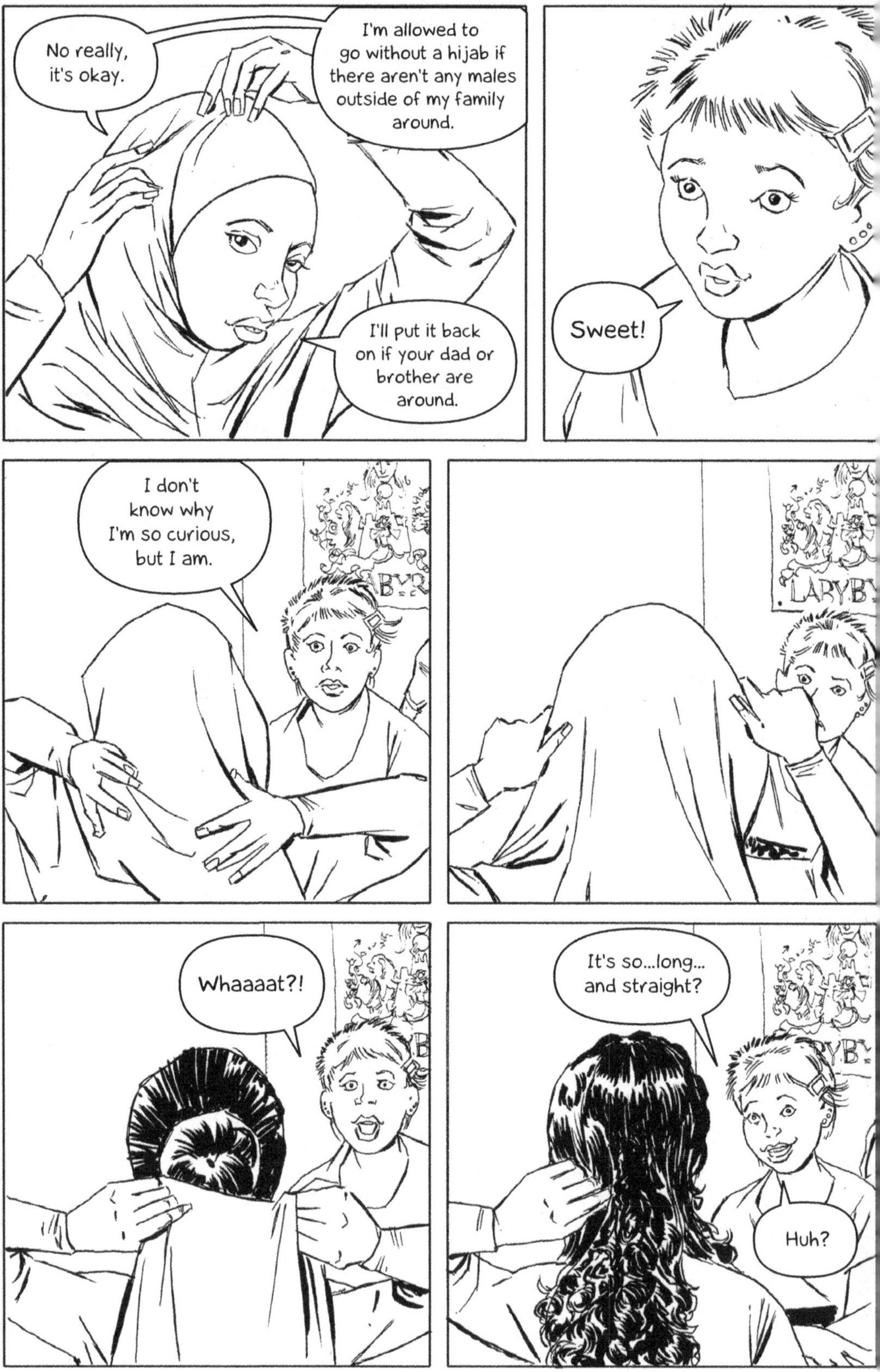

No really, it's okay.
I'm allowed to go without a hijab if there aren't any males outside of my family around.
I'll put it back on if your dad or brother are around.
Sweet!
I don't know why I'm so curious, but I am.
Whaaaat?!
It's so...long... and straight?
Huh?

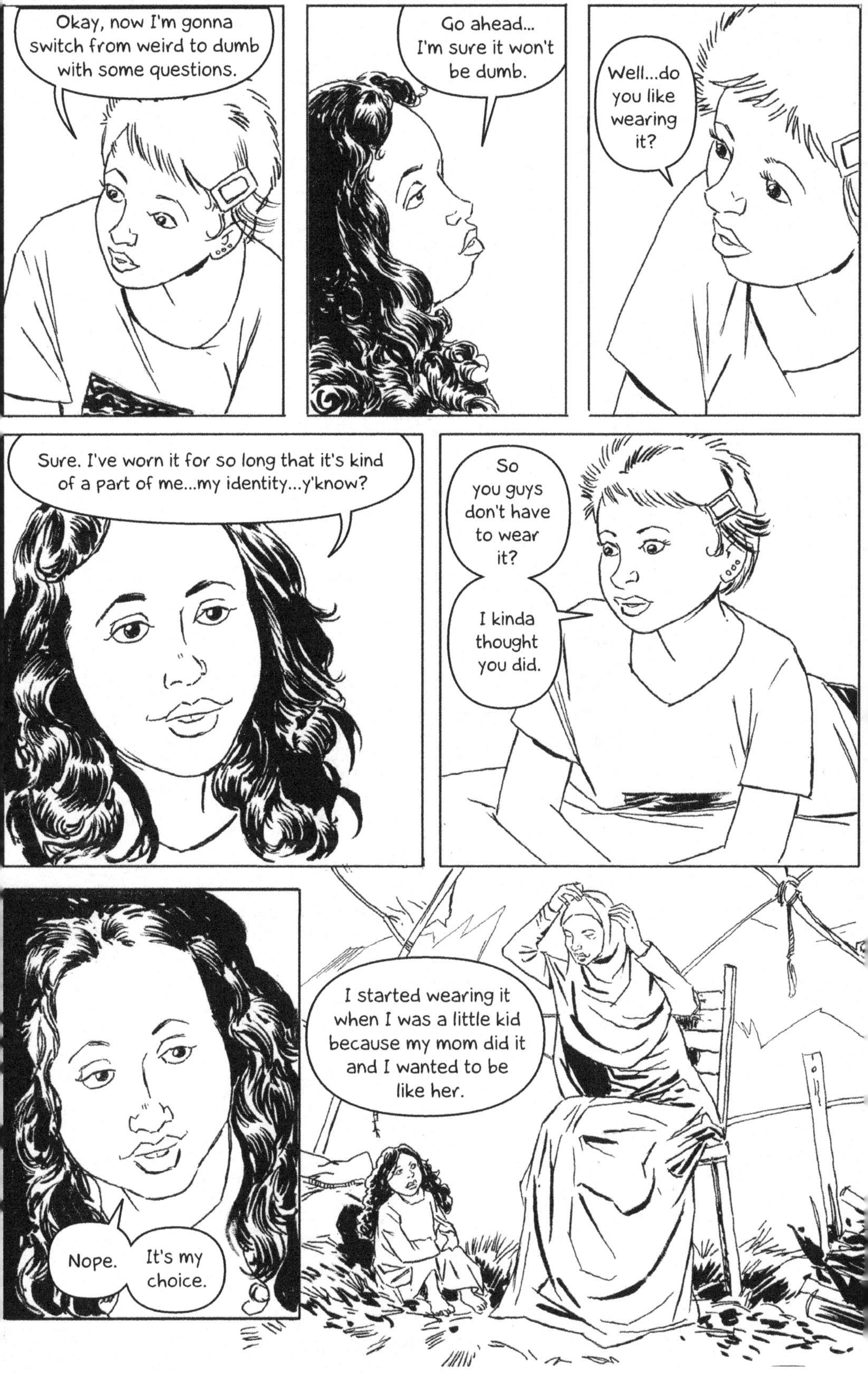
Okay, now I'm gonna switch from weird to dumb with some questions.
Go ahead... I'm sure it won't be dumb.
Well...do you like wearing it?
Sure. I've worn it for so long that it's kind of a part of me...my identity...y'know?
So you guys don't have to wear it?
I kinda thought you did.
Nope.
It's my choice.
I started wearing it when I was a little kid because my mom did it and I wanted to be like her.

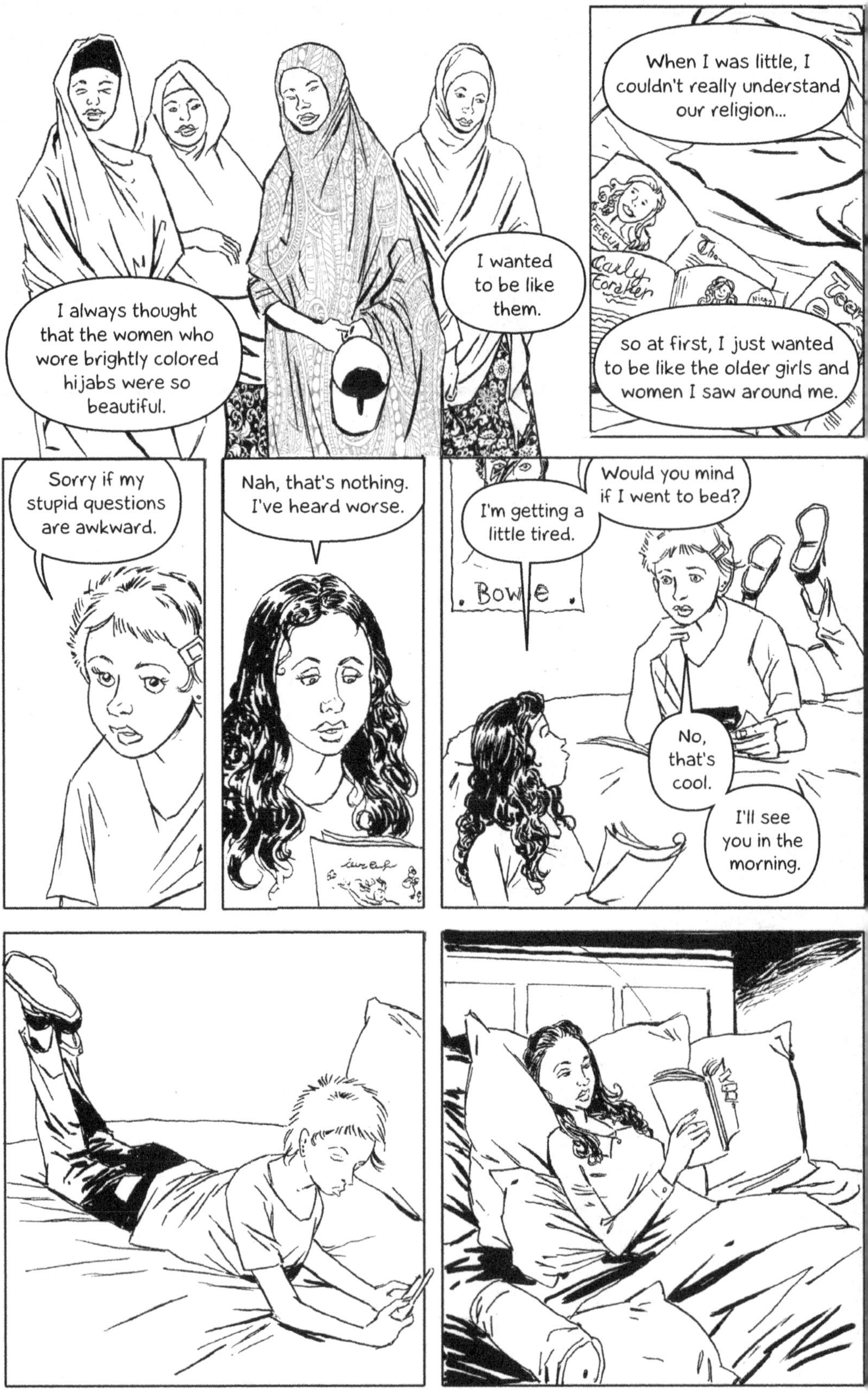
I always thought that the women who wore brightly colored hijabs were so beautiful.
I wanted to be like them.
When I was little, I couldn't really understand our religion...
so at first, I just wanted to be like the older girls and women I saw around me.
Sorry if my stupid questions are awkward.
Nah, that's nothing. I've heard worse.
Would you mind if I went to bed?
I'm getting a little tired.
No, that's cool.
I'll see you in the morning.

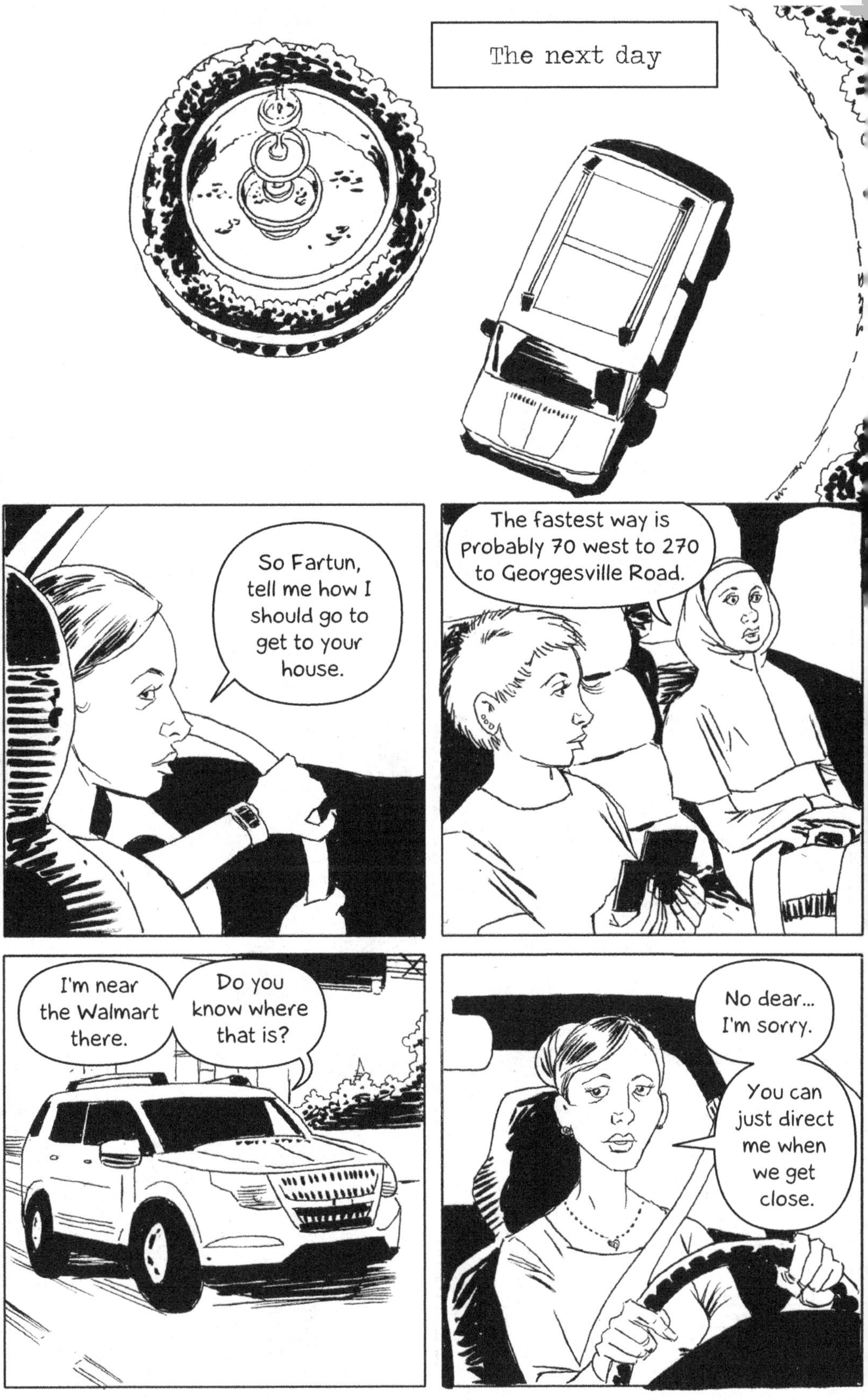
The next day
So Fartun, tell me how I should go to get to your house.
The fastest way is probably 70 west to 270 to Georgesville Road.
I'm near the Walmart there.
Do you know where that is?
No dear... I'm sorry.
You can just direct me when we get close.

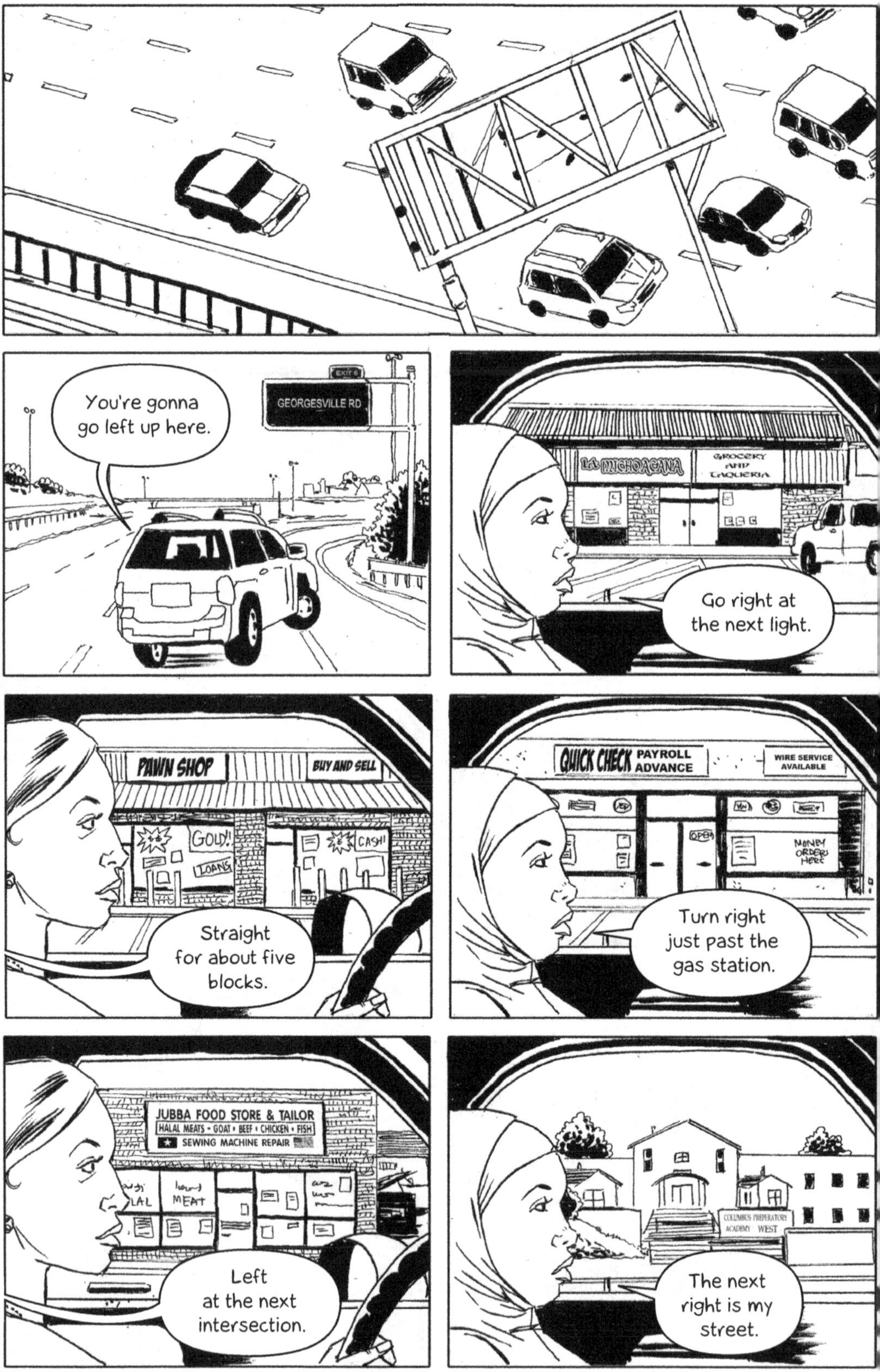
GEORGESVILLE RD
You're gonna go left up here.
LA MICHOACANA
GROCERY AND TAQUERIA
Go right at the next light.
PAWN SHOP
BUY AND SELL
GOLD!
LOANS
CASH!
Straight for about five blocks.
QUICK CHECK PAYROLL ADVANCE
WIRE SERVICE AVAILABLE
OPEN
MONEY ORDERS HERE
Turn right just past the gas station.
JUBBA FOOD STORE & TAILOR
HALAL MEATS • GOAT • BEEF • CHICKEN • FISH
SEWING MACHINE REPAIR
MEAT
Left at the next intersection.
COLUMBUS PREPARATORY ACADEMY WEST
The next right is my street.

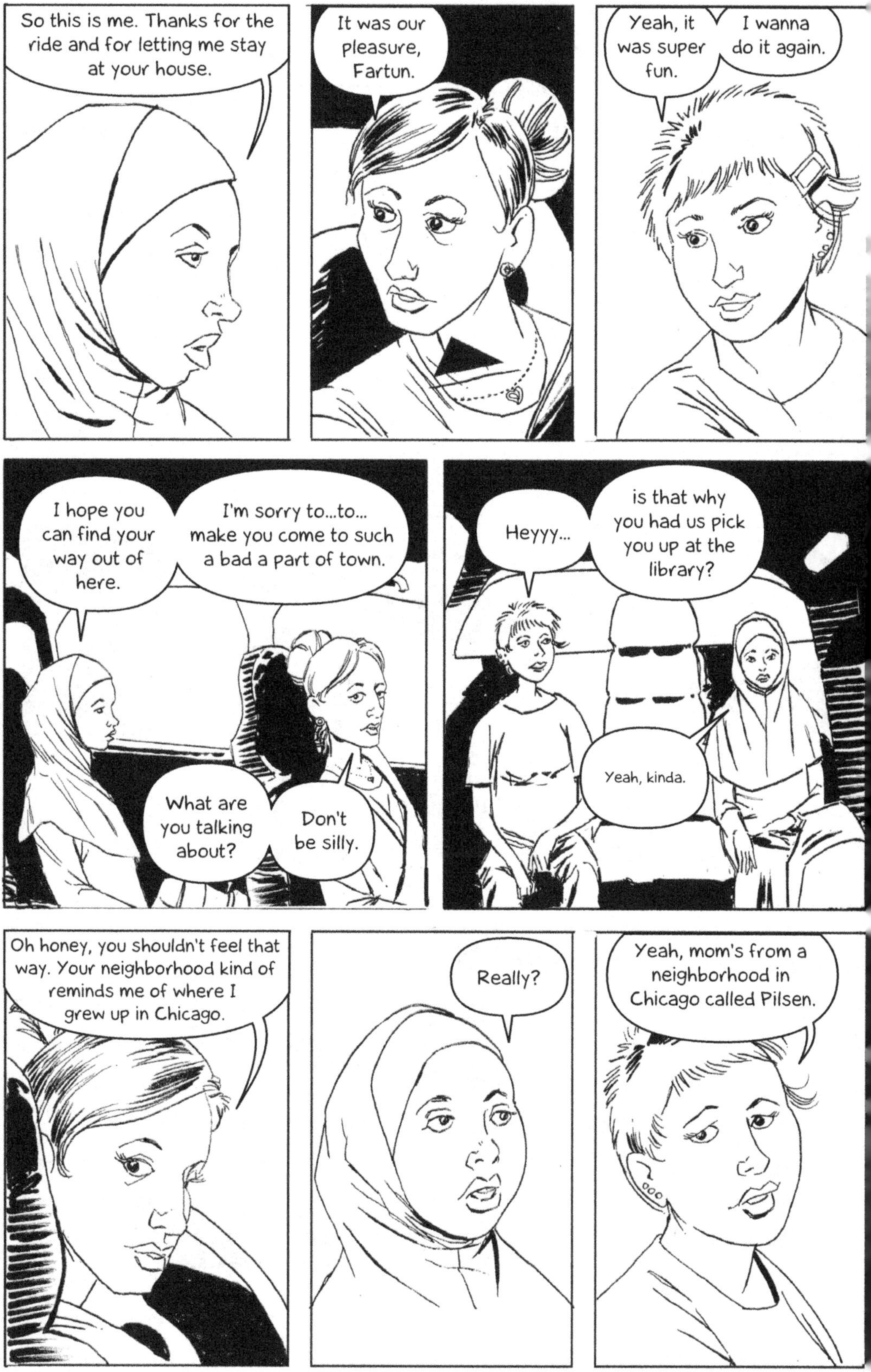
So this is me. Thanks for the ride and for letting me stay at your house.
It was our pleasure, Fartun.
Yeah, it was super fun.
I wanna do it again.
I hope you can find your way out of here.
I'm sorry to...to... make you come to such a bad a part of town.
What are you talking about?
Don't be silly.
Heyyy...
is that why you had us pick you up at the library?
Yeah, kinda.
Oh honey, you shouldn't feel that way. Your neighborhood kind of reminds me of where I grew up in Chicago.
Really?
Yeah, mom's from a neighborhood in Chicago called Pilsen.

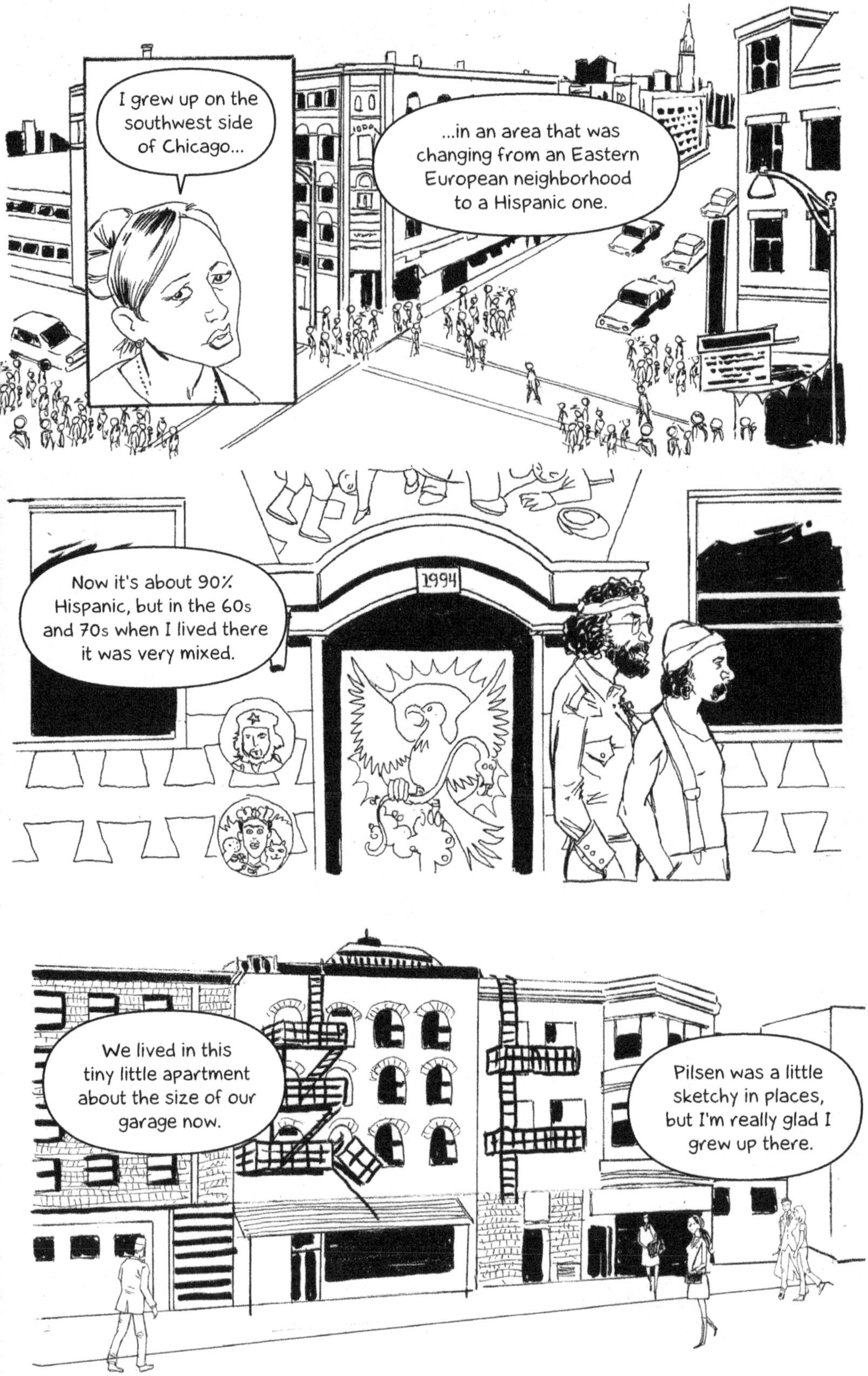
I grew up on the southwest side of Chicago...
...in an area that was changing from an Eastern European neighborhood to a Hispanic one.
Now it's about 90% Hispanic, but in the 60s and 70s when I lived there it was very mixed.
1994
We lived in this tiny little apartment about the size of our garage now.
Pilsen was a little sketchy in places, but I'm really glad I grew up there.

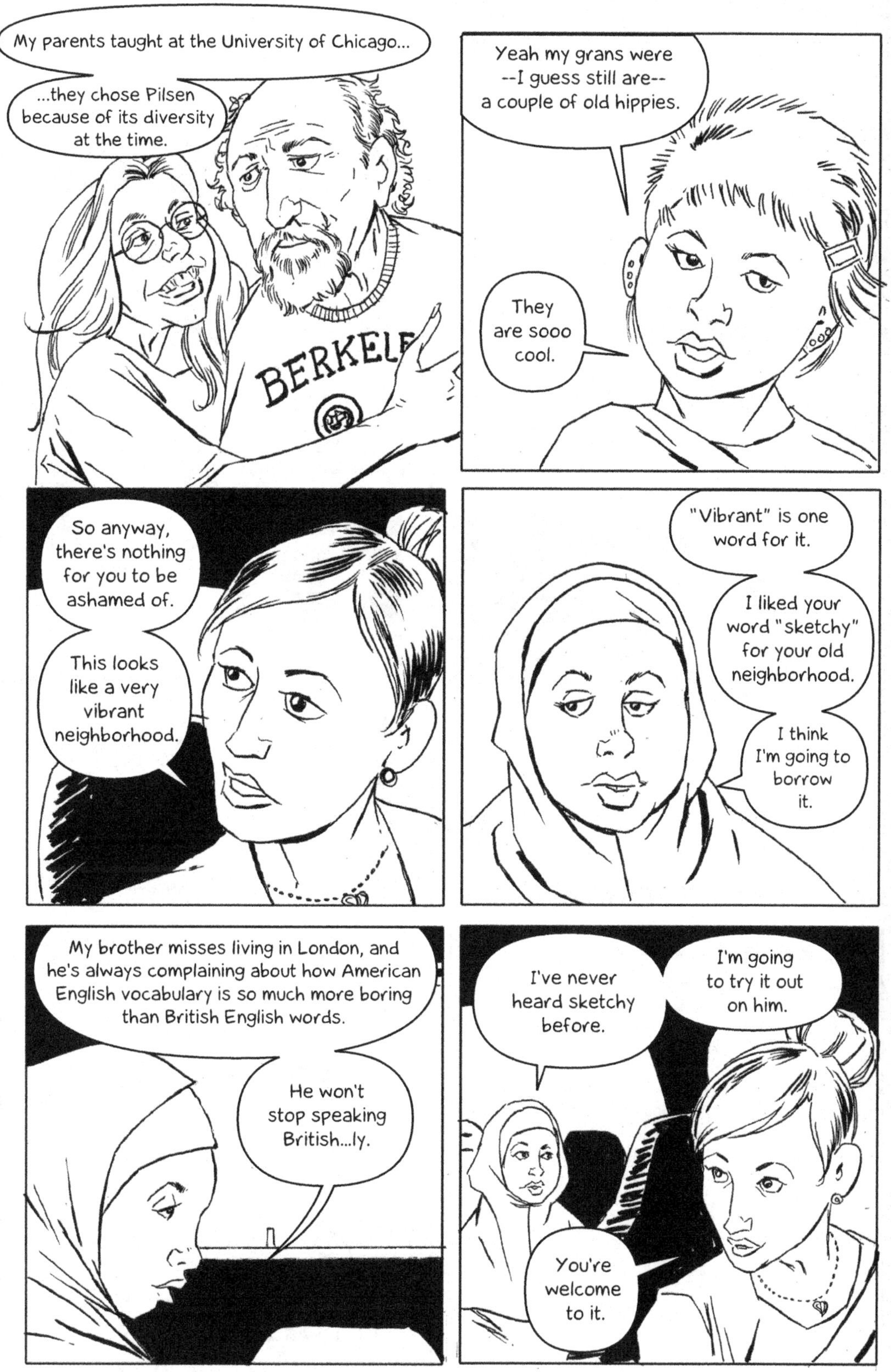
My parents taught at the University of Chicago...
...they chose Pilsen because of its diversity at the time.
BERKELE
Yeah my grans were --I guess still are-- a couple of old hippies.
They are sooo cool.
So anyway, there's nothing for you to be ashamed of.
This looks like a very vibrant neighborhood.
"Vibrant" is one word for it.
I liked your word "sketchy" for your old neighborhood.
I think I'm going to borrow it.
My brother misses living in London, and he's always complaining about how American English vocabulary is so much more boring than British English words.
He won't stop speaking British...ly.
I've never heard sketchy before.
I'm going to try it out on him.
You're welcome to it.

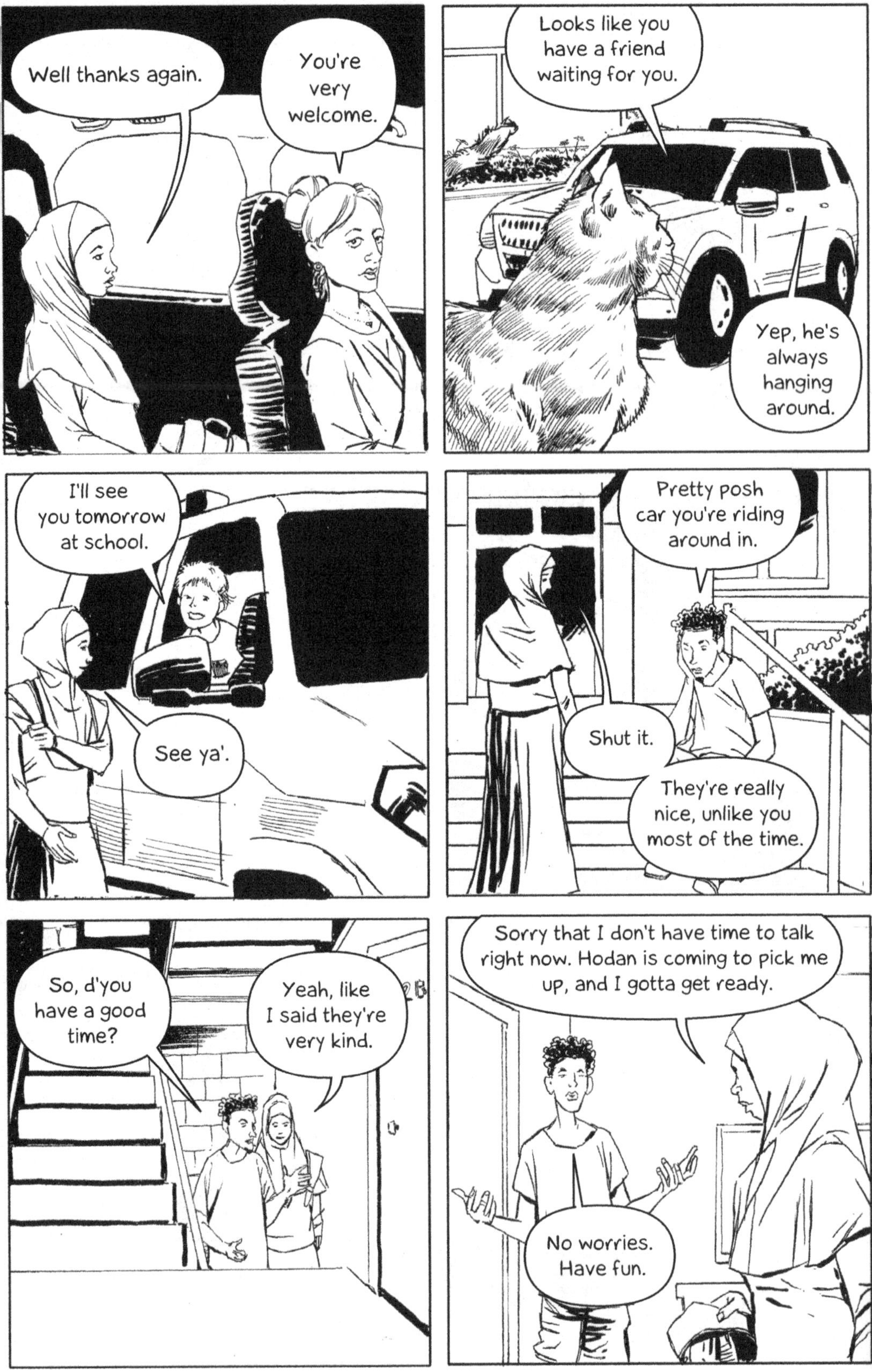
Well thanks again.
You're very welcome.
Looks like you have a friend waiting for you.
Yep, he's always hanging around.
I'll see you tomorrow at school.
See ya'.
Pretty posh car you're riding around in.
Shut it.
They're really nice, unlike you most of the time.
So, d'you have a good time?
Yeah, like I said they're very kind.
Sorry that I don't have time to talk right now. Hodan is coming to pick me up, and I gotta get ready.
No worries. Have fun.

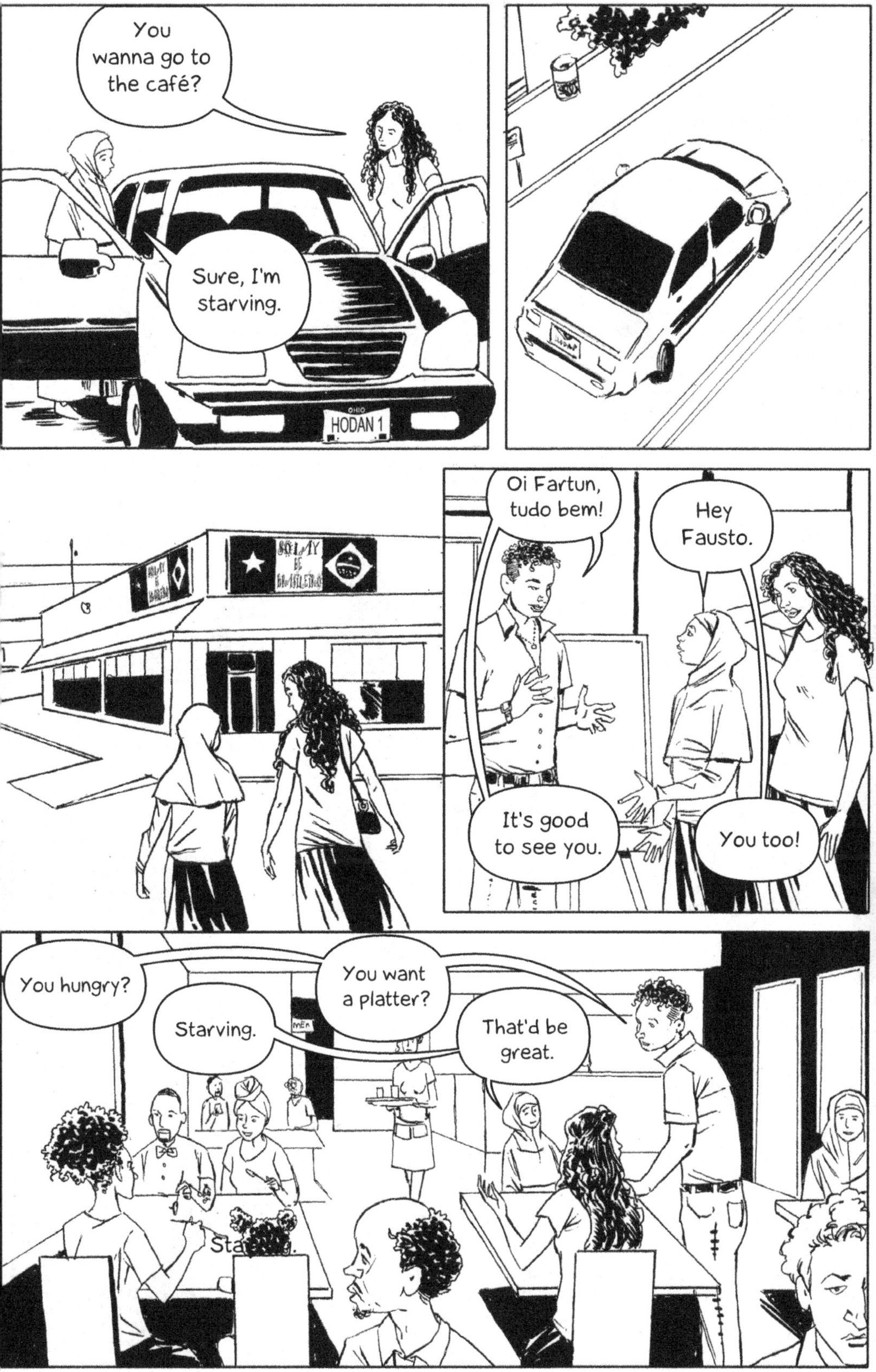

You wanna go to the café?
Sure, I'm starving.
OHIO
HODAN 1
Oi Fartun, tudo bem!
Hey Fausto.
It's good to see you.
You too!
You hungry?
Starving.
You want a platter?
That'd be great.

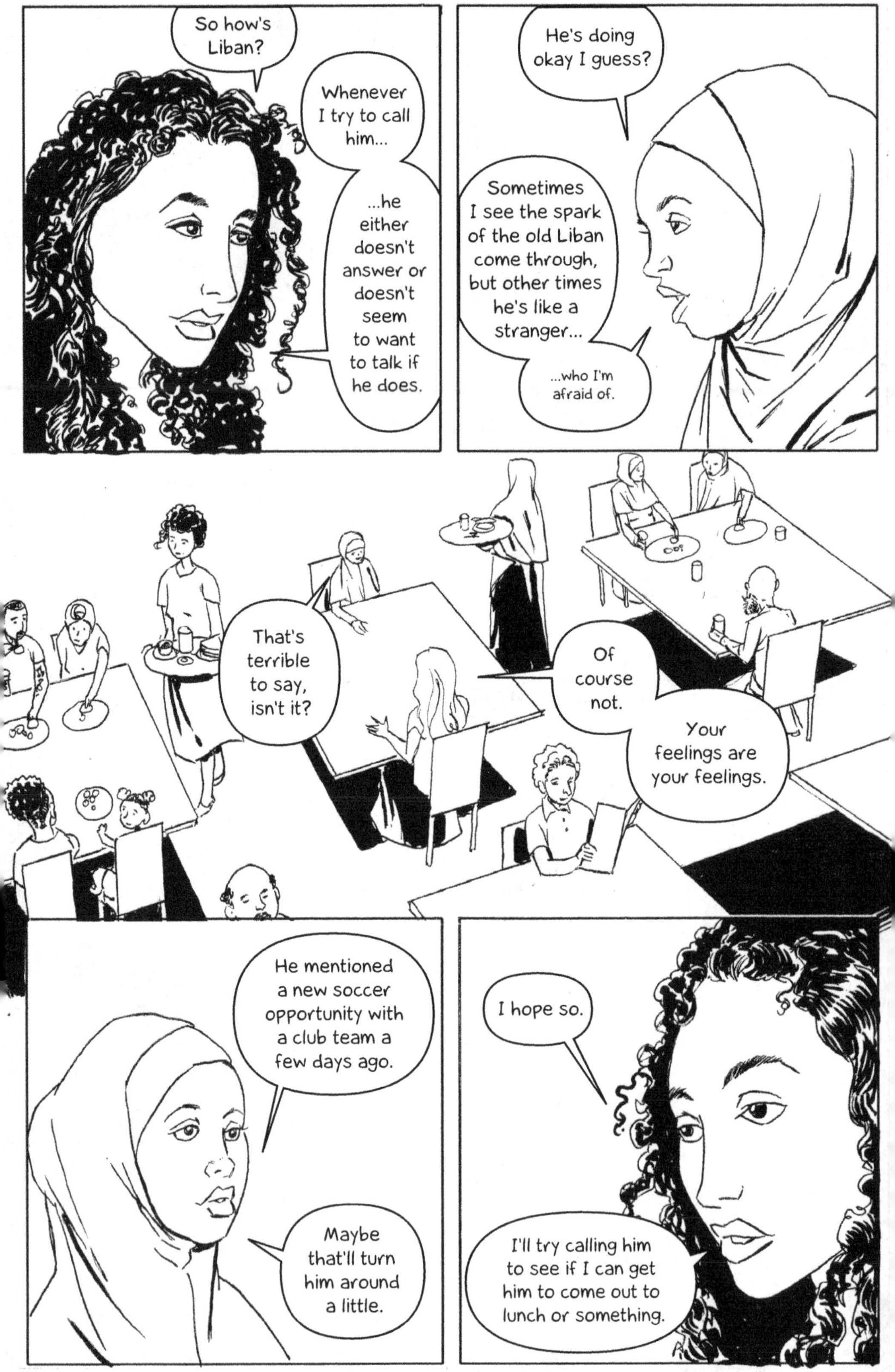
So how's Liban?
Whenever I try to call him...
...he either doesn't answer or doesn't seem to want to talk if he does.
He's doing okay I guess?
Sometimes I see the spark of the old Liban come through, but other times he's like a stranger...
...who I'm afraid of.
That's terrible to say, isn't it?
Of course not.
Your feelings are your feelings.
He mentioned a new soccer opportunity with a club team a few days ago.
Maybe that'll turn him around a little.
I hope so.
I'll try calling him to see if I can get him to come out to lunch or something.

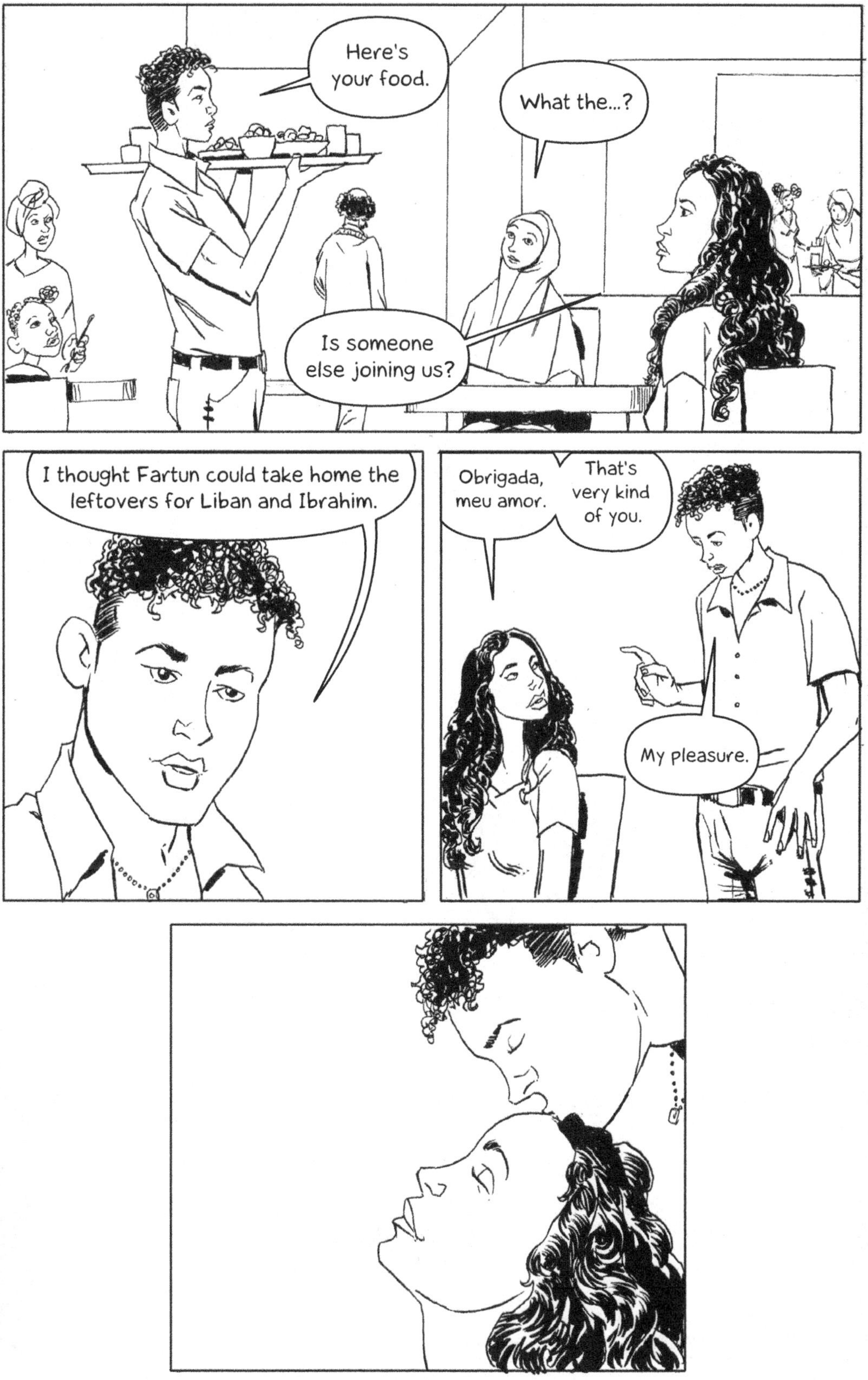
Here's your food.
What the...?
Is someone else joining us?
I thought Fartun could take home the leftovers for Liban and Ibrahim.
Obrigada, meu amor.
That's very kind of you.
My pleasure.

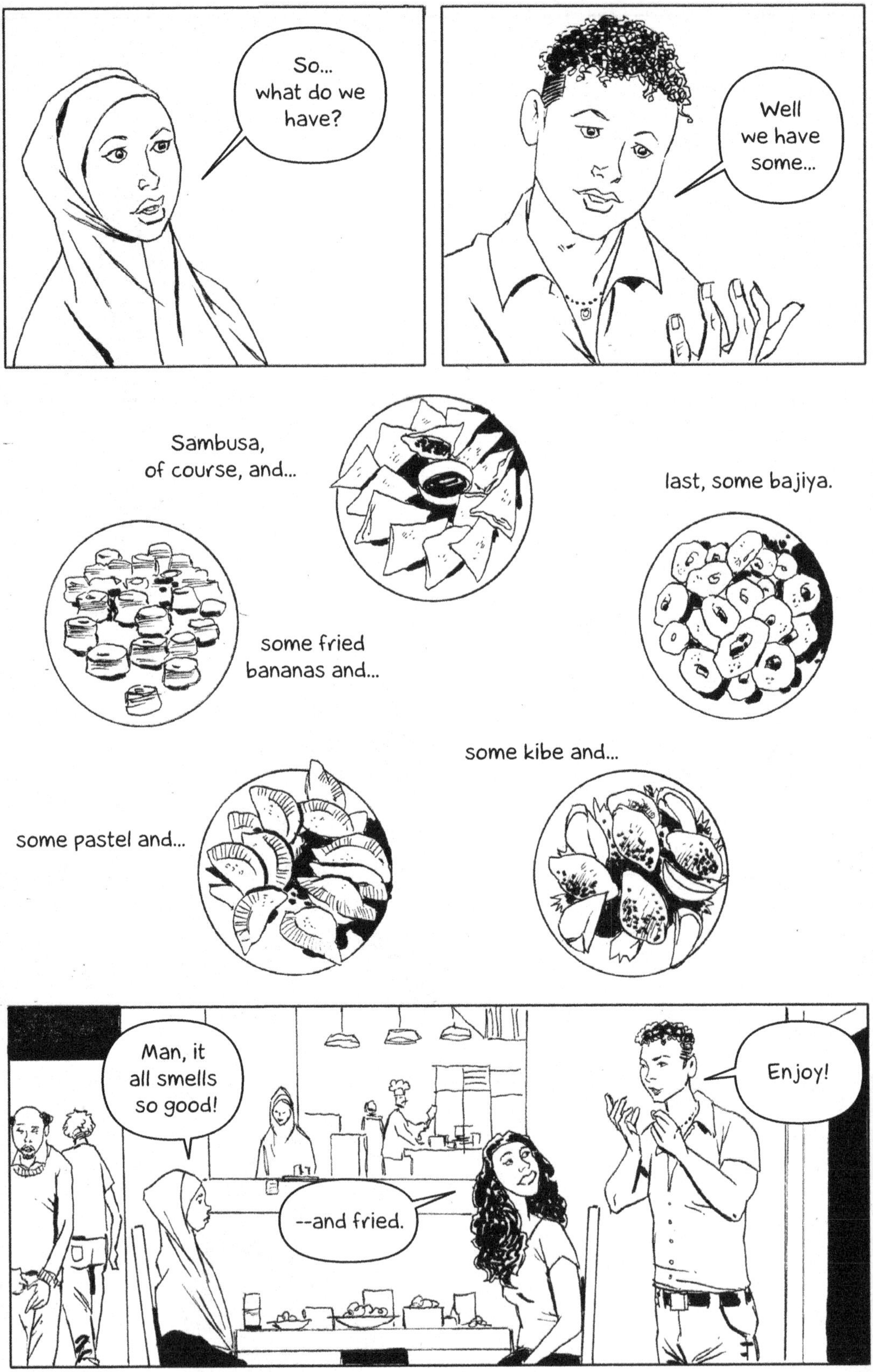
So... what do we have?
Well we have some...
Sambusa, of course, and...
some fried bananas and...
some pastel and...
some kibe and...
last, some bajiya.
Man, it all smells so good!
--and fried.
Enjoy!

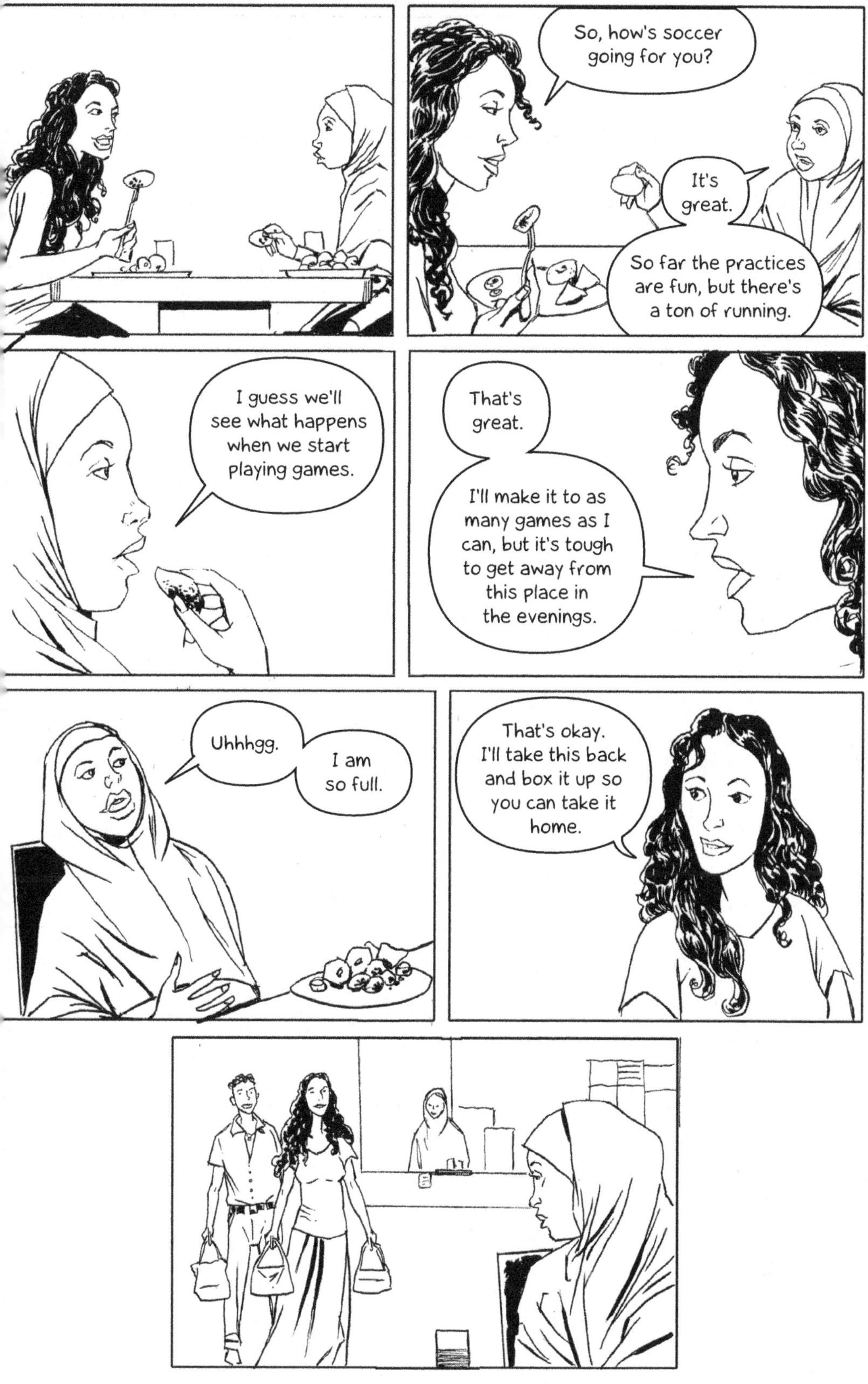
So, how's soccer going for you?
It's great.
So far the practices are fun, but there's a ton of running.
I guess we'll see what happens when we start playing games.
That's great.
I'll make it to as many games as I can, but it's tough to get away from this place in the evenings.
Uhhhgg.
I am so full.
That's okay. I'll take this back and box it up so you can take it home.

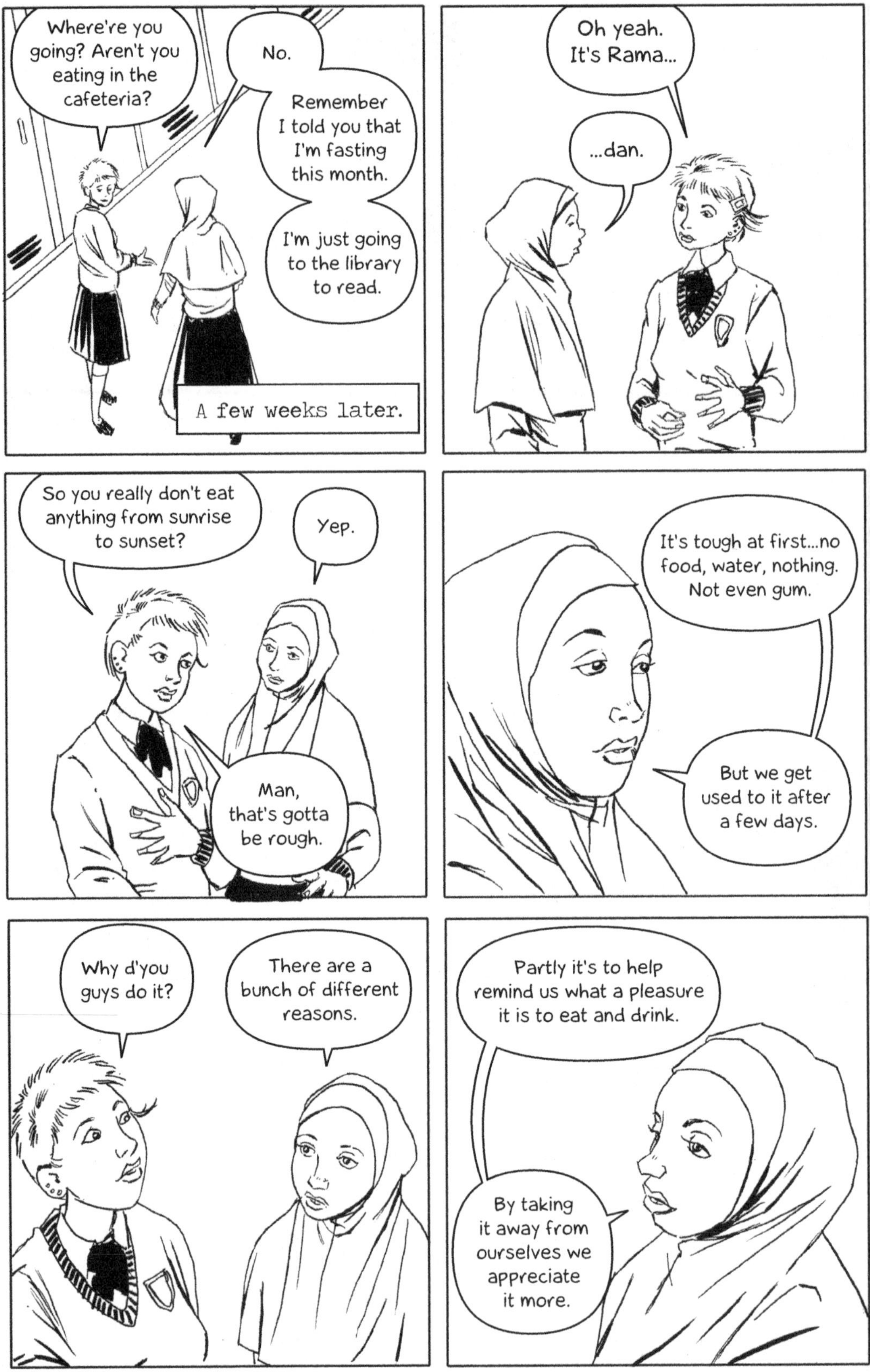
Where're you going? Aren't you eating in the cafeteria?
No.
Remember I told you that I'm fasting this month.
I'm just going to the library to read.
A few weeks later.
Oh yeah. It's Rama...
...dan.
So you really don't eat anything from sunrise to sunset?
Yep.
Man, that's gotta be rough.
It's tough at first...no food, water, nothing. Not even gum.
But we get used to it after a few days.
Why d'you guys do it?
There are a bunch of different reasons.
Partly it's to help remind us what a pleasure it is to eat and drink.
By taking it away from ourselves we appreciate it more.

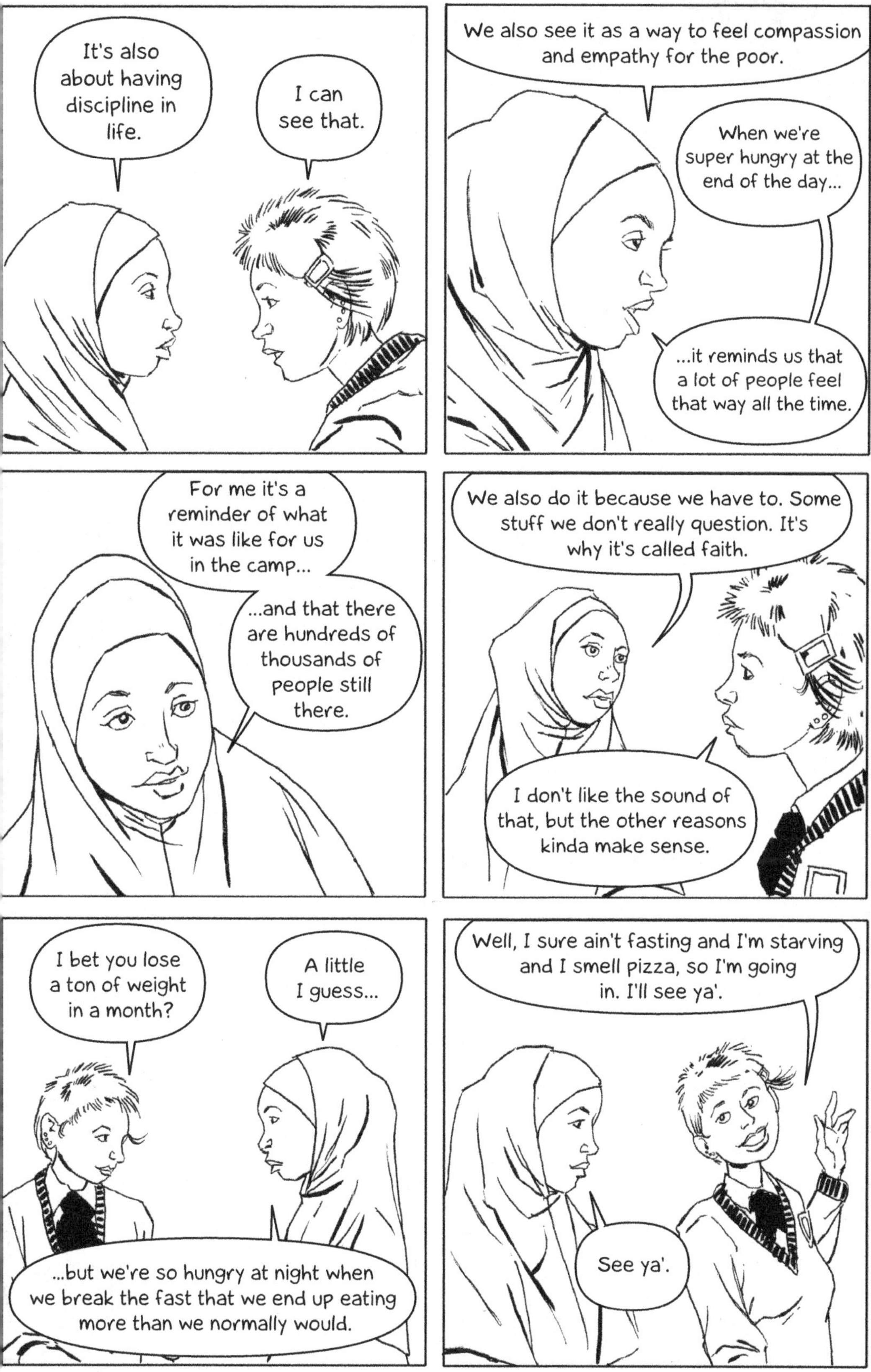
It's also about having discipline in life.
I can see that.
We also see it as a way to feel compassion and empathy for the poor.
When we're super hungry at the end of the day...
...it reminds us that a lot of people feel that way all the time.
For me it's a reminder of what it was like for us in the camp...
...and that there are hundreds of thousands of people still there.
We also do it because we have to. Some stuff we don't really question. It's why it's called faith.
I don't like the sound of that, but the other reasons kinda make sense.
I bet you lose a ton of weight in a month?
A little I guess...
...but we're so hungry at night when we break the fast that we end up eating more than we normally would.
Well, I sure ain't fasting and I'm starving and I smell pizza, so I'm going in. I'll see ya'.
See ya'.

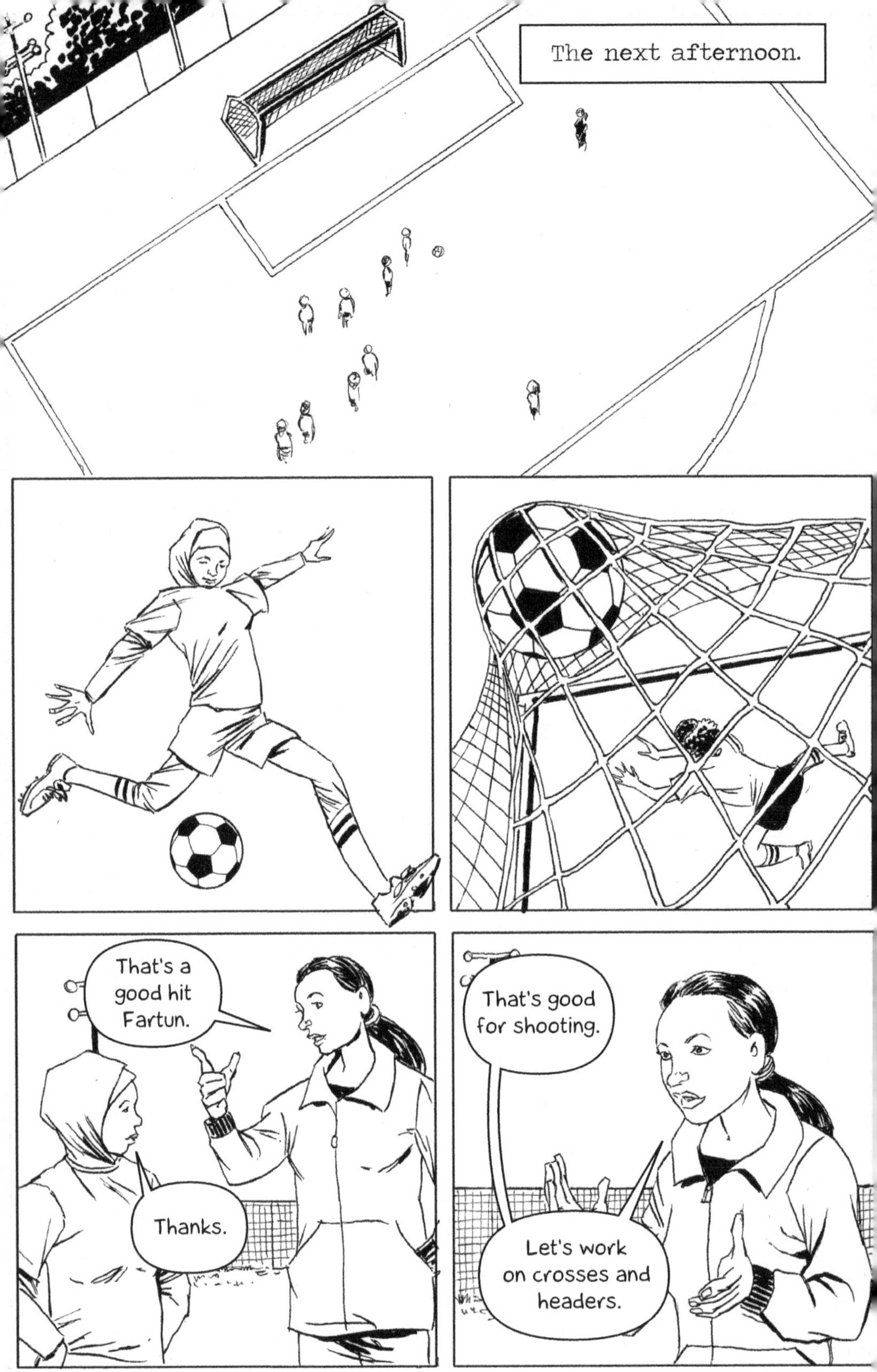
The next afternoon.
That's a good hit Fartun.
Thanks.
That's good for shooting.
Let's work on crosses and headers.

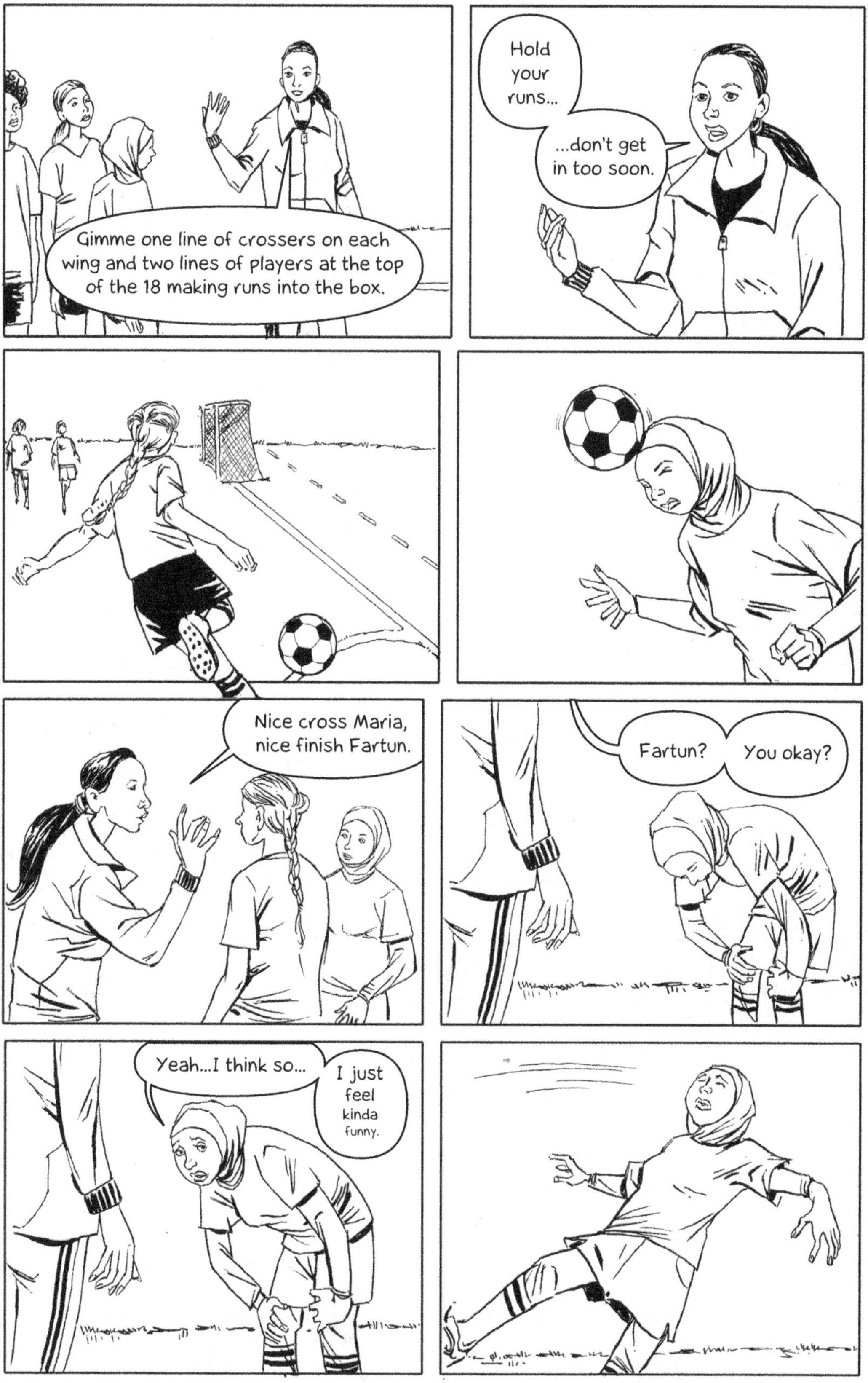
Gimme one line of crossers on each wing and two lines of players at the top of the 18 making runs into the box.
Hold your runs...
...don't get in too soon.
Nice cross Maria, nice finish Fartun.
Fartun?
You okay?
Yeah...I think so...
I just feel kinda funny.

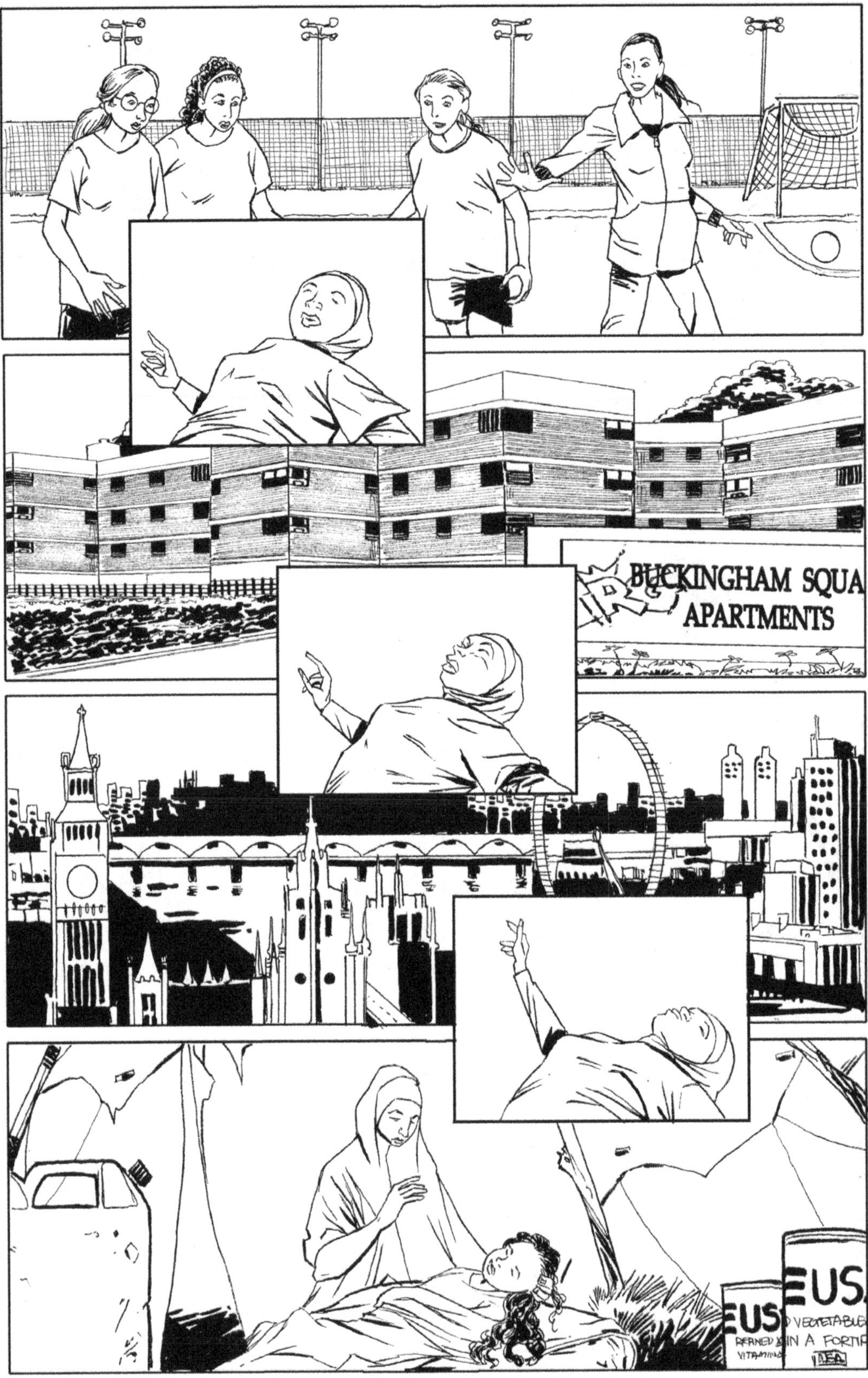
BUCKINGHAM SQUA
APARTMENTS

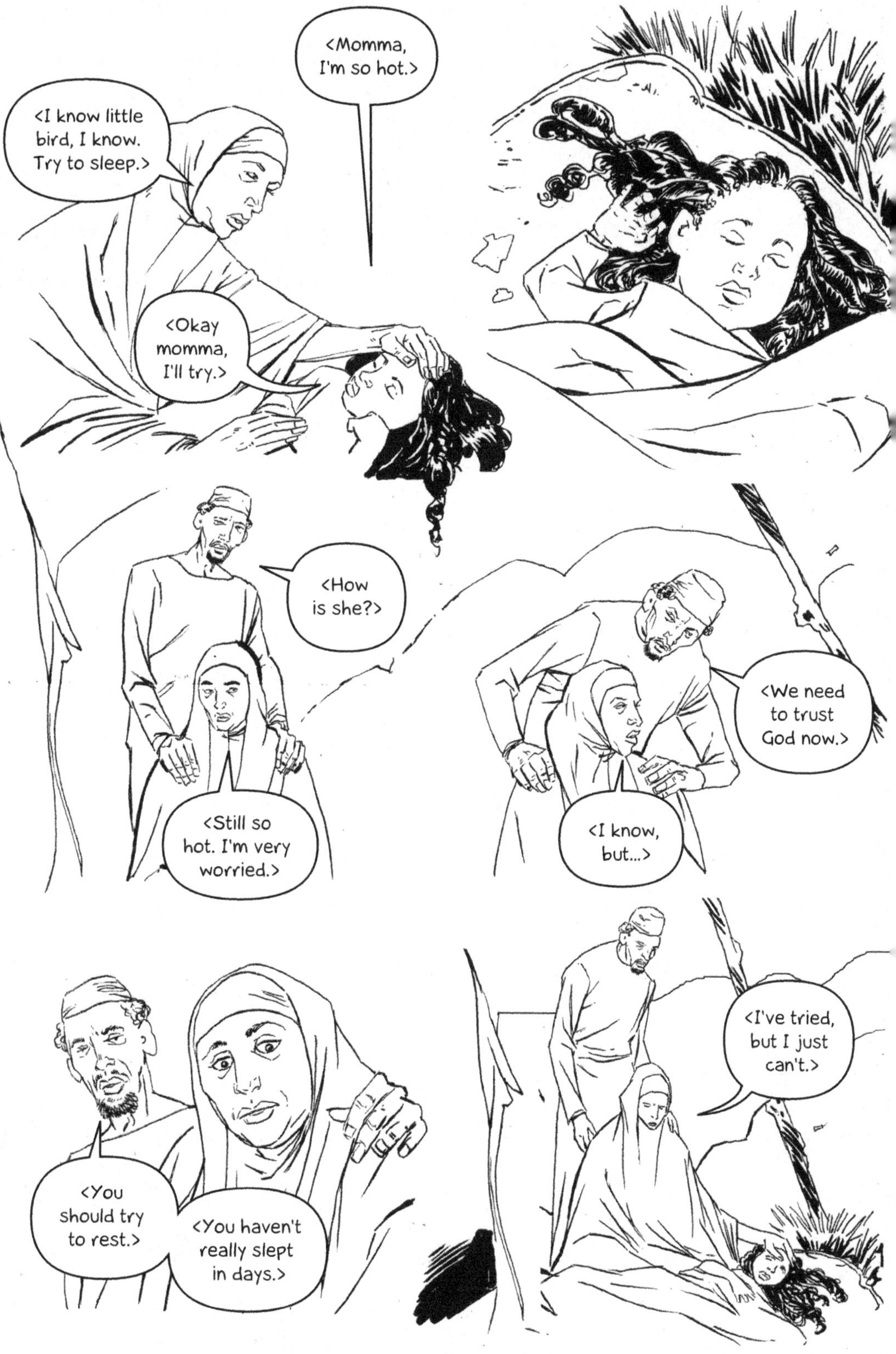
<Momma, I'm so hot.>
<I know little bird, I know. Try to sleep.>
<Okay momma, I'll try.>
<How is she?>
<Still so hot. I'm very worried.>
<We need to trust God now.>
<I know, but...>
<You should try to rest.>
<You haven't really slept in days.>
<I've tried, but I just can't.>

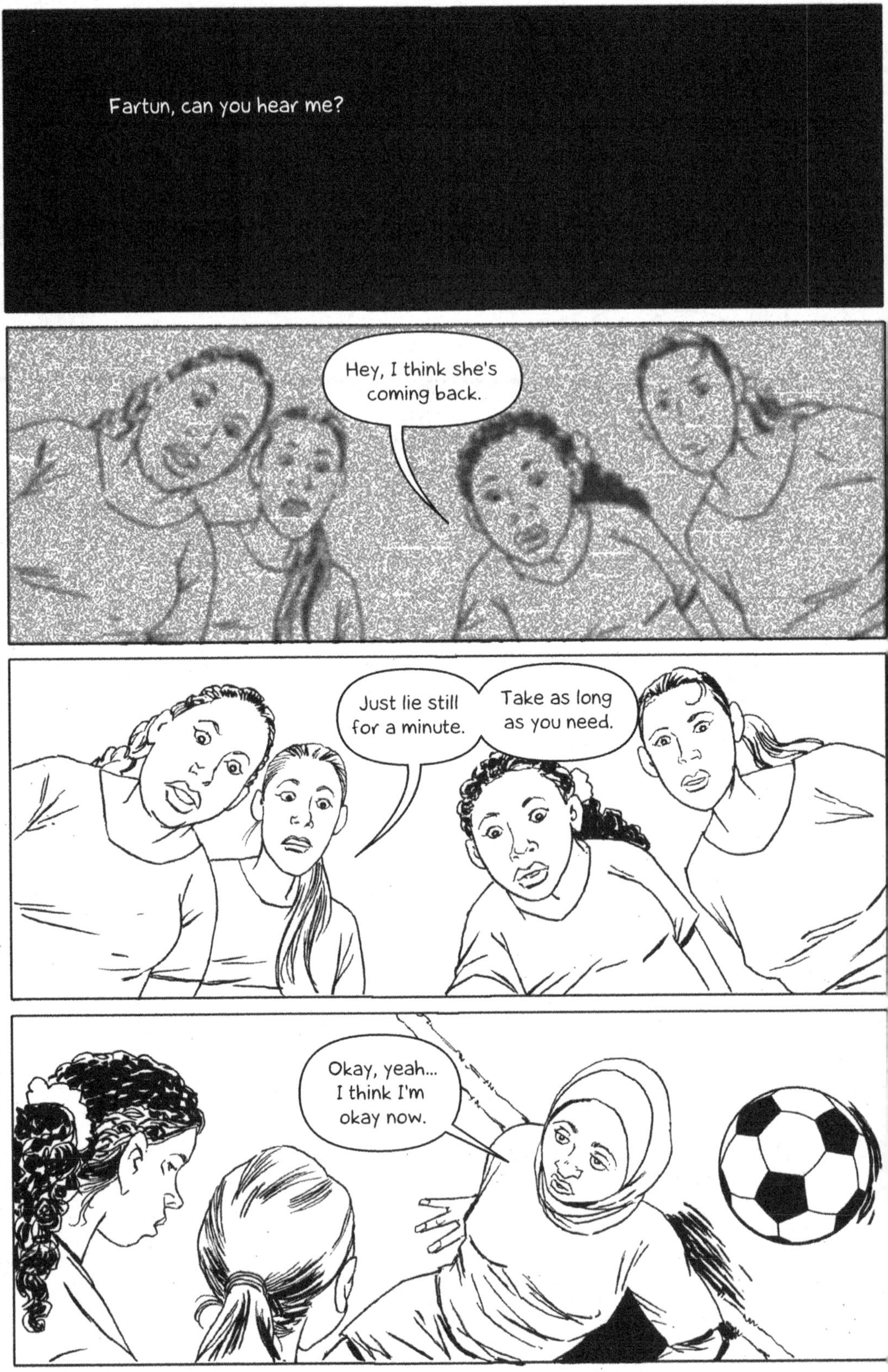
Fartun, can you hear me?
Hey, I think she's coming back.
Just lie still for a minute.
Take as long as you need.
Okay, yeah... I think I'm okay now.

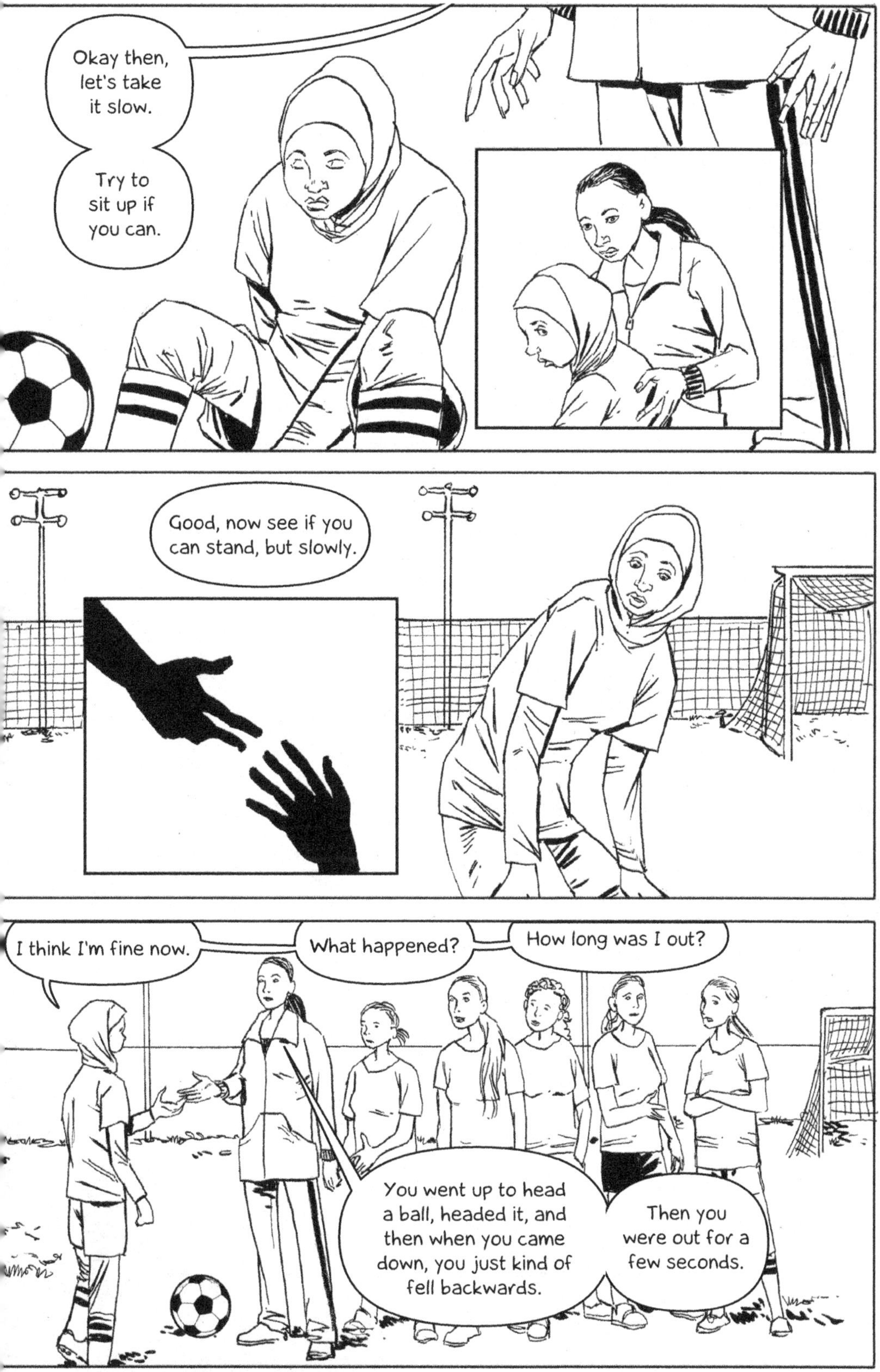
Okay then, let's take it slow.
Try to sit up if you can.
Good, now see if you can stand, but slowly.
I think I'm fine now.
What happened?
How long was I out?
You went up to head a ball, headed it, and then when you came down, you just kind of fell backwards.
Then you were out for a few seconds.

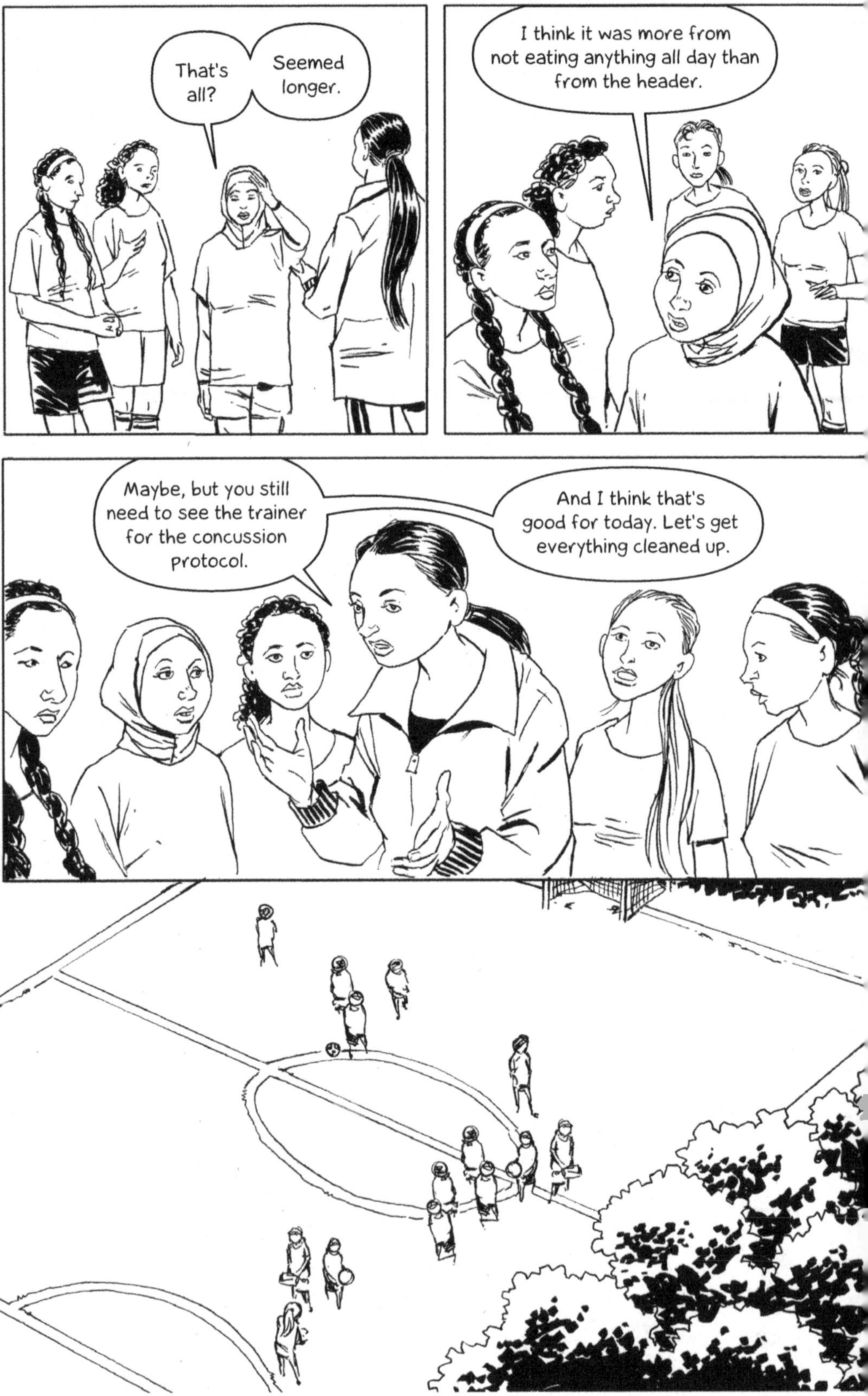
That's all?
Seemed longer.
I think it was more from not eating anything all day than from the header.
Maybe, but you still need to see the trainer for the concussion protocol.
And I think that's good for today. Let's get everything cleaned up.

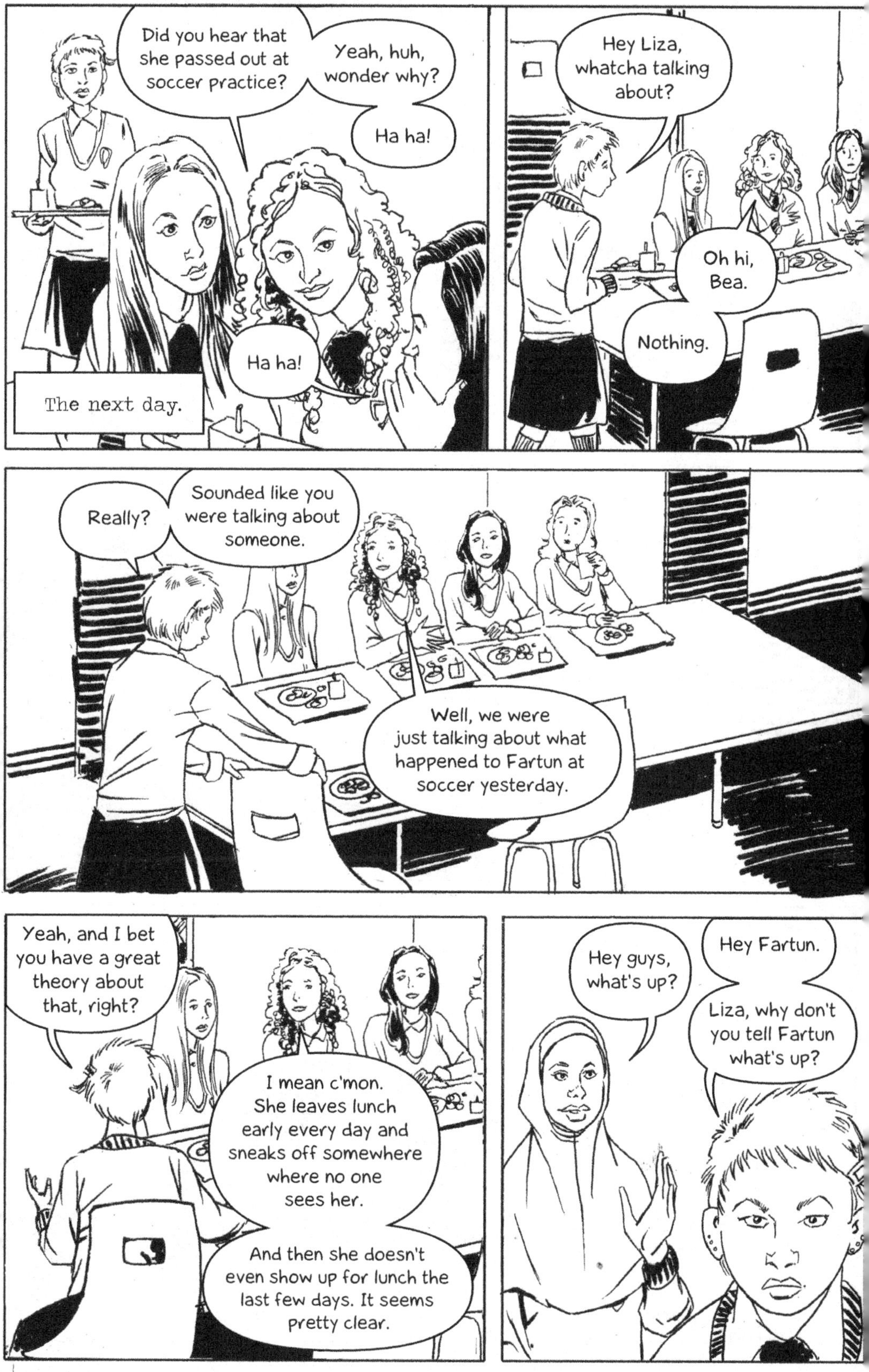
Did you hear that she passed out at soccer practice?
Yeah, huh, wonder why?
Ha ha!
Ha ha!
The next day.
Hey Liza, whatcha talking about?
Oh hi, Bea.
Nothing.
Really?
Sounded like you were talking about someone.
Well, we were just talking about what happened to Fartun at soccer yesterday.
Yeah, and I bet you have a great theory about that, right?
I mean c'mon. She leaves lunch early every day and sneaks off somewhere where no one sees her.
And then she doesn't even show up for lunch the last few days. It seems pretty clear.
Hey guys, what's up?
Hey Fartun.
Liza, why don't you tell Fartun what's up?

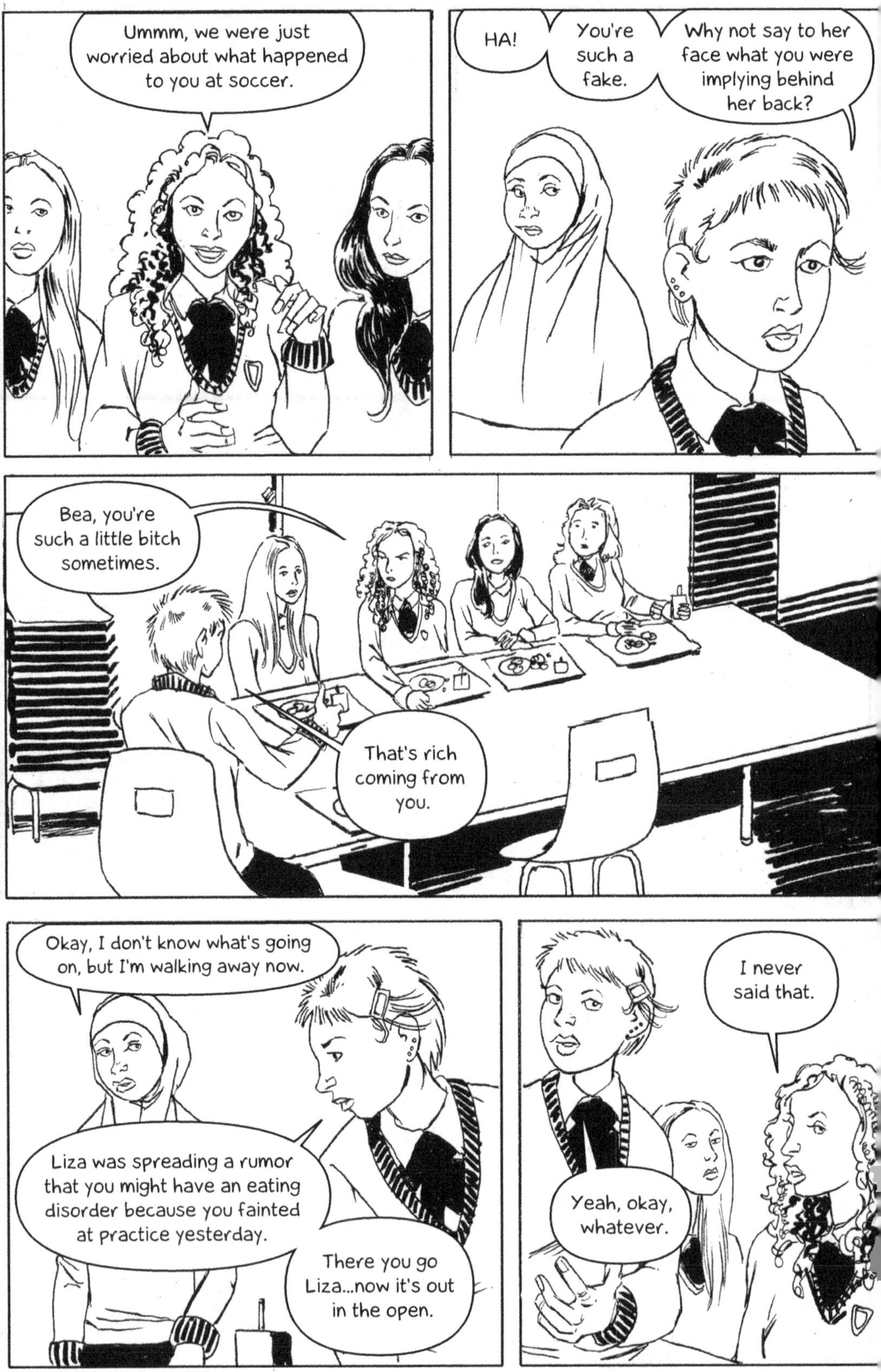
Ummm, we were just worried about what happened to you at soccer.
HA!
You're such a fake.
Why not say to her face what you were implying behind her back?
Bea, you're such a little bitch sometimes.
That's rich coming from you.
Okay, I don't know what's going on, but I'm walking away now.
Liza was spreading a rumor that you might have an eating disorder because you fainted at practice yesterday.
There you go Liza...now it's out in the open.
I never said that.
Yeah, okay, whatever.

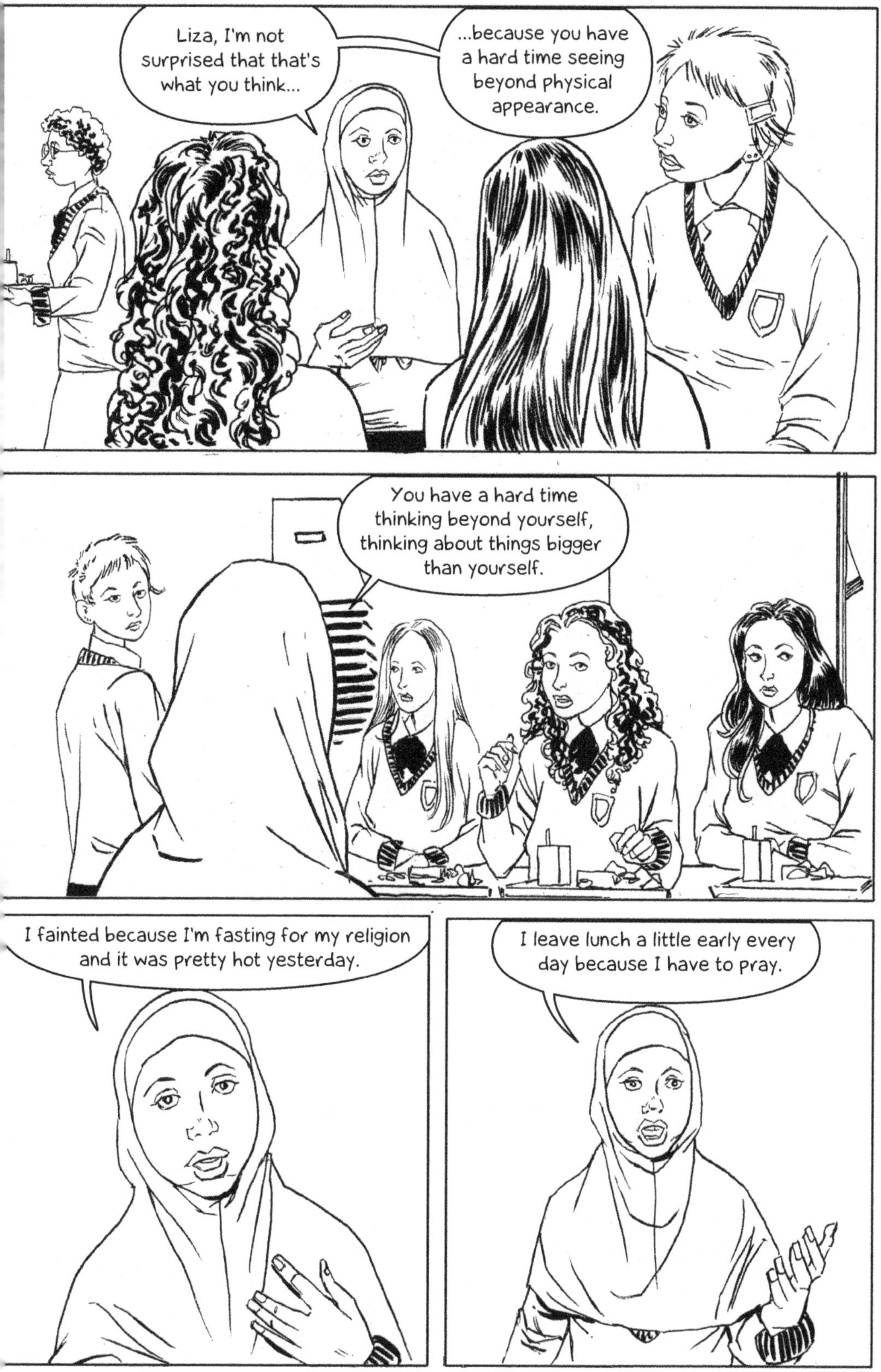
Liza, I'm not surprised that that's what you think...
...because you have a hard time seeing beyond physical appearance.
You have a hard time thinking beyond yourself, thinking about things bigger than yourself.
I fainted because I'm fasting for my religion and it was pretty hot yesterday.
I leave lunch a little early every day because I have to pray.

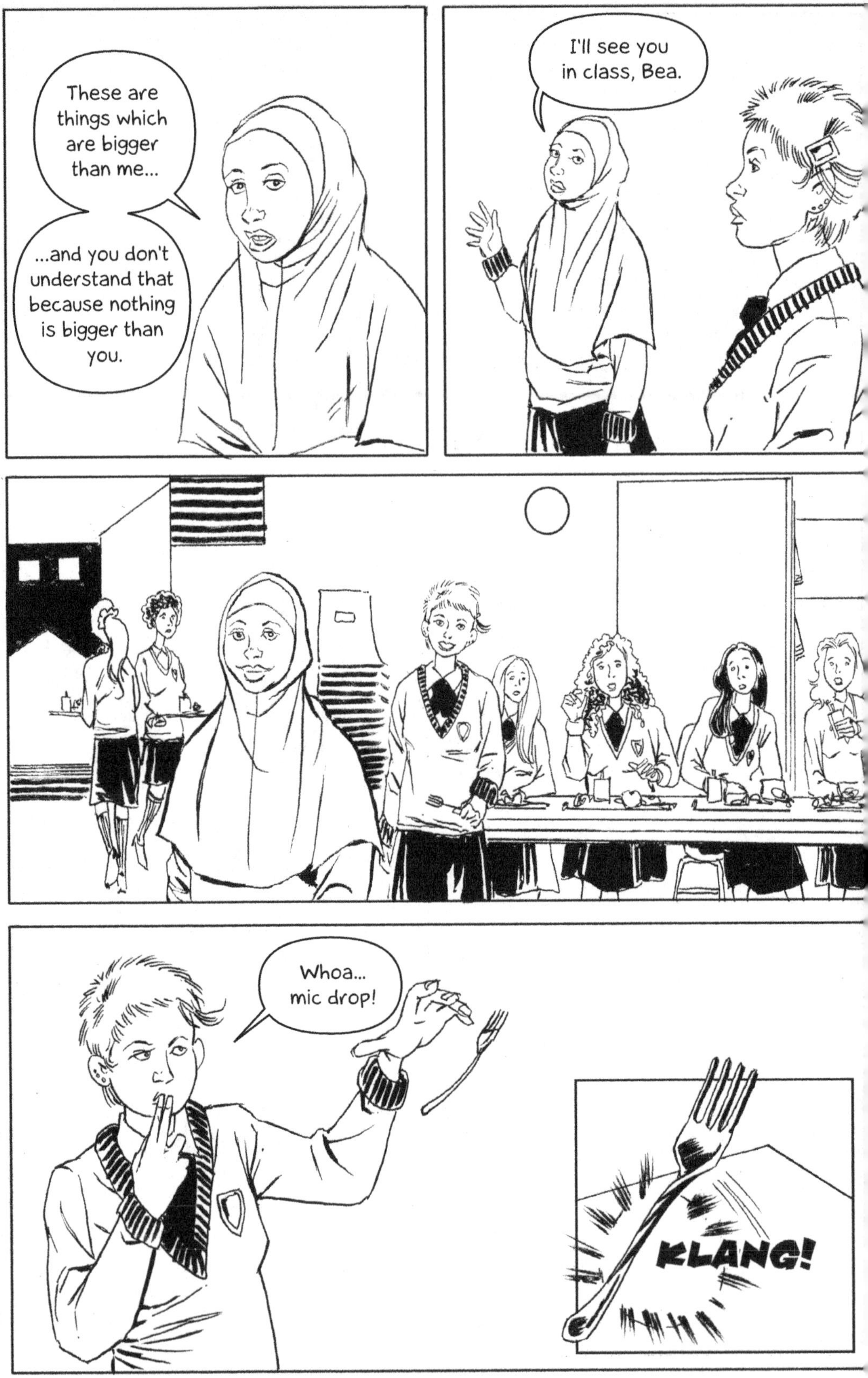
These are things which are bigger than me...
...and you don't understand that because nothing is bigger than you.
I'll see you in class, Bea.
Whoa... mic drop!
KLANG!

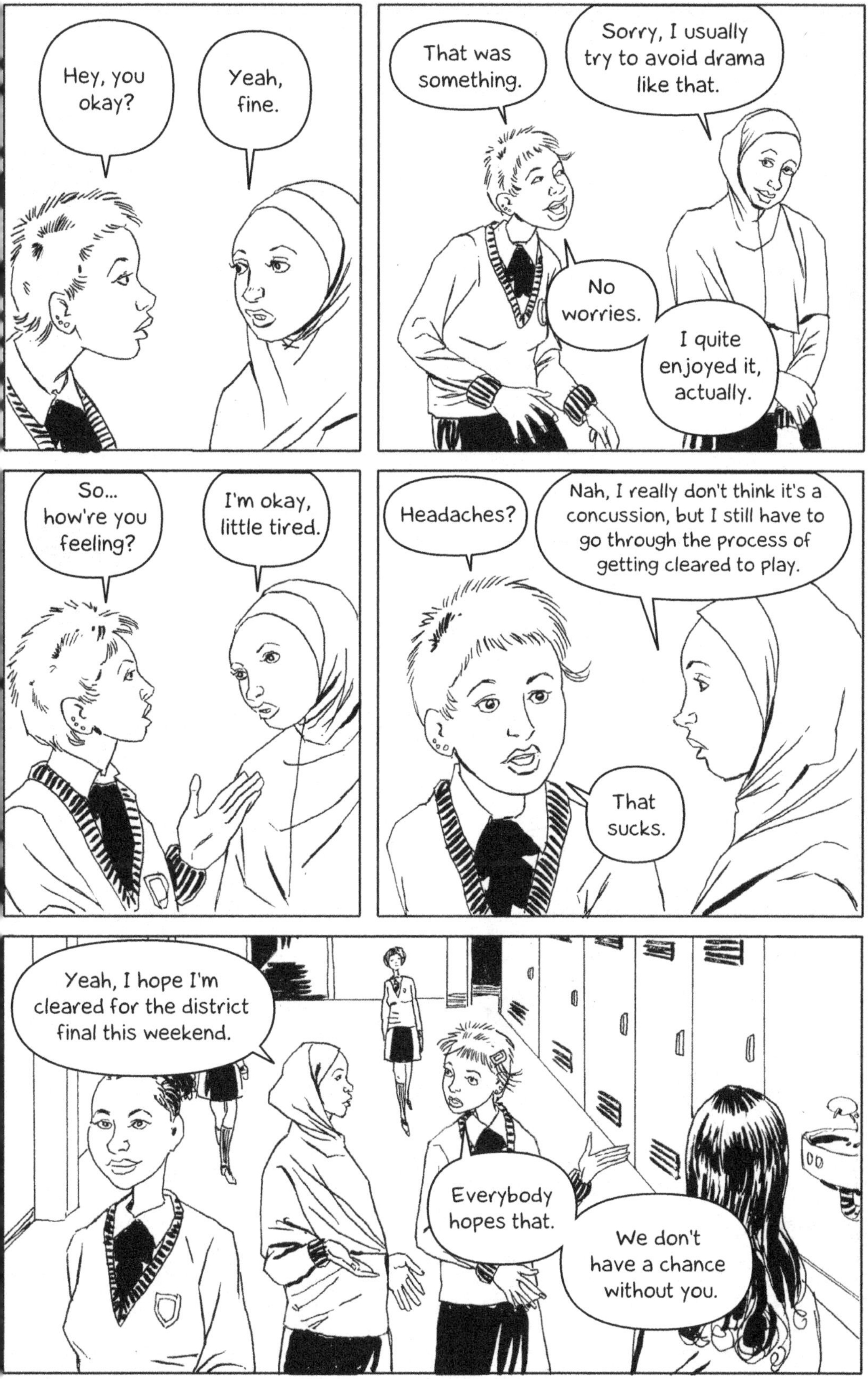
Hey, you okay?
Yeah, fine.
That was something.
Sorry, I usually try to avoid drama like that.
No worries.
I quite enjoyed it, actually.
So... how're you feeling?
I'm okay, little tired.
Headaches?
Nah, I really don't think it's a concussion, but I still have to go through the process of getting cleared to play.
That sucks.
Yeah, I hope I'm cleared for the district final this weekend.
Everybody hopes that.
We don't have a chance without you.

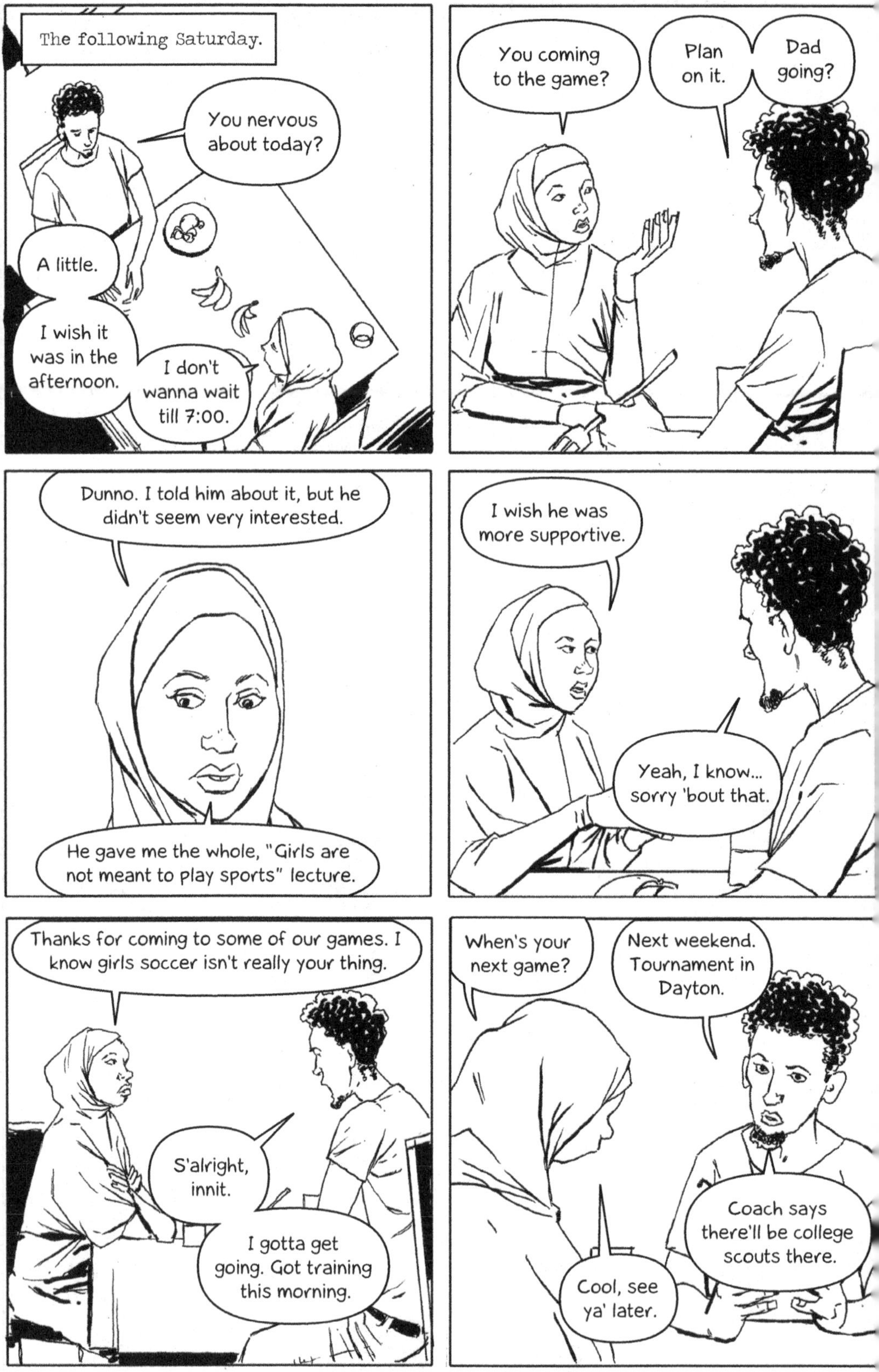
The following Saturday.
You nervous about today?
A little.
I wish it was in the afternoon.
I don't wanna wait till 7:00.
You coming to the game?
Plan on it.
Dad going?
Dunno. I told him about it, but he didn't seem very interested.
He gave me the whole, "Girls are not meant to play sports" lecture.
I wish he was more supportive.
Yeah, I know... sorry 'bout that.
Thanks for coming to some of our games. I know girls soccer isn't really your thing.
S'alright, innit.
I gotta get going. Got training this morning.
When's your next game?
Next weekend. Tournament in Dayton.
Coach says there'll be college scouts there.
Cool, see ya' later.

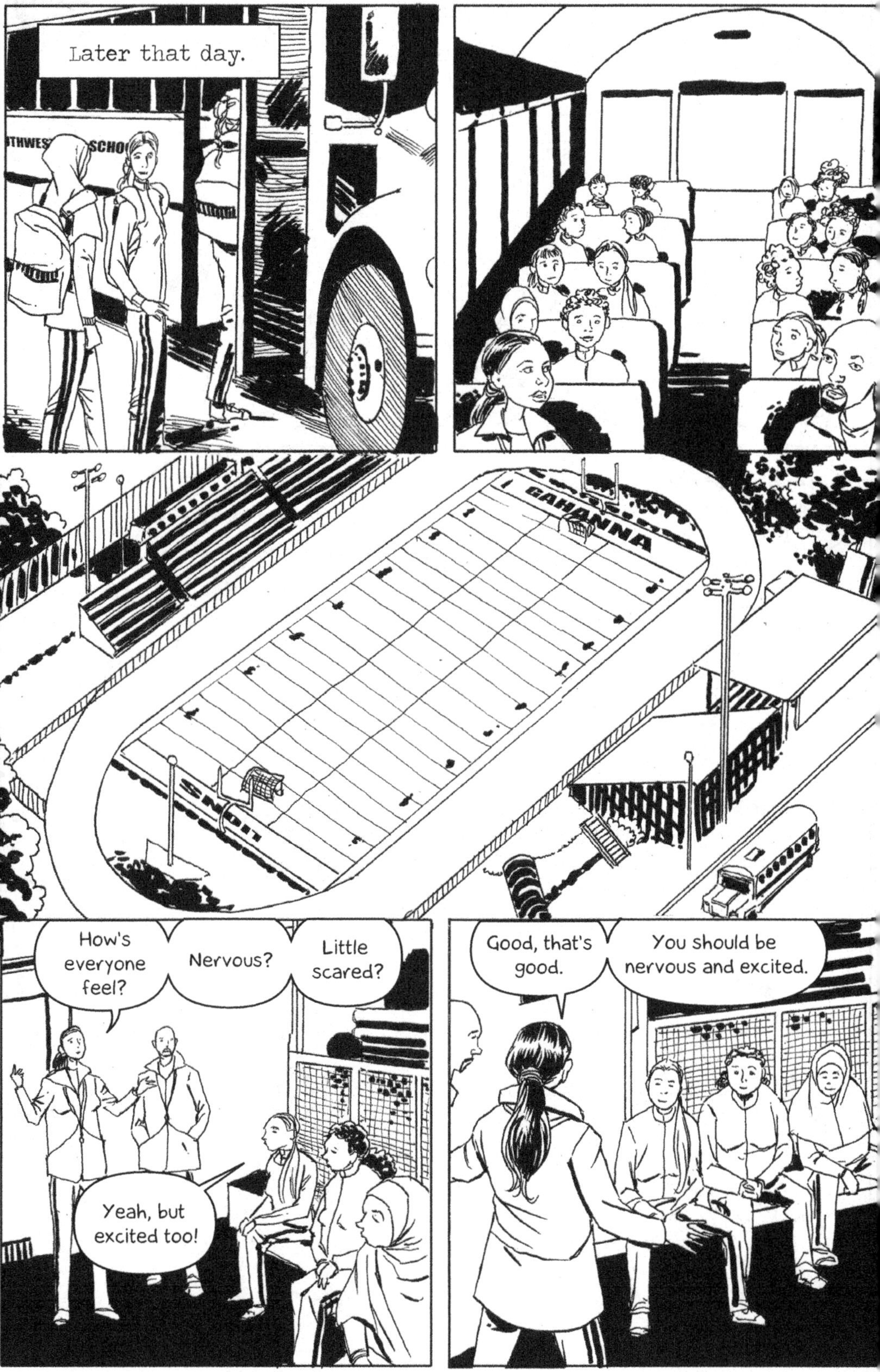
Later that day.
THWES
SCHO
GAHANNA
How's everyone feel?
Nervous?
Little scared?
Yeah, but excited too!
Good, that's good.
You should be nervous and excited.

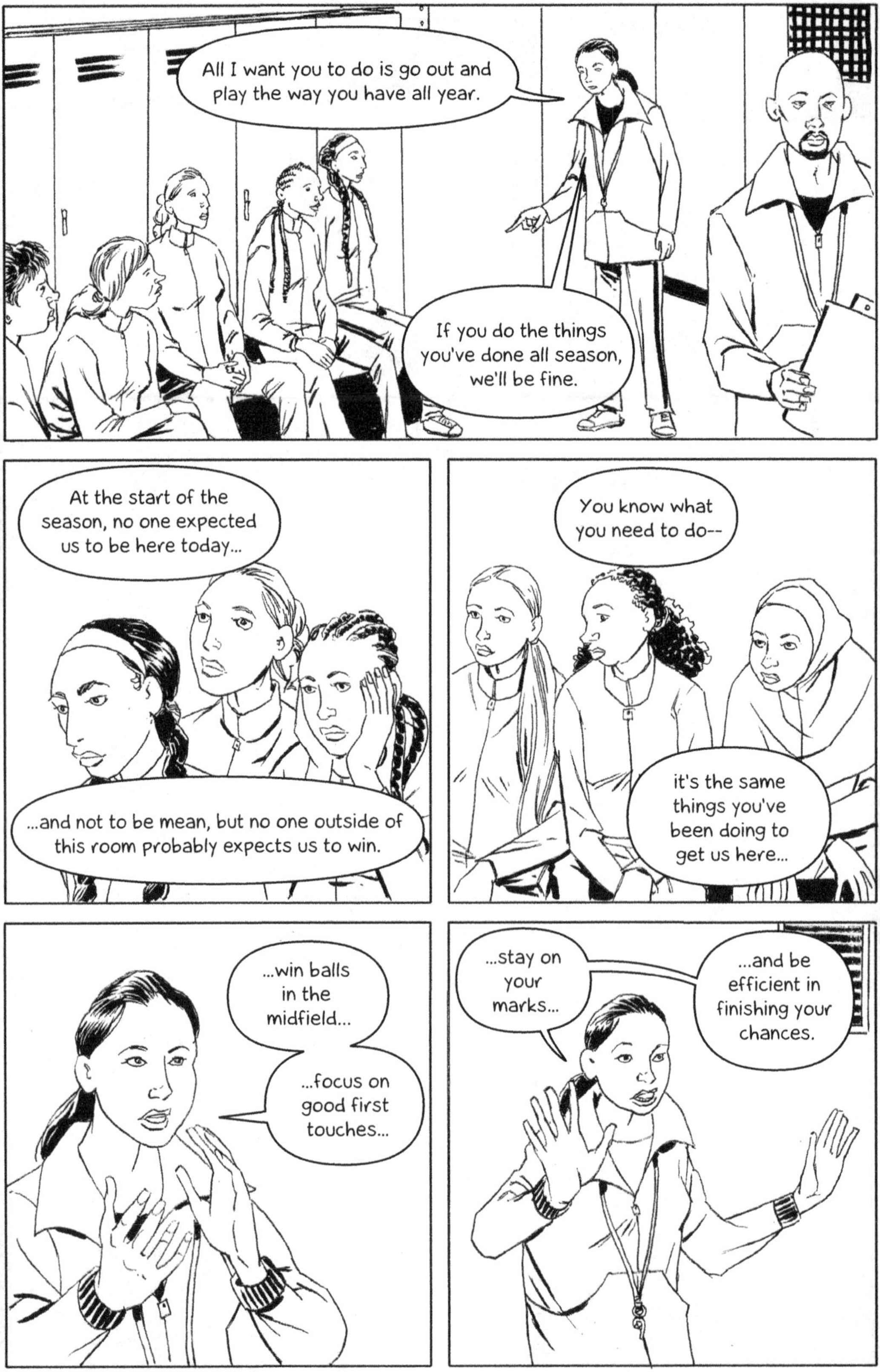
All I want you to do is go out and play the way you have all year.
If you do the things you've done all season, we'll be fine.
At the start of the season, no one expected us to be here today...
...and not to be mean, but no one outside of this room probably expects us to win.
You know what you need to do--
it's the same things you've been doing to get us here...
...win balls in the midfield...
...focus on good first touches...
...stay on your marks...
...and be efficient in finishing your chances.

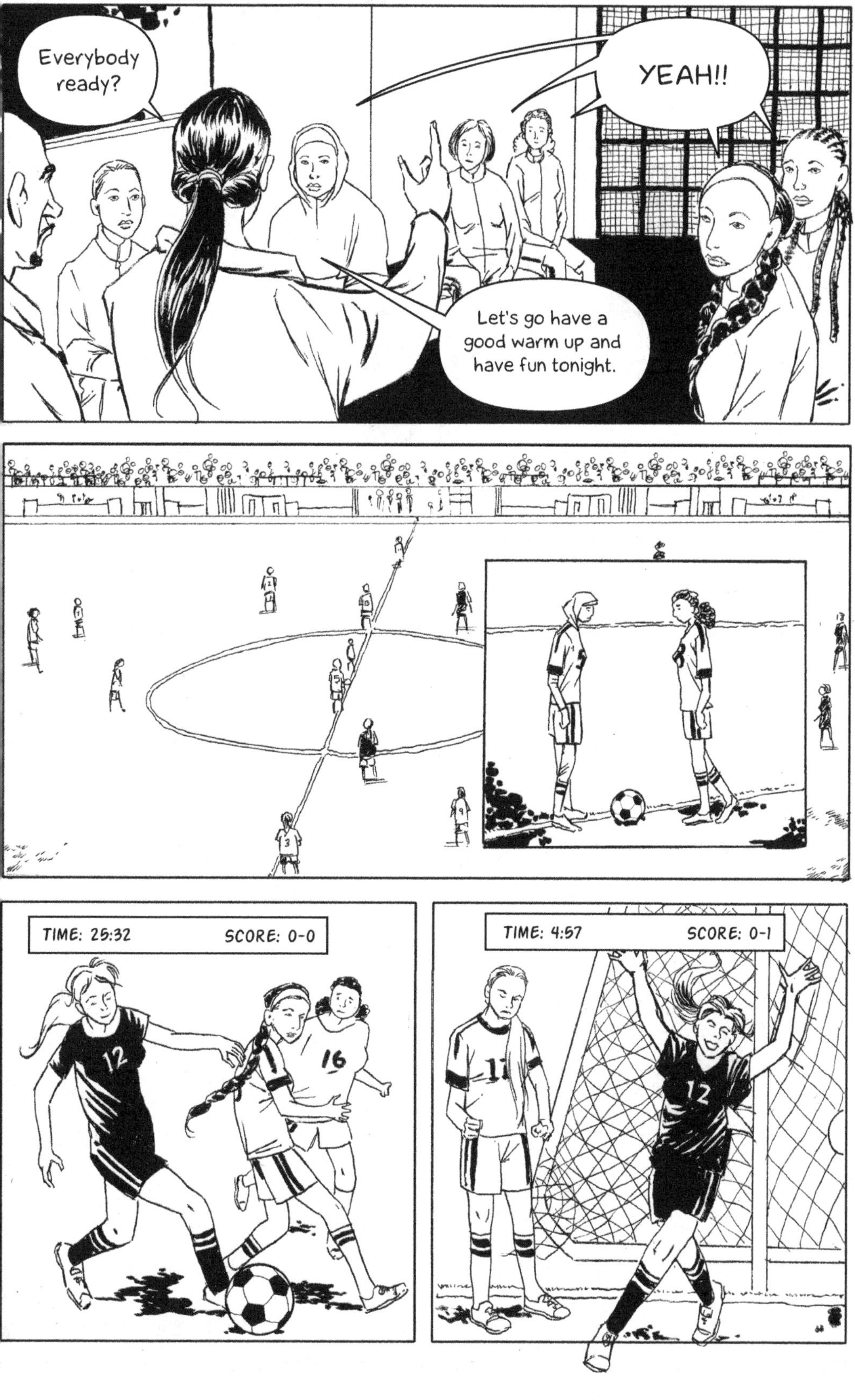

Everybody ready?
Let's go have a good warm up and have fun tonight.
YEAH!!
TIME: 25:32
SCORE: 0-0
TIME: 4:57
SCORE: 0-1

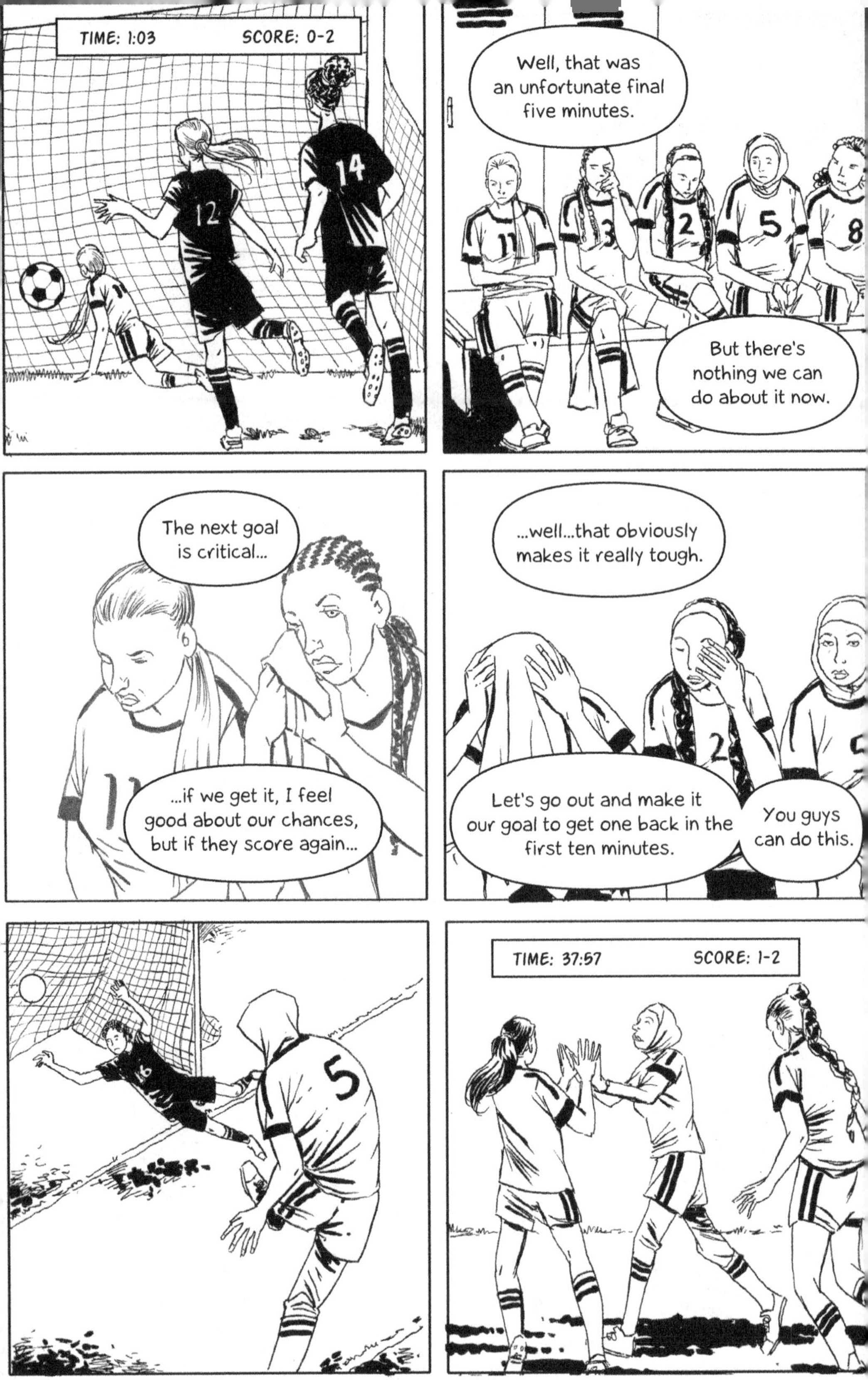
TIME: 1:03
SCORE: 0-2
Well, that was an unfortunate final five minutes.
But there's nothing we can do about it now.
The next goal is critical...
...if we get it, I feel good about our chances, but if they score again...
...well...that obviously makes it really tough.
Let's go out and make it our goal to get one back in the first ten minutes.
You guys can do this.
TIME: 37:57
SCORE: 1-2

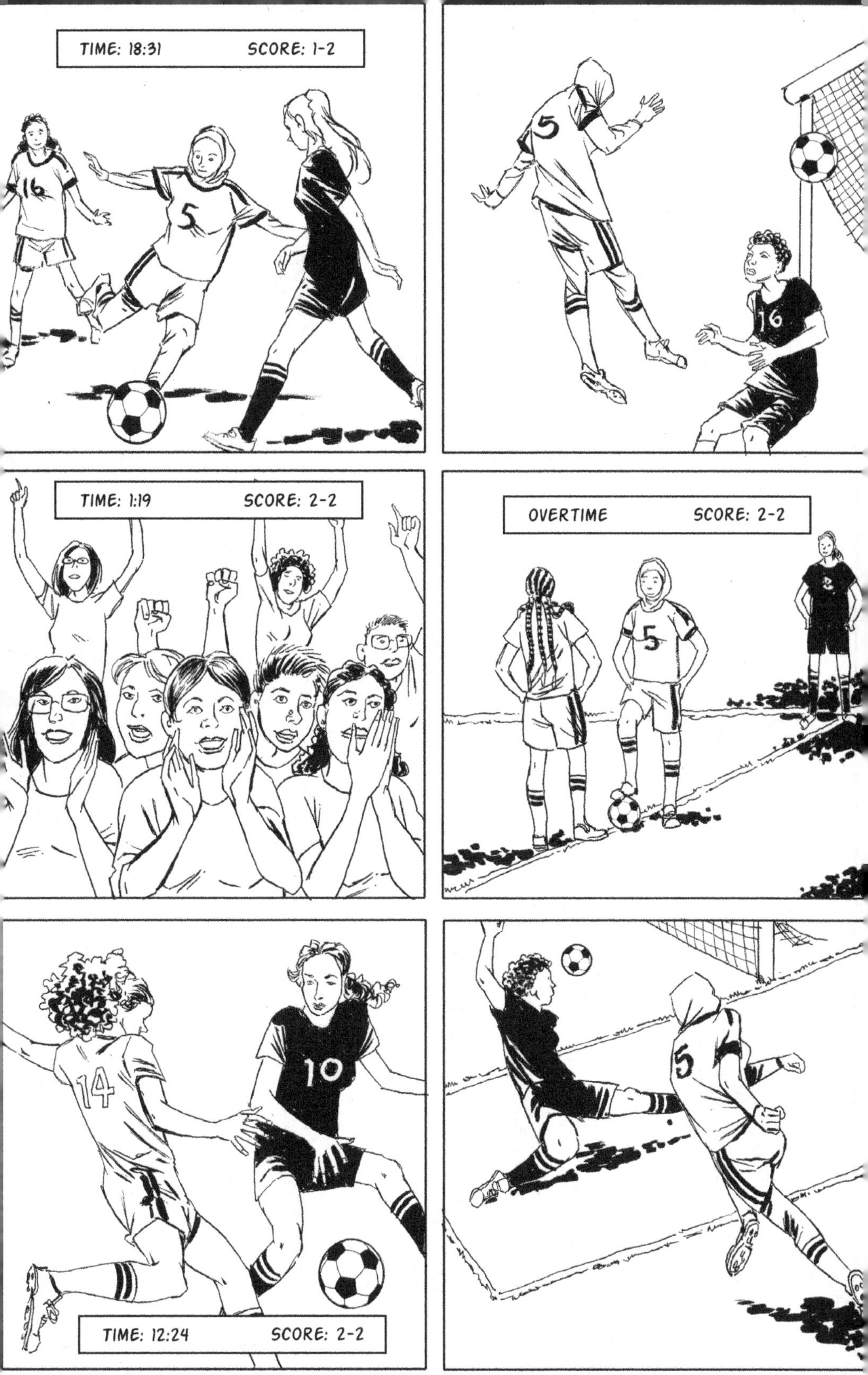
TIME: 18:31 SCORE: 1-2
TIME: 1:19 SCORE: 2-2
OVERTIME SCORE: 2-2
TIME: 12:24 SCORE: 2-2

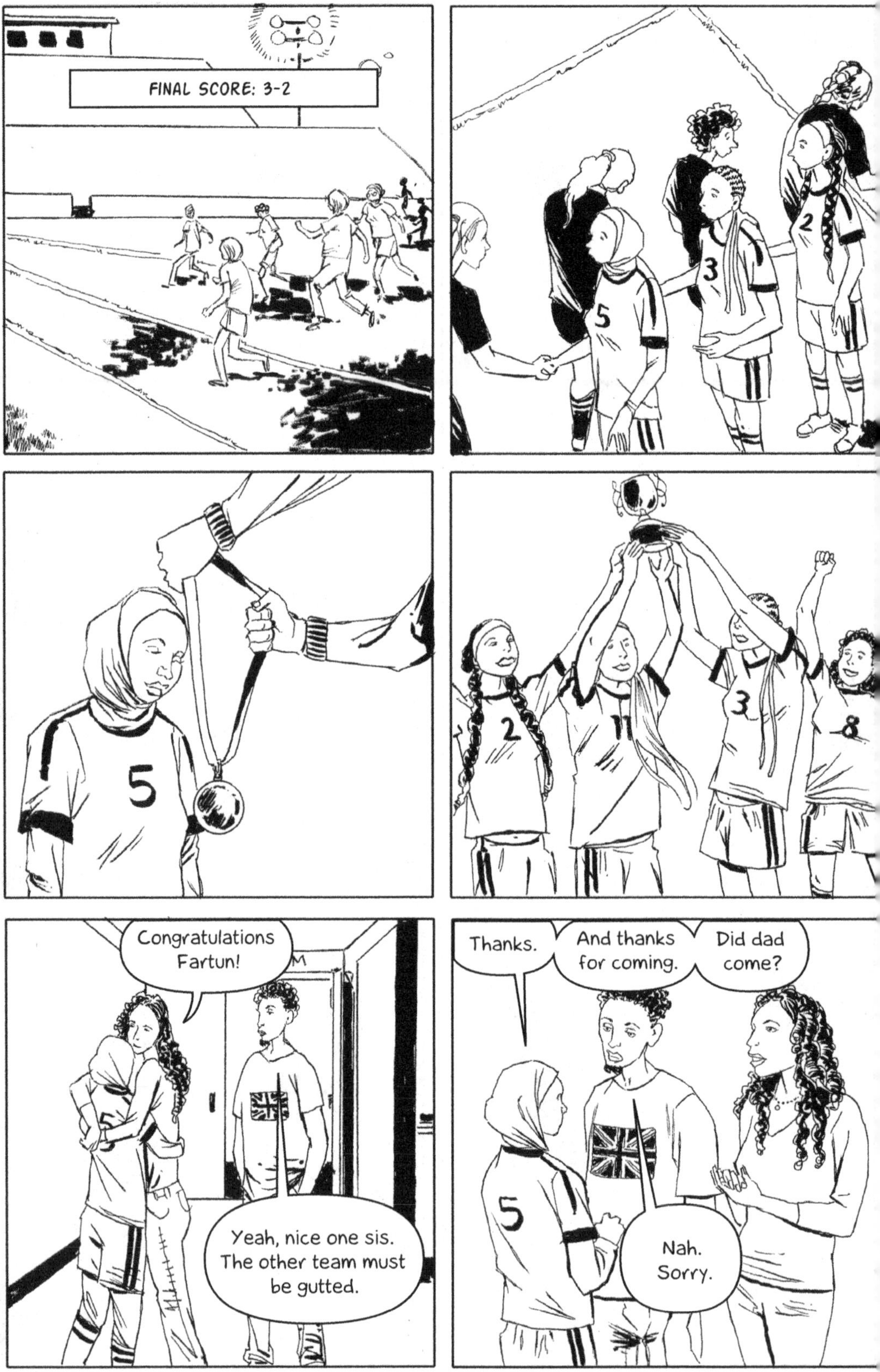
FINAL SCORE: 3-2
Congratulations Fartun!
Yeah, nice one sis. The other team must be gutted.
Thanks.
And thanks for coming.
Did dad come?
Nah. Sorry.

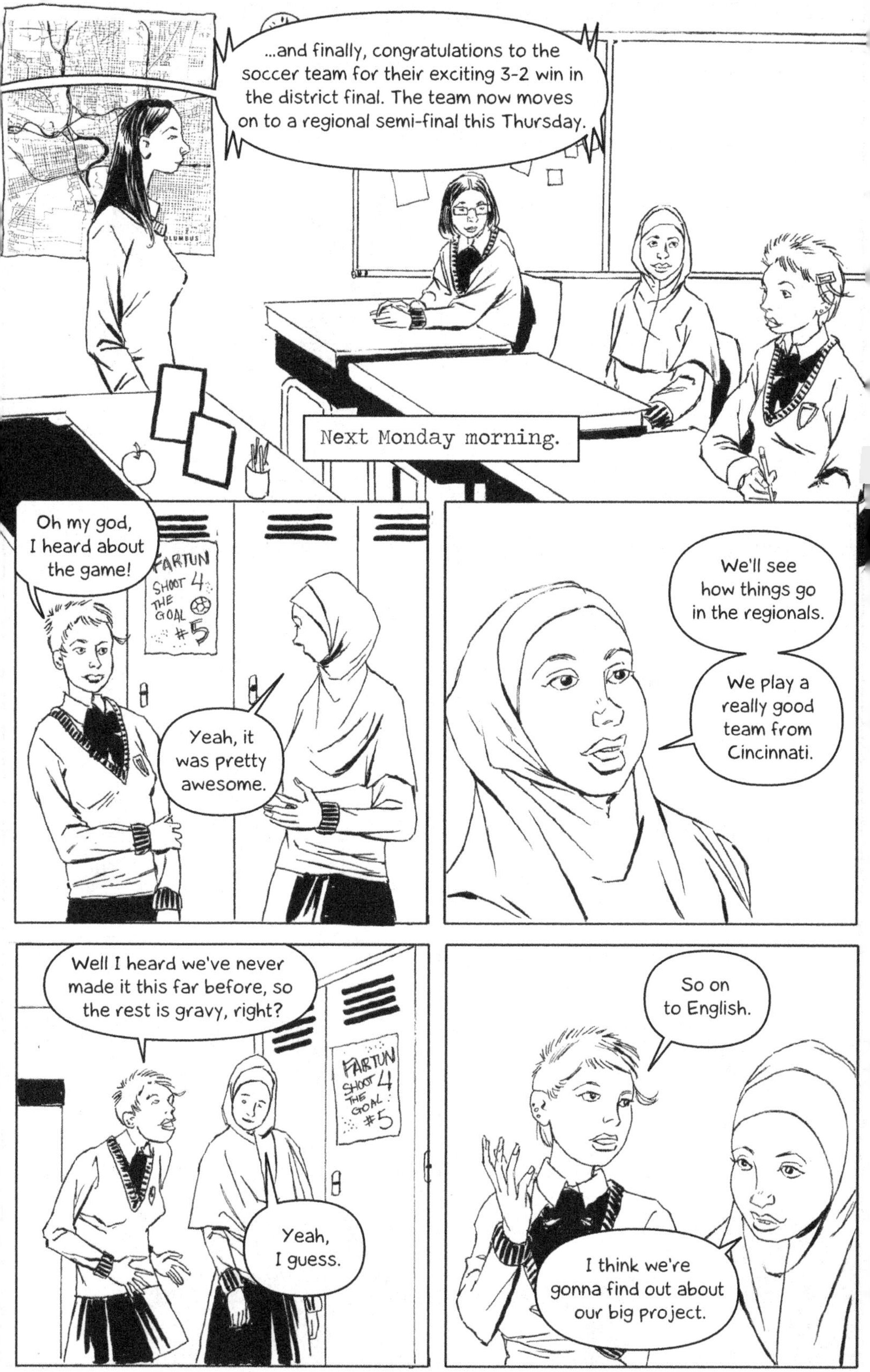
...and finally, congratulations to the soccer team for their exciting 3-2 win in the district final. The team now moves on to a regional semi-final this Thursday.
COLUMBUS
Next Monday morning.
Oh my god, I heard about the game!
FARTUN SHOOT 4 THE GOAL #5
Yeah, it was pretty awesome.
We'll see how things go in the regionals.
We play a really good team from Cincinnati.
Well I heard we've never made it this far before, so the rest is gravy, right?
FARTUN SHOOT 4 THE GOAL #5
Yeah, I guess.
So on to English.
I think we're gonna find out about our big project.

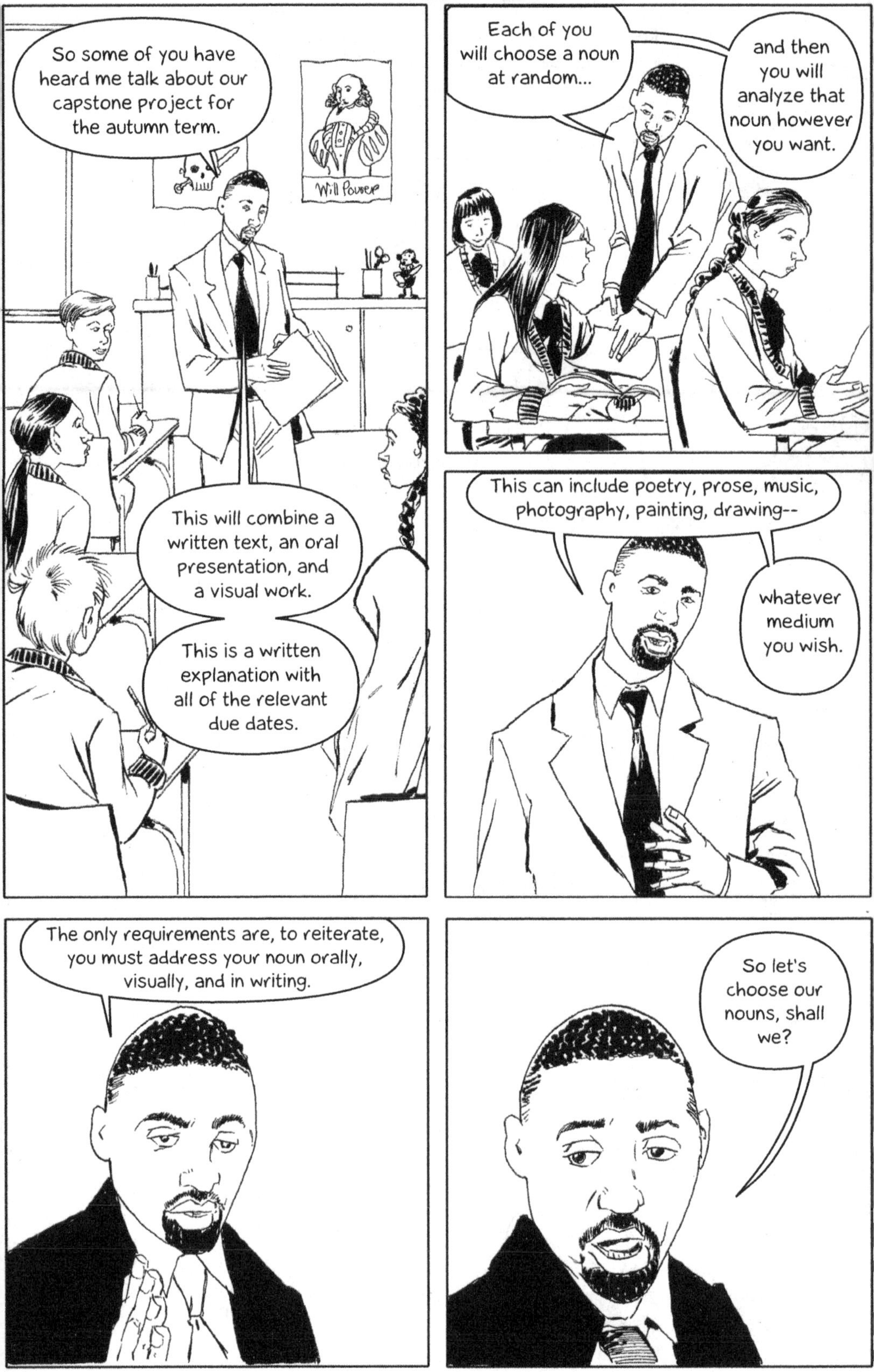
So some of you have heard me talk about our capstone project for the autumn term.
Will Power
This will combine a written text, an oral presentation, and a visual work.
This is a written explanation with all of the relevant due dates.
Each of you will choose a noun at random...
and then you will analyze that noun however you want.
This can include poetry, prose, music, photography, painting, drawing--
whatever medium you wish.
The only requirements are, to reiterate, you must address your noun orally, visually, and in writing.
So let's choose our nouns, shall we?

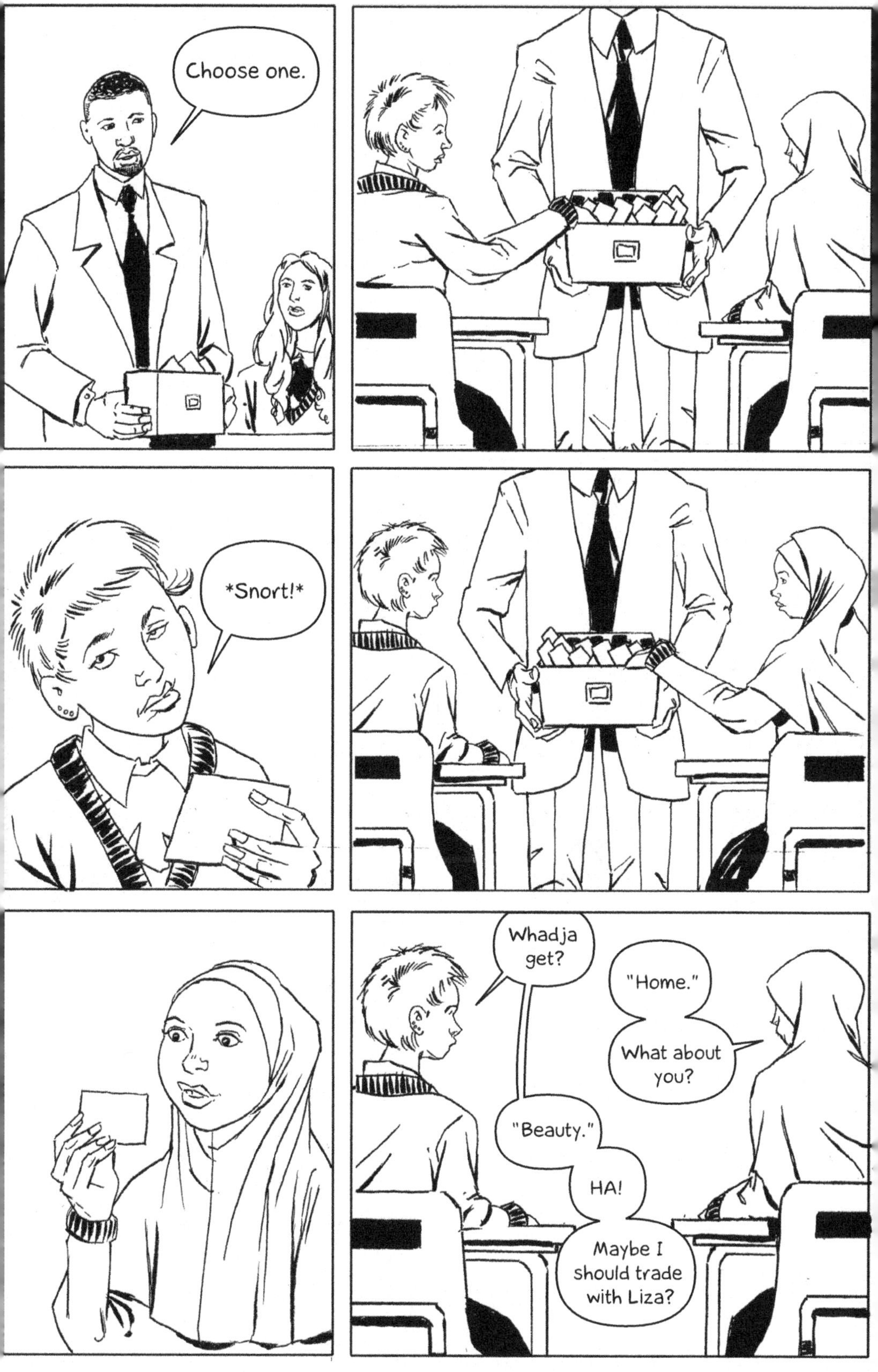
Choose one.
Snort!
Whadja get?
"Home."
What about you?
"Beauty."
HA!
Maybe I should trade with Liza?

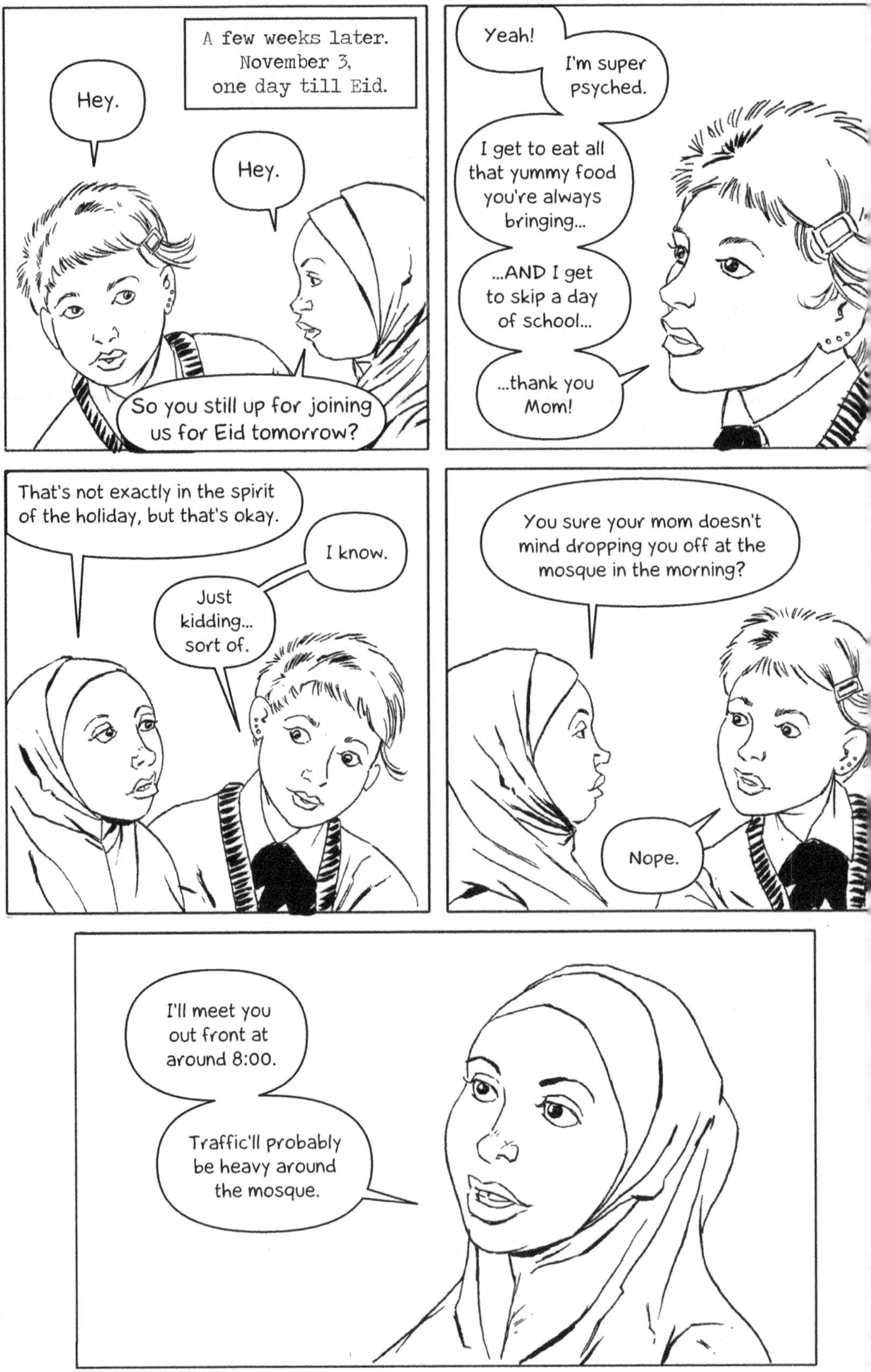
A few weeks later. November 3, one day till Eid.
Hey.
Hey.
So you still up for joining us for Eid tomorrow?
Yeah!
I'm super psyched.
I get to eat all that yummy food you're always bringing...
...AND I get to skip a day of school...
...thank you Mom!
That's not exactly in the spirit of the holiday, but that's okay.
I know.
Just kidding... sort of.
You sure your mom doesn't mind dropping you off at the mosque in the morning?
Nope.
I'll meet you out front at around 8:00.
Traffic'll probably be heavy around the mosque.

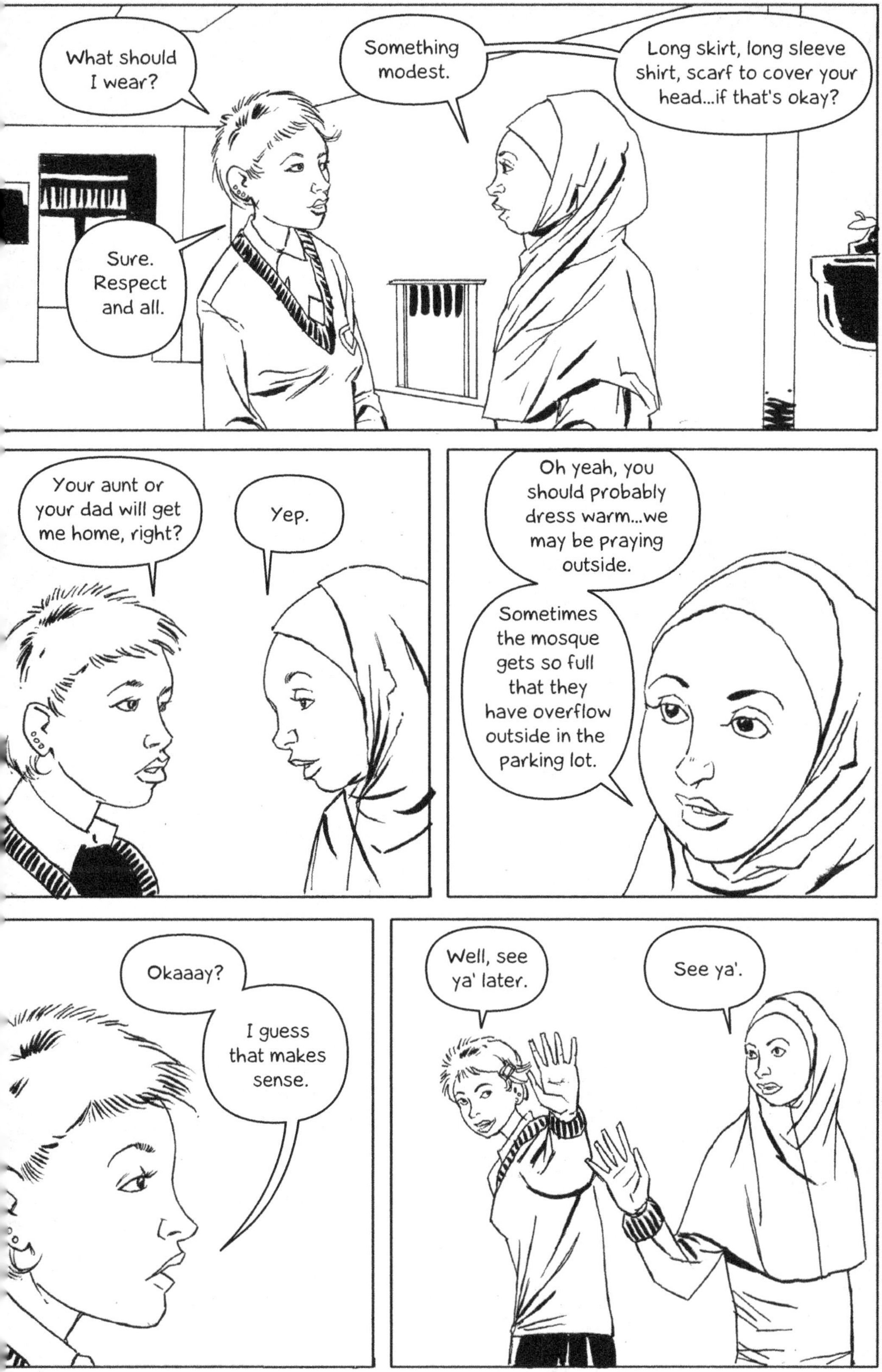
What should I wear?
Something modest.
Long skirt, long sleeve shirt, scarf to cover your head...if that's okay?
Sure. Respect and all.
Your aunt or your dad will get me home, right?
Yep.
Oh yeah, you should probably dress warm...we may be praying outside.
Sometimes the mosque gets so full that they have overflow outside in the parking lot.
Okaaay?
I guess that makes sense.
Well, see ya' later.
See ya'.

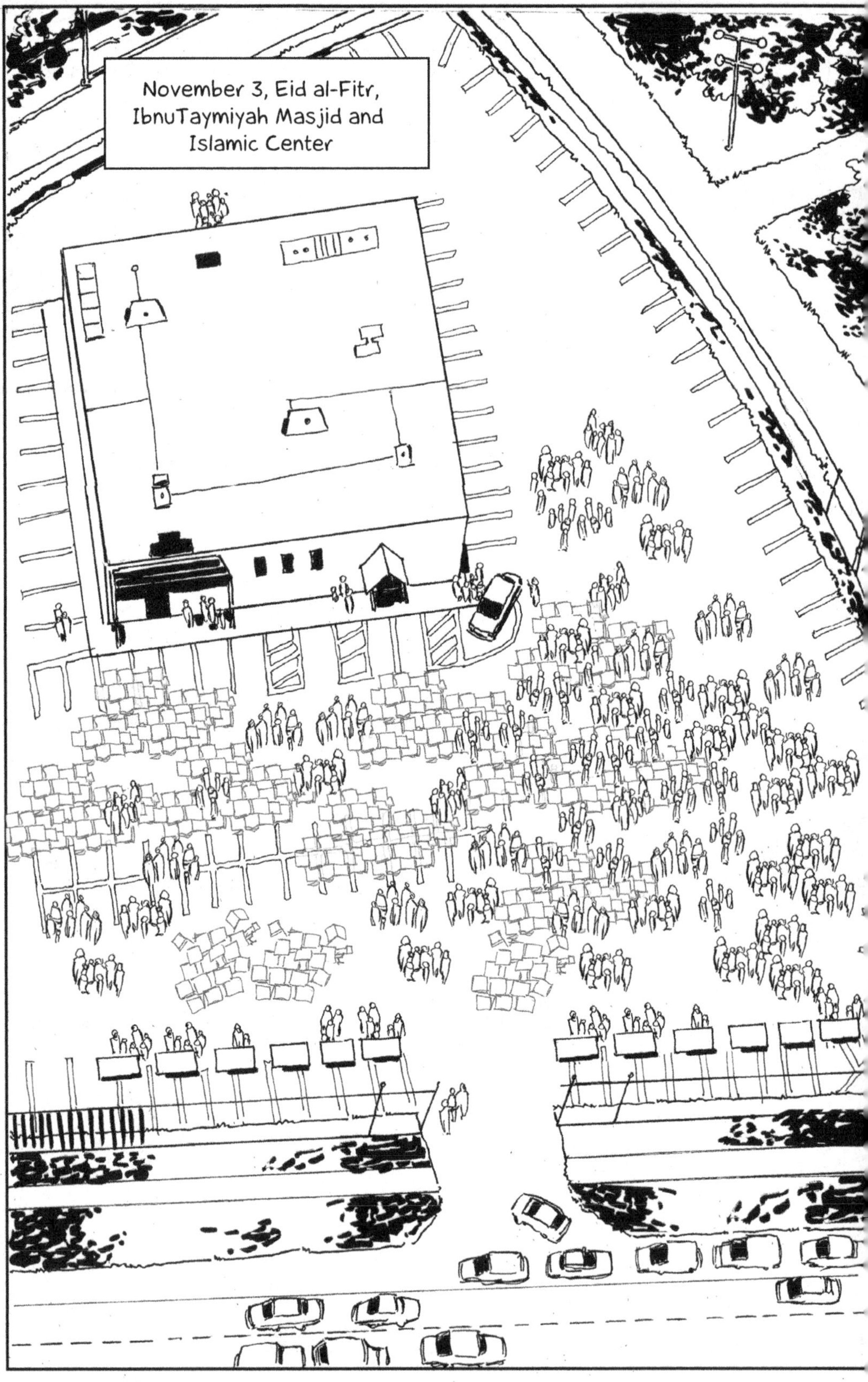
November 3, Eid al-Fitr,
IbnuTaymiyah Masjid and
Islamic Center

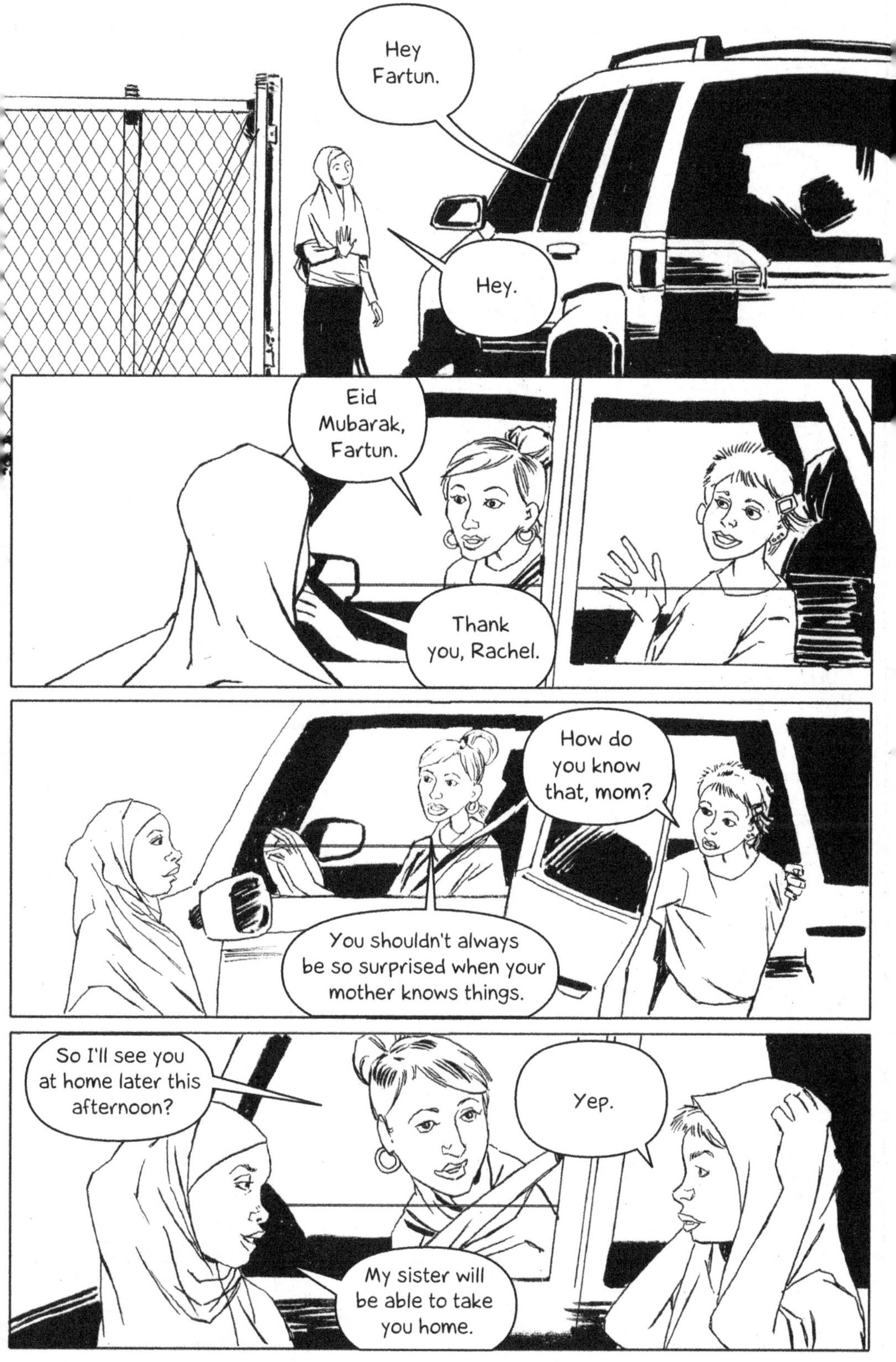
Hey Fartun.
Hey.
Eid Mubarak, Fartun.
Thank you, Rachel.
How do you know that, mom?
You shouldn't always be so surprised when your mother knows things.
So I'll see you at home later this afternoon?
Yep.
My sister will be able to take you home.

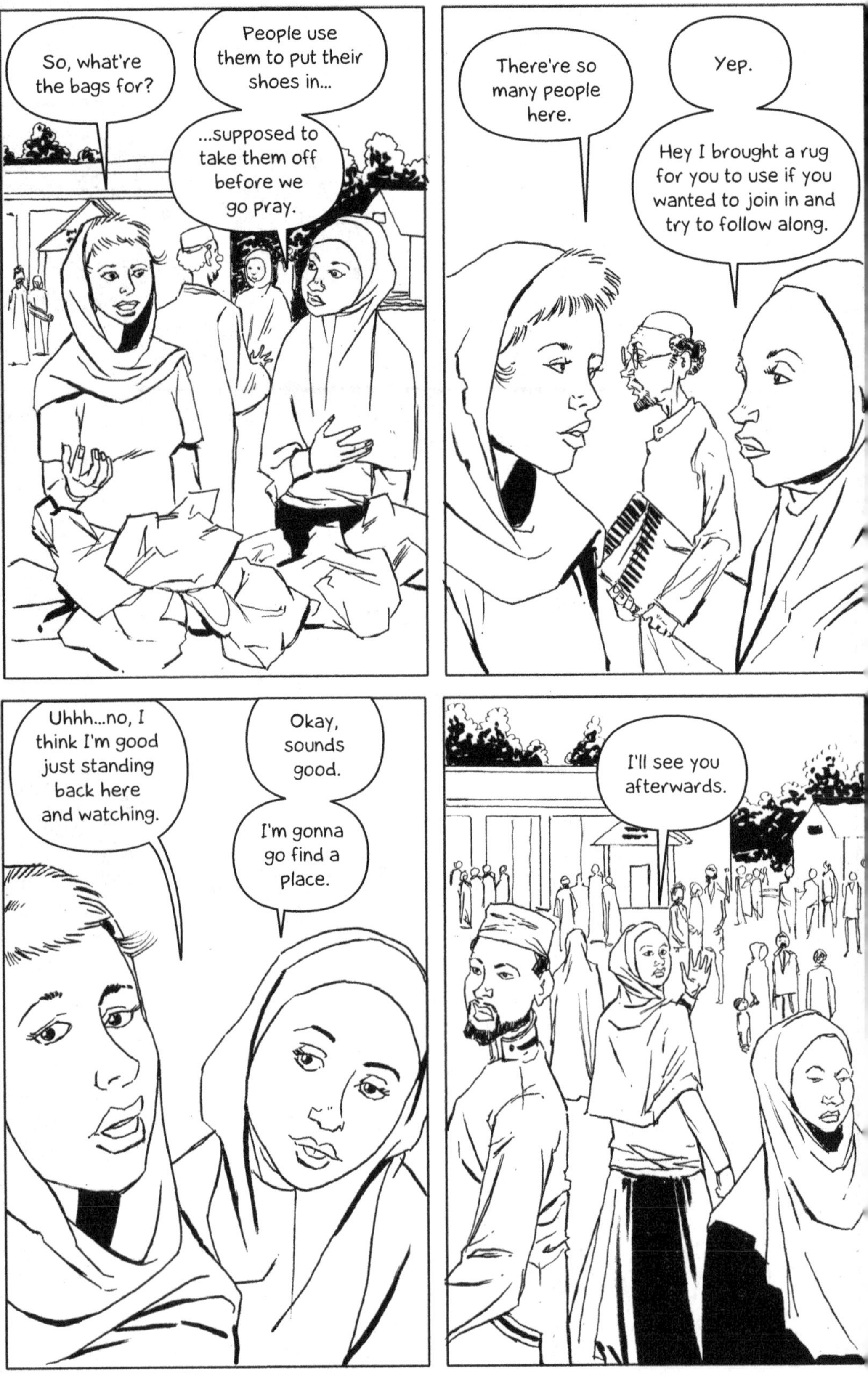
So, what're the bags for?
People use them to put their shoes in...
...supposed to take them off before we go pray.
There're so many people here.
Yep.
Hey I brought a rug for you to use if you wanted to join in and try to follow along.
Uhhh...no, I think I'm good just standing back here and watching.
Okay, sounds good.
I'm gonna go find a place.
I'll see you afterwards.

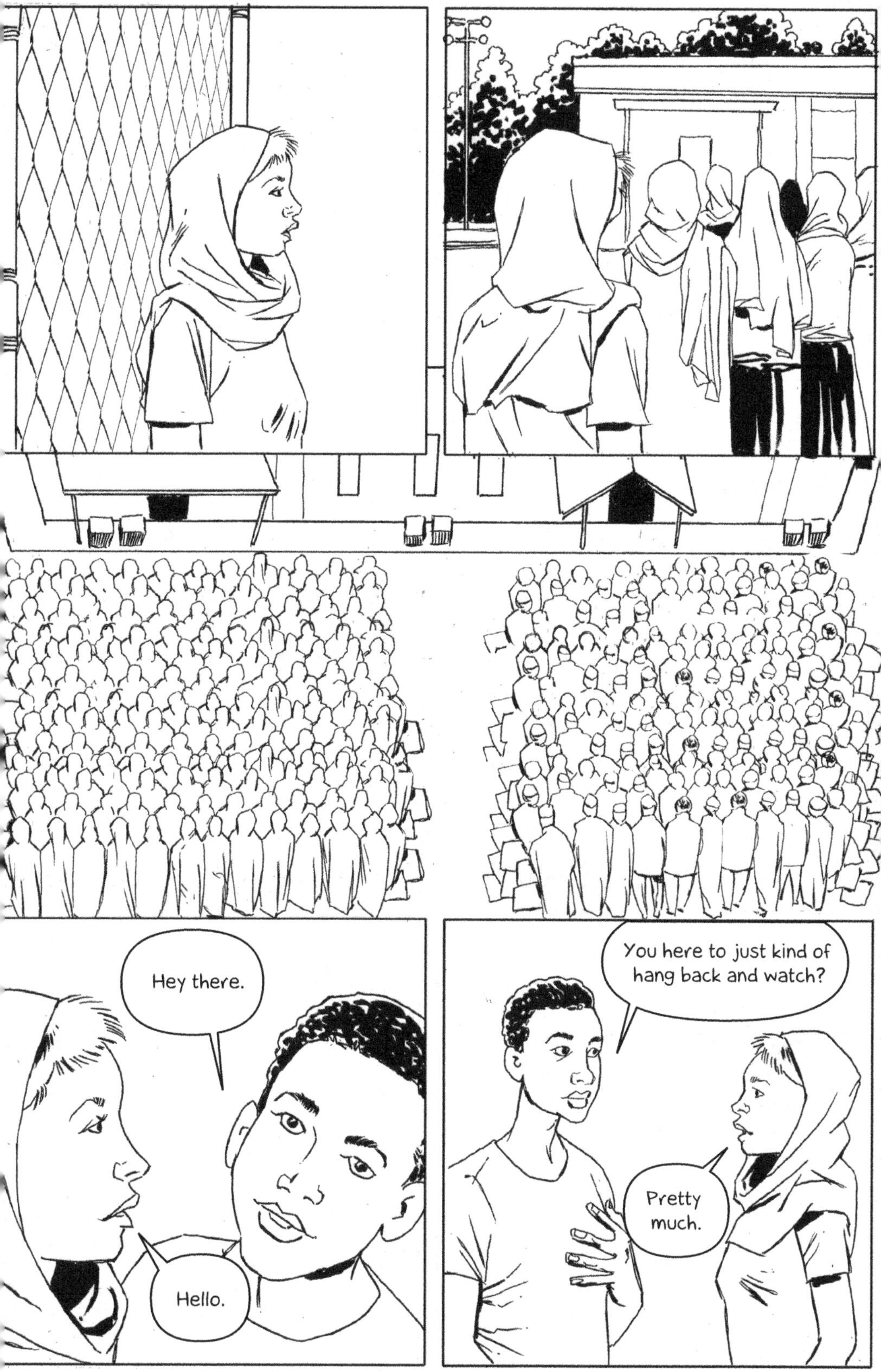
Hey there.
Hello.
You here to just kind of hang back and watch?
Pretty much.

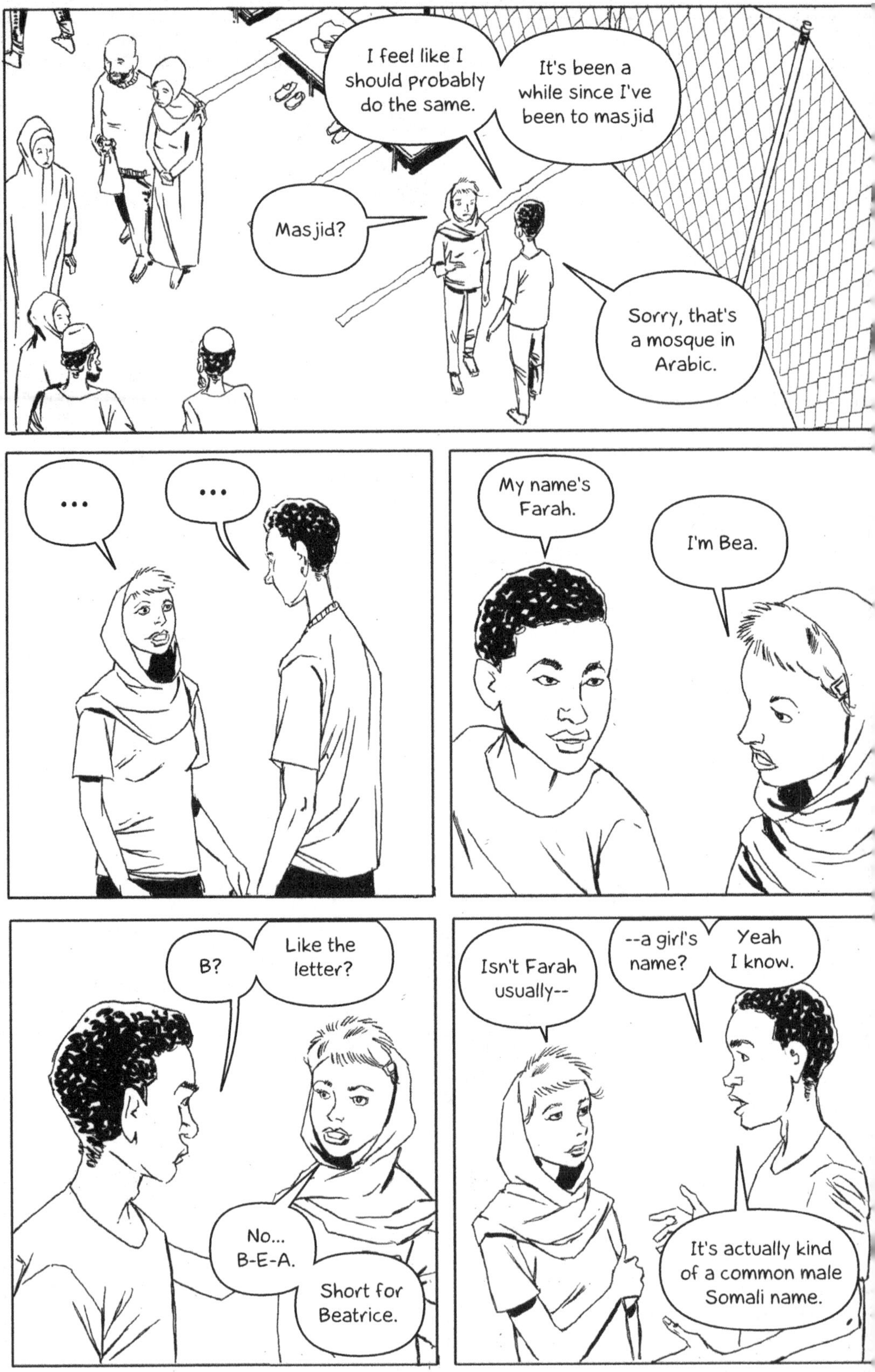
I feel like I should probably do the same.
It's been a while since I've been to masjid
Masjid?
Sorry, that's a mosque in Arabic.
...
...
My name's Farah.
I'm Bea.
B?
Like the letter?
No... B-E-A.
Short for Beatrice.
Isn't Farah usually--
--a girl's name?
Yeah I know.
It's actually kind of a common male Somali name.

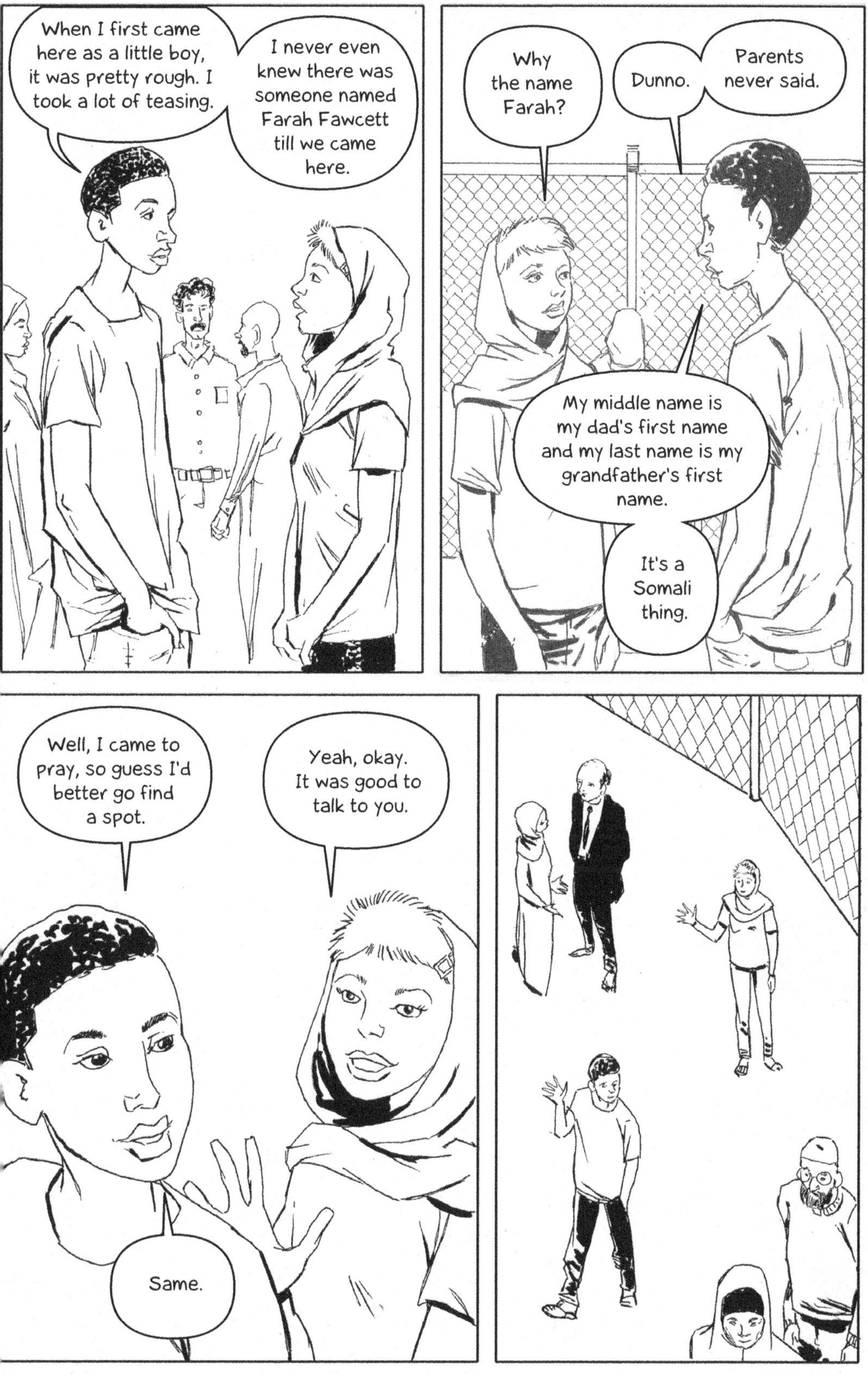
When I first came here as a little boy, it was pretty rough. I took a lot of teasing.
I never even knew there was someone named Farah Fawcett till we came here.
Why the name Farah?
Dunno.
Parents never said.
My middle name is my dad's first name and my last name is my grandfather's first name.
It's a Somali thing.
Well, I came to pray, so guess I'd better go find a spot.
Yeah, okay. It was good to talk to you.
Same.

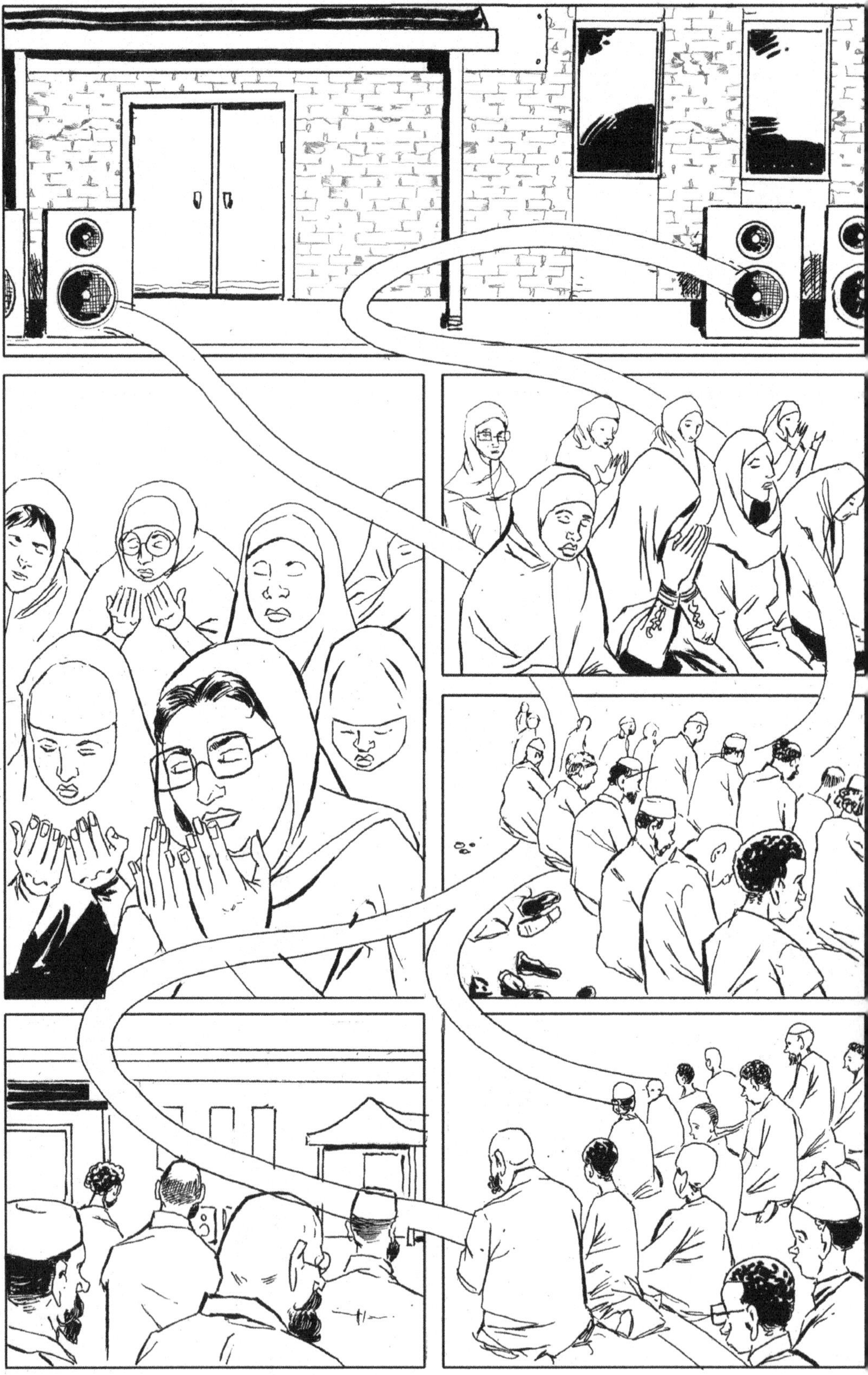

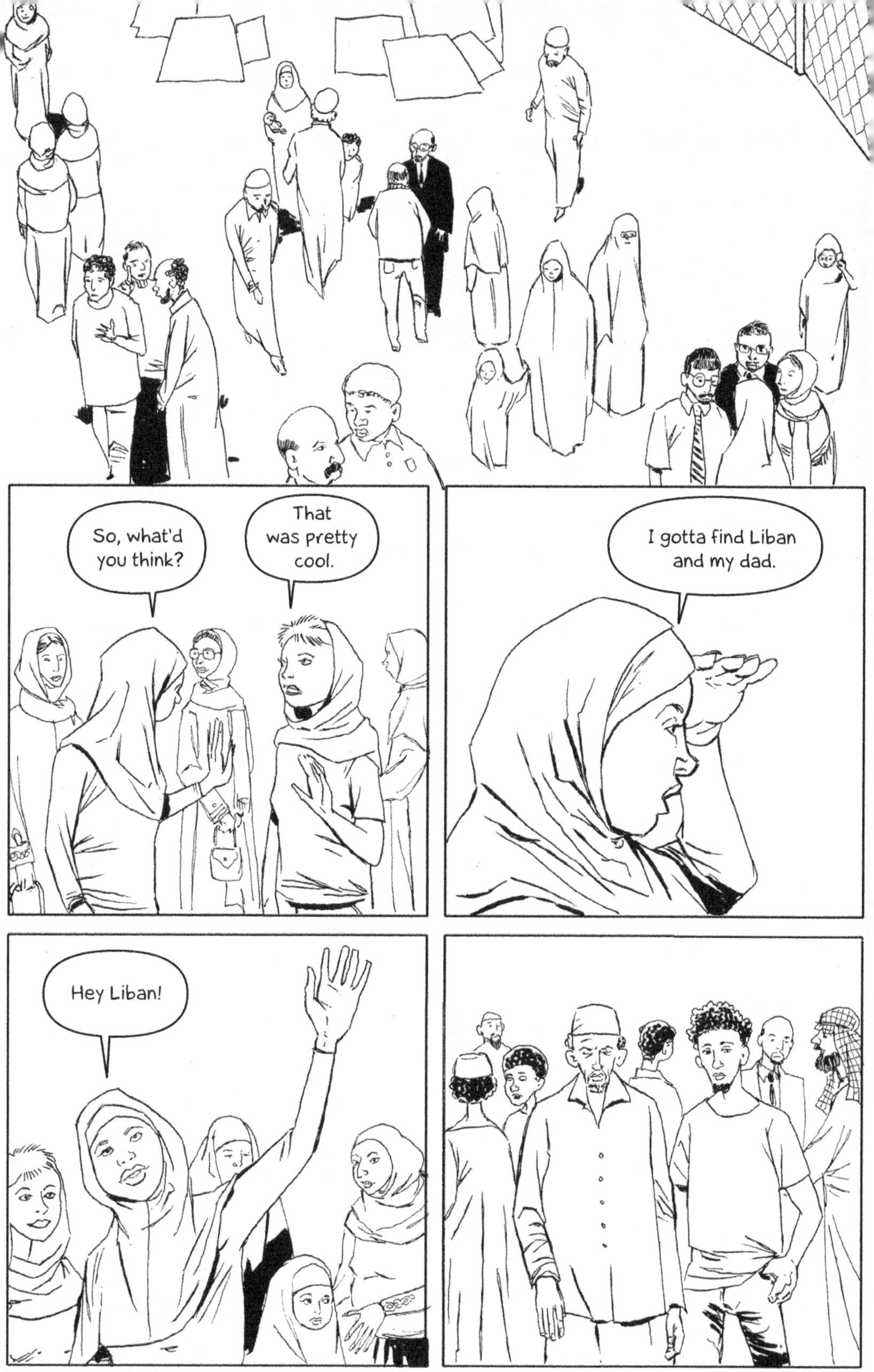
So, what'd you think?
That was pretty cool.
I gotta find Liban and my dad.
Hey Liban!

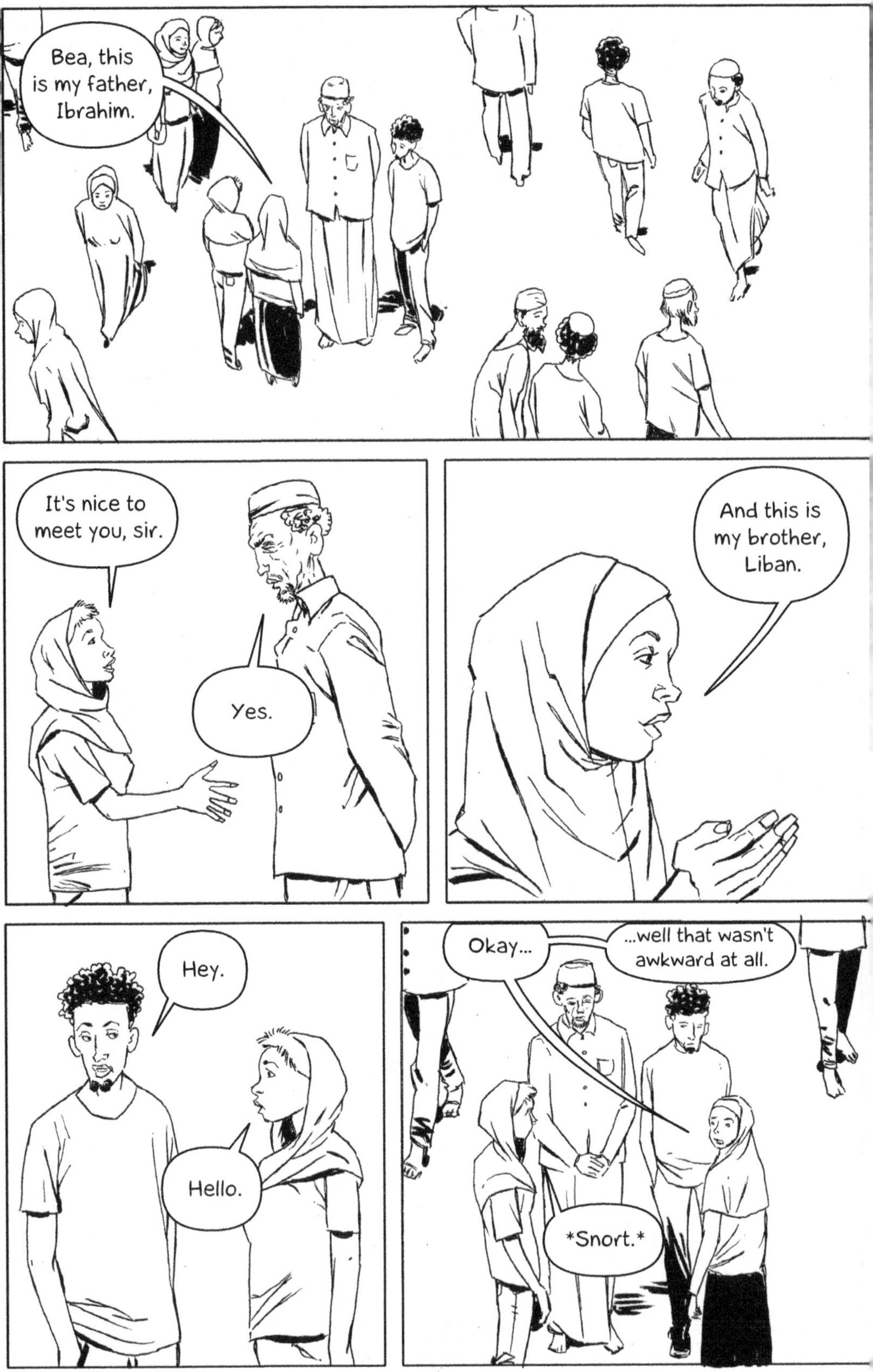
Bea, this is my father, Ibrahim.
It's nice to meet you, sir.
Yes.
And this is my brother, Liban.
Hey.
Hello.
Okay...
...well that wasn't awkward at all.
Snort.

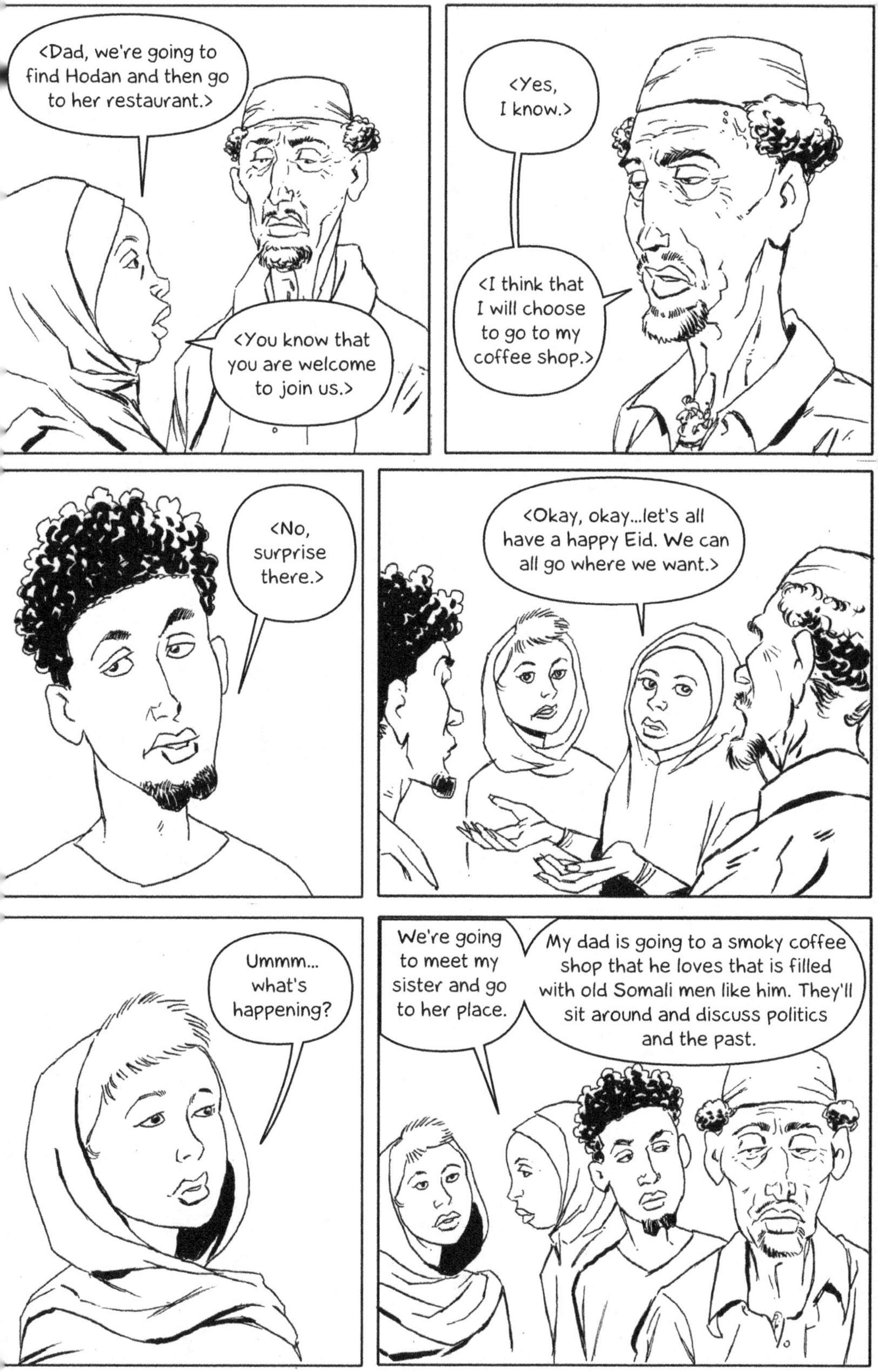
<Dad, we're going to find Hodan and then go to her restaurant.>
<You know that you are welcome to join us.>
<Yes, I know.>
<I think that I will choose to go to my coffee shop.>
<No, surprise there.>
<Okay, okay...let's all have a happy Eid. We can all go where we want.>
Ummm... what's happening?
We're going to meet my sister and go to her place.
My dad is going to a smoky coffee shop that he loves that is filled with old Somali men like him. They'll sit around and discuss politics and the past.

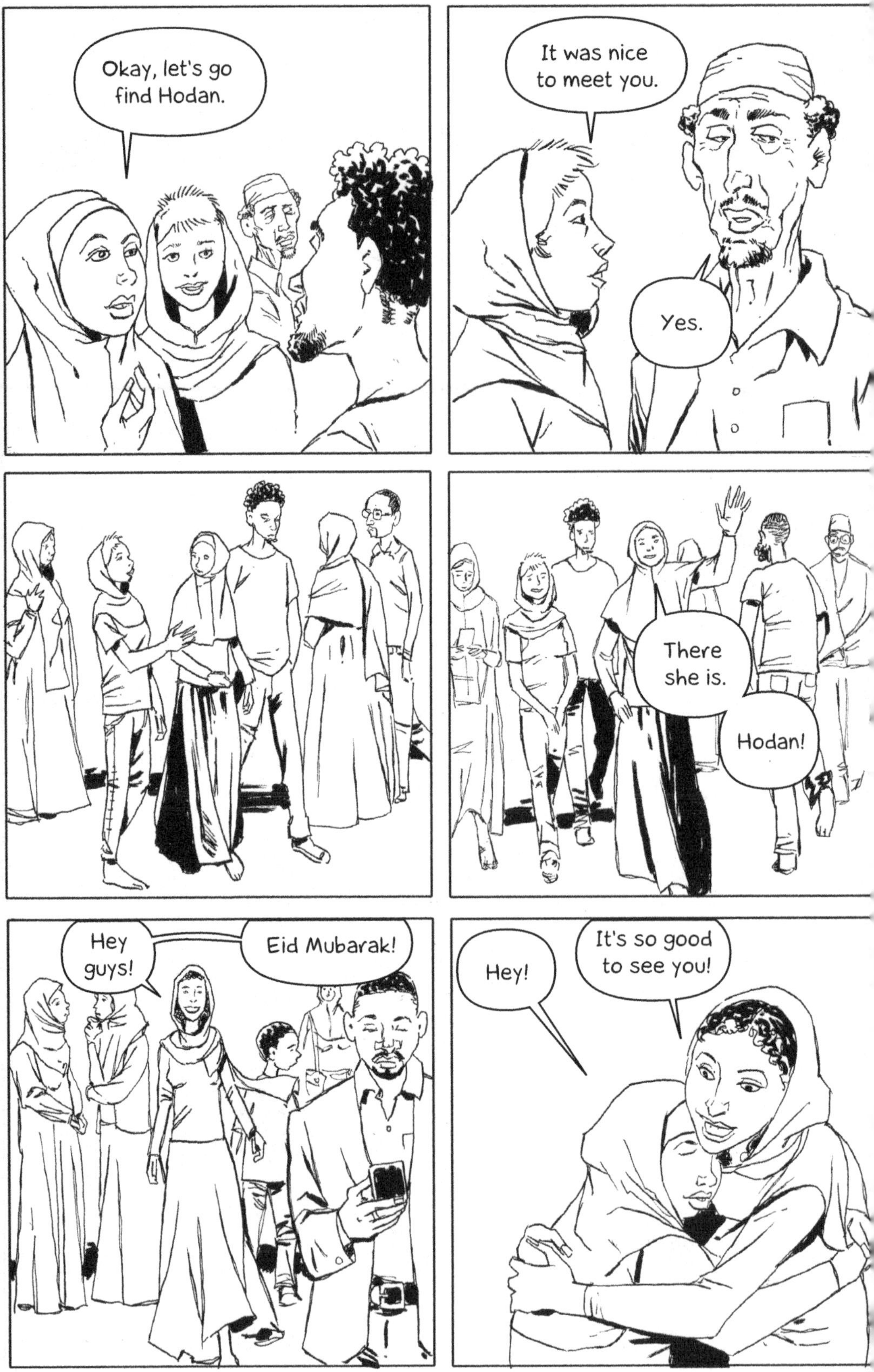
Okay, let's go find Hodan.
It was nice to meet you.
Yes.
There she is.
Hodan!
Hey guys!
Eid Mubarak!
Hey!
It's so good to see you!

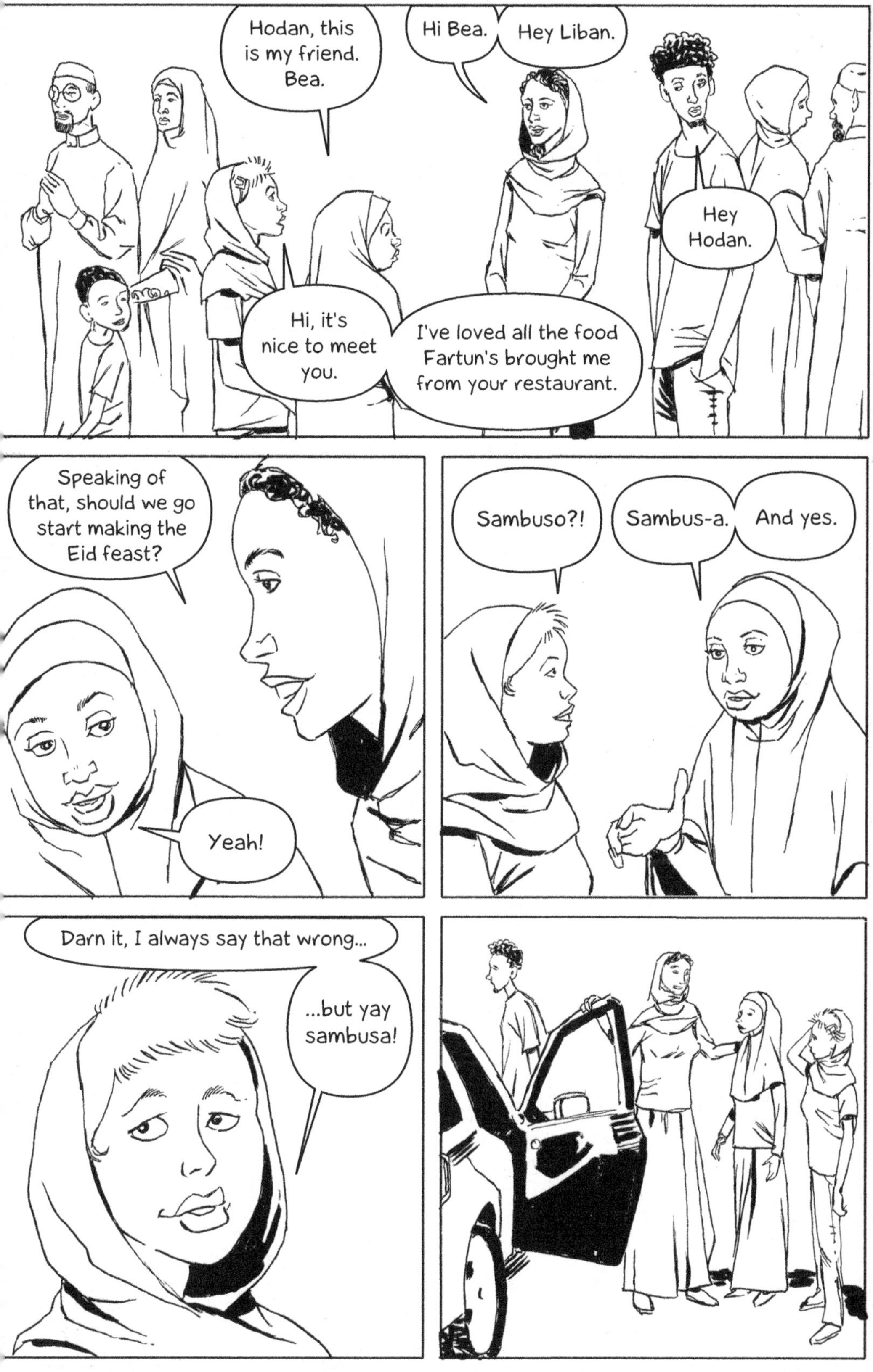

Hodan, this is my friend. Bea.
Hi Bea.
Hey Liban.
Hey Hodan.
Hi, it's nice to meet you.
I've loved all the food Fartun's brought me from your restaurant.
Speaking of that, should we go start making the Eid feast?
Yeah!
Sambuso?!
Sambus-a.
And yes.
Darn it, I always say that wrong...
...but yay sambusa!

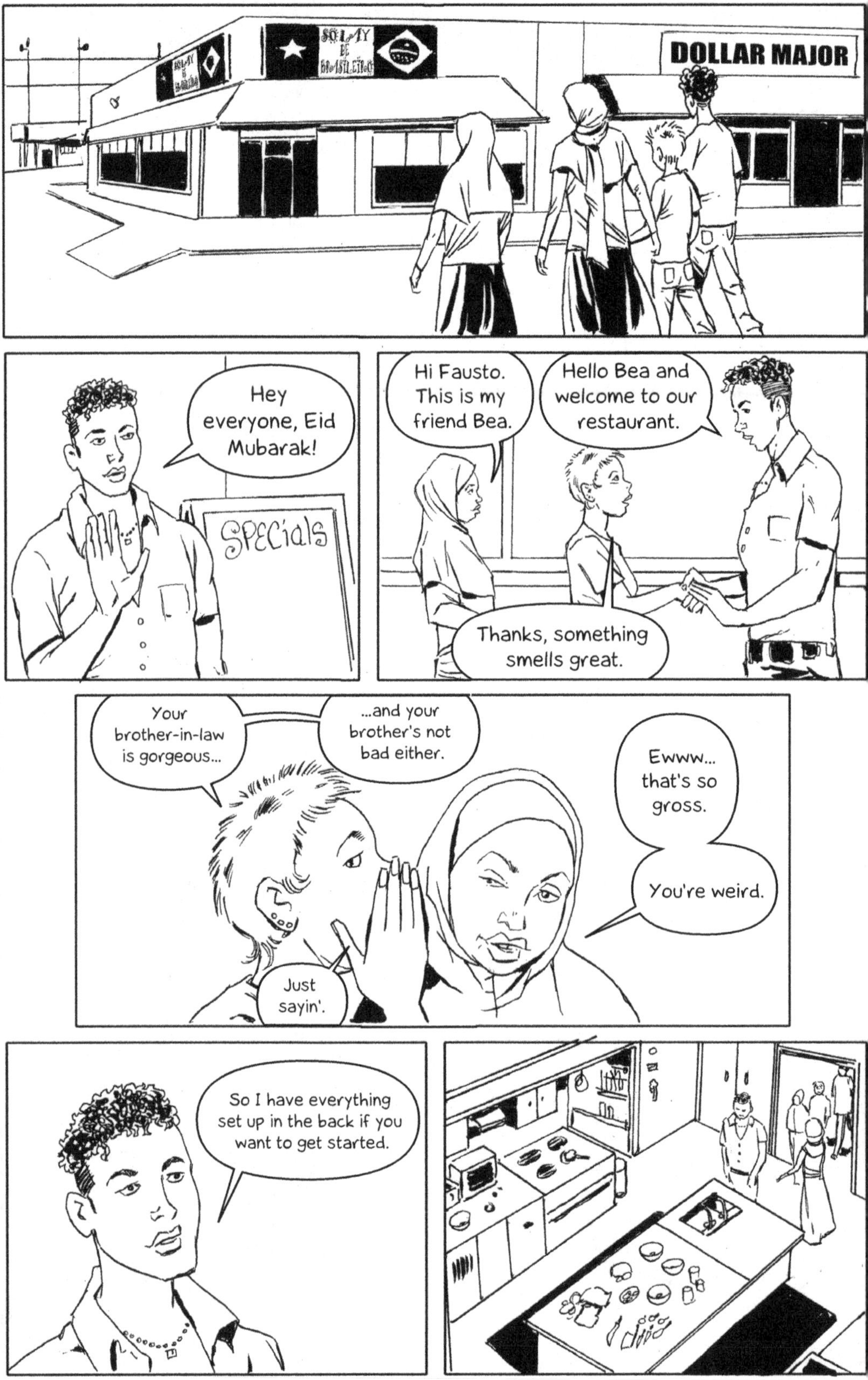
DOLLAR MAJOR
Hey everyone, Eid Mubarak!
SPECials
Hi Fausto. This is my friend Bea.
Hello Bea and welcome to our restaurant.
Thanks, something smells great.
Your brother-in-law is gorgeous...
...and your brother's not bad either.
Just sayin'.
Ewww... that's so gross.
You're weird.
So I have everything set up in the back if you want to get started.

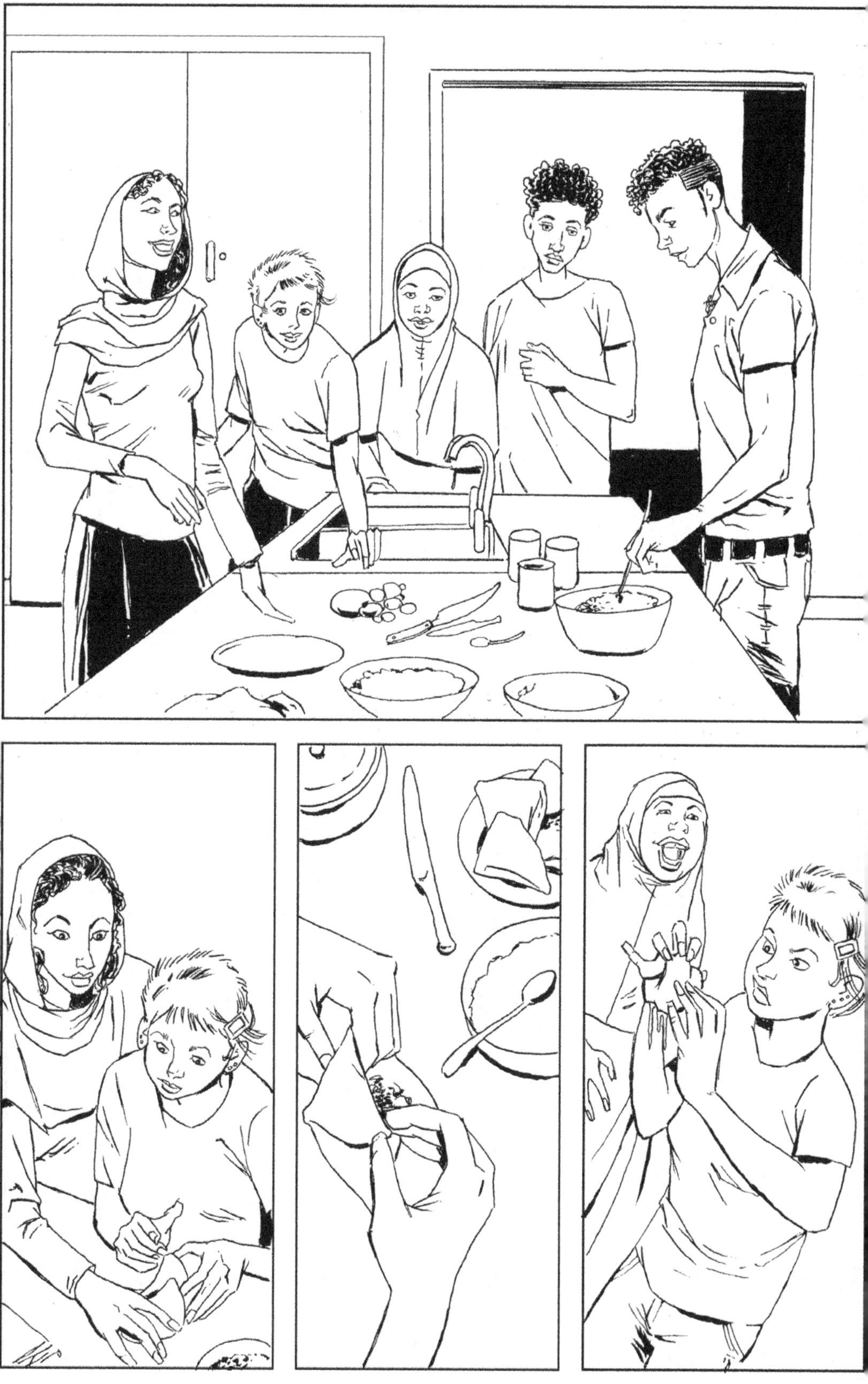

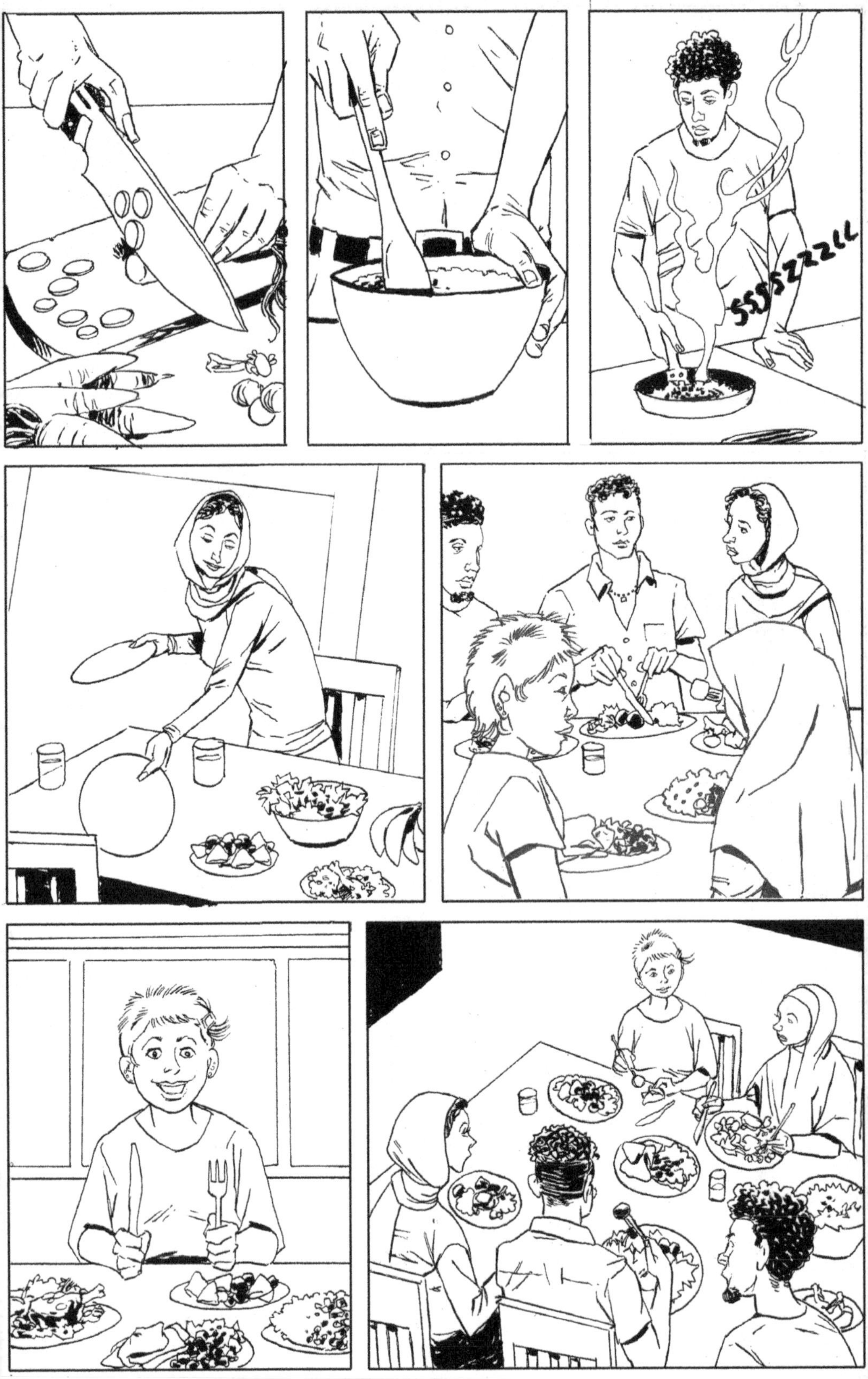
SSSSZZZZLL

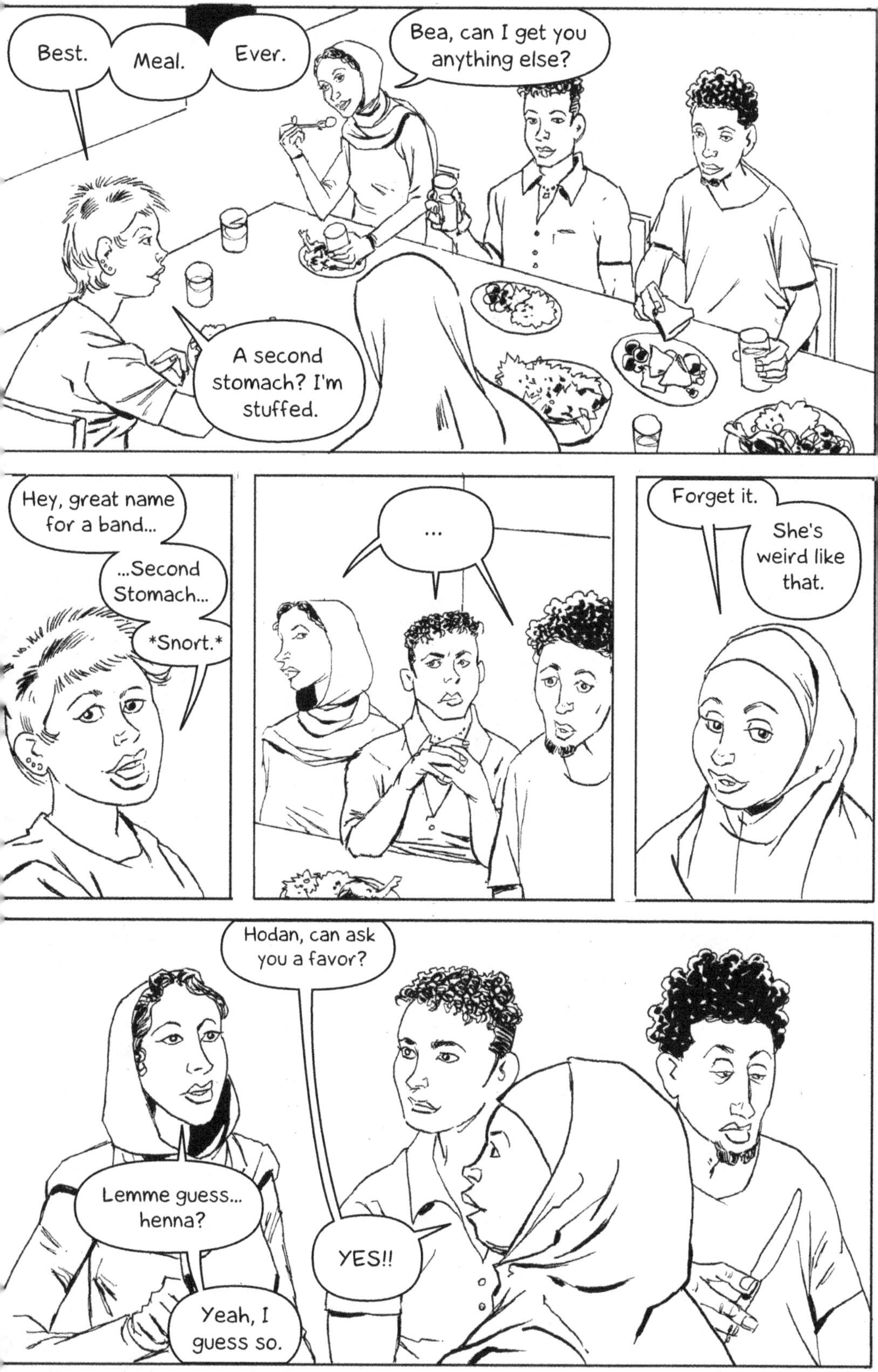
Best.
Meal.
Ever.
Bea, can I get you anything else?
A second stomach? I'm stuffed.
Hey, great name for a band...
...Second Stomach...
Snort.
...
Forget it.
She's weird like that.
Hodan, can ask you a favor?
Lemme guess... henna?
YES!!
Yeah, I guess so.

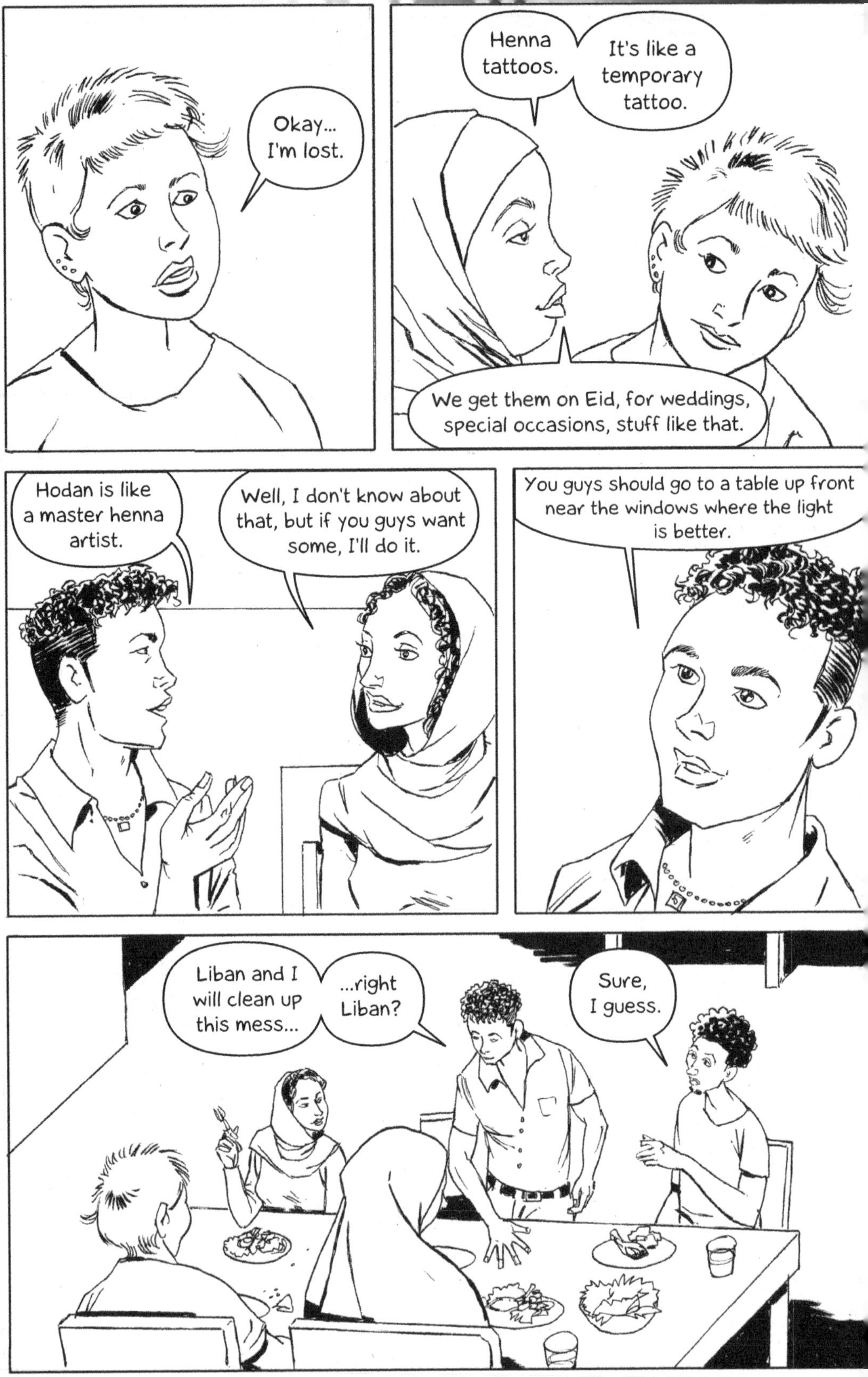
Okay...
I'm lost.
Henna tattoos.
It's like a temporary tattoo.
We get them on Eid, for weddings, special occasions, stuff like that.
Hodan is like a master henna artist.
Well, I don't know about that, but if you guys want some, I'll do it.
You guys should go to a table up front near the windows where the light is better.
Liban and I will clean up this mess...
...right Liban?
Sure, I guess.

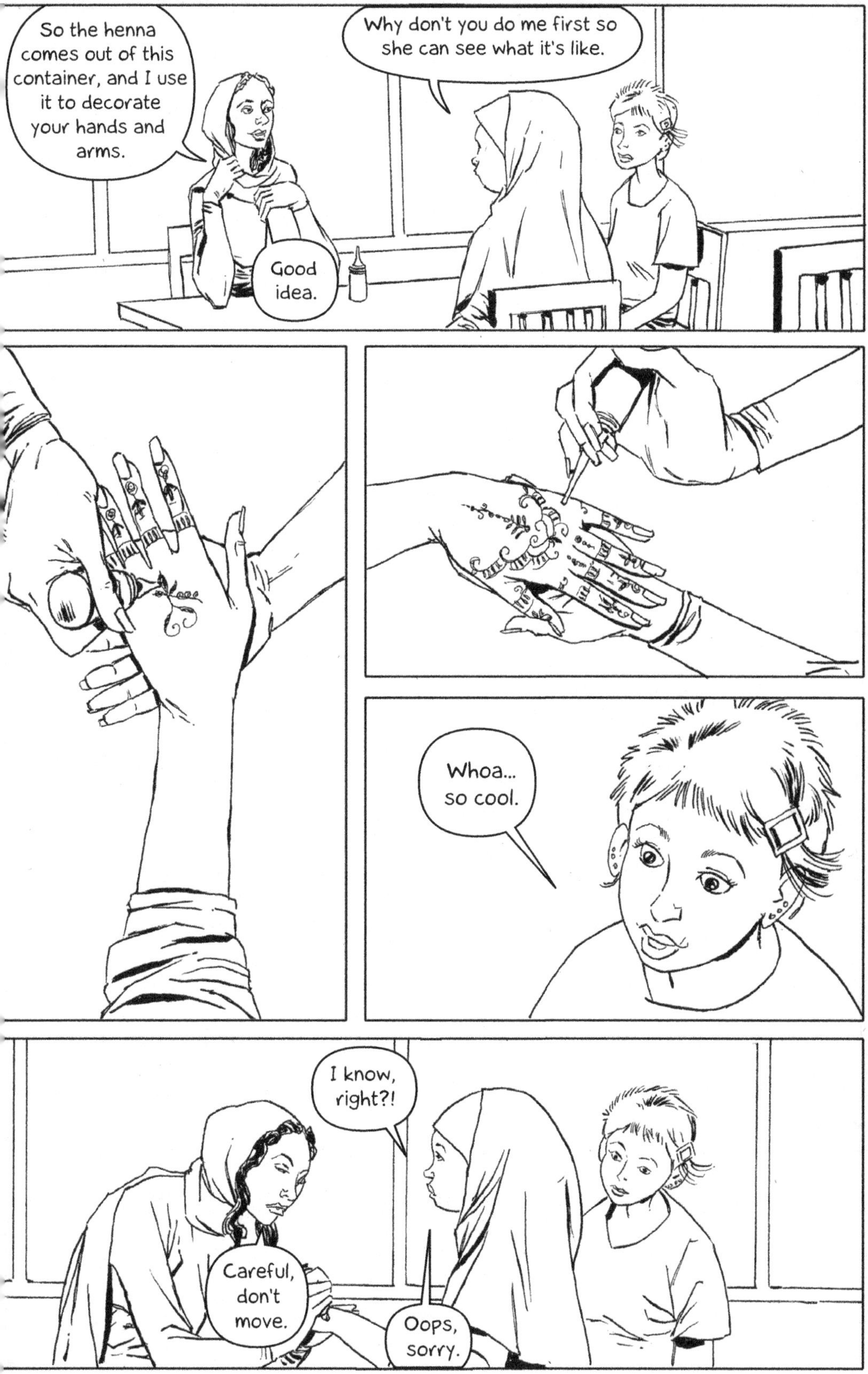
So the henna comes out of this container, and I use it to decorate your hands and arms.
Why don't you do me first so she can see what it's like.
Good idea.
Whoa... so cool.
I know, right?!
Careful, don't move.
Oops, sorry.

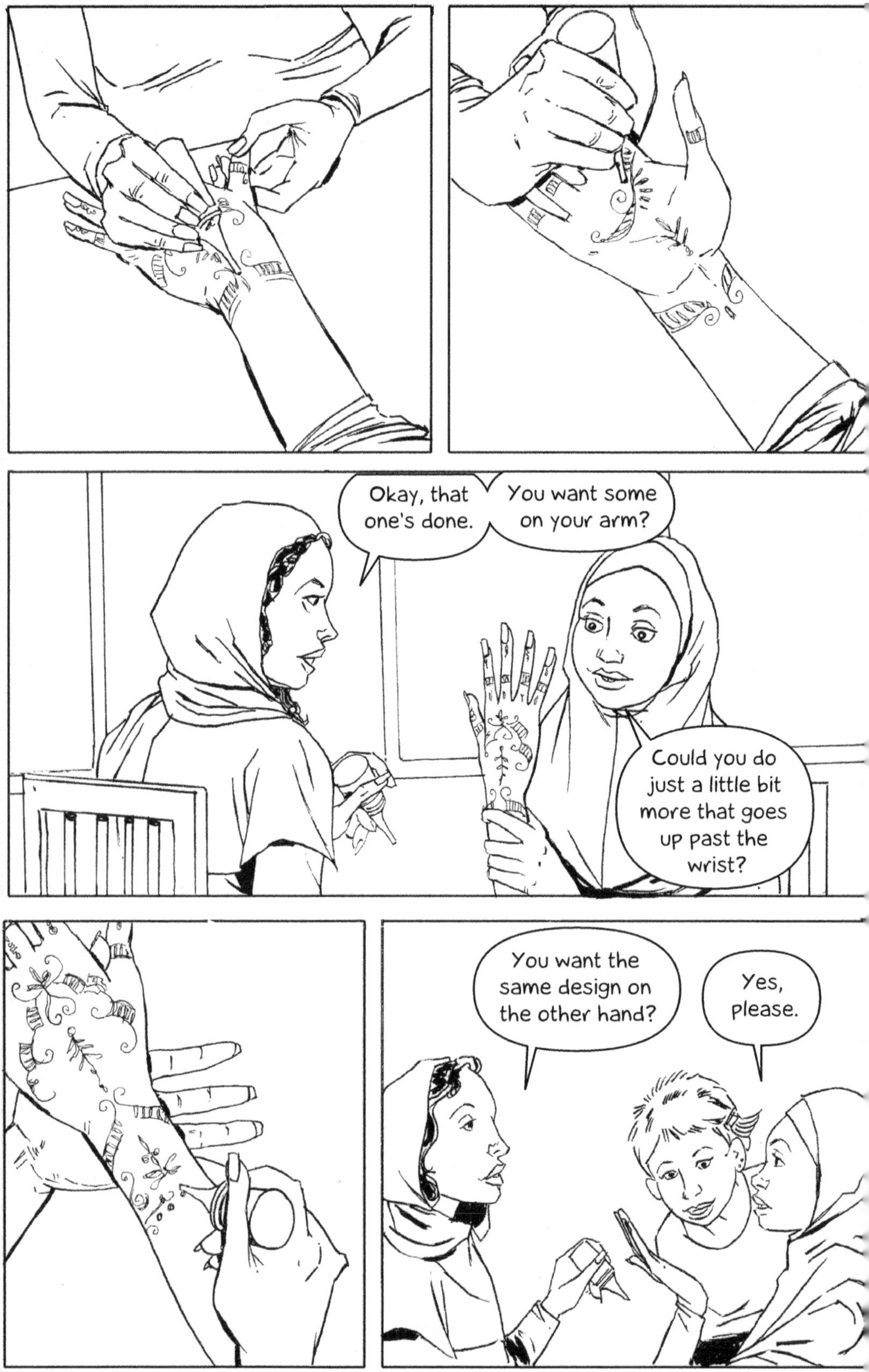

Okay, that one's done.
You want some on your arm?
Could you do just a little bit more that goes up past the wrist?
You want the same design on the other hand?
Yes, please.

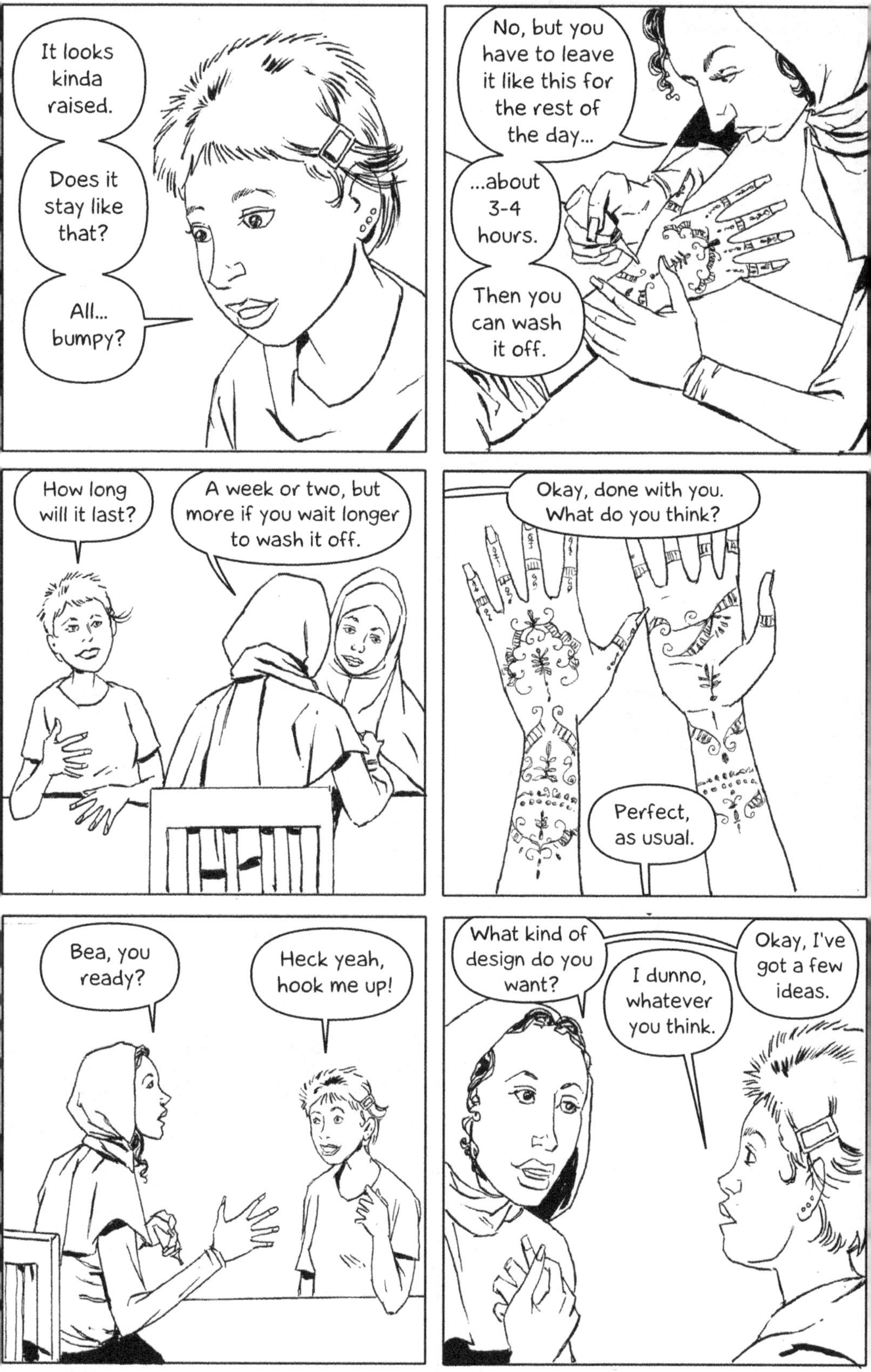
It looks kinda raised.
Does it stay like that?
All... bumpy?
No, but you have to leave it like this for the rest of the day...
...about 3-4 hours.
Then you can wash it off.
How long will it last?
A week or two, but more if you wait longer to wash it off.
Okay, done with you. What do you think?
Perfect, as usual.
Bea, you ready?
Heck yeah, hook me up!
What kind of design do you want?
I dunno, whatever you think.
Okay, I've got a few ideas.

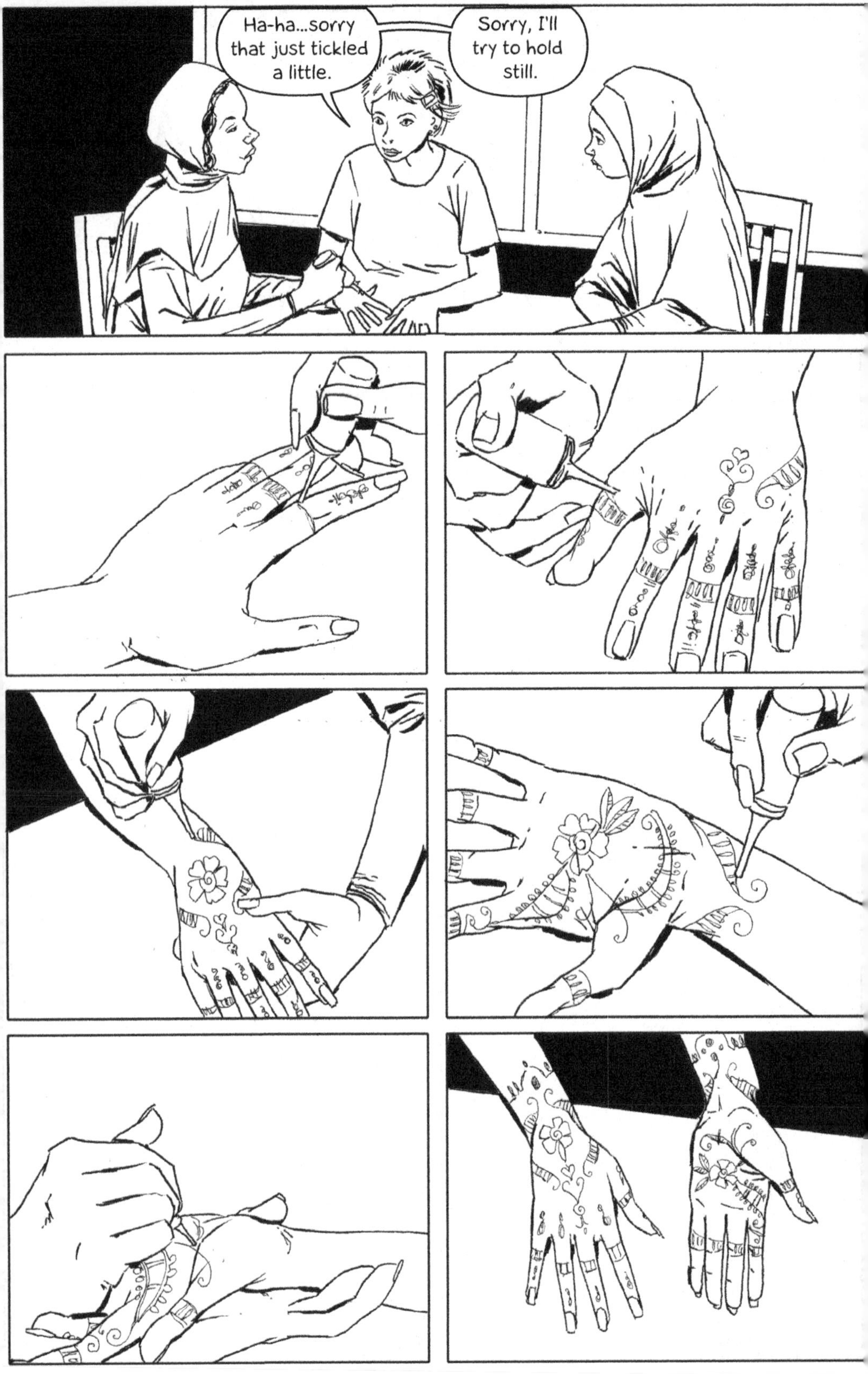
Ha-ha...sorry that just tickled a little.
Sorry, I'll try to hold still.

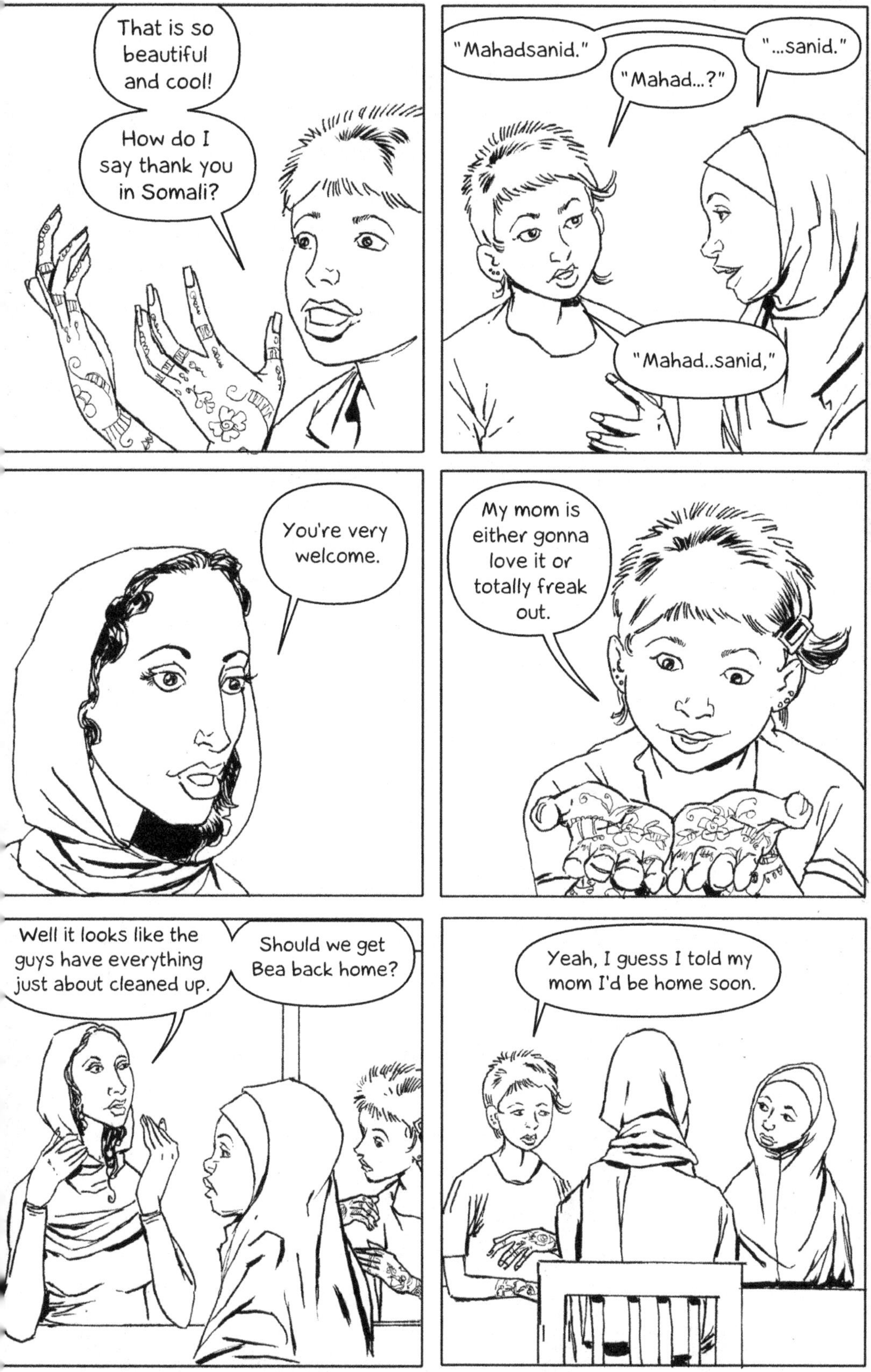
That is so beautiful and cool!
How do I say thank you in Somali?
"Mahadsanid."
"Mahad...?"
"...sanid."
"Mahad..sanid,"
You're very welcome.
My mom is either gonna love it or totally freak out.
Well it looks like the guys have everything just about cleaned up.
Should we get Bea back home?
Yeah, I guess I told my mom I'd be home soon.

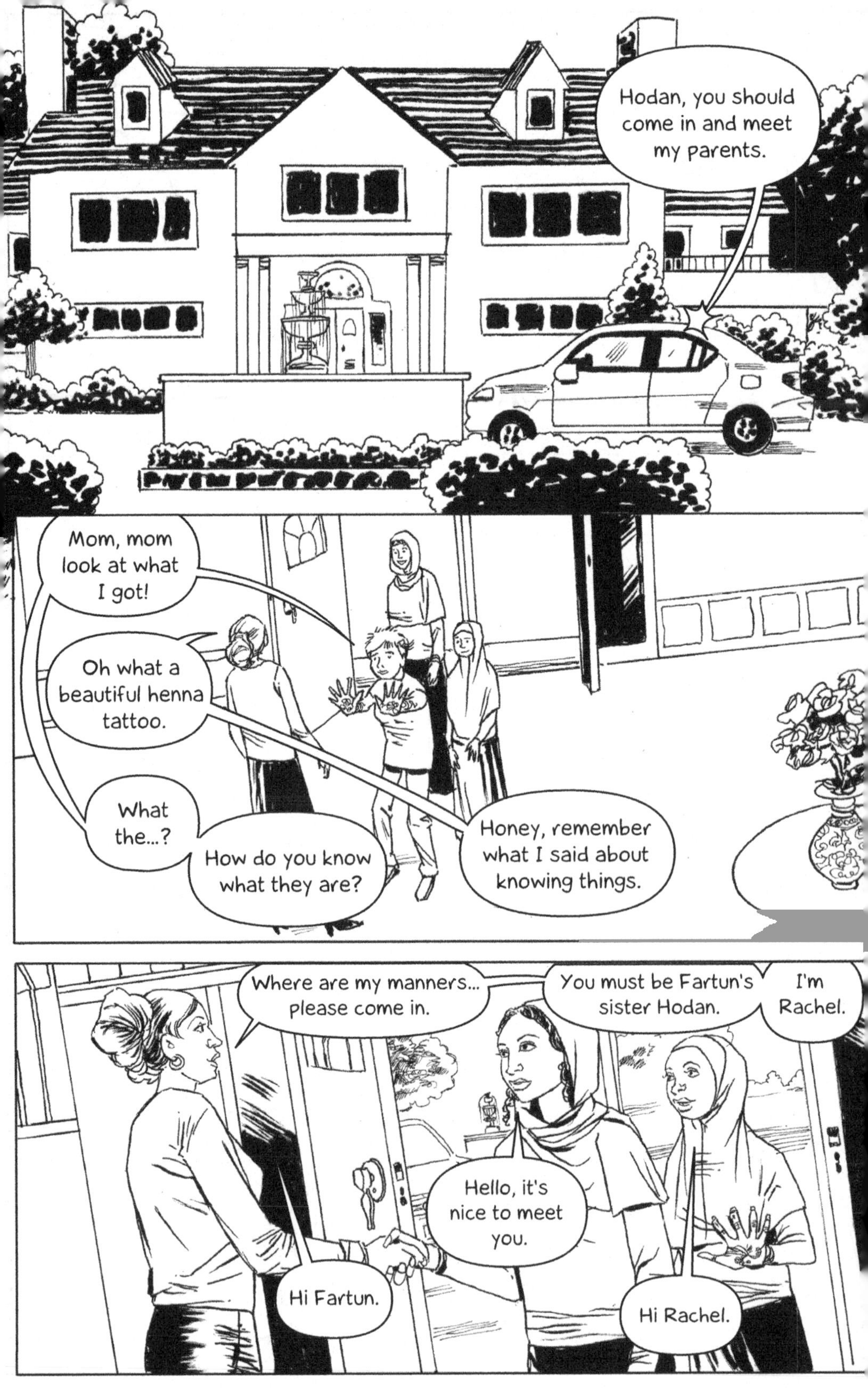
Hodan, you should come in and meet my parents.
Mom, mom look at what I got!
Oh what a beautiful henna tattoo.
What the...?
How do you know what they are?
Honey, remember what I said about knowing things.
Where are my manners... please come in.
You must be Fartun's sister Hodan.
I'm Rachel.
Hello, it's nice to meet you.
Hi Fartun.
Hi Rachel.

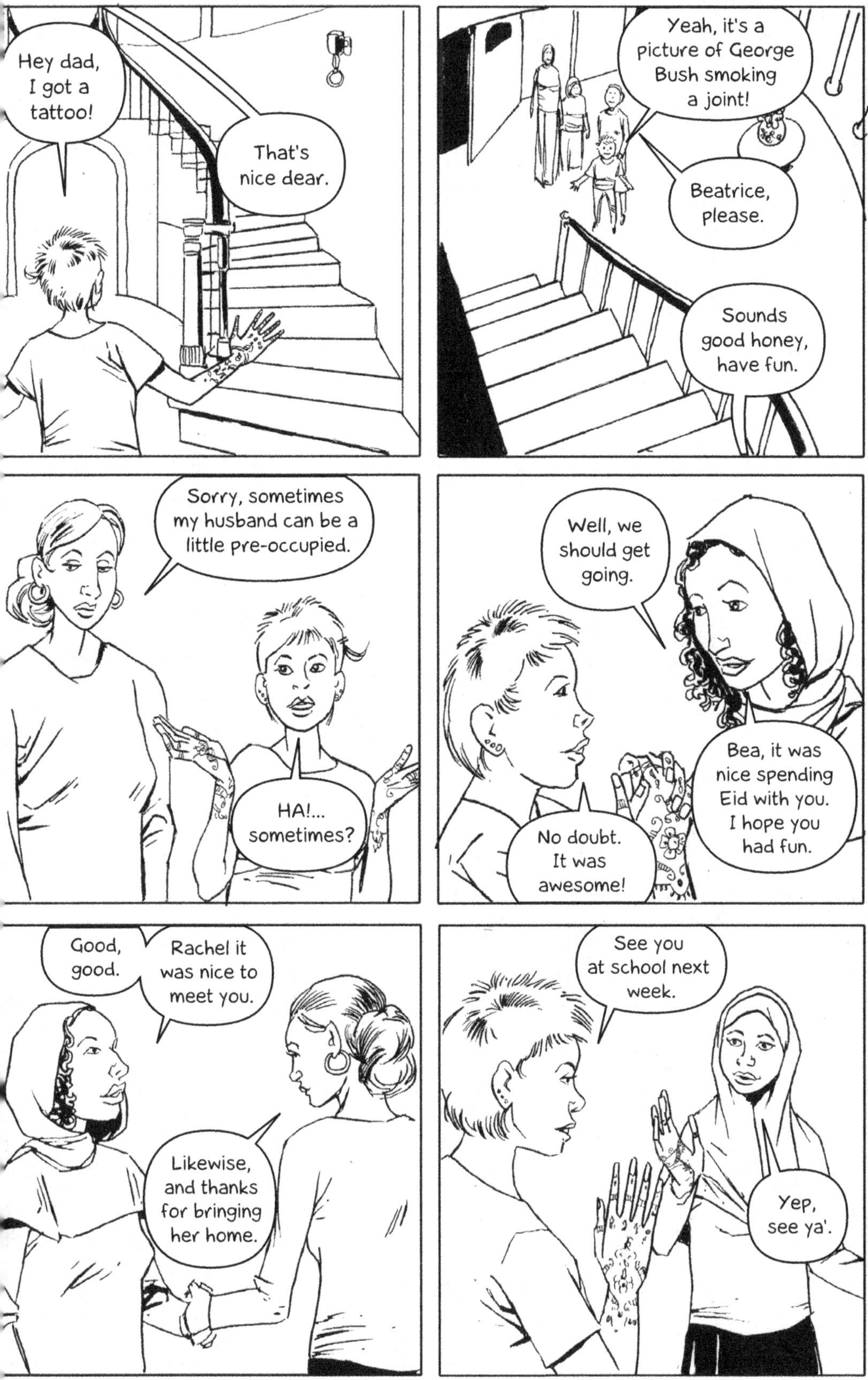
Hey dad, I got a tattoo!
That's nice dear.
Yeah, it's a picture of George Bush smoking a joint!
Beatrice, please.
Sounds good honey, have fun.
Sorry, sometimes my husband can be a little pre-occupied.
HA!... sometimes?
Well, we should get going.
Bea, it was nice spending Eid with you. I hope you had fun.
No doubt. It was awesome!
Good, good.
Rachel it was nice to meet you.
Likewise, and thanks for bringing her home.
See you at school next week.
Yep, see ya'.

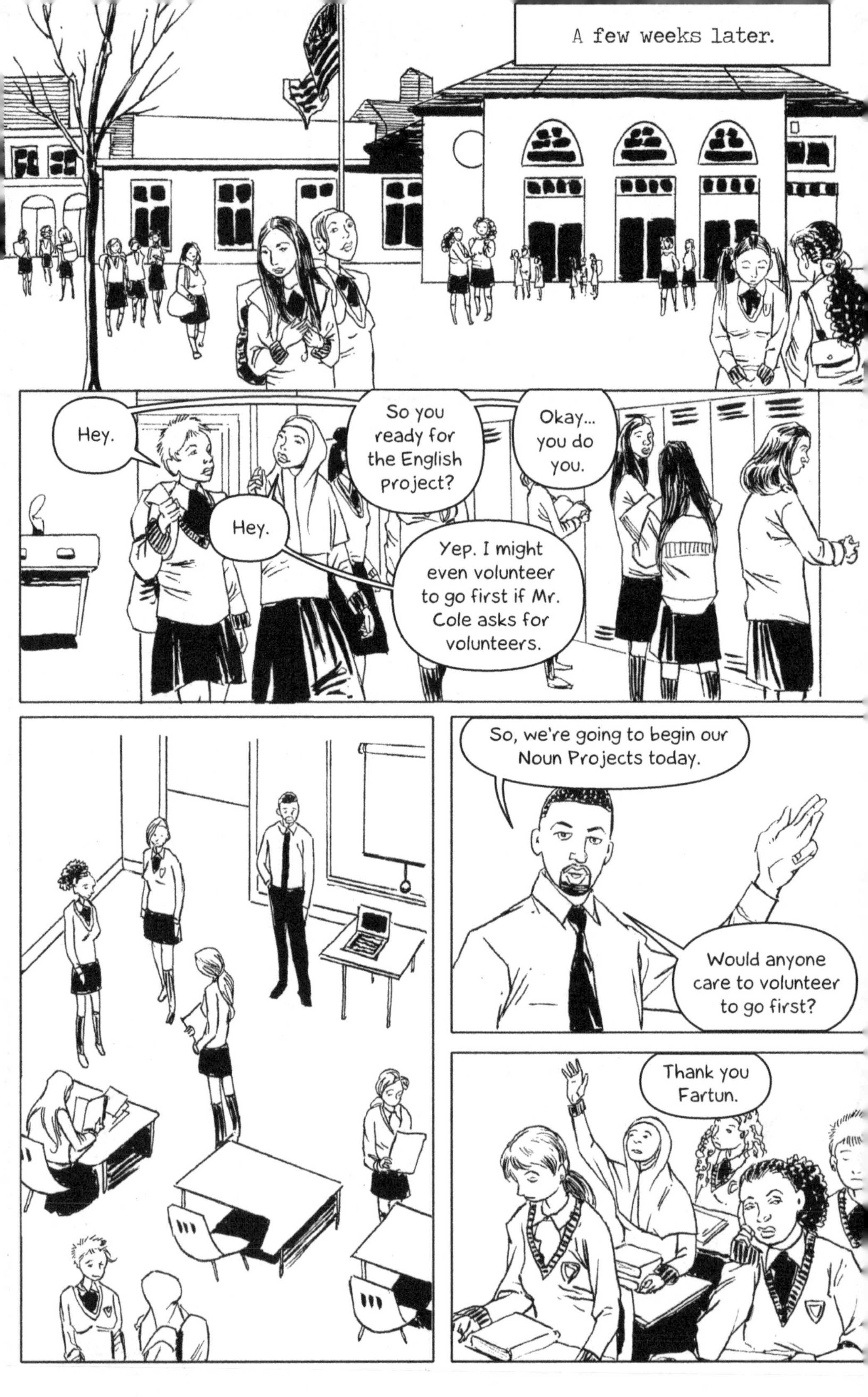
A few weeks later.
Hey.
So you ready for the English project?
Okay... you do you.
Hey.
Yep. I might even volunteer to go first if Mr. Cole asks for volunteers.
So, we're going to begin our Noun Projects today.
Would anyone care to volunteer to go first?
Thank you Fartun.

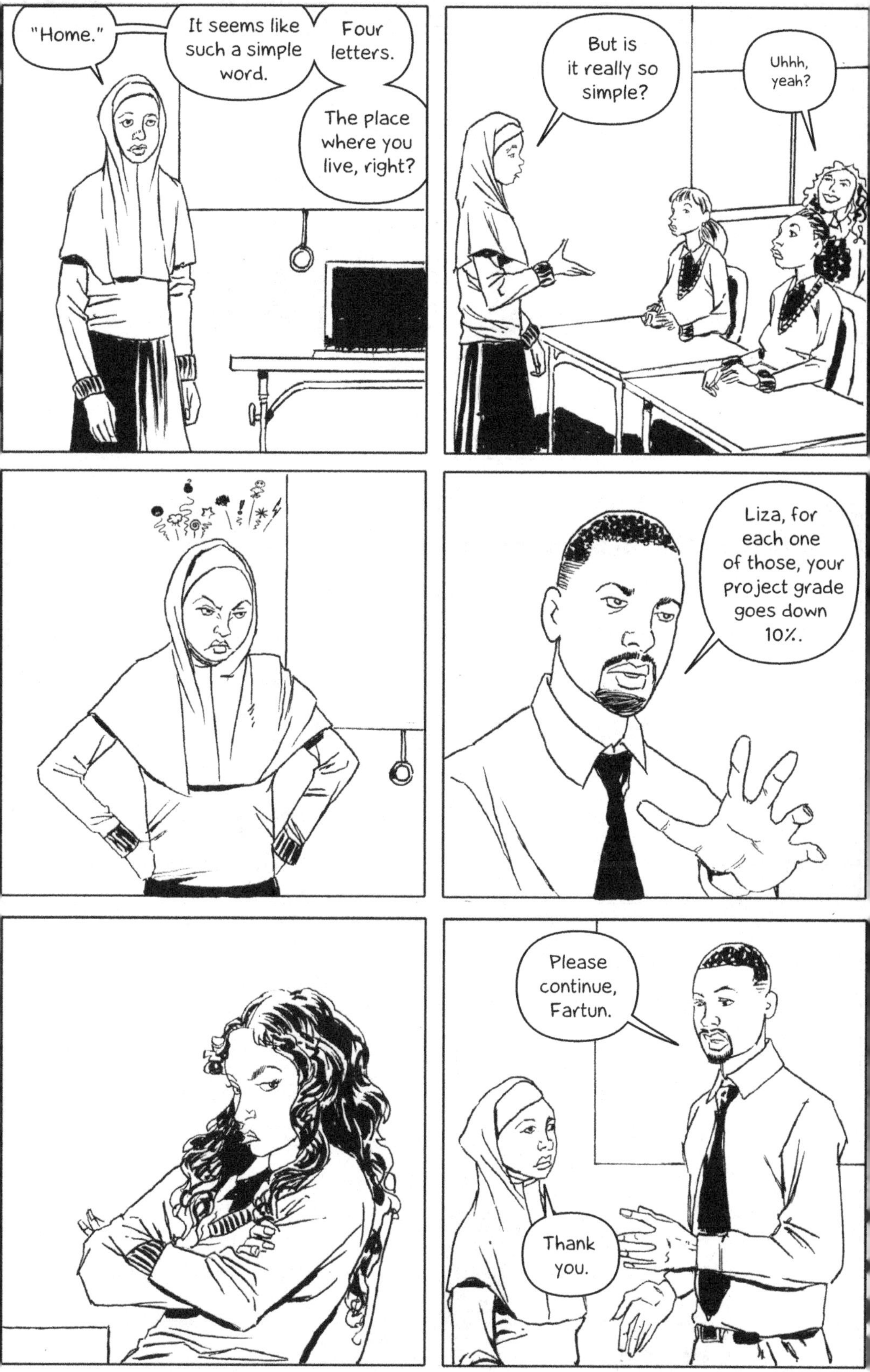
"Home."
It seems like such a simple word.
Four letters.
The place where you live, right?
But is it really so simple?
Uhhh, yeah?
Liza, for each one of those, your project grade goes down 10%.
Please continue, Fartun.
Thank you.

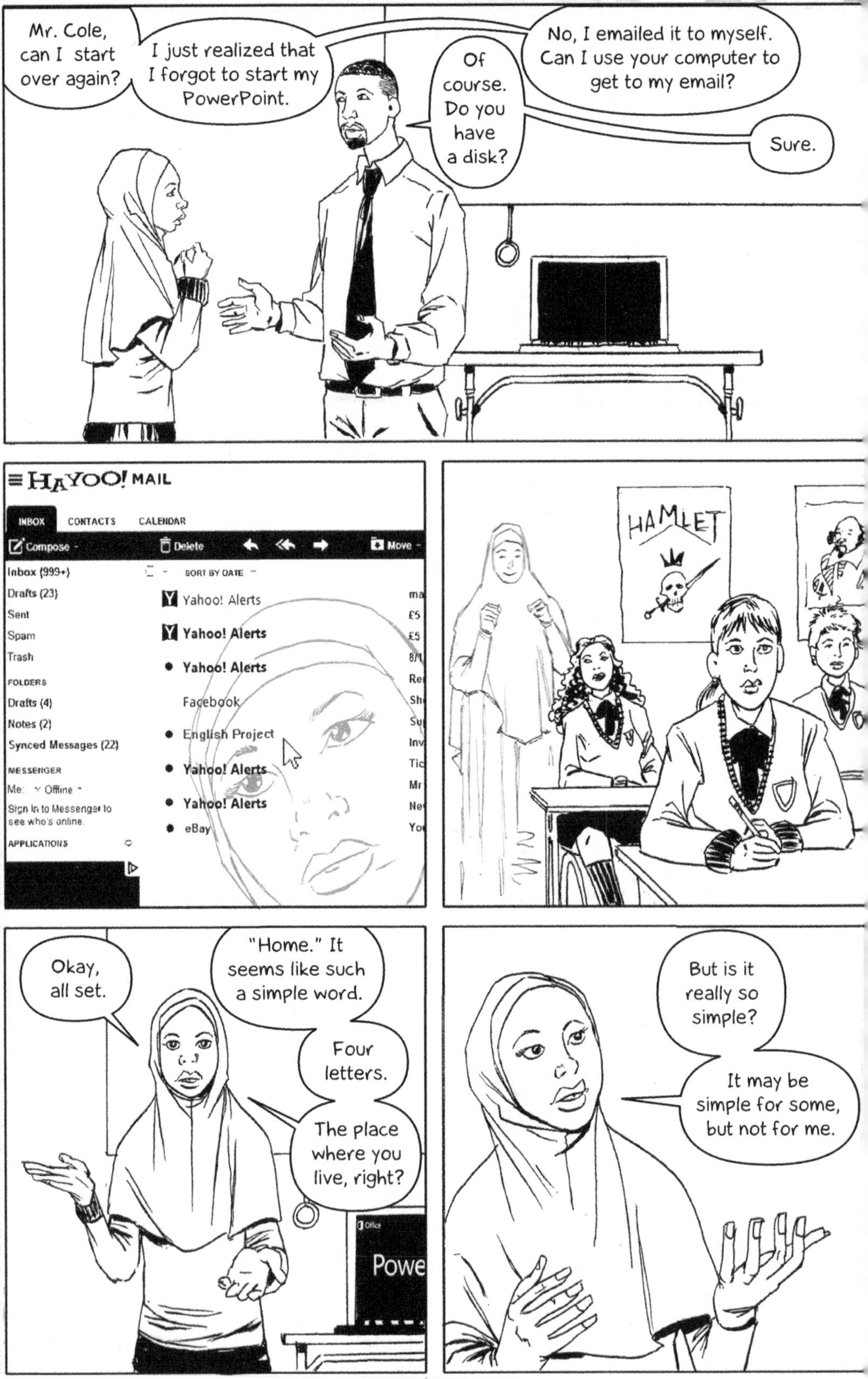

Mr. Cole, can I start over again?
I just realized that I forgot to start my PowerPoint.
Of course. Do you have a disk?
No, I emailed it to myself. Can I use your computer to get to my email?
Sure.
HAYOO! MAIL
INBOX
CONTACTS
CALENDAR
Compose
Delete
Move
Inbox (999+)
Drafts (23)
Sent
Spam
Trash
FOLDERS
Drafts (4)
Notes (2)
Synced Messages (22)
MESSENGER
Me: Offline
Sign In to Messenger to see who's online.
APPLICATIONS
SORT BY DATE
Yahoo! Alerts
Yahoo! Alerts
Yahoo! Alerts
Facebook
English Project
Yahoo! Alerts
Yahoo! Alerts
eBay
HAMLET
Okay, all set.
"Home." It seems like such a simple word.
Four letters.
The place where you live, right?
Office
Powe
But is it really so simple?
It may be simple for some, but not for me.

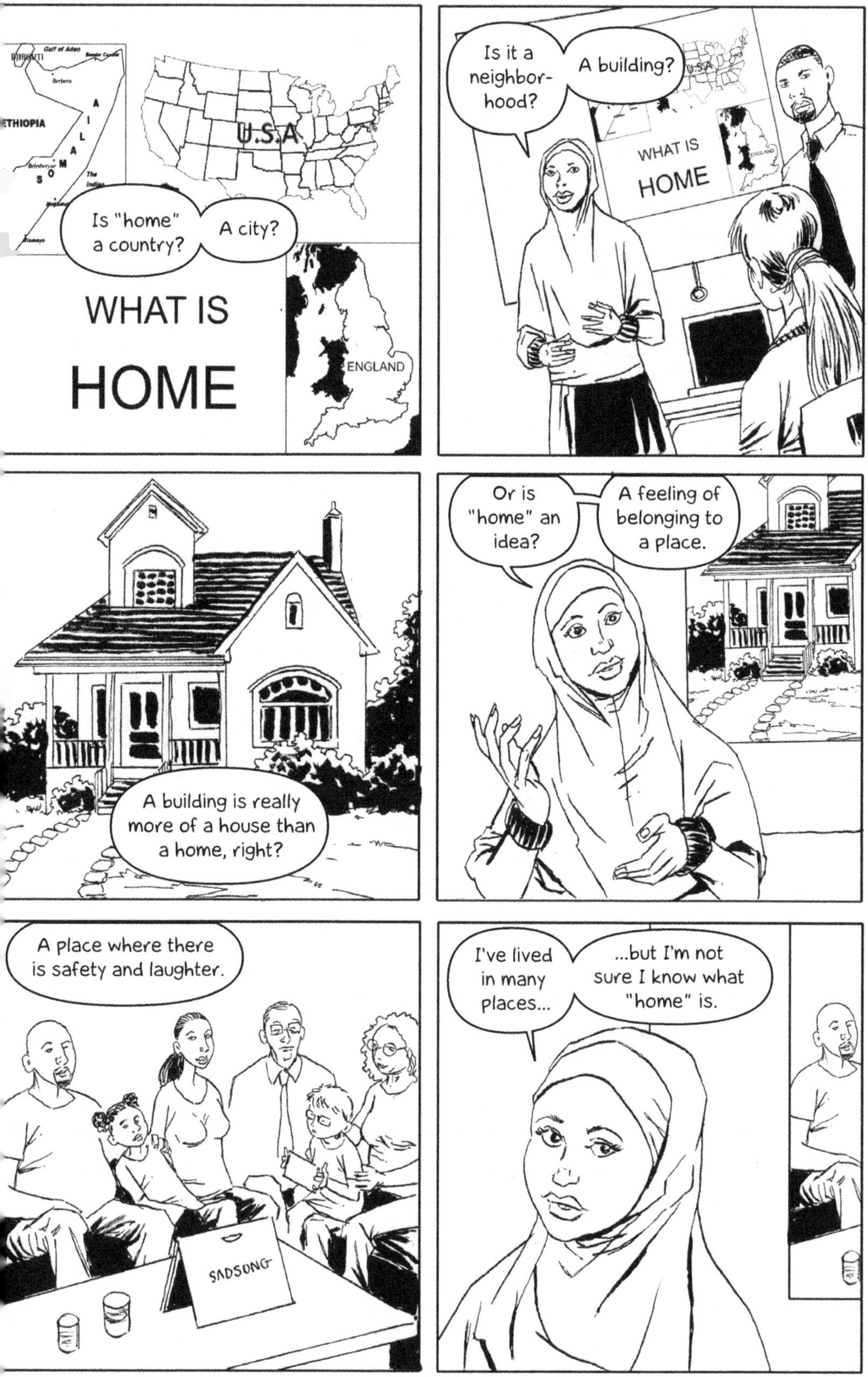
Gulf of Aden
ETHIOPIA
U.S.A
ENGLAND
WHAT IS
HOME
Is "home" a country?
A city?
Is it a neighbor-hood?
A building?
WHAT IS
HOME
A building is really more of a house than a home, right?
Or is "home" an idea?
A feeling of belonging to a place.
A place where there is safety and laughter.
SADSONG
I've lived in many places...
...but I'm not sure I know what "home" is.

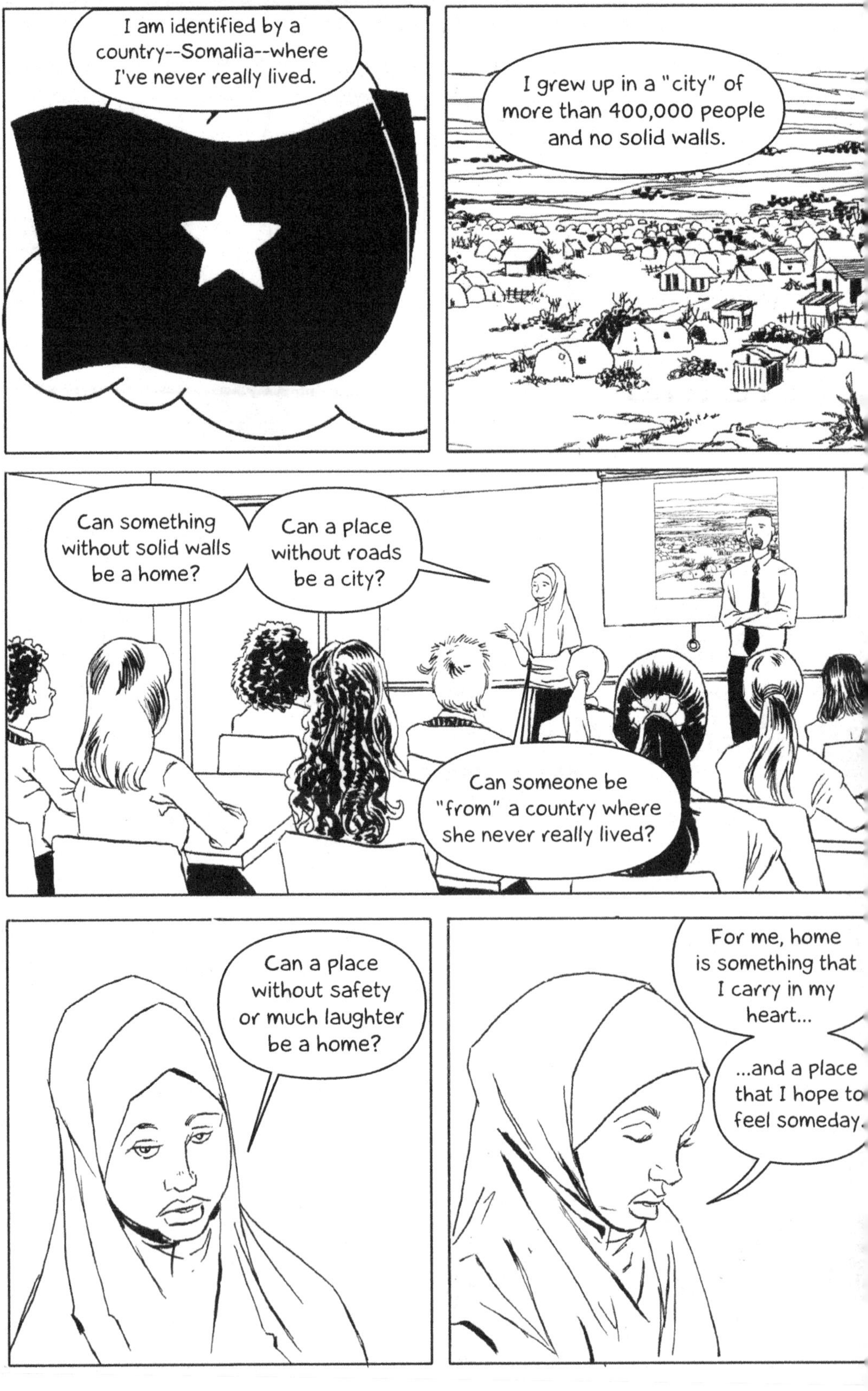
I am identified by a country--Somalia--where I've never really lived.
I grew up in a "city" of more than 400,000 people and no solid walls.
Can something without solid walls be a home?
Can a place without roads be a city?
Can someone be "from" a country where she never really lived?
Can a place without safety or much laughter be a home?
For me, home is something that I carry in my heart...
...and a place that I hope to feel someday.

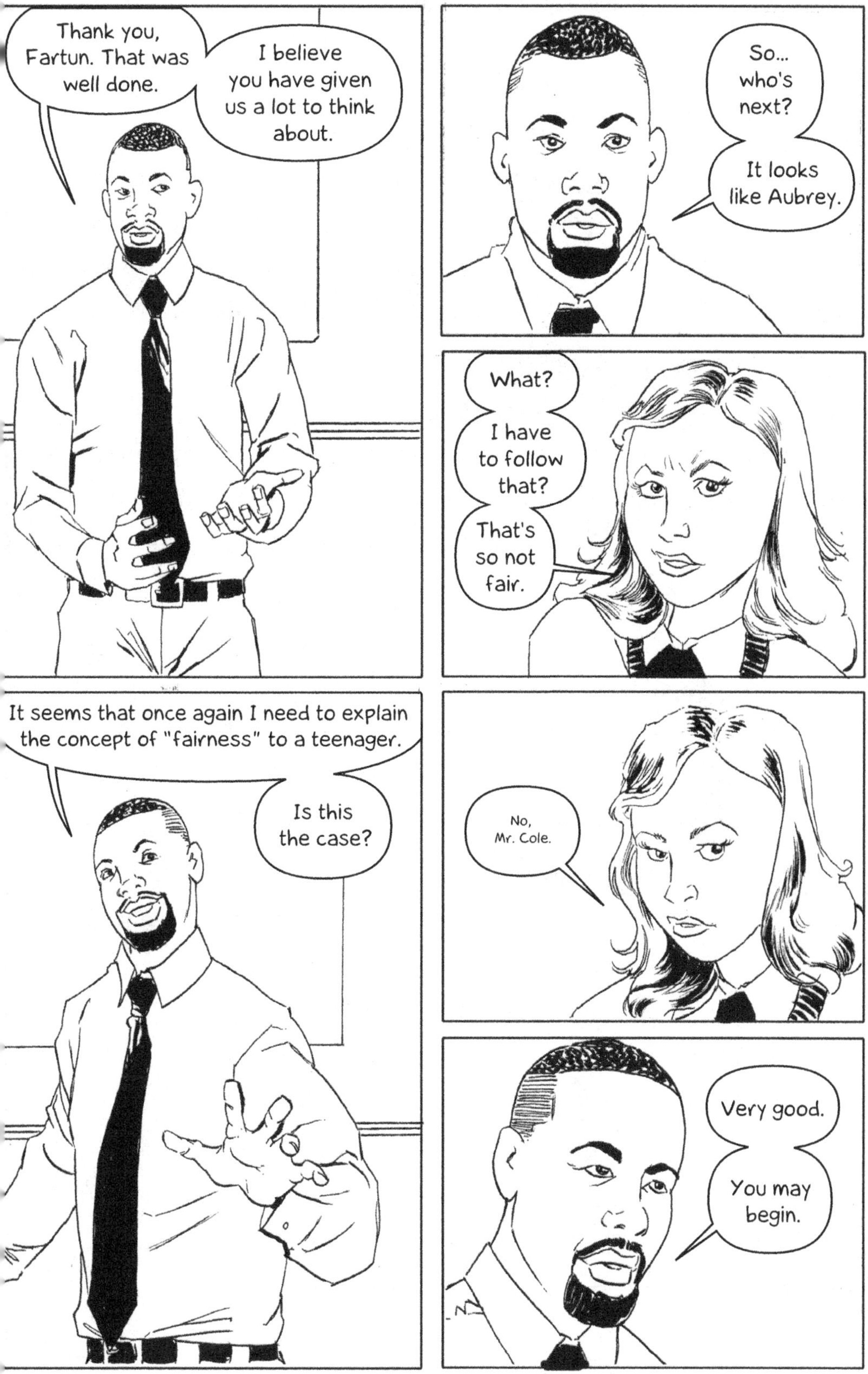
Thank you, Fartun. That was well done.
I believe you have given us a lot to think about.
So... who's next?
It looks like Aubrey.
What?
I have to follow that?
That's so not fair.
It seems that once again I need to explain the concept of "fairness" to a teenager.
Is this the case?
No, Mr. Cole.
Very good.
You may begin.

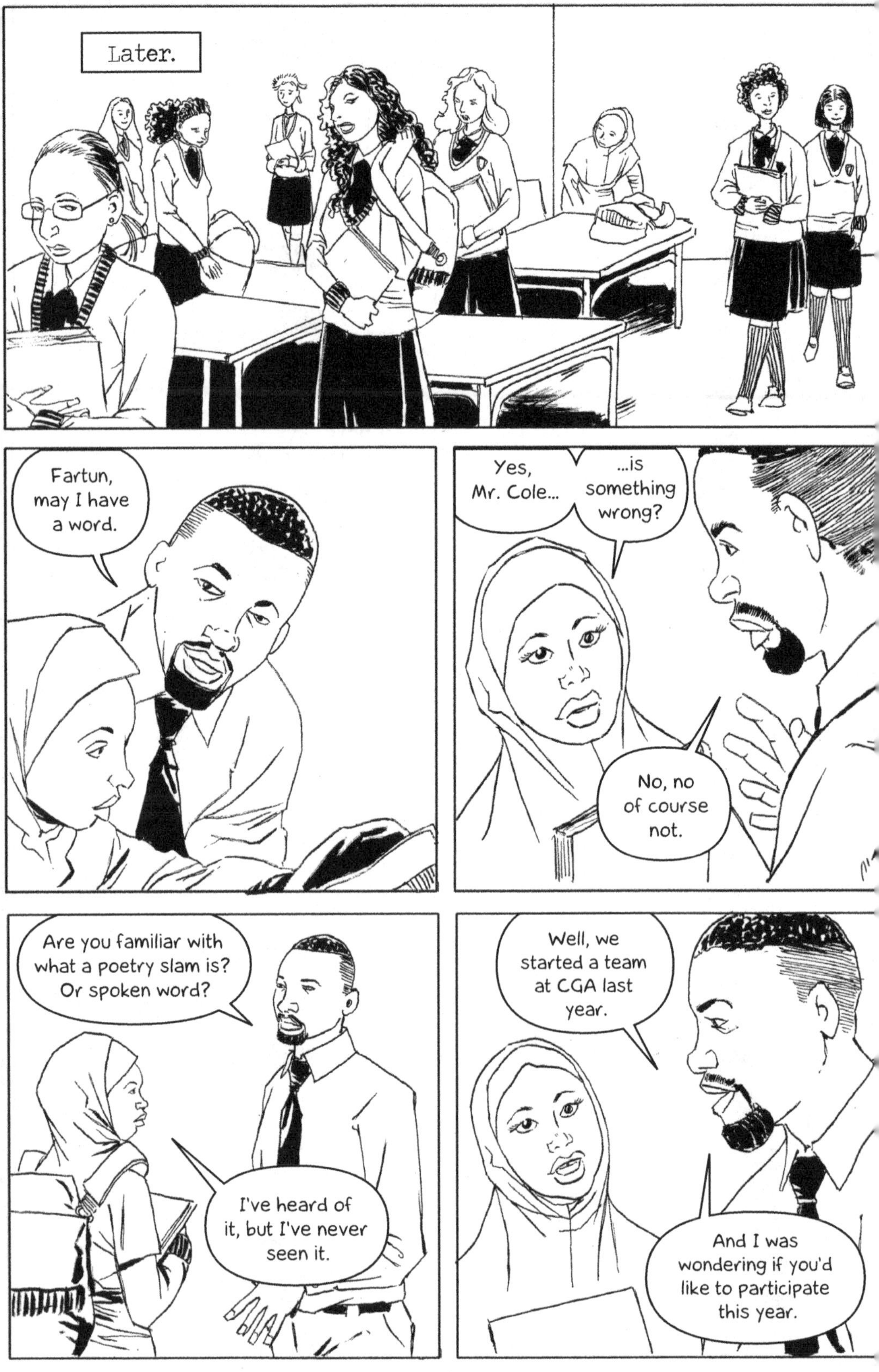
Later.
Fartun, may I have a word.
Yes, Mr. Cole...
...is something wrong?
No, no of course not.
Are you familiar with what a poetry slam is? Or spoken word?
I've heard of it, but I've never seen it.
Well, we started a team at CGA last year.
And I was wondering if you'd like to participate this year.

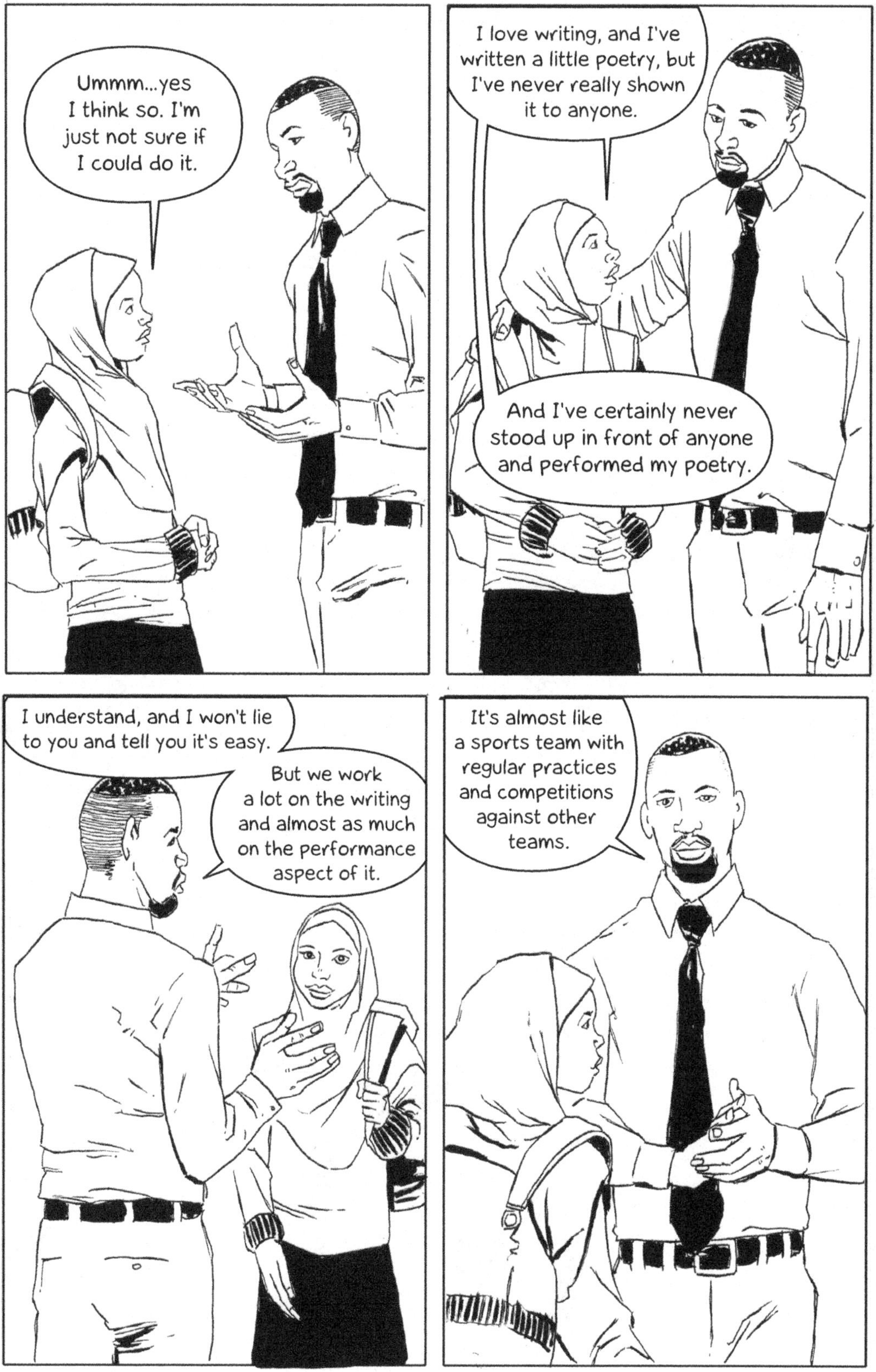
Ummm...yes I think so. I'm just not sure if I could do it.
I love writing, and I've written a little poetry, but I've never really shown it to anyone.
And I've certainly never stood up in front of anyone and performed my poetry.
I understand, and I won't lie to you and tell you it's easy.
But we work a lot on the writing and almost as much on the performance aspect of it.
It's almost like a sports team with regular practices and competitions against other teams.

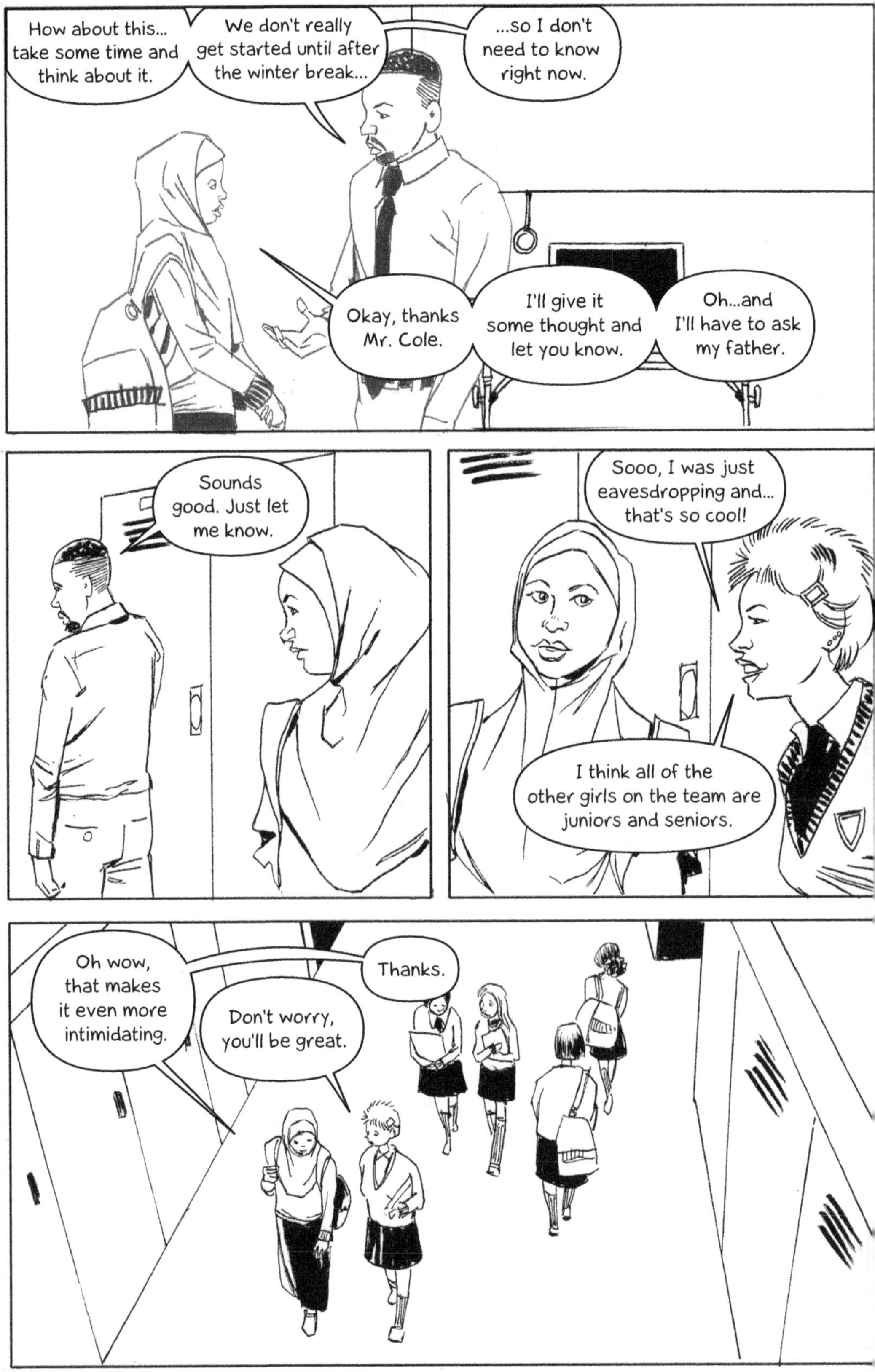
How about this... take some time and think about it.
We don't really get started until after the winter break...
...so I don't need to know right now.
Okay, thanks Mr. Cole.
I'll give it some thought and let you know.
Oh...and I'll have to ask my father.
Sounds good. Just let me know.
Sooo, I was just eavesdropping and... that's so cool!
I think all of the other girls on the team are juniors and seniors.
Oh wow, that makes it even more intimidating.
Don't worry, you'll be great.
Thanks.

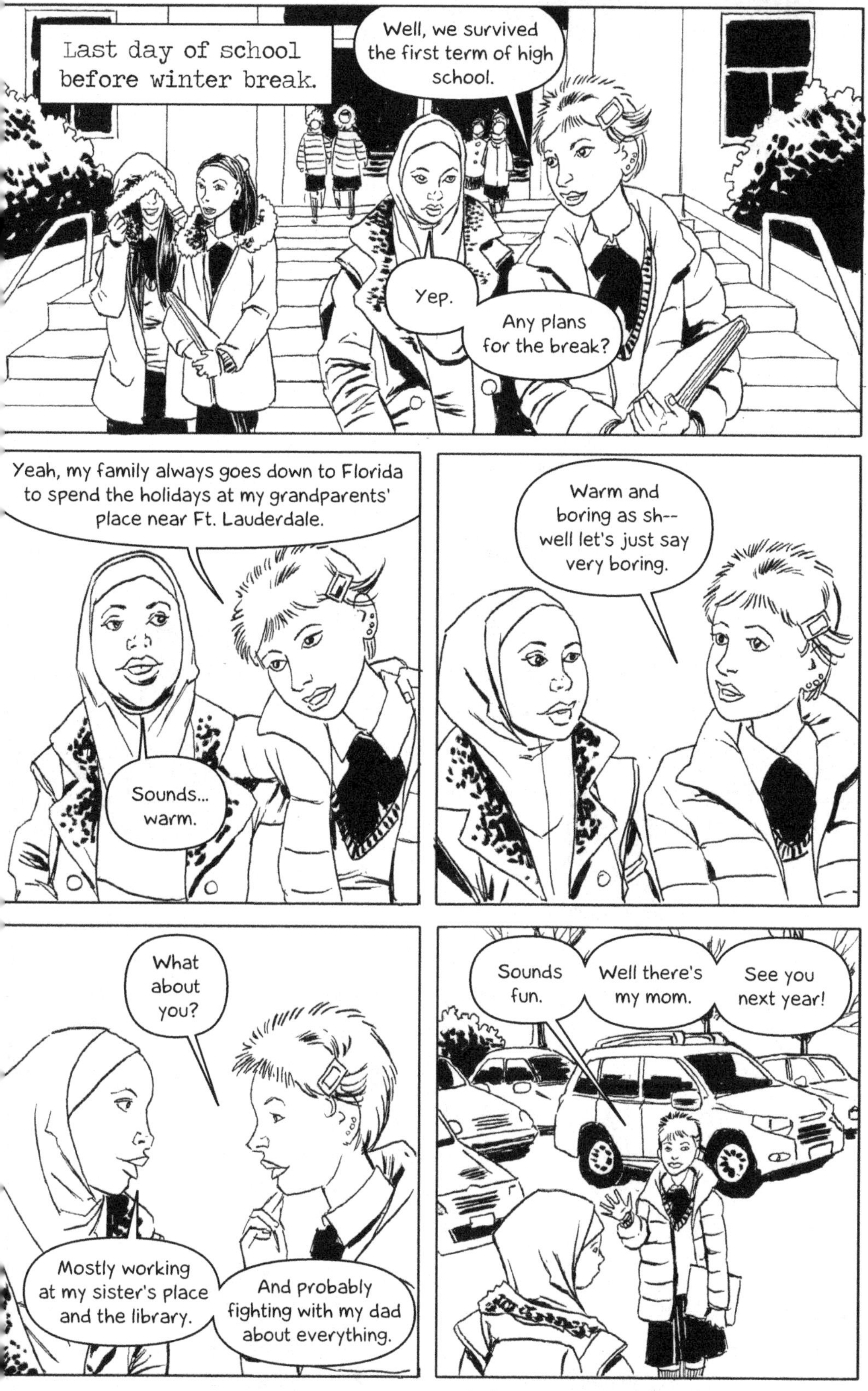
Last day of school before winter break.
Well, we survived the first term of high school.
Yep.
Any plans for the break?
Yeah, my family always goes down to Florida to spend the holidays at my grandparents' place near Ft. Lauderdale.
Sounds... warm.
Warm and boring as sh-- well let's just say very boring.
What about you?
Mostly working at my sister's place and the library.
And probably fighting with my dad about everything.
Sounds fun.
Well there's my mom.
See you next year!

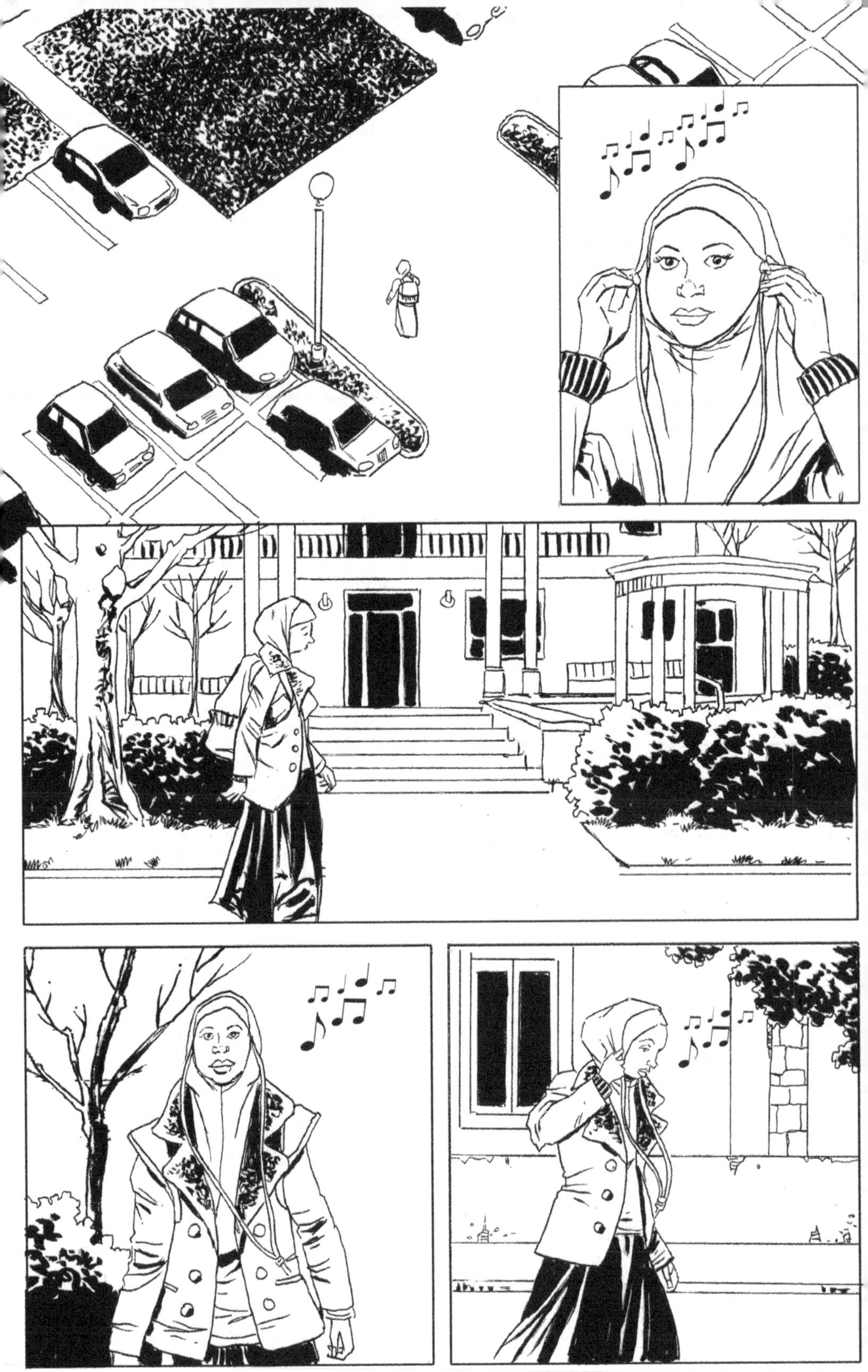

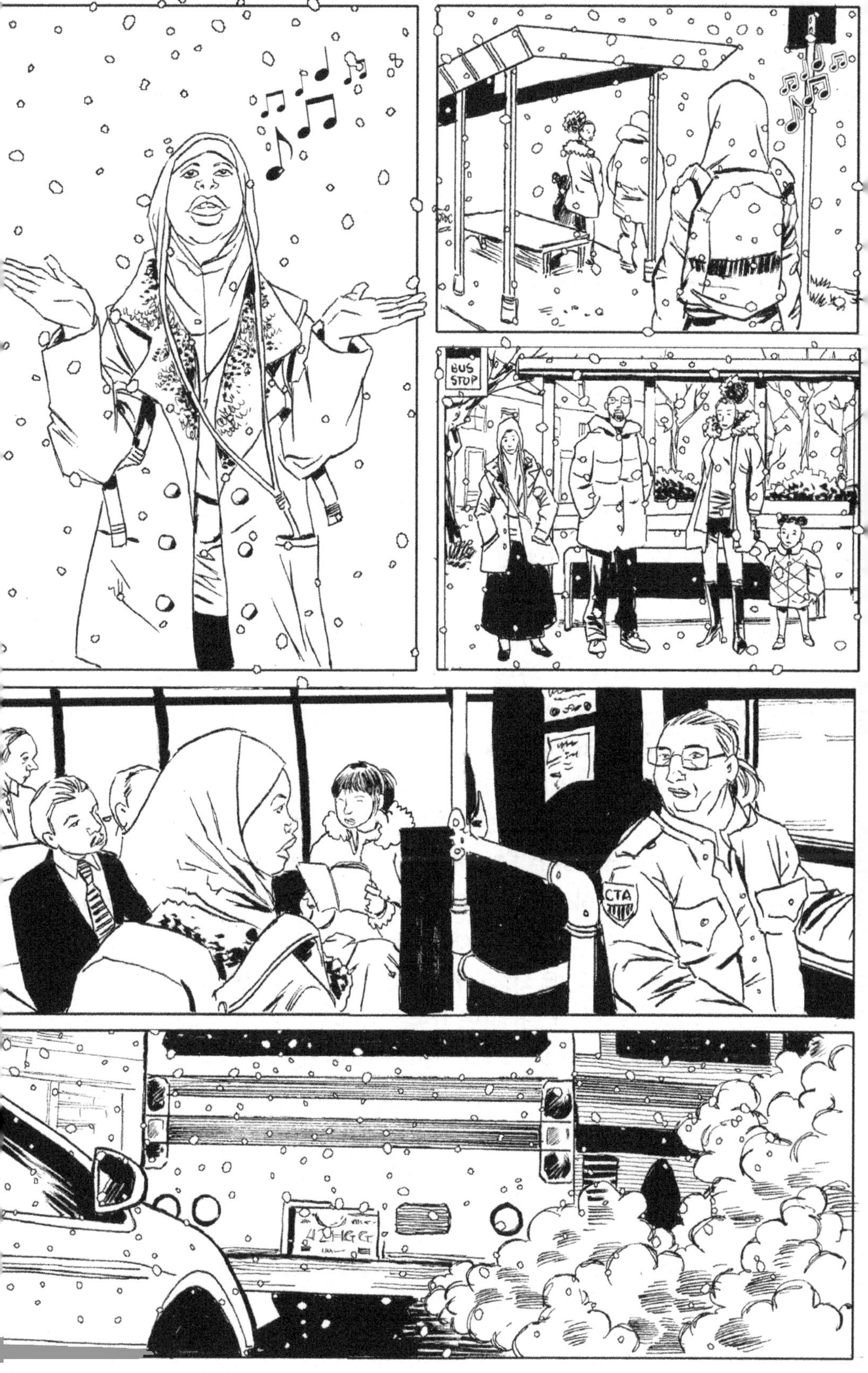
BUS STOP
CTA

T.E.

-This book would not have been possible without the help of the following. Thank you to Mohamed Hashi, Abdirashid Abdalla, Fardowsa Abdalla, Farhio Abdalla, Asia Mohamud, Halima Suleiman, Sontow Mayow, Najmo Abdinur, Qorsho Hassan, Muhammad Arifeen, Abukar Arman, Dara Naraghi, John Novak, Liz Neal. Thanks to Brent for his wonderful art, which really does the heavy lifting on this book. And finally a special thank you to my wife, Michelle.

B.B.

-To Holly and the boys, thanks for your unwavering love and support. Nevan, thanks for making sure you got the first copy of every book I make. To my parents, thanks for believing in me and letting me pursue my dreams. To my teachers, I appreciate all you inspired me to do. For all of my friends and family who've read my books and love my art, thank you. Nayson, thanks for going to my comics shows with me, you are always and inspiration to be around. I love that you love art as much as I do. Thanks to Dara for giving me my big break. Thanks to my old pal Noor Jama for introducing me to sambusa and teaching me Somali, although I am far from fluent. And of course thanks to Terry for giving me this opportunity to help make this fantastic creation.

Made in the USA
Monee, IL
11 January 2020